"So, Liam, you really were the problem child."

"That I was."

"Your parents must be relieved."

"They are. And I'm sorry I gave them so much trouble. They're good, good people. It wasn't their fault. Sometimes if you're good at something, it can get you in trouble. You follow the path because it's easy for you, and sometimes you're in over your head before you realize it."

He understood then that he'd been sitting here sharing his life story with her easily, without even thinking about it. How had Ria managed that? She'd given him one tiny bit of her own history, and suddenly he was pouring his own out by the bucket? When what he'd meant to do was get that distance between them?

"I'm surprised that Dylan didn't pour his soul out to you on request," he said with a grimace.

"I can have that effect," she said with a laugh. "It's my honest face."

Yeah, your face is honest. Among other things. Like beautiful. Fascinating.

Trouble.

* * *

Be sure to check out the rest of the books in this miniseries.

Cutter's Code: A clever and mysterious canine helps a group of secret operatives crack the case.

* * *

If you're on Twitter, tell us what you think of Harlequin Romantic Suspense! #harlequinromsuspense

Dear Reader,

When you've been through some battles of your own, you tend to be more aware of how dealing with adversity works. In my case, it made me very aware of the truth of the old saying "Be kind. Everyone you meet is fighting a battle you know nothing about."

This was brought home to me once more in the writing of *Operation Alpha*. Because Liam Burnett, that laid-back, ever-cheerful Texas guy, had always seemed just that to me. It wasn't until I got into his story that I found, somewhat to my surprise, that there was a great deal I didn't know about him. That nobody knew about him. And it took the persistence of a good, loving woman and a certain very, very determined dog to get him to face the past he hid behind that carefree facade.

Happy reading!

Justine

OPERATION ALPHA

Justine Davis

HARLEQUIN®ROMANTIC SUSPENSE

Recycling programs
for this product may
not exist in your area.

ISBN-13: 978-0-373-40203-8

Operation Alpha

HARLEQUIN®
www.Harlequin.com

Printed in U.S.A.

Justine Davis lives on Puget Sound in Washington State, watching big ships and the occasional submarine go by and sharing the neighborhood with assorted wildlife, including a pair of bald eagles, deer, a bear or two and a tailless raccoon. In the few hours when she's not planning, plotting or writing her next book, her favorite things are photography, knitting her way through a huge yarn stash and driving her restored 1967 Corvette roadster—top down, of course.

Connect with Justine at her website, justinedavis.com, at Twitter.com/justine_d_davis, or on Facebook at Facebook.com/justinedaredavis.

Books by Justine Davis

Harlequin Romantic Suspense

Cutter's Code

Operation Midnight
Operation Reunion
Operation Blind Date
Operation Unleashed
Operation Power Play
Operation Homecoming
Operation Soldier Next Door
Operation Alpha

The Coltons of Texas

Colton Family Rescue

Redstone, Incorporated

Just Another Day in Paradise
One of These Nights
In His Sights
Second-Chance Hero
Dark Reunion
Deadly Temptation
Her Best Friend's Husband
The Best Revenge
Redstone Ever After

Visit the Author Profile page at Harlequin.com, or justinedavis.com, for more titles.

The biggest love sometimes comes in the smallest packages...

Dexter was a Chihuahua, black with a little white on his neck. He came to us from a puppy mill, although we didn't know that until later. Despite that start in life, he was such a loving dog in so many ways. He was always giving hugs and kisses. He particularly loved being on his dad's lap. There is a big picture of him sleeping on his dad's lap in our living room. When we would watch TV in the dining room, he would want up and then put his head on the table and fall asleep until Dad moved. Many times we stayed there watching TV until late so we wouldn't disturb him. If he was left in the car even for a few minutes, and whoever was in the car with him told him that Mom or Dad was coming, he would whine so loud you could hear him before you got there.

We were blessed with Dexter's light in our lives for twelve years. When the end came, we wrapped him in the baby blanket I made him to lay him to rest. There is a marker and a heart made of stones in the backyard, with wildflowers planted around it so every summer Dexter has wildflowers, and a solar cross so he always has light.

We miss him still, and he will never be forgotten.

Peggy, Tim and DeeDee

Chapter 1

"Hi, Mr. Foxworth."

Quinn Foxworth looked at the blonde, sweet-faced teenager standing in the doorway of the Foxworth northwest headquarters. She wasn't alone, but he focused on her because she looked familiar. He couldn't quite place her; yet she obviously knew him.

Before he could speak, his dog, Cutter, trotted around the far corner of the building. Foxworth tracker Liam Burnett was at his heels, giving a playful swipe at the dog's plumed tail. Liam had volunteered for fetch duty this afternoon, and while summer might have ended, it was still warm enough that he'd worked up a sweat. Cutter, however, showed no sign he'd even had a workout.

The instant the dog caught sight—or scent—of the newcomers, his head came up and he broke into a run. He came to a halt at the girl's feet, sat politely and gave her a tongue-lolling, old-friend sort of greeting. The girl tilted her head to look at him, smiling widely. His tail began to wag happily, again as if this were a long-lost friend.

And suddenly Quinn knew.

"Emily?" he asked, startled.

She turned her gaze back to him. "I didn't think you'd recognize me."

"It took a moment. It's been—"

"Six years. I know." She reached up and touched the locket that was on a gold chain around her neck. "I still wear it every day."

Quinn smiled. "Good," he said quietly to the girl—young woman now—who had been the inspiration for starting the Foxworth Foundation. They had kept in touch by phone and email, but he hadn't seen her in person since the day Emily Parker and her adoptive parents had come to once more thank him for recovering the precious piece of jewelry that had been all she had from her dead mother. The change in her from age ten to sixteen was astonishing.

Liam had caught up with the dog now, and Emily turned and politely gestured the other person with her forward. "This is Ms. Connelly. She teaches at my school."

Quinn had only a moment to take in the petite brunette, but he was used to making quick assessments. Dressed in tan jeans and a loose white shirt that had a shine to it, she didn't look that much older than Emily. But he'd learned not to judge age just by looks; Liam looked years younger than he was. He was also smart and tough, and he had become someone Quinn would trust with his life.

"Ria, please," the woman said, holding out a hand. Quinn shook it. She had a steady grip, but her hand felt delicate in his.

"Liam Burnett, our tracker and resident tech guy," he said with a nod in the direction of the man who was quickly yanking his T-shirt back over his head. After, Quinn noted, a moment of stock-still staring at the woman who had arrived with Emily. He had recovered quickly, but Quinn was certain he'd seen it.

"Hi," Liam said with a nod to them both, "I'd shake hands, but I've been throwing his grubby baseball."

The woman laughed. And Liam seemed to stop breathing. "Not a tennis ball?" she asked.

"He likes those," Quinn explained, "but he loves the baseball. It's heavier, goes farther. And it was a gift from my wife's brother."

"Doesn't it hurt his teeth?" Emily asked.

"He knows the difference, knows not to try and catch this one in midair."

Emily smiled at the dog. "So he's smart and beautiful."

"He's Cutter," Quinn said simply. "Although judging by his greeting, I'm not sure he needs to be introduced to you. He's acting like he's known you all along."

"I thought he was just friendly," Emily said, sounding pleased as she stroked the dog's head. Cutter leaned into her as if she were long-lost family.

"He's not like that with complete strangers, at least not right away. It's almost like he knows."

"Knows?" Emily asked.

"How important you are to us."

The girl blushed.

"You're the locket girl," Liam said suddenly.

Emily looked surprised. "You know about me?"

"We all do," Liam said with a warm smile. "You're still Quinn's favorite case. He says you're why they made Foxworth official."

"But you've done so many things, big things, much more important than finding my locket," she said.

"No," Quinn said gently. "Nothing's been more important than that. Bigger maybe, louder, but not more important."

Emily glanced at her teacher. Ria Connelly smiled, and nodded. "As advertised," she said.

Quinn lifted a brow. "I've been telling her about Fox-worth," Emily said. "I think she thought I was exaggerating."

And why, Quinn wondered, would she be telling one of her teachers about us?

In the moment he thought it, Cutter shifted. He moved over to Ria and glanced up at her, wagging his tail. Clearly both of their visitors were more than accepted—they were welcome. Already. The woman smiled and immediately bent to him, quickly finding that spot behind his right ear that he loved having scratched. The dog blissfully tilted his head into her fingers, but after a moment, as if at some unseen signal the animal suddenly eyed both women intently. And then he turned and, in front of both of them, sat facing Quinn.

And gave him The Look.

Well, well.

"Come in," Quinn said. "Hayley will want to meet you."

The girl smiled even wider. "I want to meet her, too. I'm sorry I couldn't come to the wedding."

"We understood. A chance to go to Australia doesn't come along every day."

"No. Oh, and my folks said to say hello."

"How are they?"

"They're good." Emily looked at him steadily for a moment before adding, "And I love them very much. I'm very lucky to have them, that they chose me."

Quinn felt the last bit of concern he'd always carried about that fade away. The Hardings were wonderful people, but he'd always worried if the devastated child who had lost first her father, and then the mother she had been so close to, would be able to really adjust. It was a credit to them that she'd gone from withdrawn child to an obviously bright, outgoing teenager.

He smiled at both women—for the ten-year-old he remembered had certainly become that—as he gestured them inside. Cutter and his ball-thrower followed, and Quinn noted with interest that Liam's gaze was once more on the woman accompanying the teenager.

"Hayley's got lemonade out on the patio. Let's join her." Quinn put a gentle hand on Emily's shoulder as he added, "And then you can tell us what you need us for."

The girl looked up at him, clearly startled that he'd guessed this wasn't just a social call. "I'll explain later," he said as Cutter escorted the women inside.

Quinn held back a moment. "Might want to work on that nonexistent poker face of yours," he whispered to Liam.

Liam grimaced. Quinn grinned.

"Don't blame you," he said. And he didn't. Ria Connelly had the same kind of attractiveness Hayley did, the quiet kind that wasn't glamorous or flashy but lasted forever.

But he also knew—because Hayley often pointed it out—that Liam was rather determinedly uninvolved, watching with amusement as first Quinn, then fellow Foxworth colleague Teague Johnson, followed by their friend Detective Brett Dunbar and finally Hayley's long-lost brother Walker had joined the ranks of the attached, thanks in large part to the uncannily clever and apparently matchmaking Cutter. And that didn't even include the couples he'd brought together on their cases.

Quinn had even overheard him warning the dog once. *Don't you be turning those eyes on me, hound. I've tried that, and it always ends badly.*

Quinn knew the bare bones of Liam's story, what could be gleaned from dry, emotionless reports of facts and what he'd had to know before taking him on at Foxworth but not much more. Someday he was going to get all of it out of the guy, Quinn thought as he shut the door behind them. Or more likely Hayley would; she had them all confiding in her. Well, except Rafe, but he didn't confide in anyone.

In the meantime, it was clear Emily had a problem she thought they could solve. Or perhaps it was Ria. Or both, he thought, remembering how the dog had sat in front of both of them. Cutter hadn't been wrong yet. Which he was going to have to explain yet again, he thought as he led them out to the patio to join his wife.

Life with a dog who kept forgetting he was just a dog was very interesting.

Chapter 2

Cleaned up and cooled down now, Liam Burnett stood in the bathroom and stared at his own rueful expression in the mirror. He ran a hand over his hair. He'd been letting it grow out a bit from his usual buzz cut. He hated haircuts and usually just did it himself, short enough he didn't have to worry about it for a while. But now he laughingly admitted it was fun, because he went to Teague's fiancée Laney's dog grooming shop and she did it with her variable-length clippers, shorter on the sides, a little longer on top. He liked her, and it was fun telling people he got his hair cut at a dog groomer's.

Teague had gotten really lucky, he thought. Laney was the real deal. And good for him. The frequent sparring partner who helped Liam stay sharp was a good guy. The ex-marine with the easy grin deserved to be happy. Former marine, Liam corrected. Both Teague and Rafe had sternly told him there was no such thing as an ex-marine.

And what do you deserve, exactly?

He answered his own question. *Not that.*

He thought of the group out on the patio. The girl with the locket, who had started Quinn Foxworth on the path that had led him to the Foxworth Foundation. It was the story they had each heard when they'd joined up, to illustrate that it wasn't the size of the case that determined what they took on, or the importance of the person. To Foxworth, helping a ten-year-old girl devastated by the loss of a single memento was just as important as taking down a crooked politician.

And then there was the woman. He didn't remember ever having a teacher who looked like her. That sleek swing of dark hair that gleamed in the sun, those eyes the color of today's sky, that petite, nicely curved figure... nope, nothing like that in his memory banks. Of course, if he'd paid more attention in school he might have noticed if one had been there. Not to mention he never would have started down that road to—

He caught himself before going down that snake hole. Barely, because he'd gotten out of the habit. His life now was good, so good he rarely thought of those days anymore, the days before Quinn had yanked him off a bad path. Had given him a final choice.

"And saved your sorry ass," he muttered to the reflection in the mirror.

And that, he thought, was enough self-absorption for the week. He wasn't sure what had set him off now. Maybe it was the girl, Emily. Maybe he was just hoping she wasn't in trouble. But she'd seemed happy enough. Maybe the problem wasn't hers.

The teacher? Had Emily brought her because she was the one with the problem Foxworth could fix?

He found he liked that idea even less. Which in turn unsettled him even more. She was a complete stranger; why would it bother him to think she had a problem that would need Foxworth? He was always glad to help people in trouble, he loved what they did, but this was a different sort of feeling, and he didn't like it.

He caught himself looking in the mirror again. His mirror gazing was usually limited to making sure nothing was grossly wrong, like dirt on his nose or pizza sauce on his cheek. Yet he stood there wondering how he had appeared to her, all grubby and sweaty from playing with Cutter.

All right, that's it. Now you've gone over the edge. Get the heck out of here.

As he donned clean clothes from his locker on the back wall of the bathroom, he pondered. Maybe he should just go about his business. Maybe Quinn wouldn't need or want him on this one, he reasoned. Emily was special to his boss, being the first case and all. He'd probably want to handle whatever this was himself.

Besides, Liam had other things to do. Some stuff to send to Ty. He and the tech guy at Foxworth headquarters in St. Louis had been working on improving the in-house tracking system, installed on all the Foxworth vehicles. And he hadn't been to the shooting range in a while; he needed to do that, too. He'd never had to actually use the handgun Quinn insisted he be proficient with, but it had been close a couple of times and he wanted to be sure he was up to speed. Even though he was much more at home with rifles, he'd turned out to be a decent shot with the Colt. But that didn't mean he didn't need to practice. And he'd promised Rafe he'd do an electronics check on the backup generator while Rafe was off in Alaska on that sabotage case. So he could do that, and then he could…he could…

His list of reasons to avoid joining the group on the patio sputtered to a halt. He was trying to decide where to start when a low woof outside the bathroom door startled him. He hastily yanked on his boots—custom-made back

home, his one splurge when he'd accepted the job here—
and opened the door. Cutter stood there, waiting.

"What's up, hound?"

The dog turned and trotted a few steps toward the patio,
stopped and looked back over his shoulder. The customary
"follow me" canine body language. Cutter's vocabulary
was much larger than most dogs, and given that Liam's
folks raised them he had some basis for that observation.
But this one was pretty standard to most dogs. What wasn't
standard was how impossibly inventive the animal was
when it came to getting his point across.

And how impossibly stubborn he was when it came to
getting people to do what he wanted.

"Boss didn't ask for me," Liam pointed out, even though
he knew resisting was useless if the dog's mind was set.
And the look Cutter gave him then was the canine equiva-
lent of "Seriously? That's what you're going with?"

Maybe Quinn had sent the dog for him, to hurry him
up, Liam thought.

He had a sudden vision of taking this guy home to meet
his parents' rather rambunctious pack of mostly tracking
hounds and hunting dogs. Cutter would have them orga-
nized and herding longhorns, whether they were bred for
it or not.

The image gave him the laugh he needed and, feeling
silly over his uncharacteristic burst of self-contemplation,
he followed Cutter who, as he'd expected, headed straight
for the patio where the others were gathered.

Ria Connelly was glad she had a glass of Hayley Foxworth's delicious lemonade—no powdered mix here—to
focus on when the Foxworths' dog came back. Because
he had with him the other Foxworth…agent? Operative?
Whatever they called themselves. The one she'd met outside. Liam. Who had obviously been playing with said

dog quite cheerfully. Part of his job? Maybe, but judging by the way he'd been laughing as they came around the building, it was a part he enjoyed.

Of course, Cutter was a very beautiful dog, with a lot of personality. She'd seen that even in the short time she'd been here. She liked the way his head and shoulders were black but the color shifted to a reddish brown over the rest of his body, liked the thick, soft fur and most of all the amber-flecked dark eyes, so wise and knowing.

And she wasn't usually fanciful about dogs, but this one seemed different to her. If he was a person she would have said he had an old soul. So maybe that applied to dogs, too.

As for his ball-throwing partner...

She told herself it wasn't that delightful grin or hair in that style she liked—short but a bit longer on top, where it looked like you could muss it any which way and it would still look intentional...

And thoughts of messing with his hair led down roads she had no business going. He didn't look that much older than some of her students. But, then, that was often said about her, too.

Besides, it wasn't that at all. It was simply that she liked that he'd been so happy over a simple thing like playing with a dog. Her world seemed to be overflowing with teen-age angst these days, and seeing somebody so pleased with such a simple thing was like an antidote. And it had nothing to do with the leanly muscled body or the chest—and abs—that had been on display before he'd pulled his shirt back on. Hastily enough that she found the seeming self-consciousness rather charming until she remembered this was, after all, his place of work.

When Quinn gestured to him to take a seat, he headed for one of the empty ones near his boss. The dog got in his way, though, and they seemed to try to dodge each other for a moment before he finally ended up sitting down in the chair closest to her. He gave the dog a look she couldn't define, except to say it was as wary as if the animal had suddenly morphed into a wolf.

"Cutter seems to think we'll need you for this," Hayley said, sounding amused, although Ria wasn't certain about what. She had only just met Quinn's wife, a pretty woman with lovely green eyes, but she already liked her.

"Does he now," Liam said with an expressively wry quirk of his mouth. Ria wondered where he was from, what place had put that slight drawl in his voice. "And just what is 'this'?" Liam asked, shifting his gaze from the dog to Hayley.

"We're about to find out," Quinn said equably. He looked at their two visitors. "Which of you has the problem?"

"Neither of us, really," Emily said with a glance at Ria.

Ria smiled. "I'm just the wheelman, as it were. But I understand her concern."

She also had her doubts that this vague, nebulous job was something an operation the apparent size of Foxworth would take on. This building of theirs was expansive and well equipped, including a small kitchen and bath, a living area with fireplace that could be in any nice home and even a bedroom in the back corner. She also thought she'd caught a glimpse of a helicopter in that warehouse-looking building at the other end of the gravel parking area. Foxworth was much bigger than she'd expected.

Emily's explanation played back in her head. *They used insurance money to start it, Mr. Foxworth and his sister. Their parents were killed by terrorists.*

So he understood loss. But even that seemed on a much grander scale. And yet…

He never belittled me or the smallness of my request. He understood how important my mother's locket was to me, how it was the only thing I wanted in life, to have it back, because it was the only thing I had left of hers. And he found it. He turned the thieves over to the police but only after he got the locket back.

Emily's heartfelt retelling of her story had been the final factor in Ria's decision to at least give this a try. And that's what she should be focused on—Emily's worries, not the distraction of the sandy-haired guy with the quirky grin sitting too close to her.

"Emily?" Ria liked how Quinn said it. He was a big, powerful-looking guy, but he wasn't afraid to be kind or gentle.

"I think," Emily began, hesitated, then plunged ahead. "I think a friend of mine is in trouble. Maybe bad trouble. Will you help?"

Ria thought asking that before explaining was a bit hasty. But she had, it seemed, underestimated Foxworth. It was Hayley who answered, as if she knew perfectly well what her husband would say. As she apparently did.

"Of course."

Chapter 3

"His name is Dylan," Emily said. "Dylan Oakley."

"What makes you think he's in trouble?" Quinn asked.

"He's been very different lately. I mean, he has reason, but…"

When she stopped, swallowing tightly, Ria knew why and stepped in. "His mother was killed in March, in a hiking accident."

It was a moment before anyone spoke.

"You know him? Is he a student of yours, as well?" Quinn asked Ria.

She nodded. "I've had him in classes for two years. And the difference in him is…marked."

"And it's been getting worse lately, not better," Emily said.

"Sometimes it happens that way," Hayley said, her tone gentle with understanding. "Grief has its own path, and it's different for everyone."

Emily's gaze shifted to Quinn. He nodded. "She knows, too."

Even the dog sat up from his spot near Emily and plopped his chin on the girl's knee, making her smile as she reached out to stroke his fur.

Ria felt oddly out of place. As if she'd stumbled into a club she gratefully lacked the qualifications for. She'd never lost anyone really close to her. Even both sets of her grandparents were still kicking, a couple of them off playing in a seniors tennis tournament in California. Her parents were still running the family hardware stores and her two older brothers were busy with their lives—one producing the much-desired grandkids for the parents while he managed the accounting for the stores, the other following his dream of being an airline pilot. She had aunts and uncles scattered all over the country, and cousins abounded.

She knew she was lucky, but nothing had brought it home like this moment, sitting here among people who had dealt with the kind of loss she'd never had to face. Yet.

Ria toyed with one of her earrings, the tiny silver crossed saw and hammer that was the logo for her family's stores. She glanced at Liam, wondering. But it was there, too, that look. That understanding. It changed his open, innocent appearance, and suddenly he didn't seem quite so young. But his expression was also tinged with something else. In fact, for a moment she thought she saw guilt before he lowered his gaze.

And belatedly she realized that when she had looked at him, he'd already been looking at her. She gave herself an inward shake and focused on the matter at hand.

"But Dylan used to talk to me," Emily was saying. "Because I got it. I knew how it felt, losing his mom. But he stopped. And he doesn't even talk to his best friends anymore."

"He's a smart kid and used to be well prepared. But

his grades have dropped dramatically in the last couple of months," Ria said. "He's even missed some classes, which he never did even right after she died. In fact, he seemed to dive into his studies even more."

"It's a good way to avoid thinking about it," Quinn said. His voice held the self-knowledge they all seemed to share but her.

"I read tons of books," Emily said.

"So did I, after my mother died," Hayley said. "It was my escape."

Emily looked at Liam. "What did you do?"

He gave the girl a startled glance. "What makes you think—" He stopped, and Ria saw his jaw tighten and then release as he said, "Computers. And sometimes I'd take off into the hills for a few days. Find something to track."

There was silence for a moment. Ria looked at her student. She also obviously recognized he'd been through this particular hell. But, then, Emily was very perceptive.

"He's also dropped his other activities," Ria said. "He played baseball in a local league and was good at it, but he didn't sign up this year."

"And he was just starting to get really interested in martial arts," Emily said. "He was all excited, looking for a good school or coach or whatever they call them, and now he won't even talk about it."

"Withdrawing from life," Hayley said with a frown.

"Exactly," Emily said. "I'm worried about him. I even—"

She broke off, looking embarrassed.

"Truth is best, if we're to help." Quinn's tone was mild, nonjudgmental.

"I snuck a look at his phone," the girl admitted. "I was afraid he might be…thinking of doing something."

She'd told Ria about her surreptitious checking of text messages and web history, and while Ria couldn't officially condone the sneakiness and invasion of privacy, she understood the girl's motivation.

"I didn't find anything," Emily said quickly. "Nothing ominous, anyway."

"No searching for suicide hotlines or methods," Ria put in, since that had been her main concern.

"Or bomb-building information?" Quinn asked, his voice gentle.

Emily's eyebrows shot up, and Ria guessed hers had, too.

"Of course not! Dylan would never. Ever." Emily was vehement.

Ria didn't blame him for asking. How many times had people said, after some disaster, that they'd had no idea, that they couldn't believe their nice, quiet neighbor/friend/relative could have done such a thing?

"No insult intended, Emily. Just eliminating possibilities. Like before."

Ria saw the girl let out a breath, and then she nodded. Emily had told her how Quinn had asked a ton of questions, some of them shocking to her. But one had led to the awful realization that someone she'd thought a friend had been one of the thieves who had broken into their house on a night when they'd known she and her adoptive family would be gone.

"Here, I can show you."

Emily sent a picture she'd taken of Dylan at a baseball game last year to Quinn's phone, and followed it with one she'd surreptitiously taken just last week. Ria had seen them both, and the change in the boy was startling. He'd gone from a healthy, carefree, good-looking young man with a fun-loving air to a shadowed, hunched, too-thin boy who looked nothing less than haunted.

Hayley looked at them as they came in, and Ria saw her eyes widen as she took in an audible breath.

"I see why you're concerned," she said.

"I think he's not eating, too," Emily said.

"He's lost weight," Ria confirmed. "And he didn't have much to spare, since he'd already lost some after his mom died."

"He said that was his dad's lousy cooking," Emily said.

"He told you that?" It was the first time Liam had spoken. Emily nodded.

"Yes. We talked a lot, back then. And really, if he'd just stopped talking to me, I would have understood. I would have thought I was just a reminder of loss he didn't want to think about anymore. And that's fine. You have to do what you have to do to get through."

Quinn gave her a long, steady look. "You," he said, "have become everything I ever saw in you, my young friend."

Emily blushed, but she was smiling widely. And in that moment Ria quite liked Quinn Foxworth. Quinn nodded at the girl, and she picked up where she'd left off.

"But he's quit talking to everyone. And sometimes after school he goes up to the lookout—that's a spot with a bench on the hill behind the school—and just sits there. For hours."

"Sounds like a guy with a lot on his mind," Liam said.

"Has he seen a counselor?" Hayley asked.

"Yes," Ria said. "I referred him to the therapist who consults for the school. He saw Dylan for a couple of months after his mother was killed. Of course, we didn't discuss the actual sessions, but he said he was doing well. But then they stopped."

Emily looked at Ria. "He stopped going because his dad wouldn't let him go anymore. And wouldn't let his little brother Kevin go at all, said he didn't need it."

"Sounds like Dad could've used some counseling," Liam said rather sourly. Ria nearly smiled at that.

"And four months later he's like that," Emily said, gesturing with her phone, which still showed that last, haggard photograph.

"Something's eatin' at that boy," Liam said. "He looks like he's carrying the world."

"I don't know what you can do," Emily said to him. "But—"

"We're Foxworth. We'll think of something. Right, boss?"

Ria found herself smiling. She liked Liam's easy, kind reassurance to the girl and the quiet but obvious respect for Quinn that she had a feeling was only partly because he was his boss. And she liked the hint of a drawl, as well. She wanted to ask where he was from, but this didn't seem the time. Not to mention he unsettled her a bit too much.

"We will certainly try," Quinn agreed. "That boy needs some help."

"I just don't know who he'll take it from," Ria said. "We've all tried. Almost everybody he knows has."

"Maybe," Hayley said slowly, "it needs to be someone he doesn't know."

Quinn looked at his wife. "Meaning?"

"People under stress sometimes resist someone pushing to 'help.' And it can be easier to open up to someone who doesn't know about all your baggage."

"That's true," Emily said and then looked at Quinn. "Remember how I poured my heart out to you when my poor parents couldn't even get me to tell them what was wrong? I was afraid of hurting their feelings by wanting this—" she fingered the locket "—back so much."

Quinn looked thoughtful. Ria thought she saw him flick a glance at Liam, but then he quickly got down to business. Details like Dylan's address, his family situation—just his father, little brother and a distant uncle left now—and the names of his friends.

"I'll get on those names," Liam said. "See if anything pops."

"Liam's not just our best tracker in the physical world," Quinn explained at her questioning look. "If it's out there in cyberspace, he'll find it."

"Or Ty will, but it won't come to that," Liam said with a grin. That grin.

"Ty?" Emily asked.

"Our tech guy at headquarters," Hayley said. She smiled. "They have a bit of a competition going on. But together, there's never been anything they couldn't find."

"He won't know, will he?" Emily asked anxiously. "If Dylan knew we were poking into his life…"

"Not a trace," Liam assured her.

Quinn went on then, asking about any new friends Dylan might now be hanging around with that he hadn't before.

"None at school at least," Emily said with assurance. "Cove Academy is small, I'd have noticed."

"We'll have to see about elsewhere, then," Quinn said briskly.

"Dylan's good with tech stuff," Ria said with a quick glance at Liam that felt oddly as if she were sneaking a peek at something tempting but forbidden. "And math. But he does—or did—well in English, too. He won a state prize last term for an essay he wrote." Her mouth tightened. "His mother died the same day it was announced. He never even went to get it."

"Does he drive?" Liam asked.

"He doesn't have his license yet, just his permit," Emily said.

"So no car?"

Emily frowned. "No. He thought he would get his mom's car, after, but his dad got rid of it." The frown deepened. "Practically gave it away, Dylan said. He was really upset."

"His father was grieving, too," Ria said. "Maybe he couldn't bear to see it."

"I get that, but he should have thought how Dylan would feel, too."

"Clear thinking and grieving don't always go together," Liam said. "Sometimes they fight each other so hard neither wins, but you lose."

Ria drew back slightly. That had been an almost lyrical way of putting it. And she saw by Emily's expression that he had reached her. Slowly the girl nodded.

"So what do we do?" Liam asked, looking at his boss.

"Computers, martial arts, a stranger," Quinn said, summing up the discussion as he looked at Liam. "I think you may need to go back to school."

"What?" Liam looked so startled Ria almost laughed.

"We'll think of a good cover. Ria will help, I'm sure."

"Of course," she said, barely masking her amusement at his reaction.

Then she realized that this meant she would now apparently have Liam Burnett in her world. Up close and personal.

And that was a lot more unsettling than funny.

Chapter 4

Liam caught himself, realized he'd once more been staring at his laptop screen without seeing a thing. This was
at least the third time since he'd come upstairs to begin
this session that his mind had drifted off task and started
wandering through the underbrush.

"How's it coming?"

He managed not to jump when Hayley spoke from
barely three feet behind him. He had no idea how long
she'd been in the room. Talk about woolgathering, as his
grandmother always used to say.

"It's coming," he said cautiously. "I have the basics.
Dylan used to be semi-active on social media, even after
a break when his mother died, but faded out over the summer."

"That fits. Withdrawing."

He nodded. "No real official, cop-type trouble that I could
find."

"Quinn called Brett, so he's checking that for us," she said.

He nodded and went on. "Friends are pretty typical. Lots of selfies and talking to each other. A couple of mentions of him but mostly asking where he is or if he's coming somewhere. Then, later, a couple more mad because he didn't show up somewhere he was supposed to."

"Progression," Hayley said.

Liam nodded. "Emily asked about him, as well, a couple of times, but she apparently isn't much for yammering on social media."

"I'm not surprised. Ria said she was focused more on her studies."

She had? He didn't remember that.

Probably because you were too busy trying not to stare at her. You'd better start thinking of her as Emily's teacher, nothing more.

He made himself focus and continued. "When she does post something, it's usually not fluff. Serious stuff. She's big into animal welfare, supporting the local shelter, that kind of thing."

"Speaking of which," Hayley said, "Cutter's stuff is ready."

He blinked. "What?"

"His go bag. You can keep it in your truck for when he's with you. And if you need to take him home with you, we've cleared it with your apartment manager." Liam stared at her, brow furrowed. Hayley tilted her head. "He's going with you, remember?"

"He is?"

She drew back slightly, looking concerned. "Do you not remember that discussion?"

He flushed because the only answer was no. He didn't remember much after Quinn had said he was going to school. Ria Connelly's school.

He snapped his gaze back to his laptop before she could read anything in his expression. "Must have zoned out. Sorry."

"Hmm." Hayley didn't say anything more, but then she wouldn't. She explained patiently, "You're taking him because Emily said Dylan really likes dogs, but his dad would never let him have one."

He seized on the mention of Dylan's father to get past the awkward moment.

"Haven't found much on Dad in the public record. A couple of traffic tickets and one road rage incident that was mentioned in a police activity blog, but I don't know yet if he was the aggressor."

"Brett will find that out for us," Hayley said. "When?"

"Since his wife's death," Liam said, confirming what he knew she suspected. "Before that, he seems squeaky clean."

"So those incidents could be grief messing with his judgment."

"Could be," he agreed and went on. "He has no social accounts. In fact, he doesn't have an online presence at all that I can find."

"Emily did say that Dylan says his father's a bit of a technophobe. Doesn't even have a smartphone."

"You still usually end up somewhere, via somebody else, friend or job, something. But I haven't dug deep yet. Professional sites, checking for fake names or profiles with the same IP, all that."

"If he's a credit counselor, that's someplace to start."

"He is?"

Hayley's mouth quirked. "Missed that, too?"

"I guess I was already thinking about this," he muttered, gesturing at the laptop. It wasn't really true, but since he wasn't even sure himself what had him so rattled he couldn't explain. It would be fine, he'd get in in some capacity, try to get Dylan to open up to him, they'd put Emily's mind at ease and he'd be done.

"We've been brainstorming how to get you and Dylan together," she said.

He gave her a sideways look. "Just don't say I look young enough to go in as a student."

Hayley laughed. "While you could probably do it, we decided it would take too long and stand out too much if you came in as the new kid and zeroed in on him. We need a way to get Dylan to be interested right off."

"Cutter?" he asked. "Isn't that what that's about?"

"Yes, but even clever as you both are that could take a while."

Liam's mouth twisted up at one corner. "Him, yes. Me, not so sure."

"That's okay," Hayley said breezily. "We're sure."

He smiled at her easy, sincere compliment. But before he could respond there was the sound of footsteps on the stairs, and a moment later Quinn, Emily and her teacher—somehow thinking of her that way wasn't helping as much as he thought it would—came into the big meeting room. Quinn and Emily immediately gravitated to the big wall of windows that looked out on the clearing. Quinn must have told her about the eagles because she was scanning the tree line intently.

"Dylan said his mom loved eagles," Emily said sadly. "That's why she loved hiking so much. She loved seeing them out in the wild."

Quinn gave the girl a one-armed hug. He left her to watch for the eagles as he turned to head toward Hayley and Liam.

"I think we've got it," he told them as he joined them on the other side of the room, where their tech equipment was set up.

Liam had the feeling he should have stuck around for that discussion downstairs, instead of bolting to another room. Then again, he'd clearly been so distracted he wouldn't have been much use anyway. He glanced at Emily's teacher—no, still not working—wondering how such a petite woman could take up so much space in a room this big.

She smiled at him. And suddenly Liam felt like he had the time he'd gone to the mountains above Denver, simply because he'd never seen mountains so high in person. He had found himself out of breath merely going up a flight of stairs, but was never sure if it was the exertion or the view.

"Liam never quits once he's on the scent," Quinn was saying, in the tone of a promise.

He yanked his gaze back to his boss. "What do I have to do?" he asked warily.

"Brush up on your judo and Muay Thai. Ria's going to get you in as an after-school coach."

He blinked. "But I don't know anything about teaching it."

"Ria will help with that."

Oh, great.

"You'll manage," Quinn said at his expression. Then he added with a grin, "After all, you were taught by one of the best."

The old joke—he'd been taught mostly by Quinn himself—helped him get a grip. "And put him on the ground more than once," he pointed out, his customary response.

"That's when I knew you were ready," Quinn said. "And you've got that sudden-strike thing going for you."

"Sudden strike?" Ria asked.

Quinn's grin widened. Emily had just rejoined them, and he gave her a wink as he answered. "He strolls in all relaxed and leisurely, lolls around like he couldn't move fast even if he wanted to. Just when you start thinking he's half-asleep he explodes and takes you out before you can blink."

Ria laughed. It was a light, lilting sound that gave him

that high-altitude feeling again, even more than Quinn's warming words.

"I'll remember that," she said.

"Dylan will like that," Emily said. "He really did want to learn. It's the only thing he still mentions now and then."

"And teaching something concrete, physical-like—that is different than having to teach English or math or history," Ria said in a reassuring tone. "You can actually show what needs to be done."

Liam just looked at her for a moment. Made himself do it. Made himself ignore that odd feeling. No one spoke. If he was going to do this job—and it looked like he had no choice—it might be best to draw a line right here and now. He couldn't get it done if he let her keep him off balance. He didn't like admitting that this woman he hadn't even known existed two hours ago could do that, but there it was. So he needed some space. He'd figure out why later.

"Martial arts," he said formally, "are as much mental as physical. If you don't understand the concept behind them—and each one is different—you won't be able to utilize them to their full potential. You can go through the moves and even be effective, but unless you understand the mind-set you'll only be mimicking. It won't be instinctive, and it may let you down when you need it most."

She was staring at him. He supposed it was because he'd given what was, for him, practically a speech. And then she surprised him.

"Your drawl was gone."

His mouth twisted. Figures a teacher—an English teacher—wouldn't like his drawl. So he exaggerated it when he said, "I c'n actually talk like a guy who done went to school, iffen I need to."

She drew back slightly. When she spoke, it was in the same kind of tone and cadence he had used in his little speech on the martial arts. "And I put on glasses when I feel I need to be taken more seriously by people who tend to judge on appearance alone. That was not a criticism. Nor was it an assumption that you were not educated based on a regional accent. In fact, I rather missed it."

He'd started to tighten up when it was clear she was mimicking him, but her last sentence disarmed him.

"And might I suggest," she added, "that you remember that speech? It would be a great introduction to what you're trying to teach." She looked at Quinn then. "Was that the verbal version of that sudden strike?"

Quinn was watching them with amusement, Hayley with great interest. Too much interest. So, he realized belatedly, was Cutter. *Oh, no. Uh-uh. No way.*

"I'm not sure," Quinn said. "I've never seen anybody get to him like that before."

Because nobody has, Liam thought with an inward grimace, glad she was still looking at Quinn.

"Should I be flattered, or worried?" Ria asked.

"That," Hayley said, "I think is going to be up to you to figure out."

Liam wanted to ask which of them she meant. But he didn't, because he was afraid she meant the both of them. Together. And being linked with that woman, even jokingly, set off alarms.

He shifted his gaze to Cutter, who was looking up at him with his most innocent expression. But the knowledge of the dog's track record was emblazoned in his mind as if in neon. Glowing. Immutable.

Oh, no, you don't, hound. This is not happening.

Chapter 5

Liam was a little surprised at how easily it all came together. Within two days Ria had the okay for him to utilize the school's gym for after-school meetings starting on Monday.

He looked at her, sitting in a shaft of sunlight at the outdoor coffee stand a couple of miles down the road from the Cove Academy, where they'd met to work out the details before he arrived at the school. The plan was to spend this weekend working up his approach and to get as many tips from her about teaching as he could. It was only Saturday and he already knew he was going to regret that plan.

"That was quick," he said when she told him things were set.

"All I had to do was ask," she said, taking a sip of her coffee. A vanilla blend, he noted, wondering if it was significant. He hadn't slept worth a damn, so went for a double shot of espresso.

Her hair gleamed dark and smooth, those blue eyes were

thankfully—or maybe not, since he couldn't tell where she was looking—masked with sunglasses. Since he was wearing them, as well, they could easily be staring at each other and neither of them would know it.

"Your Head of School knows I'm not really a teacher, right? Just a guy who knows some stuff?"

Ria nodded. "She knows. And she wants to meet you first, of course. But I think what really sold her was your little speech."

He blinked. "What?"

"I quoted it to her. She was intrigued."

"Oh." He wasn't sure what to say to that. Or the fact that she remembered enough to quote him. "I'd say your boss trusts you."

"Dr. Halvorson picks instructors very carefully," she told him. "She knows what she wants, and she generally gets it."

No, he thought, she wouldn't be staring at him. That seemed to be only his problem. Despite convincing himself she really wasn't all that, and that his reaction had been a fluke. He'd even thought about calling a couple of casual female acquaintances, thinking maybe an unfussy, no-strings date would set him to rights again. But when he realized how long it had been, he discarded that idea as unwise. He wasn't sure he was interested anyway.

"How did you end up as a teacher?" he asked, trying to divert his thoughts.

He saw her brows rise above the dark glasses. "I ended up as a teacher because that was always my goal."

"Always?"

She nodded. "It's all I ever wanted to be, since sixth grade and Mr. Matta. He made everything come so alive that kids ran to get to class not because they were late but because they loved it. That's the kind of teacher I try to be."

And if I'd had you, I might have paid more attention...

"From what Emily has said, you are."

"I hope so. I'm lucky to be at Cove. Once we get through Dr. Halvorson's lengthy process, we pretty much have free rein. And she's always open to suggestions like this one." She flashed a grin that nearly stopped his breath. Again. "And that you're volunteering helps on the budget end."

"Things are tight?"

"Not really, but she does have an administrative board to account to." She took another sip of coffee. "How does Foxworth do that, anyway? Do what they do, for free?"

Glad for the ordinary question, Liam answered easily. "Quinn's sister. Financial genius. Took the insurance money from their parents and parlayed it into enough to keep them going probably forever."

"What a sad way to start but a wonderful tribute."

He nodded. "They're good people. The best."

"How did you end up there?"

"Long story."

She studied him silently for a moment. And he realized sunglasses didn't matter when you could actually feel someone's gaze on you.

"Unpleasant story?" she finally asked.

"Could have been."

He was dodging, he knew it. How he'd come to Foxworth wasn't something he dwelt on often. And then it struck him that this might be the perfect way to get that distance he wanted between them. Because he could already tell Ria Connelly was generally a straight-arrow sort, had probably never been in trouble in her life. If he told her the truth, she'd put the distance there herself.

If he told the full truth, she'd probably get up, walk away and never look back.

But then the whole case would be compromised. He'd be letting Foxworth down and, worse, Emily, which he had a feeling Quinn would not forget soon.

The sunglasses didn't mask at all that she was staring at him now. It was as if her steady gaze had some sort of tangible energy, and he could feel it flowing toward him.

"Not into mutual sharing, huh?" She said it lightly, but he had a feeling there was a sting in it anyway. "Dr. Halvorson may ask, you know. She's very thorough. Besides, once you're there Quinn thinks it will speed things up with Dylan if he thinks we're friends. And a friend would know that."

He let out a breath. Went for the digest version. "I'm good with computers. Good enough to get into some trouble. I was on a wrong path. Quinn gave me a chance to go another way."

There was more to it than that, so much more, but he couldn't go there now. He had a job to do, Foxworth had trusted him with it and he would get it done.

"And you took it."

"Quinn is...very convincing."

And the thought of being locked up was pretty persuasive, too.

"He seems like a very solid guy."

"He is. Like a rock. I owe him—" he had to unexpectedly stop, swallow, before he could finish "—everything."

She smiled at him then, a soft, warm kind of smile that, like her stare, he felt in an almost physical way. "Obviously you justified his faith. You should be proud."

Well, that wasn't the result he'd intended. "I was sitting in lockup, looking at serious jail time," he pointed out. "I'm just grateful."

"Which also takes a certain amount of grace and class, Liam Burnett. Whether you admit it or not, it wasn't all Quinn."

He nearly gaped at her. How had she turned that around? He tells her he nearly went to jail—in fact, he had for a couple of days before Quinn had stepped in—and she's complimenting him?

"You must be a heck of a teacher," he said with a rueful quirk of his mouth.

"I'm good," she said easily. "Very good."

She said it with a quiet, humble sort of confidence, the kind that had nothing to prove. And he found himself smiling at her.

"I believe that."

"I assume you hacked somebody?" she asked. "Who? Or what?"

Again the possibilities raced through his mind. He could tell her about the time he hacked school systems, to tweak the grades of student customers who paid him according to what grade they wanted. Or later when he'd rigged a contest's random draw to win. Or more, all strictly for personal benefit. The ones he wasn't proud of.

Or he could tell her about the ones that had made Quinn think he might fit at Foxworth. When he'd screwed with the records of his hometown's biggest bully and the guy had ended up on a community service road crew, taking bullying from guys much bigger and tougher than him. Or the county guy who kept harassing his parents over a property line, despite their irrefutable proof he was wrong. Or the bank that happened to be run by the county guy's brother-in-law and had started giving his folks grief.

But the last answer was the one that explained everything, so, with a wry expression and raised brows, he gave it to her.

"At one point… Foxworth."

She blinked. Reached up and pulled off her sunglasses as if to stare at him more incredulously.

"You hacked Foxworth?"

He nodded. "I didn't believe anybody would really do what they do—fight for people in the right, big or small, and do it for only the promise of help in turn down the line." His mouth curved into a smile as he remembered his own disbelief. "But they do," he added softly.

"Let me get this right…you hacked Foxworth, and Quinn hired you?"

"Crazy, huh?"

"Or very, very smart," she said. "His gamble obviously paid off."

"But it'll never be paid back." He grinned. "My folks think he walks on water. They were sure I was headed straight to hell. I was the black sheep of the family, no doubt."

"Siblings?"

"Two of each. Couple of successful corporate types, an oil exec and a doctor."

"So you really were the problem child."

"That I was."

"They must be relieved."

"They are. And I'm sorry I gave them so much trouble. They're good, good people. It wasn't their fault. Sometimes, if you're good at something, it can get you in trouble. You follow the path because it's easy for you, and sometimes you're in over your head before you realize it."

He realized then that he'd been sitting here sharing his life story with her, easily, without even thinking about it. How had she managed that? She'd given him one tiny bit of her own history, and suddenly he was pouring his own out by the bucket? When what he'd meant to do was get that distance between them?

"I'm surprised that Dylan didn't pour his soul out to you on request," he said with a grimace.

"I can have that effect," she said with a laugh. "It's my honest face."

Yeah, your face is honest. Among other things. Like beautiful. Fascinating.

Trouble.

"I only wish Dylan would," she went on. "I'm worried about him."

Time to get down to business, Liam thought. Quickly he updated her on what they'd learned, which wasn't much more than he'd gleaned that first day. Quinn had advised him to leave it there for now, until he got a feel for things after he met Dylan. His assessment, Quinn had said, would determine if they picked up the pace.

"Tell me more about him," he said then. "The more I know, the better chance I have of getting through. And maybe, more important, of not having him shut down on me."

She looked thoughtful. "You're bringing the dog, right? That will help."

He nodded. "Cutter's mine for the operation. Already have his go bag in my truck."

Her eyes widened. "The dog has a go bag?"

He gave her a crooked grin. "He's one of the team. And, believe me, it won't seem strange once you get to know him."

"What's strange was how he greeted Emily, as though they were friends already."

"I noticed that. And like I said, once you get to know him, you'll find out I've been right about him all along."

"Right about him?"

"I've been telling them since he got here that he's not a dog. He's a smart alien in a dog suit."

She laughed, and that made him feel much better than it should have.

It was going to be a long weekend.

Chapter 6

He'd underestimated.

This might turn out to be the longest weekend of his life, Liam thought as he sat on a bench at Cove Academy the next day. Even longer than the weekend he'd spent in juvie, trying to stay alive. It wasn't that it didn't go well jobwise; it did. Ria helped stir up memories of what it was like to be that age, and between them they decided he should go in less as a formal instructor and more as a guy who put his skills to actual use, willing to share. Although the idea of teaching a bunch of kids, instead of dealing with just one, was intimidating. They had progressed to that topic on this sunny Sunday afternoon as they sat, her large black bag between them. He didn't know whether to be thankful or frustrated at the barrier.

"I'm no expert in any one of the usual arts. I've just developed a style that works for me that is a combination of a lot of them," he warned her.

"But you had to learn at least parts of them all to do that, didn't you?"

"True."

"Then let your approach to them be the same…that you're going to show them bits of each so they can get an idea if there's one they'd like to pursue."

He considered that, and it seemed reasonable. But, then, most things she said did. "And hope Dylan bites."

"Yes."

If the boy didn't, Liam wasn't sure what he'd do. He'd just have to deal with that if it happened. And, in the meantime, get through the rest of today. At least once he really started on the case, he might only see her now and then, instead of for hours at a time, as they'd done yesterday and now today.

With not much sleep in-between.

Cutter, lying at their feet, lifted his head. And Liam thought of how, a couple of hours into that tossing and turning night, the dog had hopped up on the bed beside him, given a little whine and a lick to his ear and settled in. Whether it was because of the comfortable familiarity of a dog, or that talent Cutter had for soothing restless souls, Liam had finally gone to sleep for a couple of hours.

Why he was so restless in the first place was something he'd deal with later.

Or not at all, he thought wryly as he looked around again.

Ria had suggested they have today's meeting at the school so he could get familiar with the grounds. The place had once been a small farm of sorts, and the big farmhouse and various buildings had been converted into classrooms, labs, a library, several study rooms, a theater, a small coop that apparently still served as one for a few chickens and the barn that was now the gym where he'd be working.

"This is quite a place," he'd said when they'd first arrived, looking around at the campus carved out of a thick grove of evergreens.

"I think it's lovely. Peaceful. Conducive to learning."

And again Liam caught himself thinking that if he'd ever had a teacher who looked like her, he might have paid a lot more attention. Since he'd sworn off thoughts like that—apparently unsuccessfully—his tone had been a bit snarky. "Spoken like a born teacher."

"I am, I hope" was all she'd said. And thus had begun day two of this longest weekend.

If it wasn't for Cutter, bless that hound, Liam wouldn't have made it. But, as he had last night, the dog seemed to sense when he was too near the edge and then did something. Anything. Demand a break, more often to play than for a call of nature. Chase a bird, a ball if Liam would throw it, or simply start a rather manic game of tag. He included Ria in the tag, which made it both easier—it was difficult to think of anything but fun when you were playing with a dog who seemed to be working overtime to make you laugh—and harder, because she did laugh, delightedly, and it was the best thing he'd heard in years.

"He is quite a personality," she said now, after the current mad chase ended with Cutter finally stopping for a drink of water from a spigot Liam turned on for him. They sat on a different bench in a shady spot while Cutter plopped down before them, panting but clearly happy.

"He is. He's downright scary sometimes. But he's also a valuable member of Foxworth," he said.

"I imagine he gets people to talk to you. Like, hopefully, Dylan."

"He does. But it's more than that. He brings us at least half our cases."

She looked from him to the dog and then back. "He what?"

Liam explained as best he could with examples, ending by asking, "Remember when he sat in front of you and Emily and looked at Quinn?"

"Yes."

"He was giving him The Look."

She smiled but in a puzzled way. "You say that like it's capitalized."

"To us, it is. It's his 'fix it' look. Means there's a problem that needs fixing and Foxworth can do it."

Again she glanced from him to the dog and back. "That's…"

"Yeah. It is. But it's true."

She looked at Cutter with even more interest now. "He's Hayley's dog?"

"Started out that way. But he's Quinn's now, too. We knew that when he got his own bark."

"His own bark?"

She was laughing again, but it was clearly in delight, not disbelief. She only stopped when Cutter got to his feet. The dog stretched and then started walking toward the woods next to the building that housed the library.

"Do you need to go with him?" she asked.

Liam shook his head as he opened the envelope of flyers Hayley had printed up for him last night, announcing his workshop. "He'll let me know."

"He is…amazing."

"He's a different sort of critter, that's for sure."

She tilted her head as she looked at him then. "Is your accent still off-limits?"

His mind shot back to that moment when he'd both misinterpreted and overreacted to her comment on his drawl. Maybe he'd known even then how she was going to tangle him up. But he wasn't going to make that too-obvious mistake again.

"Texas," he confirmed neutrally.

"Your family is still there?"

"Most of them, yes."

"I have a cousin in San Antonio. He has a restaurant on the River Walk. He—"

She broke off as Cutter, from the corner of the library, let out a sharp, two-note bark.

"And there's my call," Liam said, lifting his head.

"That's your bark?"

"Yep."

"Amazing," she repeated and got up with him.

"Maybe you should stay here until I find out what he's onto."

"I hardly think anything's going to happen here."

"The roads are paved with dead critters who didn't think anything was going to happen."

"Well, thanks for that visual," she said, her tone dry. "If some murderer is lurking in the woods, wouldn't I be safer with you and Cutter than standing here alone?"

"I was thinking more about bears and mountain lions." But, he thought, it was interesting that her first thought was a human threat.

"Oh. We haven't seen any for a long time. Coyotes, yes."

"With that barn full of coyote bait, I'm not surprised."

"Another charming visual." She sounded a little peeved now. "Are you always so graphic?"

"Realistic," he retorted.

"Then maybe I won't tell you how I feel about orcas."

"I can probably guess."

"I love them," she admitted. "They're so beautiful, and I love that they play. They have a cohesive family unit, aunts will take care of calves if the mother dies. It's remarkable."

Again spoken like a teacher. "And they're killing machines, don't forget that. They call them killer whales for a reason."

"That, too. Very efficient."

She seemed unbothered this time, and he guessed she'd come to terms with that aspect of the striking black-and-white creatures. And he wondered if she'd set him up for that, just to show him she wasn't naïve about the realities of nature.

The bark came again, more insistent this time. But not warning, he thought. Cutter just wanted him over there; he wasn't sounding an alarm to come armed and ready to fight.

He started toward the sound. Ria followed. Of course. He'd just have to trust that if it was a threat, he and Cutter could handle it. Which wouldn't even be a question if it was only him. But Ria threw everything off balance.

In more ways than one.

He shoved the thought out of his mind as he rounded the corner of the building. Trusting Cutter, he didn't take unusual care, but he was alert and ready just the same.

The scene that greeted them was anything but threatening.

Cutter was lolling in front of someone seated on the ground. The dog was clearly reveling in enthusiastic petting and scratching. His tail was wagging energetically. There was definitely no threat here.

"Dylan," Ria breathed, so close Liam could feel the brush of it against his ear. He wondered if the shiver that went through him was visible to her, even as he confirmed the teenager's identity from the photos he'd seen.

"He's smiling," Ria said, sounding pleasantly surprised. "I hadn't realized how long it's been since I've seen him smile."

"Step one accomplished, then," he said quietly. And she smiled at him, as if her annoyance at him had been erased by a simple smile from a troubled boy. Which told him even more about her.

Dylan looked up then, still smiling at the dog. But when he saw them, the smile froze and then vanished as the boy went still. Too still.

"Here we go," Liam muttered and started forward.

"Gently," Ria suggested, right behind him.

He gave her a sideways look but quickly returned his focus to Dylan Oakley. "Hey," he called out as they got closer, "sorry. He sort of wandered. Hope he's not bothering you."

Dylan seemed to relax a little. "No, he's not. He's great."

"He's a good, smart dog."

"His name's Cutter?" the boy asked, indicating the tag on his collar.

Cutter woofed. Liam grinned. "He likes to answer that one himself."

"Cool." For a moment the smile came back. And Liam noted it didn't vanish again when Dylan shifted his gaze to Ria. So there was trust here, just not enough.

"Ms. Connelly," Dylan said with a nod.

"Hi, Dylan. This is my friend Liam. Liam Burnett. And you've already met his dog."

As if on cue, Cutter leaned in and gave the boy a swipe with his tongue. Dylan's smile widened. It was holding. Which made Liam hopeful.

"What are you doing here on a sunny Sunday afternoon?"

The boy looked instantly wary. "I forgot a book," he said, gesturing at the backpack beside him. It was larger than most he'd seen schoolkids carrying and Liam wondered if it was because Cove textbooks were bigger or if maybe Dylan had more in there than most. *Ready to run* was the phrase that popped into his mind, and he filed it away as a possibility.

"No e-reader?" Liam asked lightly. "Save your back?"

The boy seemed to relax slightly. "They believe in dead-tree versions."

"The learning process is different," Ria said. "Especially note taking. Running it through the brain and out through writing seems to make it stick better."

Dylan didn't dispute her, Liam noticed. The boy merely shrugged.

"Speaking of learning," she said, "Liam's going to be holding some workshops here the next couple of weeks, after classes."

He supposed that was a good way to put it. Better than teaching, which might put him in a don't-talk-to category in the boy's mind. She'd clearly realized that.

"Workshops?" He shifted his gaze to Liam. "You're a teacher?"

Liam laughed. "Boy, would my old man laugh his butt off to hear that. No, I'm just a guy who knows some stuff."

He thought he saw something flicker in the boy's eyes when he mentioned his father, but it vanished so quickly he couldn't be sure. "What stuff?"

He was about to just say "martial arts" when Ria touched his arm. He wasn't sure what she meant—or why it sent another shiver through him—but he let her take the lead. She knew the kid, after all.

"A few students have shown an interest in learning about martial arts. Liam's going to be helping them choose which one they might like best."

He saw what she'd done. If he'd answered as he'd been going to, it might have had Dylan thinking this was aimed specifically at him. Which it was. But she'd diluted it, said there were others, so now he couldn't be sure. But that didn't stop Dylan from regarding Liam suspiciously.

"You some kind of expert?"

Liam shook his head. "Like I said, just a guy who knows some stuff and has put it into use now and then. Enough about most of the disciplines to show the differences."

"So you don't, like, have your own dojo, or whatever it is?"

"No. I'm nowhere near that level. What I've got is a crazy combination of a lot of different styles."

Dylan considered that. "You mean like MMA?"

Liam laughed. "Only in that I use what works for me. I'm not into fighting for fighting's sake. I'm into staying alive and undamaged."

He was sure of what he saw in the boy's eyes then. And it made his jaw tighten. Because it was pure, unadulterated hope.

Chapter 7

Ria wondered if Liam had seen it, that look in Dylan's eyes. Was he that perceptive? He'd certainly taken her cue easily enough. Which said something, that he didn't feel he had to lead every step of the conversation. Of course, given the electric snap that had nearly singed her fingers when she'd touched him, she'd learned something about herself, too. She apparently had a weakness for cute, former bad-boy Texans who still had a hint of a drawl.

But now she needed to focus on Dylan. That look had convinced her more than anything that Emily had been right. And oddly, so did Cutter's reaction, which was to lean into the boy as if putting himself between Dylan and the world. Yes, he needed help. But he'd reacted so strongly to the words *staying alive* and *undamaged* that her entire assessment shifted. It didn't seem to her now that Dylan was worried about the inner threat, the kind that led to self-harm or worse, but an exterior one. Was he in some other kind of trouble?

"You should come by." Liam's tone hit just the right casual note. "Meet up in the gym lobby. I'm not into public embarrassment, either, so after I explain the plan, we'll talk one at a time, go through some things."

Again Dylan reacted but with simple interest this time. Or appreciation about the privacy. That was a good call on Liam's part, she thought.

"Just talk?" Dylan asked.

"At first. Maybe do a couple of basic exercises or I'll show some examples of stuff at the foundation of the discipline, so people get a feel for if they'll like it or hate it."

He flashed that grin and, despite having seen it before, Ria nearly gasped. His easy smile had punch enough, but that sudden grin was lethal.

"Guess I'd better bring a book," he said, nodding toward Dylan's backpack, "in case nobody shows up."

For the first time Dylan smiled. "They'll show up."

"Maybe help spread the word? I'd hate to be sitting there by myself tomorrow afternoon, reading my truck maintenance manual or something."

"I could loan you a copy of *War and Peace*," Ria suggested, encouraged by Dylan's continuing smile.

This time Dylan actually laughed at Liam's exaggeratedly horrified expression.

"Try it," Dylan suggested. "Ms. Connelly can make even that really interesting."

Ria was moved by the simple compliment. "Thank you, Dylan. You did quite well in that section."

The boy looked pleased in turn. He nodded toward the flyers Liam held. "Maybe I could help, post some of those around?"

"That would be great," Liam said, separating out several. "Just anywhere people pass by a lot."

"Well," Ria said after Dylan, with a final pat for Cutter, had gone off with flyers in hand, "that went well."

"Seemed to," Liam agreed.

"I think he'll show up. Then you can get some one-on-one time with him."

He nodded. "There's something going on with him, for sure. Question is, is it more than just being a teenager?"

"What you saw at the end there, the smile, the laugh? That's what he was like all the time, before."

"Happy kid."

"Mostly." She sighed. "Dylan was usually the peace-maker. He could talk kids out of fighting or crack a joke that would have them laughing instead."

An odd little smile turned up just one corner of his mouth, and Ria wondered if perhaps he'd been like Dylan, at that age. Before he'd gotten into trouble. She was more curious about that now than ever. She wanted to know what had sent him down that bad path he'd mentioned,

"We'll see what I find out tomorrow."

He rose and began to walk, the rest of the flyers in hand, pausing here and there to put one up as she pointed out likely spots where the most kids would see them.

"You don't mind dealing with other kids, just to get to Dylan?" she asked when he'd posted one outside the science lab.

He shrugged. "I'll be nervous, but it'll be good practice for me. We had a slow summer—which is good news, considering what we do—and I kind of slacked off."

"I'm almost afraid to ask what a busy summer would be."

He grinned. And again her stomach took that tumble. "Let's see…last summer we had a decade-old missing-person case and what turned into a hostage situation. Then a kidnapping. That was before the whole 'take down the state government' thing."

She'd known some of this, from Emily, but the scope of what Foxworth did was boggling. But she couldn't help smiling back at his grin. "Foxworth must really be something."

"We are. Champion of lost causes, people in the right and the truth."

He said it laughingly but with pride, as well. A well-deserved pride, from what she'd seen and heard so far.

"Sounds like a great job."

"Saved my life," Liam said, and there was nothing but sincerity in his voice then.

"But…kidnappings and hostages? That sounds dangerous."

"We're trained for that—Quinn sees to it—although I needed more than the others. They're mostly ex-military and I was just a borderline computer geek who happened to like to track and hunt."

"Seems there'd be some overlap there."

The grin again. *Good grief, stomach, settle down*, she ordered as she posted a final flyer on a board outside the library, where regular school notices were always placed.

"Some. Quinn took care of the gaps, although I felt a bit out of place at first. But Quinn made me see we all have our specialties."

"Like computers and tracking?"

He nodded. "Quinn's the decision guy, obviously. Hayley provides the insight into motivation and subtext. She's amazing with people. Teague's a pilot and tactician of sorts. Rafe…" His voice trailed off, and the slightest of furrows creased his brow. "Well, Rafe is Rafe."

Whoever Rafe was, Liam was worried about him, she thought. But he was clearly not inclined to go into it now, because he went on quickly.

"And Cutter, of course. He's the one who bonds us all together. He belongs to all of us, as much as any one dog can."

"That's sweet," she said.

"And he's saved us all, at one time or another. If we're smart enough to listen to him."

The dog gave a soft whuff, as if reminding Liam they should listen to him all the time. Ria couldn't stop herself from laughing. "He's really quite expressive, isn't he?"

"He gets his point across," he agreed, but he seemed to be avoiding looking at her now. She wondered if he was regretting having said so much, although to her it didn't seem as if he'd given away much that was personal.

Cutter whuffed again, this time as he rose up to put his front paws on the school bulletin board. He nosed at another flyer, a slick one for a new restaurant in the picturesque little town on the bay at the bottom of the hill. Ria hadn't been there yet, but she'd heard from various students that they had some seriously good burgers and an outrageous selection of fries with various toppings that made a meal in themselves and were cheap enough to tempt students with sometimes strapped finances.

She heard a faint sound, realized that, as Liam had looked at the menu that had Cutter's attention, his stomach had growled.

"Skip breakfast?" she asked with a smile.

"And lunch," he muttered.

"I've heard they're good." She kept her tone neutral, nonsuggestive. His stomach made a more insistent sound. He gave her a quick flick of a glance.

"You haven't been there?"

"Not yet."

She wondered, for a brief moment that annoyingly made her hold her breath, if he was going to ask her to go with him. She'd happily forego the insulated bag full of fruit and yogurt in the school fridge if he did.

He didn't.

In that moment Cutter turned, sat and stared up at Liam with what Ria could only describe as a disgusted look. Liam seemed to purposely ignore the animal, and he muttered something under his breath that sounded like "Don't even try, hound."

And abruptly he excused himself, with just enough politeness to keep it from being rude.

Just.

She watched him go, watched the dog follow with obvious reluctance and wondered what on earth had just happened here.

Chapter 8

"He doesn't look like much of a fighter."

"Doesn't look like a teacher, either."

"Hey, he's got a dog. Maybe he's blind. That would be cool, like a superhero."

"Maybe he's got the dog because he's gutless."

Liam listened without looking, since he'd already noted and mentally cataloged the trio of boys when they'd come in. They didn't join the other dozen or so who'd shown up but kept to themselves in a little knot near the door. There were always at least three, he thought. The ringleader and a couple of sycophants. And there was little doubt that the boy who had spoken first and last was the ringleader. He was the biggest of them and wore the most scornful expression.

He was also the one Cutter was watching like an errant sheep.

And Liam noticed many of the other kids who'd gathered around the mats on the floor were keeping a wary eye on the trio. Including Dylan, who was standing toward the back but appeared more intent than any of them.

"Great," he heard a boy mutter, looking at the biggest of the three. "Just what we need—Alan screwing things up."

Purposely Liam turned his back on the threesome. It went against his instincts, but the gym had several mirrors in one corner, near what he guessed was a bar for dance students to use, and he positioned himself so he could watch the three easily without looking directly at them. Otherwise he ignored them, and he saw the leader's expression change; he obviously wasn't used to being ignored.

"Hi, everyone. My name's Liam Burnett. Thanks for turning up and saving me from reading *War and Peace*."

He got a few chuckles, and all of the ones in front of him smiled. He noted Emily's absence. The girl had said she wasn't going to come because she was afraid she'd give him away somehow and Dylan would shy away.

"Y'all know why you're here," he began. He heard the snicker from behind him, no doubt at the drawl he'd purposely let through. "Well, most of you, anyway. Some don't have even a clue."

The titter that went through the group had a nervous edge to it. He kept his back turned but saw the trio, the big guy in the lead, start moving toward him. He watched the reflection, assessing. Alan was big, yes. Nearly his own height. And bulky. Probably outweighed him by at least twenty pounds. But it wasn't muscle, Liam noted, seeing the softness around the middle and in the arms beneath the T-shirt from a local bar. Wondered if the kid counted on his sheer size to intimidate. Wondered if he expected people to think he was old enough to hang out in that dive bar his shirt advertised. Or clever enough to bluff his way in.

And wondered what Alan was doing here at Cove at all. From what Ria had told him about the school and its academic standards, he seemed an unlikely fit. But maybe his folks were rich and bought his way in; money did talk, after all.

And maybe he's really a genius under all that bluster.

Liam nearly grinned at his own thought. Quinn had taught him much about making assumptions.

"I gotta figure," he said to the group, "since this isn't getting you out of class, that you want to be here. Question is, why?"

"Because it's cool?" one of the boys in front suggested.

Liam grinned at him. "It is that."

Another laugh from the group.

"You going to teach girls, too?"

Liam looked at the girl who stood up front, looking at him rather challengingly. In that moment he was glad he'd helped Quinn to train Hayley and Teague's Laney. They'd taught him as much as he'd taught them.

"Absolutely," he said. "With the right mind-set, girls can get more out of it than anyone."

She looked surprised. "You're just saying that."

"Nope. In fact, you have an advantage. If you're attacked, it's usually by someone who thinks you're weak, and if you know how, you can use that assumption against them. You usually are smaller. You can use the size disparity even more. There's an entire discipline, Brazilian jiujitsu, that specializes in just that."

Her attitude changed visibly, from one of challenge to interest. In fact, she looked downright intrigued. He counted it as a small victory.

"I'm not an expert in any one of the disciplines," he said. "What I am good at is picking what works for me. And that's why I'm here, to help you pick."

"If you're not an expert, why should we listen to you?"

"What I'm also good at," Liam said without acknowledging the bully's presence with even a glance, "is assessing an opponent. The way they carry themselves, like a true fighter or just a big ol' thug who doesn't have a clue about fighting someone who knows how to fight back."

A murmur went through the group. They got that he was talking specifically about the boy coming up behind him.

"And," Liam continued, "I'm good at assessing the real level of the threat. If it's someone who can hold their own, or someone clueless I could take down with a sneeze."

This time they laughed. He supposed he shouldn't egg the kid on like that, but he really didn't like bullies. He'd been on the short end of that experience too often, when he was this age.

In the mirror he saw the boy's hands curl into fists. A glance at Alan's face showed he wasn't quite sure he was being insulted, which was also Liam's intent. Liam wondered if Alan was foolish enough to rush him, to attack someone there to teach defense against just that, and in front of the whole group. He almost hoped he was.

He doubted Foxworth would appreciate getting sued by some irate parent over the bruising of their not-so-little boy. Unless, of course, Alan started it. In front of multiple witnesses.

"Most bullies are more scared than anything," he said, keeping Alan's reflection in the line of his peripheral vision as he stepped onto the mat. "Except for maybe that clueless thing."

Again, laughter. Liam could almost feel the big kid's rage.

"Go ahead, give it a shot," he said, without turning.

Alan stopped dead. Liam shoved his hands into his jeans' front pockets. Stood casually, as if he were completely unaware. "You've got the drop on me, right? From behind. And you're a big guy. No way you can lose."

"It's a trap," Alan muttered.

So he was smarter than he looked, Liam thought. "Just a demonstration," he said. "I need a tough guy."

Alan smiled at that; Liam could see it in the mirror. But still Alan hesitated. Then somebody in the group muttered audibly, "Coward." He felt more than saw Alan stiffen.

"Come on," he urged. "No repercussions."

He felt the moment when the boy decided, egged on by that derisive comment, heard the movement when he took that first step. And then he was charging, energized perhaps by the free rein given.

At the last second Liam dodged, spun and swept his right foot into Alan's path, carefully avoiding the knees, where he could do some real damage. The boy went down, hitting the soft mat with a thud that seemed to echo off the walls. And Liam had never taken his hands out of his pockets.

The cheer that went up told him how weary the others were of this particular bully. But he also knew the dangers of provoking one and the likelihood Alan would take out his fury and embarrassment on the first smaller, weaker prey he could find. So Liam grinned and held out a hand to Alan.

"Great job, Alan. Thanks for being a good sport about it. Oh, and for not taking my head off."

The implication that he could have if he'd wanted to seemed to mollify the boy. Liam watched him make the decision to play along. He let Liam give him the hand up.

"If you can't take out the best, what good are you?" Alan said.

Bluster, Liam thought. But he only nodded. If he was really here to teach, it might be interesting to find out what was behind the bully facade. But right now he'd served a purpose. Every other kid in that gym was on Liam's side now.

Liam almost had the mat rolled up for stowing under the bleachers along the side wall when he sensed the approach. Instead of looking behind him, he looked at Cutter, who was on his feet, tail wagging. Trusting the dog's instincts, he finished the job before straightening up and turning around.

Dylan.

"Hey," Liam said casually.

The boy nodded. "That was great. I liked the sound of the Krav Maga stuff."

Liam smiled. "It's effective. Designed for one purpose—street survival."

"Neutralize the threat, you said."

He nodded. "By whatever means necessary."

Dylan nodded. And as if it were a signal, Cutter walked up to him, tail still wagging, ears up. The boy's smile widened. He reached out to stroke the dog's head. The tail wagged faster.

"I was watching him. He didn't like Alan much."

"He's a very good judge of people."

Dylan didn't miss the implication, that Cutter clearly liked him as much as he'd disliked Alan. The boy looked pleased, which told Liam a lot.

"You want to talk about which way you want to go?" Liam asked.

Dylan shook his head. "I can't. I shouldn't even be here now. I have to get home. I'm stuck with watching my little brother, so I have to go get him."

"I hated that, being the built-in babysitter," Liam said.

Dylan's gaze shot to his face. "Yeah. Sucks."

There was something else there, Liam thought. Something deeper than just not liking being a babysitter. He glanced at Cutter, who was leaning into the boy, giving him the full-on Cutter stamp of approval. The boy continued petting the dog, smiling in a way that, for the moment at least, seemed to erase the shadows.

"You got some other time you could free up?" Liam asked. "I'm flexible."

He saw something else flash in the boy's eyes. Surprise? Even eagerness?

"Really? I mean, I have an hour-and-a-half break at eleven, between trig and English on Tuesday and Thursday."

Liam had already known this from Ria; it was part of the plan, and why he'd made the suggestion. It would give them time without other kids around.

"All right. We'll do your one-on-one session then. I'll see if the gym's available, or we'll need to find someplace else."

"Thanks," Dylan said. "A lot."

"No problem. We'll take our time, until you decide what you want to pursue."

"How about we go straight to Krav Maga?"

"If that's what you want, I know a guy. I'll hook you up. But you won't be any good at it unless you can master the mental part first. It's harder than you might think to really believe in no holds barred and no quarter given. It's not the way most people think, if they're not living in a war zone."

"Those guys are serious," Dylan said.

"They have to be. For them it's survival. But for you, it's all about control. Of the other guy, sure, but of you first. It has to be instinctive, second nature."

"Like you did with Alan?"

Liam's mouth quirked upward. "Nah. I was mainly focused on not really hurting him. Didn't want to get sued by angry parents."

"You'd have everybody there on your side, testifying that he jumped you."

"They did seem to enjoy seeing him on his back," Liam said with a grin.

Dylan smiled, and it was the most genuine one Liam had seen from him, except for when he was looking at Cutter. Which he did again now.

"Will you bring him?"

"If you want."

"Yeah. He's a great dog."

"See you tomorrow, then?"

Dylan nodded, not even trying to hide his eagerness now. And when he left, even his steps seemed lighter.

"Thanks, buddy," Liam said softly to Cutter as he watched the boy go. "We're in the door now, at least."

He reached out to scratch behind the dog's right ear, in that spot he liked. The feathery tail began to wag again. And it was a moment before Liam realized it wasn't simply the touch he was happy about. Someone was once more coming up behind him. And this one was a bigger threat than Alan had ever thought about being. To Liam, anyway.

Ria.

Chapter 9

"You're a natural."

Liam didn't look at her. He also didn't seem surprised that she'd been watching. She'd kept out of sight in the seating gallery up above, not wanting to interfere yet too curious to stay away.

She was too curious in general when it came to Liam Burnett.

"Questionable," he said.

"You are. I can tell when someone is getting through to them."

He picked up the light tan jacket that seemed to have a huge number of pockets and pulled it on. It wasn't at all chilly in here, and he seemed to be giving the simple task way too much attention as he said, "Maybe."

"And I'm sorry."

That did it. He finally looked at her, clearly puzzled. "About what?"

"I should have warned you about Alan."

"Oh." He shrugged off her concern.

"I didn't expect him, of all people, to show up." She grimaced. "And the thought of him with any martial arts skills is rather frightening."

Liam shook his head. "Could be the best thing to happen to him. The core of most of them is discipline. And the better you get, the less need you have to prove it."

There was a lot more to Liam than a cute face and that easy drawl. And the sandy-brown hair she still wanted to touch and those rich, golden-brown eyes that seemed to warm her when he looked at her.

Oh, and that great bod, don't forget that.

That body did more than just warm her; it had her wondering things she shouldn't be thinking about. He was here to help Dylan, that's all. She could appreciate, though, couldn't she? As long as she kept her silly thoughts to herself? After all, it had been a long time since a man had distracted her so.

"That would be nice," she said hastily in an effort to divert her errant thoughts. "Alan's on school probation already, which is the only thing that keeps him from being worse than what you saw."

"I wondered at first why he was here at Cove at all. But he's smarter than he acts, isn't he?"

Ria's gaze sharpened. "Yes, he is. Most people don't see that, though. They only see the bluster." And yet Liam had.

"Well, he's got plenty of that."

"It got him kicked out of public school. And I don't know how long Dr. Halvorson will put up with it here."

He gestured around generally. "His folks must be well-off. To afford this, I mean."

"They are, although we have several scholarship programs. And a few students with benefactors, like Emily."

Liam looked back at her. "Emily?"

"Yes. Didn't you know? Foxworth is paying for her schooling."

A slow smile curved his mouth. She thought it delightful. As was the mouth. And there she went again, she scolded herself.

"No, I didn't know," he said.

"But you don't sound surprised."

"Nope. It sounds like them." His mouth quirked upward at one corner. "I'm a beneficiary of some of those Foxworth principles, after all."

She was too curious not to ask. "How did you even find out about them, to hack them? Emily said they work on word of mouth only."

"They helped the uncle of a buddy of mine, who got in trouble with the government for trespassing on government land. Didn't matter that he'd done it to save a kid's life. Anyway, Foxworth stepped in and made it go away. My buddy didn't believe that's what they did all the time, and for free. So he dared me to find out."

"And did you?"

"Not that way," he said as they stepped outside. He was going to regret that jacket, she thought. As sometimes happened here, they were having more summer weather now, in September, than they'd had during summer itself. "Their security was really good, so I didn't get far."

"Then what happened?" she asked, genuinely interested, and a bit disarmed by how easily he was talking about it now.

"Quinn stepped in. Well, Rafe first, actually. I know you haven't met him, but believe me when I say he was enough to scare me straight in a big hurry."

"I would think Quinn could manage that."

"Probably. But having a sniper look at you with those long-distance eyes like you were his next target is not something you soon forget."

Ria blinked. "Sniper?"

"Yep. And a legendary one."

Pride, humor and something more echoed in his voice. Friendship, clearly, but still more. She remembered when she thought she'd heard concern in his voice when the name had come up before. Was it something specific, or was this Rafe just a guy you generally worried about?

It struck her then that Liam looked as if he felt about Rafe something like what she and Emily had felt about Dylan—that there was something wrong, something off, something that could erupt at any moment.

And she supposed she was thinking about that to avoid dealing with the fact that Foxworth had a sniper.

"Do you use his skills often?" She was aware her voice sounded rather faint.

"Actually use them? No. But there are a lot of times when we're damned glad he's there."

She suppressed a shiver at the thought of what kind of cases those must be. And once more revised her assessment of Foxworth and what they did.

"No need for him here," she said, rather fervently.

"Nah. Although it might do Alan good to just meet him," he added with a grin. That grin that still had the effect of kicking her pulse up noticeably.

"I think you handled him perfectly," she said.

"Guys who count solely on their size have weaknesses."

"To your sudden strike?" Ria asked, thinking of the way he'd done it, never even taking his hands out of his pockets.

He shrugged, looking a little embarrassed. "That's Quinn's term. I just want it over, fast."

"It was. And yet you gave him a graceful way out, as if he'd been in on it."

"I don't like bullies, enjoy taking them down, but I've found that humiliating them publically right off the bat can lead to an unpleasant aftermath. And too often it's an innocent bystander who gets hurt."

She studied him for a moment. He seemed such an odd combination, of young, drawling cowboy and wise old sage.

"That's against the Foxworth creed, too? Innocent bystanders getting hurt?"

"Absolutely."

"Even with her high praise, I begin to think Emily understated."

They were at the parking lot now, and Liam stopped beside his big gray truck and turned to look at her. "There are no words for how proud I am to work for them, how much I love what we do."

She had seen troubled kids in her time as a teacher. Knew too well how easily they could take the wrong path, how one thing or person could make all the difference either way. And she could picture Liam, looking not much younger than he did now, in turmoil, scared and trying to hide it and being offered a way out.

"I'm glad, of all places, you tried to hack Foxworth," she said quietly.

He simply stood there for a moment, looking at her. And when his next words came, they were totally unexpected.

"I was thinking of trying out that new place for dinner. Join me?"

She was probably gaping at him, she thought as she tried to find her voice.

"We could talk about ways to get Dylan to open up, once I have him alone," he added, speaking almost hastily, as if to make sure she knew this wasn't a social thing or, worse, a date.

Her heart properly chastised, her pulse dropping back to normal, she managed to say evenly enough, "All right. It would be good to have a strategy."

And it would be good if your imagination wouldn't run away with you at every opportunity around this guy.

The goal was to help Dylan, if possible. Why couldn't she focus on that? At this point, the only thing she had going for her was that he was obviously as determined as she was—or should be—to keep this strictly business.

She hoped he was better at that than she seemed to be at the moment.

As it turned out, it wasn't hard at all for her to remember this was, in essence, a strategy session. Liam so clearly was thinking of other things that it was an effort to not be insulted. After the third time his distraction became painfully apparent, she focused on the fish she'd ordered, wondering how something that had tasted so good when it arrived had suddenly lost its flavor.

It was a good thing that hadn't been a date, she thought as she headed home after an awkward good-bye. It hadn't even been very productive as a planning session, since all they'd ended up agreeing on was to get Dylan talking and hope Liam could guide the conversation to what was bothering him. Which had already been the plan anyway.

She spent the rest of her evening studiously going over her lesson plans for the next day. And scrupulously avoiding thinking about the fact that she'd just spent two hours with a very cute guy who unexpectedly fascinated her, and it had been about as romantic as washing her car.

But in the last moments before she fell asleep, in that time when she was too sleepy to keep the leash on her mind, it strayed to the bottom line of the evening. Which was that she was being an idiot, heading down a one-way street the wrong way.

It just figured that the first guy who had intrigued her in ages wasn't the least bit interested in return.

Chapter 10

Liam stood to one side of the mat on the gym floor, watching Dylan go through the moves he'd just shown him. The boy had a natural grace, and it wasn't going to take much to get him started once he decided on a direction. The question was what it would take to get him to start talking. Liam didn't want to make the kid pull back by pushing too hard.

"Good job," he called out, and Cutter accented the praise with a happy bark and a wag of his tail. The boy responded as much to the dog as to Liam, and smiled. "Let's talk."

He saw the sudden wariness in the boy's eyes. Since he had, as the team often told him, the worst poker face of any of them, he'd had to learn to accurately assess their tells. He'd gotten pretty good at it with everyone except Rafe. But he didn't think anyone could read Rafe unless he wanted them to.

"You've got speed, agility and some power. The field's

pretty much open to you. You just need to decide," he said. The wariness faded at the words, a sort of proof that Ria and Emily were right—something was bothering the kid. And clearly Ria had been right about this approach, talking about anything but what they really wanted to know, just to get the boy going.

The less Liam thought about last night, the better. It had been unnerving for him to sit across a table from Ria Connelly, barely tasting what food he managed to eat because he constantly had to yank his mind back to the matter at hand.

"I did a little looking last night," Dylan said as he left the mat and approached.

"The joy of the internet," Liam said with a grin.

The boy relaxed a little. "Yeah."

Dylan sat down on the bottom bleacher. Cutter immediately shifted to sit next to the boy and plopped his chin on his knee, earning a warm smile. Liam knew the effect the dog had on people, especially those with a troubled mind. He'd grown up around dogs, lots of them since his parents raised them, but he'd never seen one who had Cutter's knack for comforting people. He not only seemed to know when someone needed his particular brand of soothing but somehow delivered it in the appropriate dose. Dylan began stroking his fur, and Liam saw the change in him almost instantly.

"Judo's the classic," Liam said, "but it comes with a lot of study if you want the whole package. It's a philosophy as much as a sport. Karate's another."

"That's where kickboxing started, isn't it?"

"You have been studying," Liam said. "Yes."

Dylan leaned down closer to Cutter but kept his gaze on Liam. "What about Tae Kwon Do?"

"Like those head-high kicks, do you?"

Dylan smiled kind of lopsidedly. "They look cool."

"That they do. You've got the speed and agility for it. And it takes balance, since the stances are narrower. Then you've got Muay Thai, which is the every-body-part-is-a-weapon thing."

Dylan grinned then. He seemed relaxed now, and Liam decided to chance shifting the conversation slightly.

"Really, your approach depends on the why." Liam watched him steadily as he went on. "If you do it because it's trendy or cool, that's fine. It will do you good no matter your reason. You just pick the one you like most and go for it."

Dylan looked puzzled. "I figured you'd be all about deeper reasons."

"I'm working on the assumption you're just dipping your toe in now, not looking for a life's passion. If it becomes that, fine, but you need to know your choices for now. Which brings us back to why. Why are you interested?"

Dylan looked down at Cutter, seeming glad of the distraction of the dog's presence. "Maybe I just want the cool factor."

Liam waited until the silence made the boy look back up at him. "I'd believe that with some," he said quietly. "But I think you are, as you said, deeper than that."

The boy looked pleased, but the expression quickly vanished. Liam went on conversationally.

"There's the physical side, of course—the great exercise. There's also learning that control, of your body and mind. There's the self-confidence that comes with knowing you can protect yourself or others."

Dylan went very still. Strike, Liam thought. But before he could pursue it, a rather raucous guitar riff sounded. Dylan grabbed a cell phone out of his backpack, looked and grimaced.

"Yeah?" he answered and then listened. Liam saw the

kid was keeping a wary eye on him, as if he were trying to decide whether to walk away to keep the call private. In the end it was short, and he didn't. "Wait there. I'll come get you."

He ended the call with a swipe and stuck the phone back in his pocket. He glanced at Liam and shrugged.

"I gotta go get my little brother."

"Now? Where?"

"Down by the marina." He gave Liam a sideways look. "He cut school again."

"Again? Has he done that a lot?" Liam asked.

Dylan hesitated, then shook his head. "Just since our mom died. In March."

"That's rough. You need a ride?" Dylan gave him that wary look again, and Liam shrugged. "If we're done I'll be leaving anyway."

"Sorry, I know you only came for me—"

Liam cut him off with a wave. "No problem. Family comes first."

"Yeah. Right."

Liam knew he hadn't mistaken the bitter undertone in Dylan's voice that time. "Come on. I'm parked right over there. Hound?"

Cutter jumped up and trotted ahead of them toward where the truck was parked as if he'd understood the conversation. Once in the truck, Cutter settled in the small backseat of the crew cab. It was a moment before the boy spoke again.

"That thing you did with Alan," he said. "What was that?"

"Besides cool, you mean?"

He got a grin for that one. "Yeah."

"That was just geometry and physics." Dylan blinked, clearly startled. "Angle of attack and the tendency of a... large body in motion to remain in motion."

Dylan made a strangled noise that sounded like a smoth-ered snort. Liam counted it as success. The too-serious boy had laughed a few times, loosened up a bit, so there was definitely progress.

"You can drop me off here," Dylan said as they reached the street that led slightly downhill to the picturesque ma-rina. Again a sideways look. "Kevin's kind of scared of strangers."

It was too early to push, Liam thought and let it go. "Okay. But take my number. I've got a couple of things to do here, so I'll be in town for a bit. In case you want a ride home or back to school or something."

They exchanged the numbers, but Dylan said, "No, we're good. I know what buses to take. Thanks for the ride." Then he hefted his backpack and reached to give Cutter a good-bye pat.

"See you Thursday?"

The boy seemed oddly relieved. "Yeah. Sure."

Liam watched him go, but when the boy looked back over his shoulder he figured he'd better move along. He drove down a block, parked on a side street, put his hunt-ing jacket on for some camouflage and sprinted toward the water. In the shelter of the entrance of the souvenir shop on the corner, he scanned the people along the waterfront. He spotted Dylan sitting next to a small boy on one of the bright blue city benches. Kevin was slumped but upright. There was little resemblance between them. With his blond hair and fair skin, the younger boy looked much more like the photos Liam had found of their mother.

Dylan had his arm around him. Protectively.

It was, in a way, a reassuring scene. But every instinct Liam had developed since coming to Foxworth was clam-oring. There was definitely something going on here. And while it might simply be two boys trying to adjust to life without their mother, those instincts were saying it was more. He watched until the two boys walked up to the main street and caught one of the smaller county buses heading north, toward where Emily had said they lived.

"I think you're right, hound," he said to Cutter when he got back to the truck. "Dylan's not the problem. He's the one trying to deal with it."

Cutter woofed approvingly from the backseat.

"And thanks for the help," Liam added, knowing the dog was half the reason Dylan had opened up at all.

Cutter leaned forward and swiped his tongue over Liam's cheek. As a "you're welcome," it was pretty clear.

"Definitely a smart alien," Liam said with an inward grin.

He'd just started the truck when his cell rang. He hit the button above his head for the Foxworth system.

"Burnett."

"Hi. It's Ria." His pulse took a leap before she even said her name. He'd recognized her voice instantly, even though he'd half expected it to be Dylan or maybe Quinn or Hayley. "Just wondering how it went with Dylan."

"Oh." Of course. He should have known. Only when she spoke again did he realize he'd been quiet long enough that she felt she had to explain.

"I have Emily in two classes tomorrow. I'm sure she'll ask."

"I just dropped him off at the marina. His brother called Dylan to pick him up."

"You're at the marina?"

"I parked out of sight so I could keep an eye on them, so I'm downtown now."

"So am I."

"Oh." *Brilliant conversationalist, aren't you, Burnett?*

"Lunch break," she explained. "Can we meet and you can update me?"

His pulse did that crazy thing again. He frowned. This

was crazy. Sure, she was attractive, he liked the way that glossy dark hair of hers gleamed in the sun, he bet she looked cute in those glasses she'd mentioned and, more than all that, he liked how much she cared for her students, but that didn't explain this.

"I'd like to stay in the loop," she said from the speaker, and he realized he'd again left her hanging.

"I…sure." He was going to regret it, he was sure, but he didn't know how to get out of meeting with her. Quinn had said they would need to communicate, that she and Emily would be more likely to notice any changes in Dylan.

"Java Hut?" she suggested.

Liam sighed. He could see the sign for the popular coffee stand from where he sat in his truck.

"Okay. I'm practically there."

"I'm at the drugstore. I'll head that way."

In the silence after the call he just sat for a moment. This made no sense to him. He just didn't react this way. He was lighthearted, never-get-too-close Liam Burnett. In his way, he stayed as unentangled as Rafe. And women didn't see him as a challenge, not the way they did with his dark, brooding partner. That was the reason he cultivated the lighthearted, joking demeanor; it was a good shield. Nobody expected him to be serious. Or get serious.

With a sharp shake of his head he got out of the truck and locked it after rolling the windows all the way down for Cutter.

"I won't be long," he promised the dog. Anybody who tried to take advantage of the open truck would regret it.

He took a quick glance inside when he got there, at the line to the counter and the few, full tables. He saw a woman with dark hair, but it was longer, didn't have the sleek swing Ria's did. Saw another sitting at a table with her back to the door, but she was hunched over her phone, focused solely on it despite apparent friends sitting with her, and that just didn't fit with what he knew of Ria.

He backed out of the doorway and leaned against the wall just outside. He looked toward the small drugstore. There were several people walking along the main street, taking advantage of the lingering sunshine, although the air was already cooler with the hint of oncoming fall. But when he spotted her, they all seemed to fade away.

For some reason he could hear Rafe's low, rumbling voice in his head. *Target acquired.*

What a crazy thing to think. And yet it was sort of like that, when you were focused on someone and the rest of the world became merely periphery. At the same time it was different, because Ria wasn't the focus, and certainly not a target; she was merely connected loosely to the case.

He nearly snorted out loud as she stopped a few yards away, smiling, to bend gracefully to pet a passing dog. Ria Connelly wasn't *merely* anything.

She straightened, looked his way and obviously spotted him. And smiled again as she tapped her phone and then slid it into a pocket. It was a different smile this time than when she greeted the dog. Wider. More pleased. And the difference made his pulse kick up again, no matter how he ordered himself to stand down.

She was carrying a small bag from the drugstore. Not, he noticed, the white paper bag from the pharmacy in the back. So not sick, or at least not prescription-sick. As she got closer he could see the square shape of a box in the plastic bag.

Just about the right size for a box of condoms.

A sensation he'd never felt before blasted through him, a combination of heat and surge and, at the same time, recoil and dread. The heat for her and the dread from wondering who she needed them for.

Cutter's steady gaze shot through his mind and the way the dog had tried to herd him toward Ria at Foxworth.

Damn. Hell.

And *no.* A big, neon-light no.

Chapter 11

Ria saw him push away from the wall just outside the door to the Java Hut. He looked odd, his expression something she couldn't quite put a name to. He took a step toward her and then stopped, apparently deciding to wait until she threaded through the group of patrons that always seemed clustered around the popular stop. By the time she got to him, the strange expression was gone.

There was a man with his hands full of the fancier Java Hut concoctions coming toward the door. Liam stayed holding it until he was clear. The man nodded and said thanks as he went out. Definitely good manners, Ria thought.

"You're not sick, are you?"

His unexpected question threw her, but after a moment she figured it out. She'd called him from the drugstore when she'd glanced at the clock and realized his session with Dylan would be over.

"No." She gestured with the bag. "Just some lozenges. My throat gets dry by the end of the day. All that talking."

His expression was so peculiar she stared at him. Relief and a touch of…disappointment? But he clearly wasn't going to explain, because without a word he headed for the end of the short line.

"Cutter?" she asked, moving along with him.

"On guard duty in the truck. He'll be fine unless this takes too long."

He sounded like a man facing an onerous task. Irritation flicked through her. She had every right—they had all agreed—to be updated on what was going on. But, perhaps fortunately, they were at the counter before she could put her irritation into words.

She ordered her favorite chai tea latte, while Liam stuck to black coffee. No froufrou for him, she thought, unsurprised.

"Shall we take them down to the water, so Cutter can come with us?"

His brow furrowed as if she'd asked him a difficult question.

"I promise this will be short," she said sweetly. "I don't expect you to exert yourself."

His expression shifted as if that had stung, as she'd meant it to.

"Yeah, sure," he muttered, finally answering her question.

He was behaving unusually, very different from the good-natured, cheerful guy she'd first met at Foxworth. Whatever was bothering him, she didn't want it to interfere with helping Dylan. And it wasn't like he was going through anything like her own silly internal battle. He barely looked at her, while she couldn't help stealing glances at him every chance she got.

One of the great—and hardest—lessons of life, she thought. Attraction isn't always mutual.

She walked alongside him, taking a sip of her drink as

they turned a corner. Feeling a chill at the sudden drop in temperature as they walked into the shade of the big art gallery on the corner, she spotted his truck. Cutter gave a happy whine as they neared the vehicle, and she shifted her cup to her other hand so she could greet him properly with a scratch of his ears. Liam dug a leash out of a side pocket on the door and snapped it onto the dog's collar, next to the blue ID tag.

"Civilization, hound," he told the dog as he jumped down to the sidewalk. "City manners on."

At her laugh, he glanced at her. "I'm not sure this qualifies as an actual city," she explained as they started toward the water; the town had less than ten thousand people.

"I'm from the wide-open spaces. Anything bigger than a couple hundred people is a city to me."

He said it with a smile so she laughed again. And when he didn't seem to take offense, she asked, "Where?"

"Little town about halfway between San Antonio and Austin famous mainly for being in some music video. Population, last I heard, was still under a thousand. But even it's a city now." He paused as they entered the waterfront park, looked at the small marina with its rows of boats, both power and sail. "Nothing like this, though."

"It is pretty, isn't it?"

They'd reached one of the bright blue city benches. She looked at the plaque that was secured to the backrest. She lifted her cup and murmured, "Here's to you," before taking another sip.

"You knew that guy?" Liam asked as they sat down.

"No. But the person whose name is on that memorial plaque was very important to someone or several someones. Just acknowledging that."

"You do that every time you sit on one of these?"

"Yes. And I'm working on the bricks in the courtyard. Try to add a new one every time I go through there."

"That's a lot of bricks," he said. It was. The entire walkway between the two rows of businesses was paved with bricks that held names or nicknames in tribute to someone lost.

"It doesn't seem right to just walk over them without even noticing." For a long moment he just looked at her. She supposed he thought she was foolish, overly sentimental or perhaps even a bit odd. She didn't care. Not about this. "I do it out of respect and gratitude that I haven't had to think about such things, yet."

"You're really something, you know that?"

He said it softly, but the tone of his voice was unmistakably admiring. And she realized she'd been wrong; she did care what this man thought of her.

Before she could slip further down that dangerous path, she spoke. "I've never met the brother, but it's in Dylan's records that he has just the one younger one. Several years younger. Shouldn't he be in school?"

He took another swallow of coffee before saying, "Apparently he's been cutting school. Dylan told me that much, and I didn't want to push him for more, not this soon."

"You're right," she agreed. "Although if he already trusts you enough to ask for a ride, that's a good sign."

"I offered, and he accepted, a bit hesitantly. He's pretty wary."

"And he never used to be," she said, frowning. "Will he come back to school? I have him in last class today."

"I don't know. Like I said, he didn't want to talk about it. Said he'd get back to school on the bus, though."

"How did his brother look?"

He thought about that for a moment. "Lost," he finally said. "And Dylan seemed pretty protective of him."

She nodded. "That fits with the old Dylan."

She realized that, whatever his reservations had been

about meeting with her, they had apparently vanished. He finished his coffee and looked thoughtful as he crumpled the cup and put it in the adjacent trash receptacle.

"Something's definitely eating at him. It may just be grief, but…"

"You think it's more?"

"My gut does. And so does his," he added, gesturing toward Cutter.

She glanced at the dog, who indeed had his "city manners" on, plopped on the grass beside the bench and merely watching the parade of people and even other dogs. He would stretch his neck and sniff if one came over to him, but he never budged from that spot.

She looked back at Liam. "So…you're taking that as proof?"

"I know it sounds crazy, if you don't know Cutter's track record."

"What, he's never wrong?"

"Never has been. He can read people like no dog—or person—I've ever known. He knows if they're on the side of the angels, so to speak. Just like he knows when somebody has a problem that's Foxworthy."

She laughed at that; she couldn't help it. "Foxworthy?"

He grinned. That blessed, heart-jumping grin. "Even Quinn liked that one."

"And he takes the dog's…word for it?"

He shrugged. "Quinn has the final say, of course, on whether we take something on. But Cutter's never brought us a case he's said no to." A grin flashed for a moment. She should be used to it by now, but it still sent that jolt through her again. "After he learned it was wiser to just go with it, that is."

She couldn't quite picture the commanding, powerful Quinn Foxworth taking his lead from a dog. But, then,

Cutter was obviously not an ordinary dog. Maybe not the alien in a dog suit Liam joked about, but hardly ordinary. But, then, neither was Liam Burnett.

Chapter 12

"So, are you and Ms. Connelly dating?"

Liam froze as Dylan finished taking off his shoes and stepped out onto the mat.

"What?"

The boy shrugged. "Saw you two talking this morning. You seem pretty tight."

"I—" He stopped, fighting off all the images Dylan's question had brought on. It was a moment before he could say firmly, "No. We're not. We're just friends. That's why she recommended me for this." He stepped onto the mat himself. Cutter had taken as his spot the corner between the mat and the wall. He often chose places like that, making Quinn joke that he was like a cop who couldn't sit with his back to the door. Liam tried a joke himself. "That, and because she's sure I won't let any of you get hurt. Or she knows my first aid training will be up to it."

"Oh." Dylan didn't laugh but darted a glance at him. The boy made no comment on the cowboy boots he was pulling off. *Points for you,* Liam thought. "Wouldn't blame you if it were true. She's pretty hot, in a quiet sort of way."

"Mmm." Liam made the sound because there was no way in hell he wanted to try and answer that in actual words. And because explaining to Ria about Cutter's perfect track record with cases, he hadn't been able to avoid thinking about his other perfect track record of bringing couples together. And no matter how thoroughly Liam convinced himself that was not happening, it was still getting on his nerves.

"And she's good with people," Dylan said. "She cares."

Liam thought of the other day at the marina and her quiet respect for the loss of people she didn't know anything about except that someone loved and missed them.

"Yes. Yes, she does."

"She worries, too. About us, I mean. Her students."

"Yes," he repeated. He thought about saying she was specifically concerned about Dylan himself but didn't want the boy to suspect anything so he decided not to. "Speaking of worries, how's your brother?"

Dylan shrugged. "Okay." Liam watched him steadily, and after a moment the boy lowered his gaze to his bare feet. He shifted them a couple of times before admitting, "Not really. He's kind of acting out."

"More than cutting school?"

A silent nod.

"What does your father say?"

Dylan sucked in an audible breath as he assumed the position they'd been practicing from. Liam couldn't tell if he was prepping for the practice, or if it had been his question about their father.

"He doesn't pay much attention. He's...been kind of out of it. Since Mom died."

"Understandable," Liam said as he joined the boy.

"Yeah." Then Dylan added, "He's moody, though. He

doesn't talk to us anymore. Well, he talks to me a little but not Kevin."

"He's probably scared. Thinking of having to raise you on his own now."

Something flashed in Dylan's eyes. "He doesn't need to raise me, I'm old enough to be on my own. But Kevin isn't. Can we get started?"

Clearly he was impatient with talking. At least about this. Liam decided it was time to let the boy get some of his obvious nerves settled. Nothing like a good scrap to do that. He nodded and turned to face the boy.

"Come at me."

"What?"

"Give me your best shot."

"But I don't know any of this stuff yet."

"I don't mean that. I mean just try to put me on the floor."

Dylan's expression was wary. He glanced at Cutter. "I don't want him going for my throat."

"He won't. He gets this is different."

"But—"

"Come on, man. It's not every day I give a guy who's pissed at the world the chance to take it out on me."

"I'm not pissed at the—"

"The hell you're not," Liam said softly.

He gestured with his hand, waggling his fingers toward himself, urging the boy on.

Dylan charged.

Just because she didn't have a class this hour didn't mean she had to be here every time Dylan and Liam had a session, Ria told herself. And yet here she was, hiding once more—well, not really hiding, but trying to go unnoticed—on the upper-level gallery that had once been the hayloft of the big barn.

She was here for Dylan, she told herself. And Emily, who was so worried about her friend. Observing, that was all. Not like she was even eavesdropping, because she couldn't hear normal conversation from up here. She could tell Liam was getting more response out of Dylan Oakley than she or even Emily had been able to. But they weren't much closer to finding out what was wrong.

It's only been four days, she reminded herself. *Don't expect miracles.* And wouldn't she and Emily both feel silly if they'd started all this and it turned out it really was all related to Dylan's mother's death last year? She'd been worried then, but his grief had seemed normal, and after about two months he'd seemed to level off. He would never be the same, she supposed, but he'd been doing all right, considering.

Until this nose dive.

But she was no expert. Maybe grief sometimes worked that way. Fading away only to come back with a vengeance.

Liam would know. He hadn't said anything, but she knew he did.

So ask him.

Sure, that would be a nice, casual topic of conversation. "So, Liam, who died and how did it affect you?"

Or maybe it was someone else who knew the path of grief. Someone close to him. Girlfriend? Even a wife? He didn't wear a ring, but that wasn't proof. It rattled her that this hadn't even occurred to her until now, to even wonder. How could she not realize that a guy like him—cute, funny, doing admirable work—likely had been grabbed up long ago?

And what did it matter if he was? It made no difference—

An explosion of movement snapped her wandering thoughts back to the scene below. A split second ago Liam had been standing casually on the mat, his posture relaxed and even a bit lazy, as if he had nothing to do but stand there and chat. And then Dylan rushed him, and he unwound from that laid-back stance and erupted into a sort of grace and power that stopped her breath.

He strolls in all relaxed and leisurely, lolls around like he couldn't move fast if he wanted to. Just when you start thinking he's half-asleep, he explodes and takes you out before you can blink.

Quinn's words echoed in her head as she saw Liam put Dylan—with exquisite care, twisting so that the boy came down flat and on the mat—on the floor with what looked like merely a twist of his waist and a flick of his wrist.

Dylan lay still for a long moment, maybe as startled as she. Only when the boy sat up did she breathe again. He was staring at Liam, who seemed to be watching how he would take it.

Dylan scrambled to his feet. Even from here she heard his exclamation.

"Damn, that was cool! Show me how to do that."

It was the most enthusiasm she'd seen from Dylan in weeks. And that alone made it all worth it.

Even if she was thinking like a fool about a guy she barely knew anything about.

So find out.

That contrary voice in her head seemed to be chiming in a lot these days. Since about the time she'd seen Liam racing around the corner of the Foxworth building on Cutter's heels. If you'd told her a week ago all it would take was seeing a nicely built guy with his shirt off to send her tumbling over an edge she'd avoided for a very long time now, she would have laughed.

And yet here she was. And no amount of reassuring herself that he'd be gone once they found out what Dylan's problem was and fixed it seemed to help.

She looked over to where his dog was positioned sphinxlike, seemingly aware this had only been practice and so not moving to protect Liam as she imagined he would under real circumstances.

Cutter was staring up at her, steadily, and she had the whimsical thought that he had somehow willed her to look at him. The intensity of the dog's gaze was almost unsettling, yet at the same time reassuring. Understanding. Soothing. Or something.

Deciding her silly thoughts were now completely out of control, she quietly got up, grabbed her lunch bag and left them to finish the session alone.

"Shakespeare, huh?"

Liam watched Dylan pull the book for his next class out of his backpack. He'd walked along with the boy, Cutter at their heels, wanting to keep the conversation going. They'd had a good session. The boy was quick, stronger than he looked and coordinated. He could use some more muscle and to learn to draw in his movements a bit, but that would come with time.

"Yeah," Dylan said. "I used to think it was pretty lame, but Ms. Connelly makes it fun. She gets the class to translate it into modern language, so we understand it better. Makes us do it like a movie script, with directions and all."

"Wow," Liam said. "Shakespeare was a lot more boring when I was in school."

Dylan grinned. "She's fun. Sometimes she'll be writing our translations on the board and turn around and say 'Why the heck would he *do* that?' To get us thinking about motivation and stuff."

…made everything come so alive kids ran to get to class not because they were late but because they loved it. That's the kind of teacher I try to be.

Her words ran through his mind. It seemed she had cer-

tainly succeeded. But then Ria Connelly seemed the sort
to succeed at anything she truly put her mind to.

"Told you." Dylan was looking at him, grinning.

"What?"

"Every time I mention her, you get all dreamy-eyed.
You're crushing on her, aren't you?"

"I wasn't thinking about her like that," Liam insisted,
glad he could say it honestly for once, because he'd just
been wondering what it must have been like to be so sure
about what you wanted to be from childhood. He'd been
anything but certain, chafing at a small-town life that was
as flat as the land around it, yet repelled by the big city.
That was one of the reasons he was so happy here, where
he'd found the perfect—in his view—combination of small
town and endless things to do.

"Coming in, Dylan?"

Dylan whirled in surprise as Ria came up behind them
but relaxed when he saw she was smiling. Liam wasn't
startled. He'd sensed her approach before she arrived. And
so had Cutter, who had risen from his polite sit outside the
door. Not surprising. You didn't become a superior tracker
without total awareness of your surroundings. And Cutter
was indeed that, the only one of the Foxworth team who
could beat him. But, then, Cutter had that canine nose.

Not that Liam's wasn't functioning just fine. Because
he'd known it was her without looking. He'd caught the
light scent that reminded him of his mother's roses, sweet,
delicate and so light that as a child he'd been afraid he'd
sniff it all away if he smelled it too often. Then later he'd
been embarrassed to admit he liked it; it was such a girly
thing.

"And where did you go just now?"

Ria's voice cut into his memories and he snapped back
to the present. Realized Dylan had gone ahead into the

classroom. So much for the superior tracker, he thought wryly.

"My mother's rose garden, actually," he said.

It took her only a split second. She smiled as she lifted a hand to her throat. Where she'd put the scent?

Need hit him like a blow harder than any Dylan had landed today. Need to breathe in more deeply, to get more of that fragrance. Need to touch that silken skin, as she was touching it. And yet he couldn't seem to breathe at all, and he didn't dare touch her. Not when simply thinking about it nearly sent him spiraling out of control.

"I'm going to take that as a compliment," she said quietly.

He clamped down, grasped for control. Thought he had it. "Do. That garden was beautiful. And smelled as good."

He saw the faint rise of color in her cheeks. So much for control, he thought, wondering why the hell he'd said that.

Because it's true? that annoying voice in his head suggested.

"Thank you." She left it simply at that, sparing him any embarrassing explanation. "You made good progress with Dylan today."

Reality snapped at him again. And he suddenly wondered just how much she'd heard of their conversation. Ran back in his head what he'd said about her. Had she heard him denying he had a crush on her? That he'd been thinking about her in that way Dylan had accused him of? Should he hope that she had heard? Or that she hadn't?

"He's opening up a little," he said, ignoring his own ridiculously tangled thoughts. "Nothing that's much of a clue yet, though. His family's kind of messed up, but we expected that."

She nodded just as the chime to mark the half hour pealed out across the serene campus.

"A lot nicer than those old fire-alarm-sounding bells at my high school," Liam said.

"Mine, too. They were quite rude." She was grinning, and he found himself grinning back. "I'd better go. *Hamlet* awaits."

"So I heard. And that you make it fun."

She looked as pleased as she had with his rose compliment. Which told him she valued this one just as much. No surprise there. But again she left it at merely, "Thank you," as she turned to walk back into her classroom. He turned to go, as well, but he couldn't help hearing the remarks rising from the students, the loudest of which seemed voiced by the whole group.

"Woo, Ms. Connelly's got a boyfriend!"

He kept going. He didn't want to hear what she said to that.

Chapter 13

"She's quite charming, your Emily," Hayley said.

The girl and her adoptive parents had left Foxworth just a few minutes ago; the Hardings had wanted to see Quinn again and meet Hayley.

"She's changed a lot," Quinn said as he poured a cup of coffee in the kitchen. "She was so quiet, almost lost, and now..."

"She's a bright, stable, outgoing young woman. The kind of kid who gives you hope for the future. And you should be proud, since you were a big part of that."

Liam listened to the exchange but said nothing. He had been about to give Quinn an update when Emily arrived with her parents, a warm, lively couple who clearly couldn't adore the girl more if she were their biological daughter. He'd shaken hands with them and noted they had both bent to formally greet Cutter, which was how Foxworth tended to begin their assessment of people these days.

He'd excused himself, as they talked about other things,

to ask Ty to check into the problems Dylan's younger brother was having at school. Kevin was a bit young to take to cutting school, but he was also far too young to have lost his mother.

Liam had returned to the others just as the conversation landed on the case.

"I can already see a difference," Emily had been telling them happily. "Dylan's enthused about something again." She flashed a shy glance at Liam. "He talks about you a lot. I can tell he likes you."

"Now I just have to get to what's eating at him."

"You will," Emily had replied confidently.

He hoped she was right.

"They seem to get along really well," Liam said now that they'd gone. "Better than most teenagers that age with their parents."

Quinn nodded and then gestured with the coffeepot, asking if Liam wanted his mug topped off. Liam shook his head no.

"I think when you go through tragedy so young, it matures you early," Hayley said. She didn't look at her husband, but Liam knew he was in her mind when she said it. But, then, as far as he could tell, Quinn was always in her thoughts, as she was in Quinn's. It was almost scary. Heck, it *was* scary. When you let someone in that deep, it just opened the door for pain.

Hayley had a point. Liam had been twenty when he'd brought his own world down around him. He couldn't imagine dealing with that kind of thing at the age Quinn had. Or Emily.

"Is it going as well as Emily hopes?" Quinn asked.

"He's starting to talk to me," Liam said, yanking his mind back once again. "But not about what's wrong. Other than his little brother acting out."

"Not surprising," Hayley said thoughtfully. "There were

times I wanted to act out after my mother died, and I was a lot older than Emily. Or Dylan."

"Instead you got spirited off in the dead of night in a black helicopter," Quinn joked.

"And found my life," Hayley said, giving him a look that made Liam faintly envious, for all that he didn't want that kind of relationship in his life.

"If you two need some privacy," Liam joked in turn, making as if to leave.

"Shut up, Burnett," Quinn said lightly, never taking his eyes off his wife, "and finish the report."

"Mutually exclusive?" Liam pointed out.

"You know what I mean."

"Yeah. Well." He took a sip of coffee. It was the blend Hayley liked. Quinn had once been a straight, plain, strong black coffee guy, but Hayley had *broadened his horizons*, as she called it. And Liam had to admit he didn't mind the occasional different flavor. "I think I will get there. If he gives me enough time."

Quinn's brow furrowed. "You think he might do something before you get there?"

"I'm hoping our sessions are taking the edge off for him, in addition to getting him to trust me."

"He is on the edge, then," Hayley said.

"Of something. I think Emily and… Ms. Connelly are right—there's something deeper going on. I just don't have any idea what it is yet."

He didn't think Quinn had noticed his slight hesitation over what to call Ria, but he knew Hayley had. Women always did notice that kind of thing. He kept going, half-afraid she'd make a remark. He'd had enough teasing from Dylan and from Ria's class yesterday. Then the door chime rang.

"Saved by the bell," he muttered to himself as Quinn got up to answer.

And Liam nearly groaned aloud when he saw that the bell hadn't saved him at all.

It was Ria.

"You just missed Emily and her parents," Quinn said as he led her back into the comfortable seating area in front of the fireplace, "but Emily said you met with them this morning."

She acknowledged Hayley, then Liam and if there was any difference between the two greetings, he couldn't see or hear it. Which irked him in a perverse sort of way he didn't like.

"Yes, I did," she said as she sat down. "We do one-on-ones with parents regularly. I wish all my students' parents were as involved as they are."

"There had to be a reason she's who she is," Hayley said with a smile.

Ria smiled the warm, contented smile of someone who was utterly certain they were where they were supposed to be in life.

"Liam can give you an update on things, if that's what you need," Quinn said, and Liam felt his pulse kick up when it appeared his boss was going to leave them alone. He opened his mouth to say it wasn't necessary, that they'd been in regular contact, when Ria spoke.

"Actually, I sort of have one for you," she said. Quinn, thankfully, sat back down. "I talked to an acquaintance of mine this afternoon who works at the school Dylan's brother attends. He said Kevin has been getting into trouble and verified he's been cutting."

"I'd better call Ty back," Liam said, starting to rise. "I had him looking into that."

Quinn gave him a look that had him sitting back down. As if Quinn knew somehow that he was just grabbing the chance to get out of the room. Liam didn't think he'd shown anything, but then Quinn always insisted he had the worst poker face.

"Text him to stand down," Quinn said, mildly enough. Then he looked back at Ria. "Do you think that's what's up with Dylan? He's worried about his brother?"

"It could be," Ria said, but she sounded doubtful. "But—"

She stopped when Cutter woofed softly. A split second later, Liam's cell rang. He saw Ria look at the dog and nearly grinned despite himself; knowing a phone was about to ring was only one of the dog's rather spooky talents.

It was the generic ring assigned to callers who didn't have their own. He pulled it out, saw the most recent number added to his contact list.

"Dylan," he said.

The room fell quiet as he answered.

"Hey, Dylan."

Silence. Liam frowned. "You there?"

The boy's voice sounded shaken when he finally answered. "Yeah. Look, I'm sorry to bother—"

Liam straightened at the way Dylan sounded. Ria reacted immediately, going very still. Even Cutter got to his feet. "No bother. What's up?"

"It's my... I need... I don't know what to do."

"Two things," Liam said briskly, standing up. "Where are you and what happened?"

The boy hesitated. Ria was also on her feet now. Quinn and Hayley waited silently, letting him handle it.

"I can't help if I don't know, buddy." Liam dug into his pocket for his keys.

"I shouldn't have called you."

"Yes, you should. Are you hurt?" He heard Ria's breath catch.

"No," Dylan said quickly. "No. Not me."

"Kevin?"

The catch in the boy's breath told him he was right. And he headed for the door, Cutter at his heels. Ria was right behind him, and he was too focused on Dylan to tell her he'd handle it.

"Are you at a hospital?" It didn't sound like it, but he had to ask.

"No. It's not that bad. Just a bad scrape, I think. But…"

"Cutter and I will come get you both. Then we can decide what to do."

The boy finally gave in. Maybe at the mention of the dog.

"We're in the waterfront park where you dropped me off that day, only at the playground down past the end of the boardwalk."

He had no idea where that was, but he'd find out. "I'm on my way. Just stay there, okay?"

When Dylan hung up, he looked at the others. "Is there a playground in the marina park?"

Ria answered instantly. "Yes. Some swings and stuff, down near the head of the bay. I'll go with you."

His protest was reflexive. "I'm not sure—"

"It only makes sense. I know where it is. Dylan knows me. Likes me, I think."

He had to admit it made sense. Dylan did know and like her, and it might take two of them to handle both boys, depending on the situation.

"And," Hayley put in, "Ria can see to his brother, give you and Cutter the chance to get Dylan to talk. Younger kids tend to trust women more. Between you and Cutter, they'll both be safe."

"Roll?" Quinn suggested, rather firmly.

Liam nearly flushed. Quinn was right; he was letting his emotions interfere with the job. That had never happened before, and he didn't like that it had now.

He opened the door, and Cutter raced ahead of them

out to his truck. Parked next to it, Liam saw what had to be Ria's car, an older but well-maintained little coupe in a surprisingly flashy red, with a parking sticker that said Cove Academy. The idea to suggest she drive separately flitted through his mind, but when she went to his passenger door—and he realized he was still letting his feelings interfere—he slammed the door on the thought.

Dylan had reached out to him, the goal of this entire operation, and he'd damned well better get his head back in the game.

Chapter 14

Ria wondered if he just liked working alone or if it was something more personal. She was confused. Sometimes they seemed to get along well—almost too well—and then he'd get like this, acting as if having her around even to help was a pain.

At least Cutter liked her, she thought as the dog stuck his head over her seat and gave her a quick swipe of his tongue on her ear. She laughed in spite of her tangled thoughts.

"Aren't you just the cleverest boy," she crooned to the dog, reaching up to stroke his soft fur. She hadn't missed that, despite the fact that Quinn and Hayley's car was parked outside, along with her own, he'd known to head for Liam's truck. And that was over and above the fact that he seemed to have somehow known that Liam's phone was about to ring. Maybe cell phones let out some kind of vibration or hum inaudible to human ears before they actually rang.

Or maybe Cutter was clairvoyant.

She nearly laughed again at her own thoughts. And out of the corner of her eye caught Liam glancing at her.

She decided to ignore his mood, whatever it was. "I'm so glad Dylan reached out to you. That he already trusts you that much."

"I'm surprised. I thought maybe he'd have called you or…what's his math teacher's name?"

"Jim Darnton. Likeable, but… Jim's hardly the call-in-an-emergency sort, not like you. He's no alpha male. He gets woozy at a paper cut."

He smiled. He didn't comment on the implied compliment, she supposed because he knew it was a given that he, and Foxworth, were the kind of people you wanted around in a crisis, no matter the size. And despite his laid-back, casual demeanor, Ria sensed this man was one-hundred-percent alpha male when necessary.

She just hoped it wouldn't be necessary.

"Did he say what happened?" she asked. And after he'd relayed the conversation, she frowned. "Ten-year-old boys get scraped up all the time. I wonder why this time has him so upset?"

"Hopefully we'll find out. If he'll talk to me."

"He called you. We have to hope that means he will." She gave him a sideways look. "And I promise I'll stay out of your way."

She liked that he looked chagrined. Did he think she wouldn't notice that he hadn't wanted her to come?

"I didn't mean—"

She cut him off with a wave. "I get that my job is to take care of Kevin while you deal with Dylan. You're the one with the rapport. And that was always the plan. I'm just glad it's working."

"Worked faster than I thought." He sounded grateful that she'd moved on as he halted at the corner stop sign.

"Why wouldn't it? You're just the type kids his age find cool."

He chuckled. "Kids I went to school with would laugh at that thought."

"We all have an awkward phase. If that's what that was, you obviously outgrew it. You're doing good work now."

He shrugged. "Some days it's the only thing that gets me through, knowing what we do. I know who I am, now. Thanks to Foxworth." He glanced at her again as they waited for traffic to clear. "Not as early as you did, but…"

"Obviously you've found your niche. And I know that not everybody's lucky enough to know exactly what they want as early as I did."

"Lucky kids."

"Thank you," she said, meaning it. And warmed that he'd said it, for she sensed that the words were genuine, not just part of the easy charm that seemed to go with the drawl.

Someone in the heavy cross traffic on the main road—a ferry must have just come in—slowed to let them in. Liam made the turn, giving the other driver a wave of thanks.

"They know you really care," he said when they were moving again.

"When Emily first expressed her concerns, I'd hoped Dylan might come to me. I know he really loved his mother, and I thought he might need a woman to talk to."

The glance he gave her then was more than amused. "You, a mother figure to a sixteen-year-old boy? I don't think so."

She frowned. "I wasn't trying to be his mother."

"Good thing. You're way too hot."

In that moment she completely understood the phrase *jaw dropping*. She was sure hers had.

"I…thank you." *I think.*

The silence in the cab of the truck was suddenly fraught

with…something she couldn't name. Or didn't dare name. She wasn't sure which. But this was quite different from his subtle compliment on her favorite perfume.

And Liam wouldn't look at her after he said it. No more quick glances as he drove. In fact, his hands seemed tighter on the truck's steering wheel. Just as well, she thought. Who knew what her face must look like. It might even reflect the crazy, heated thoughts that had careened through her mind at his words. Being compared to a beautiful, lovely scented rose garden was one thing; being called "way too hot" was something else altogether.

The silence strung out in the cab. She almost wished Cutter would do something, anything, to break the mood. Couldn't he bark at something? Do one of his other clever tricks? She even looked back at the dog, who was lolling comfortably on the small backseat. He looked…

Smug.

The darn dog looked smug. She'd never seen such an expression on a dog's face before, and she wasn't one to attribute human emotions to animals, but there was no other way to describe that look.

She was grateful when they got close enough to the park that she could give him directions.

"There's a parking lot just across from the rehab center. The stairs down into the park from there come out right near the play area."

He nodded but said nothing. The small parking area was empty, and he pulled in near the wooden steps. They got out, Liam moving the seat forward to let Cutter out.

There were only a couple of people walking along the path that wound through the tall trees. When they reached the edge of the clearing that overlooked the water and held a swing set and other children's play things, she immediately saw the small boy seated on one of the swings, with his big brother crouched beside him. And it struck her just how much Dylan's life had really changed.

"He's really had to step up," Liam said softly, startling her with how closely he'd echoed her thoughts.

"Yes," she agreed. She could see the child wasn't badly hurt, so she said, "Why don't you go ahead? I'll wait until you see how Dylan feels about me being here."

He looked at her. She couldn't read his expression. But he nodded, and she watched as he walked past the last of the trees and stepped into the sunlit clearing. She had the strongest feeling that, had he stumbled upon this entire situation on his own, unrelated to his work with Foxworth, he would be doing exactly the same thing. He would step in to help. Whether it was paying forward what Quinn had done for him or just his own innate code, she didn't know, but Liam Burnett would always help if he could. She didn't even know how she could be so certain, but she was.

He let Cutter go ahead of him, and the dog raced over toward the swings. Suddenly he stopped, about four feet from the two boys. He looked from Dylan to his little brother, then back, then back again, sniffing deeply the whole time. Finally he glanced back at Liam and gave a rather curious-sounding whine. As if he were puzzled by something. She saw Liam frown, as if he, too, were puzzled, if only by the dog's reaction.

But then Dylan said something, perhaps introducing the dog and Liam to Kevin, and Cutter trotted forward as if nothing had happened. She wondered if Kevin would be frightened of the dog, but Dylan said something and the boy looked up and smiled. Ria could see the boy's cheeks were damp and guessed he'd been crying, so that smile was no small accomplishment. Cutter seemed to accurately judge his welcome and closed in to lick the child's face. Kevin's smile widened. And when Liam approached,

Kevin appeared nothing more than normally wary. Dylan must have explained about him.

On that thought her gaze shifted to the older boy. She could almost feel Dylan's tension ease from here as Liam came to a halt before them. Could see his posture change, his body language shift from protective to open. He did trust Liam. And Cutter. Or perhaps he trusted Liam so much because of Cutter.

And why not? He'd been open, encouraging and invited the boy in.

It seemed it was only her whom he got distant with.

You're way too hot.

Ria gave herself a mental shake. Putting those two thoughts together in her silly brain did not mean they were really connected. Besides, it was Dylan and his brother she needed to focus on now. Not the way this guy unsettled her.

So she waited. And hoped Liam was getting some answers.

Chapter 15

"Watch," Liam ordered Cutter.

The dog promptly sat at Kevin's feet and plopped his head on the child's knee. Kevin leaned over and buried his face in the soft fur. The child had been wary, as expected, but it eased when Dylan had told him Liam was "the martial arts guy." Liam had crouched to check the boy's injuries and found them to be messy but fairly minor: a long scrape along his right forearm that had bled some and a pair of reddened, skinned knees.

Feeling fairly sure the boy would stay put, he drew Dylan aside, noticing that the boy positioned himself where he could keep an eye on his brother.

"You said you had first aid training," Dylan said.

Liam nodded. "He'll be okay. Need to get that scrape cleaned up, but it's not deep." He glanced at the child to make sure he wasn't getting restless, but Kevin appeared much too enraptured with Cutter to move.

He looked back at Dylan. "What'd he jump off of?"

Dylan gave him a startled look. Liam's mouth twisted wryly. "Had a few of those sets of scrapes myself. Back from when I wanted to see if I could fly."

A faint smile that didn't last crossed Dylan's face. "He said he just slipped and fell on the porch steps at home, but…"

"You don't think so."

Dylan let out a sigh that was far too weary for a sixteen-year-old who should be thinking about nothing more complicated than school or getting his driver's license.

"What is it, Dylan? I can see you're worried."

"This is, like, the fourth time he's gotten hurt like that. It's happening too often."

"You think maybe he's gotten careless, reckless? It happens. Grief is pretty consuming."

Dylan looked at him. And Liam had the craziest thought that his expression reminded him of his mother's the night he'd been arrested. Full of pain. And fear. It hit him then.

"You think he's doing this to himself," he said softly.

"I don't know," Dylan said, his voice tight. "Maybe it is just not caring enough to be careful. But…"

He was out of his depth here, Liam thought. Way out.

"He won't talk to me," Dylan said. "Used to be I couldn't get him to shut up, but now he won't tell me anything. All I know about today is he cut school again, wasn't there when I went to get him. So I started looking. This was the third place I came."

Liam thought for a moment before saying, "Ria's here. Would he talk to a woman?"

"Ms. Connelly's with you?"

An undertone in his voice made Liam grimace inwardly. *Well, that just added to the hypothesis that I've got a crush on the teacher.*

"She's waiting back there. She didn't want to…intrude if it would make things worse."

Dylan shook his head. "No. She's okay." He glanced at his brother again. "And maybe he would talk to her. She's good with kids. I've seen her."

The way he put that, it was clear Dylan no longer put himself in that kid category. With reason, it would seem.

At Liam's gesture, Ria walked quietly toward them. Cutter shifted position, leaning harder against the boy, as if he somehow had assessed the addition of another person might upset a delicate balance within Kevin. But after another wary glance, Kevin went back to petting the dog.

Liam explained quickly about Dylan's fears. Ria listened, her expression growing more concerned by the moment.

"Oh, Dylan," she said, and there was so much warmth and empathy in her voice Liam thought it just had to be soothing to him. "No wonder you haven't been yourself. You've been carrying this, and alone."

Dylan did seem almost relieved to have shared the burden. "I thought he was just acting out, but…"

"What about your father? Does he realize what's going on?"

Dylan grimaced. "Kevin hides it. Besides, Dad's no use. He's out of it and mad at the world all the time."

"Understandable," Ria said, still in that warm voice that soothed. "You didn't just lose your mother. He lost his wife. And now he has to face raising you two without her."

"Yeah, I get that. Really, I do, because I know how much I miss Mom. But this is—" Dylan's gaze shifted back to his brother, who was now hugging Cutter fiercely "—different. It's something else. I can't really explain it."

"You know your brother," Liam said. "I trust your judgment."

Gratitude lightened the boy's expression as he looked back at them. He nodded toward Kevin and the dog.

"That's the happiest I've seen him since it happened."

"Shall I try to talk to him?" Ria asked.

The boy nodded. "I can't get through to him. Maybe you can."

Ria walked over to the swings, but, instead of starting right in with Kevin, she knelt down and began to pet Cutter, who welcomed her with a swipe of his tongue and some fierce tail wagging. Liam saw the child watch the dog for a moment and then shift his gaze to Ria.

"Stamp of approval," Liam murmured.

"You think he'll trust her because the dog does?" Dylan asked.

"I've found Cutter has that effect."

The boy considered that. "Yeah," he said finally. "I mean, dogs don't generally like bad people, right?"

"It's like the old saying about not trusting someone who doesn't like dogs but totally trusting a dog when he doesn't like someone."

A faint smile flitted across Dylan's face. "I hope you're right. I hope he will."

"You're scared for him, aren't you."

It wasn't really a question, since the boy's fear was almost palpable. Dylan nodded.

"He's a pain and annoying sometimes, but he's my brother. And this crap—if he's trying to hurt himself…"

His voice trailed away.

"He's all right now," Liam said. "And we'll figure out how to keep him that way."

Dylan looked at Liam straight on then, hope in his eyes, and Liam felt the weight of the boy's need to believe. For a moment he considered telling the boy about Foxworth, about the full force and strength Dylan would have behind him if it came to that. Liam's gaze flicked to Ria, who had succeeded in getting Kevin to talk to her about something, at least. And Liam found himself wanting to discuss the idea of telling Dylan with her as much as Quinn or Hay-

ley. Again he was facing that weird snarl of work with…
whatever this was. But even though it had been barely
more than a week since he'd met her, he couldn't deny he
trusted her judgment. Especially when it came to kids.

He had progressed to wondering how Dylan would feel
if and when he learned that Ria—and Emily—had come
to Foxworth about him. Would he be angry, embarrassed
or appreciative of their concern?

He already knew the boy liked Ria. So it might depend
on how he felt about Emily.

"That girl in your English class, Emily," Liam began,
thinking that Ria would likely be much better at this than
he was, despite the fact that he'd learned a bit about pry-
ing information out of people in his time with Foxworth.

Dylan looked startled. "What about her?"

"Ria says she's been worried about you." That much
was true, after all.

The boy flushed. And looked away quickly. But not before Liam saw a flash of reaction in his eyes. Pleased reaction. So the thought wasn't unwelcome. Maybe it wouldn't
be so bad when he found out what Emily had done, if it
came to that.

And then Ria was back with them, leaving Kevin once
more engrossed with Cutter, who was trying to entice the
boy into playing.

"All I could get was that he said it's his fault."

"What is?" Liam asked as Dylan frowned.

"Your mother. Does he blame himself for what happened to her for some reason?" Ria asked the boy.

Dylan looked surprised at the idea. "I don't think so. I
mean, she and my dad were hiking, and she fell. He wasn't
with them."

"She wasn't worrying about him and distracted so she
fell, or something like that? Something that, in his mind,
might make him feel responsible?"

Dylan's jaw tightened as he shook his head. "Actually, she was worried about me."

Dylan gave Ria a wary look. Liam guessed at his worry. "Off the record here, Dylan." He looked at Ria. "Right?"

"Yes," she said, picking up on his concern quickly. "This goes nowhere."

Dylan still looked uncomfortable but after a moment said, looking at Liam, "She found some pills in a backpack in my room." His gaze shifted pleadingly to Ria, as if begging her to believe him. "They weren't mine. It wasn't even my backpack. It was my friend Derek's."

"Derek Wilson?" Ria asked. Dylan grimaced. "Off the record. I gave you a promise," she said.

Dylan sighed and gave in. "Yeah. He left it there after we were studying one night. It was finals time, and we were all cramming hard, but Derek still wanted to go out and party, so he got some uppers."

"Shall I point out the obvious?" Ria asked, one brow lifting.

Dylan gave her a rueful look. "Yeah, I know. He flunked."

"But your mother didn't believe they weren't yours?"

"No, she did, but…she was worried that I was hanging with somebody who used. That's the way she was."

Ria put a hand on his arm. "That doesn't make it your fault. You know that, don't you?"

"I know. Still hurts," he muttered.

"Of course it does." She seemed to hesitate and then asked, "What about your father? Does he blame Kevin?"

Dylan frowned. "Why would he?"

"I don't know. But Kevin said it was his father who told him it was his fault, whatever he's referring to."

"That makes no sense," Dylan said, brow furrowing as he shook his head in obvious bewilderment. "Kevin's never done anything bad."

"Sometimes life doesn't make sense," Liam said.

"Sometimes life sucks," Dylan said bluntly. "Whole damn world changed the day she died." He turned his head slightly, Liam guessed to hide the moisture building in his eyes.

"And yet it keeps turning," Liam said quietly. "The sun keeps coming up, people keep doing, going along, not even realizing everything's different. It's just not right."

Dylan's head snapped back around and he stared at Liam. "Yeah. No. It's not."

After a moment Dylan looked over at his brother again. And Liam glanced at Ria, to find her watching him. She looked…something. Approving? Surprised? He wasn't sure. He didn't trust his own assessments, not with her. He was too tangled up over her. And he wasn't sure how it had happened. He usually smothered any feelings like this long before they had a chance to take root. He knew he had to. He couldn't risk it. Ever again.

And yet this woman had him wishing it could be different, that he could dare to chance it. Dare to let her in. Except he knew he couldn't, because it was never him who paid the price. He'd learned that lesson the hard way, and he'd best remember that. No matter how much he might want to forget. Which was a sure sign he should beat feet, as Dad said, away from her as soon as he could.

No matter what Cutter said.

Chapter 16

The Foxworth building was silent, and Liam's footsteps echoed a bit. Hayley was off to visit her brother and best friend Amy down in California, and Quinn had gotten a late-night message that had sent him for the Foxworth plane and a trip to headquarters in St. Louis. The trail of the mole they'd learned about almost two years ago—the leak that had nearly cost them everything on the operation that had brought Hayley and Quinn together—had suddenly heated up. It had been a long time, but Quinn's behind-the-scenes inquiries had been ongoing. They'd hit a couple of dead ends and a wrong conclusion once, but Quinn Foxworth never, ever forgot a betrayal, and Liam didn't envy whomever it was when Quinn finally found them.

He glanced back at the text Quinn had sent him.

Rafe's already in StL, but Teague will be home Wednesday if you need backup.

Liam doubted backup would be an issue in this case, but it was like Quinn to think of all the contingencies.

He topped off his mug with the last of the half pot of coffee he'd made this morning as the laptop booted up. He wasn't sure what he wanted to check, but it was his first instinct to keep learning as much as he could about all involved with a case. For a moment he thought of his father, who frequently bemoaned the loss of privacy these days, and then of Rafe, who agreed but said half of it was our own fault for plastering every move online all the time.

He supposed they were both right, but it sure made his job easier.

Well, most of the time, he corrected after he'd spent a fruitless hour chasing rabbits that led nowhere. Maybe Dylan had understated when he'd said his father was a technophobe. The only thing Liam had been able to find on his first check was an old, very brief profile on a business networking site, with a photo of an ordinary-looking guy in the typical-for-those-pictures suit and tie. It had told him no more than he already knew, except that there was a vague resemblance to Dylan.

He'd also done a check on Dylan's mother when they'd first taken the case, as a matter of routine. There was more on her. She, at least, had a social media presence, and he found himself staring at the last photograph, a shot of a shady, deep green forest trail, posted about an hour before her fatal fall.

There was something eerie about the thought that she'd sent this photograph off into the ether to turn up on the screens of friends and followers but that she'd never see any of the "Oh, pretty!" responses or answer any of the "Where is that?" questions. That an hour later she'd be dead.

He'd looked into her accident, too, as a matter of routine. Thanks to Brett Dunbar, who had a friend in the neighboring county's sheriff's office, they had a copy of the investigation into that fall. It was thorough and documented Barton Oakley's distraught statement, including how he, in the lead, had warned his wife to be careful as they approached the part of the trail that came close to the edge of the precipitous drop that had moments later taken her life. There was also a witness statement, another hiker who had actually been up ahead talking to Barton when they'd heard a scream and come running back down the trail. They'd tried frantically to get to her, but the drop was too steep. In the end a rescue team had to rappel down the cliff to recover her body.

A reminder tone from his phone thankfully brought an end to the grim images going through Liam's mind. He'd suggested an extra session with Dylan today, after checking with Ria to see if she could arrange for them to use the gym on a Saturday, using the excuse that the previous session had been cut short.

No better off than before, he whistled for Cutter, who, after satisfying himself that Hayley and Quinn truly were not here, had settled on his bed on the floor near the windows while Liam did his online searching. Liam was still pondering that last photograph when he reached the school campus, so it took a half second for the presence of another car to register. A familiar red coupe.

Ria.

When she'd said somebody would unlock the gym for them, he hadn't expected it to be her.

Cutter's soft, questioning woof snapped him out of a haze. He realized he'd been sitting here in his truck trying to think of a way out of this. Several appellations came to mind, not the least of which was *coward*. Angry at himself, Liam yanked the truck's door open and stepped out. Cutter was on his feet already and jumped out the moment the front seat was forward enough to give him room.

Liam felt disconcerted when he got to the gym and found only Dylan waiting. His mind churned. How would he have reacted had he not seen her car and known it was her? Would he have even wondered who had unlocked the building and where they were? Or just assume arrangements had been made and gotten down to business?

And then Liam got angry at himself all over again when he found himself avoiding asking the obvious question about where Ria was, because it would only add fuel to Dylan's teasing about him having a crush on the pretty teacher.

"You okay, man?" Dylan asked. "This was your idea—"

"No, I'm good," Liam said, shaking his head sharply as if that could clear out the chaos. "Sorry."

"Ms. Connelly's upstairs in the gallery," the boy said casually.

Liam barely stopped himself from looking. Dylan didn't laugh, but Liam had the feeling it was a near thing. The absurdity of it hit him—that he had a sixteen-year-old reading his muddled mind. The sixteen-year-old he was supposed to be helping, he reminded himself firmly.

"I saw her car," he said neutrally, hoping the boy would take it as explanation.

He seemed to and said rather glumly, "She's grading papers. Probably our essays."

Liam did look up then. The sole occupant of the upper seats, she wasn't hard to spot, but he thought he could have found her in a crowd just by the rich gleam of her smooth, dark hair. He liked the way the sides swept forward to points just above her shoulders, and how it moved, all silky and flowing, when she did. She wasn't looking at them; she was bent over a thick file in her lap, propped up by the large, black leather bag that apparently served as both purse and briefcase.

Tearing his gaze away, he looked at Dylan again. "Not optimistic?"

"I think I did okay," Dylan said, "but I was kind of distracted yesterday."

"Can't imagine why," Liam said dryly.

Dylan glanced down at the polished wood of the gym floor. "Thanks again for coming for us."

"No problem. I'm glad you called."

"You got any brothers? Sisters?"

"Two each. Older brothers. Younger sisters. And let me tell you, a little sister is an entirely different set of problems."

Dylan laughed, and Liam counted it a win, while silently apologizing to his sisters, who in fact had presented a lot fewer problems to the Burnett family than he himself had.

"Let's get to it, then. I thought we'd try some Tae Kwon Do. The movements are different—you know they go for the high kicks, the spinning stuff. And there's the whole theory-of-power thing. Too much for some, so don't feel bad if it doesn't appeal." He'd found his focus now. He gave the boy an encouraging smile.

"I want to try everything," Dylan said.

"That's why I'm here."

"So where do we start?"

"We won't get into the theory of power now. My physics and biomechanics are a bit rusty. If you choose it as your discipline you'll have to, but right now we'll just go through some—"

Cutter leapt to his feet, letting out a sharp, warning bark that made Dylan start. Liam spun around. In the next instant there was a loud slam of door against wall. He wasn't really expecting a threat, but the countenance of the man who stormed into the building made him reconsider. A split second later Liam placed the man from the photograph he'd seen, even though it had obviously been taken some time ago.

Dylan's father.

"Hold," he ordered Cutter under his breath as his mind registered the resemblance to Dylan, much more pronounced in person, in the shape of his jaw and the blue of his eyes. But Liam was assessing him on another level, too. A little shorter than himself, but not much. Heavier. But it was soft weight, not muscle. Still, weight was weight, and a factor. Average arms and legs, so no exceptional reach. Not noticeably light on his feet; in fact, rather heavy. Mouth set in a scowl that looked permanently engraved.

But the main factor stayed the same. Anger put everything on a different level. People did crazy things when they were mad, things they might never do otherwise. And Liam thought of the road rage incident, where Dunbar had confirmed Barton Oakley had gone off on someone who had nearly sideswiped him, even though that driver had been dodging a large piece of debris in the roadway.

Came close to slugging the guy. Deputies almost cuffed him, he was that out of control. They let him go when they learned he'd buried his wife the day before. Grief does crazy things.

"What the hell is going on?" the man demanded as he halted before them. Cutter growled at his tone. The man looked at the dog, warily enough to tell Liam that he wasn't completely out of control.

"I left you a note, Dad," Dylan said. He sounded a bit beleaguered but not frightened, Liam noted. So he wasn't afraid of the man.

"I found it. I thought when you said you were coming here you were meeting with that damned busybody teacher." He turned on Liam. "Who the hell are you?"

"He's the one I told you about, Dad," Dylan said, while

Liam wondered what teacher he'd been talking about. Ria? Was that how he saw her being worried about his son?

The senior Oakley frowned. "You? You're just a kid yourself."

Liam didn't react to the familiar assessment. "I'm old enough to be the guy who's teaching Dylan how to rip somebody's head off," he said mildly, purposefully choosing the ominous phrase that had nothing to do with what he was really doing. He held the man's gaze steadily, wanting to know just how angry he was.

And, more important, why?

"Oh. You're the martial arts guy." Slightly calmer. So he wasn't out of control, Liam thought. Or at least he was calm enough to question the wisdom of tackling the guy teaching his son that particular subject. And Liam was glad of that when he heard the quiet sound of footsteps on the stairway just behind them. Ria, probably coming down to intercede, since he guessed she knew the man.

"Yes, I'm helping kids decide if it's something they want to do and which kind."

"I'm Barton Oakley," the man said, definitely calmer now. "Dylan's father."

"I could tell. There's a resemblance."

The man almost smiled, but then something flared in his eyes and the anger rekindled. Interesting shift, Liam thought.

"Dylan could be really good, once he chooses what he wants to pursue."

"I'm sure he could." Oakley sounded proud. "He's athletic."

Except he quit baseball, which he loved, Liam thought. But this didn't seem the time to bring that up, so he just nodded.

And then Ria was there. "Mr. Oakley, I'm glad you came to see what Dylan's—"

"You!" The anger was suddenly back at the level it had been at when he'd come in. "*You* are here!"

So he had been talking about her, Liam thought as he instinctively tensed, ready to spring with a swift ferocity that almost startled him. Cutter's hackles rose, and this time when he growled it was that half step between warning and attack. And this time Liam didn't order him to hold. He did not like the way Oakley had spoken to her.

Great. Dylan'll love it if I have to take his father down. That'll really get us to the goal now, won't it?

But if the man made the slightest move toward Ria, take him down Liam would. And to hell with the consequences.

Chapter 17

Liam marveled at Ria's utter calm as she responded to Barton Oakley's angry tone.

"I arranged these sessions for the students, so, yes, I am here."

Liam hadn't thought about that, that she'd feel responsible because she'd been the one to set all this up. That put her regular presence here in a whole different light and made him feel silly for being so antsy about it. But he shoved the feeling aside, not liking at all the way Oakley was glaring at her. Liam shifted position just slightly, enough to give himself a clear path to the man if necessary. Oakley didn't seem to notice.

"You're the one who put those silly ideas in my son's head," he said angrily to Ria.

"Dad—"

Liam cut Dylan off but in the same easy tone. "Being able to defend yourself isn't a silly idea, Mr. Oakley."

The man glanced at him, looking puzzled. "I didn't

mean that." Then he was glaring at Ria again. "I meant you. What are you doing, getting a kickback from that shrink?"

"Dad! Stop it." Dylan was starting to sound stressed.

"If you mean, did I suggest Dylan and his brother might benefit from further grief counseling, then, yes, I did," Ria said, still in that ultracalm tone that made Oakley's sound even harsher. "It's part of my job to be aware of the needs of my students beyond the classroom."

"I'll thank you to stay out of it." He practically snarled it. Ria ignored his tone, but Cutter took a step forward, looking at Liam as if begging for permission to take a chunk out of the man. Liam stifled the urge to give it.

"You're paying a lot for your son to attend Cove and I'd hate to think you weren't getting your money's worth in staff attention," Ria said.

Liam marveled at her cool dignity and the jab she managed to put into such measured words. Apparently she knew the man's mentality well enough to emphasize what mattered to him, because Liam saw the words register, taking the anger down a notch.

"In fact," she added, "you might want to set up a family session. You've all suffered a horrible loss."

Liam sensed the man's rigidity snap back to an even higher pitch than before. Cutter growled. Liam shifted his own weight to the balls of his feet, ready to react if the man made any move he thought was in any way threatening.

"You don't know the half of it," Oakley muttered.

He heard the pain in the man's voice. He felt for the guy; his life had been shattered. But at the same time he wondered what in Ria's calm words could have caused the sudden escalation. She'd merely made a helpful suggestion and offered empathy. And yet Oakley was reacting as if she'd slapped him.

"You," Barton Oakley said through clenched teeth, "can just mind your own business."

"That's enough," Liam said. "I think you'd better go cool off."

The man opened his mouth, and Liam was sure another cogent suggestion was coming, but Cutter added emphasis to his words with another ominous growl. The man shut his mouth, glanced at the dog and then back at Liam. He didn't say whatever had been on the tip of his tongue, but he looked even less happy than before.

"I'm sure Mr. Oakley is just concerned for his son's welfare," Ria said, and Liam couldn't believe how unruffled she appeared. Even Oakley seemed to realize the contrast wasn't making him look good. Liam saw the moment when he gave in, and a few seconds later Oakley took the out she'd offered him.

"I am. He's my son."

He said the last part as if each word were a complete sentence, with an odd sort of emphasis.

"Of course," Ria said, smiling at him. How any man breathing wouldn't be disarmed by that smile, Liam didn't know. "Perhaps you'd like to stay and watch them work? Mr. Burnett is really quite good."

Mr. Burnett?

He realized she was just countering Oakley's perception of him as too young, but it still niggled at him, coming from her. Dylan made a pained face, and Liam could see that he wasn't thrilled with the idea. But Liam could also see Oakley's anger was fading,

"Don't you have to get home, Dad? Where is Kevin, anyway?"

Just as quickly the anger was back, nearly as fierce as it had been before. "That boy isn't your problem."

Liam had the feeling he was angrier at Dylan's little brother than anyone else. Kevin taking off like that yesterday must have really scared his father. Some people didn't handle being frightened well, and nothing was scarier than your kid vanishing.

"You left him home alone?" Dylan asked.

"He's locked in his room, where he'll be all weekend," Oakley said sharply. "And I expect you to come straight home when you're done here, understand?"

"Yes, sir," Dylan said.

Dylan gave both Liam and Ria a darting glance that told Liam he was embarrassed as hell. Whether it was the dressing down in front of them or just his father's attitude that had done it, Liam wasn't sure. Obviously Kevin had been grounded, but at least their father hadn't ordered Dylan to come with him now; he was going to let him finish the session. So Barton Oakley didn't seem to blame the older brother for the transgressions of the younger.

When he was gone, Liam looked at the disheartened Dylan, letting his mouth twist wryly at one corner. "Wow. And I thought my old man was bad about embarrassing me in front of my friends."

Liam didn't know whether it was the commiseration or the fact that he'd classified them as friends that did it, but Dylan managed a half smile.

"He didn't used to be like that."

"So he hasn't always had such a short fuse?"

"Not before Mom…"

His voice trailed off. Liam got it, really. He understood the anger part of grief, perhaps better than the other parts. He'd spent a long time there himself. Compounded by guilt, it was an ugly place to live. And Barton Oakley had reason, after what had happened.

"I'm sure Kevin running off like that yesterday scared him," Ria said softly. "He's already lost your mother. I'm sure that makes him more protective of you boys than ever. He'll get better, Dylan. It's just going to take time. Grief isn't something that's predictable."

"And that you're all going through it doesn't help," Liam added. "There are going to be times when you're all at your lowest point at the same time, and it gets ugly."

After a moment Dylan nodded and then asked if they could finish up. He wanted to go check on Kevin.

"You're a good big brother," Ria said with a smile before leaving to return to the gallery and her grading.

Liam noted Dylan was a little wilder in his movements today, a little less controlled, which Liam interpreted as Dylan working through all the emotions his father's surprise visit had stirred up.

"One of the things this will do for you, once you narrow your focus to a particular discipline," he said as they finished and Dylan looked a bit dejected, as if he knew he hadn't done well, "is give you the mental strength to control your emotions."

Dylan flushed. "I'd like to just get rid of them."

"Not possible." *I've been trying since I was younger than you are.* "But you can learn to control when to let them go." *Unless you get sloppy, like I have.*

Dylan nodded, but he didn't look convinced. He hastened to put his shoes back on. Liam heard the faint sounds of steps on the stairs and found himself mentally bracing for Ria's presence. That he even had to do that was yet another reminder he should heed his own advice.

He tried to focus on the boy. "Worried about your brother?"

"He's really gotten kind of accident-prone."

Something in the way he said it, and in the phrase itself, snapped Liam's instincts into vigilance. "So you think that's what they are, now? Accidents?"

Dylan nodded. "I asked him. After we talked. If he was…hurting himself. Being careless. He said he's just always bumping into stuff. Falling."

"It can happen," Liam said neutrally. Because he'd heard

Ria coming he managed to stay steady, although his senses wobbled a bit when he caught that sweet scent again.

"Yeah." Then, with an attempt at a grin, Dylan added, "Maybe he's just a klutz."

Misgiving bit into Liam's mind. And a new possibility he didn't want to believe. Had that shift in Dylan's tone of voice been guilt? Was he hurting Kevin? Was Dylan Oakley taking his own tangled, grief-laden emotions out on his much smaller, skinny and relatively helpless brother?

That would change everything.

The moment the idea that Dylan was the cause of Kevin's supposed new-found clumsiness entered Liam's mind, Cutter got to his feet, looking straight at Liam. He met the dog's steady gaze, watching as the animal walked over and leaned into Dylan as if he were his best friend ever.

Cutter couldn't have said, "Trust him," more clearly if he'd spoken.

Liam offered Dylan a ride home so he didn't have to wait for the bus that came less frequently on the weekends, but the boy shook his head and, after a good-bye to Ria and a ruffle of Cutter's fur, left to walk down to the bus stop. Probably still smarting from embarrassment, Liam thought.

At least Liam's own old man had had reason. Like your kid being arrested in front of half the population of your small town. He'd deserved some embarrassment after that. Probably more than he'd gotten. Or maybe his father had known his mother would handle the final humiliation, that look only a mother could deliver.

But Dylan didn't have that anymore. He had only a father who was clearly struggling, full of the anger and fear of grief.

Chapter 18

"I don't envy him, going home to that," Ria said.

"Me, neither." Liam kept watching Dylan as he answered. He would need to keep tabs on the senior Oakley. Yes, it was most likely grief messing with his mind, but Liam didn't like the size of his anger.

"You were really good with him. You said just what he needed to hear. That he's not the only one who's been mortified by a parent, and we're still his friends."

Liam smiled at her praise but turned and lifted an eyebrow at her. "Teach, that was nothing compared to the way you handled his father. Talk about cool under fire. I would have wanted to punch him. I did want to."

I'd want to punch anyone who talked to you like that.

He had to look away again, afraid she'd read too much in his expression. She was too damned perceptive sometimes. It was, he was sure, part of what made her such a good teacher, but it made keeping his distance damned hard.

"I'm used to angry parents," she said, but she looked pleased. "And I'm glad you didn't punch him."

"I'm always for diplomacy first, if it works." He managed a grin. "Quinn kind of preaches that."

"But you're ready to fight if it doesn't?"

"He preaches that, too. That, in the end, it's the only way to back up peacekeeping." He shrugged. "I prefer to think of it as strongly encouraging good behavior."

She laughed. Damn, but he liked that sound. He looked away, saw Dylan through the open doors of the gym, making the turn off the campus and heading down toward the road where he would catch the bus. He didn't realize he was frowning until she spoke.

"What?" she asked.

"Dylan said his brother was accident-prone."

Ria paused in shifting the stack of papers she held. "Not a phrase I like to hear," she said. He was sure, as a teacher, she knew to watch out for those stock phrases that sometimes masked a much darker, deeper problem.

He let out a breath. "For a minute there, I wondered if maybe Dylan's problem was feeling guilty."

Her brows rose at that. "You mean you thought he was hurting his brother?"

"Wondered. Guilt can really turn you inside out."

"Firsthand knowledge?"

He didn't bother to deny it. "Yes."

"Your budding-criminal past?" she asked lightly.

His guilt came from more than that. Much more. And, if she knew, she wouldn't take it so lightly. For the first time since Ria Connelly had walked into his life, he thought maybe he had the tool to deal with his roiled emotions, maybe even to quash the stupid feelings he had around her. Because he knew her well enough now to know that, while some juvenile hacking for slightly illicit reasons was something she might be able to get past, the other things that had happened because of his actions would be far, far beyond the pale in her eyes.

"But you're not wondering anymore?" she asked.

It took him a moment to realize she meant Dylan. How the hell did she short-circuit his brain like that?

"No," he said. "Cutter gave him the seal of approval."

She drew back slightly. "What?"

"The moment I thought it, he made it very clear Dylan's to be trusted."

Ria looked at the dog. "You mean, when he went and leaned all over him?" Liam nodded. "So what, he's a mind reader?"

She sounded doubtful but not mocking, so he answered honestly. "Seems that way, sometimes. He's a million times better at reading people than any dog I've ever known, and I've known a few. My folks raise them. But I've never seen one like him."

She gave him a curious look. "Your parents raise dogs? Back in Texas?"

He nodded. "Hounds and hunting dogs." He glanced at Cutter. "Whole different mind-set."

"I don't even know what kind he is," she said.

"Even Hayley isn't positive, although they think he's mostly a Belgian. A Terv, my mom calls them. They could do a DNA test, but I think Hayley decided things were fine as they are. If it ain't broke and all."

Ria smiled at that. "I can't blame her. He's quite remarkable."

"He's pretty good at getting people to do what he wants. Herding-dog thing, I guess."

"People and sheep do sometimes have much in common," she said.

He couldn't help laughing at that. "Too often."

"I hope he's right this time, too. I'd hate to think Dylan would hurt anyone but especially his little brother."

"I'm betting he's right." Cutter stretched in that doggy way, front end down and tail in the air, and then he trotted toward the door. "I think my partner's ready for some fresh air."

"And I need to finish grading those essays. It's going to take me until late."

"Sounds like…" He wasn't sure what it sounded like to him, so he just let it fade away. She laughed.

"Like an exciting Saturday night? Welcome to my world."

"No hot date?" *Damn, you went there, Burnett. Idiot.*

"Gave those up. Ideas of what was hot too often diverged."

He had some ideas about what would be hot with her. And the less time spent thinking about them, the better.

"What's your idea of hot?" The words were out before he could stop himself.

"Not clubbing and getting drunk or worse every night," she said firmly.

He studied her for a moment. He was wading into dangerous waters but couldn't seem to stop that, either. "That sounded pretty specific."

"It was," she said. "I hate being a cliché."

He blinked. "What?"

"The old story. I loved, he cheated. Repeat ad infinitum."

"Idiot," he said and meant it. Something in his tone made her smile, a kind of smile that made him feel a shiver as if she'd touched him.

So now he knew there was no boyfriend in the picture. *What you should be thinking about is why the hell you felt the need to establish that.*

But there was no denying the low, hot burst of satisfaction he'd felt. However, he could ignore it. At least, he thought he could. And he'd better.

It was nearly eight; she'd been at it two hours but was having no luck at all finishing this grading. Usually Ria found her students' essays entertaining, at the least, and truly enjoyed some of the tangents they took off on. But nothing was holding her attention tonight.

Nothing except Liam Burnett asking if she had a hot date tonight.

She tried to convince herself that it was her lack of a dating life—even though this was intentional—that had her unsettled, but she knew better. It was quite simply the fact that it was Liam who had asked. And no amount of telling herself he'd simply been teasing her about her Saturday-night plans, or lack thereof, seemed to be helping. Because she couldn't seem to stop wondering if he'd asked because he'd wanted to know if she was seeing someone. And that way lay folly.

If you're going to obsess about anything, obsess about Dylan. And Kevin. They're the ones with a real problem.

That made her think of the heart-sinking moment when Liam said he had wondered if Dylan had been hurting his brother.

Which made her think of his trust and faith in Cutter's judgment. Somehow she found that…endearing.

As if you needed anything more to be attracted to. A guy who helps people for a living, with a history he's overcome, a sharp brain behind that hint of a drawl and a body that just happens to also be sexy as…as…

She had no comparison, she realized. She couldn't even isolate what it was about him. Great eyes, cute nose, that sandy-brown hair, tall but not so tall he towered over her own five-foot-four. And if she wanted to delve into sex, as it seemed she did, a great body, muscled yet lean, with a backside that had her thinking about back pockets in an entirely new way.

And that mouth. Yes, there was that. That mouth had her thinking about many things in an entirely new way.

She threw down her pen, rubbed at her eyes. Glanced at

the clock; it hadn't changed. Then at the remaining stack of essays. Two hours, and she'd barely made a dent.

Of course, if her brain would stick to the task at hand and quit lapsing into lengthy ponderings of the sexiness that was Liam Burnett, she'd be further along. But she couldn't seem to help it. And she truly did like the way he'd handled Dylan today. She liked the way he'd handled this whole thing. He'd only been at it a week and he already had Dylan liking and trusting him enough to call him when he needed help. Of course, Liam was a likeable guy.

And thinking that brought her full circle to the sexiness of Liam Burnett. And where exactly that could get him. And probably did, when he decided it was somewhere he wanted to go.

Eleven days ago you didn't even know he existed.

The phrase *blissful ignorance* slipped into her mind. Except she hadn't really been blissful. Not since Chad. But she hadn't been crushed, either. She'd simply taken herself out of that particular pool. She'd vowed to give herself at least six months to get it and him out of her system, to get over the fact that she had foolishly given her heart when it wasn't wanted. It had taken longer than six months, but she'd eventually accepted—most of the time, anyway— that it had been a case of her own poor judgment, not evidence that all men were such jerks.

Idiot.

Liam's short, sharp assessment of a man he'd never met had shocked her with its vehemence and warmed her for the same reason. She cautioned herself against reading too much into it. Maybe he thought all men who cheated were idiots. He seemed honorable enough.

Like you're any judge. If you were, you wouldn't have fallen for a cheater.

Or maybe Liam just thought Chad was an idiot for getting caught.

When her phone chimed with an incoming text, she was glad of the interruption to this hamster wheel she seemed to be caught on. This was from someone who didn't have an assigned notification tone, so not family or friends. She'd take a stranger, even a wrong-number text, over one of her brothers ribbing her for being home at eight o'clock on a Saturday night.

She laughed at herself as she got up and went to the kitchen counter, where she'd left her phone beside the thermal lunch bag she always used. She picked up the phone and tapped the text bubble icon. And then froze.

Liam.

She unlocked the phone with a haste she was glad no one was there to see. Opened the texting app.

Wow, two whole words.

Still working?

She supposed it was polite of him to text rather than call at this hour. He probably just had a question about Dylan or something, or he wanted to ask her about what had happened today.

She sent back, Yes and no.

Moments later the generic ring sounded. She found herself taking a deep breath before answering. And trying to ignore the tiny leap her pulse took when she heard his voice, deep, a little rough around the edges and sweetened with that hint of a drawl.

"Not going well?"

"Let's just say I'll be working tomorrow, too."

"I shouldn't have called then, but—"

"No, it's all right. I welcome the break, really." That wasn't strictly true, she thought, since you had to be actually working before you took a break, but she welcomed the interruption anyway. And tried not to admit she would welcome an interruption from him just about any time.

"I just wanted to…" His voice trailed off. As if he'd started to say one thing and gotten distracted. "I just…"

Definitely distracted.

And do not *read anything personal into that.*

Right. Good luck with that.

Wonderful, now she was arguing with herself. "Wanted to what?" she asked, and if her voice was more brisk than usual it was because she was trying to chide herself into common sense.

"Talk."

Well, obviously. Phone calls generally meant that.

The moment the words formed in her head she nearly burst out laughing at her own silly snark. She never acted like this. And she realized she could either be angry or amused that he got to her so easily. Given her worry over Dylan and his brother, anger would be easiest. And so she chose amusement.

"I'm sorry," she said with a laugh. "I'm upset with myself for not getting these essays done, but that's no reason to take it out on you." *Well, other than you're half the reason I can't focus, which I will keep to myself, thank you.* "Has something else happened?"

"No. I just need to…kind of assess the situation, and it would be better with someone who knows Dylan."

"So you need a sounding board?"

"Something like that."

"I can do that," she said. "It would certainly be more productive than I have been tonight."

She walked toward the refrigerator, thinking more caffeine was going to be in order. And if it kept her awake all night, maybe she'd actually get the work she was supposed to be doing done.

"Can you meet me?"

Her hand froze on the refrigerator door handle. Meet him?

"Ria?" he said when she didn't answer.

"I…fine. Where?" *Well, you've done it now, haven't you…*

"The Line? It's close and they aren't buried yet."

The place that had begun as a place for people stuck in long weekend lines for the ferry back to the city side had become popular with the locals, too, when it became known they had quick service, reasonable prices and great appetizers. She'd always thought it clever of them to focus on the quick-to-eat dishes people could grab in the time they were waiting.

He just wants to talk about the case.

If she'd said it to herself once as she drove, she'd said it a half-dozen times. And it was only when she was parking— a handy three blocks down—that she realized the obvious.

It's close.

How had he known it was close for her, that she lived barely three miles from the popular spot?

"Because Foxworth is obviously very thorough," she muttered to herself as she got out of the car. And obviously they had done all their homework on everyone involved. Except Emily, of course, since they already knew her.

She took out her phone, silenced it and put it back in her pocket as she passed the ice cream stand where a cluster of teenagers were gathered. Although it wasn't dark yet, the twilight was fading, and she acknowledged once more how much she loved living here, where she could walk alone unmolested and where she knew that, if something happened, strangers would jump in to help. They had their problems, of course, but she wouldn't trade her small town and life here for anything.

She nearly jumped when a figure stepped out of the darkness of the entrance overhang.

"Now that's a great smile."

He said it like a guy greeting a date would. But this was not a date. It was *not*. Nor was he responsible for the crazy places her mind always seemed to want to go around him. That was her, and her alone.

And it was going to be a long night.

Chapter 19

"You beat me here," she said, still a little disconcerted by both his sudden appearance and the compliment.

"Actually," he said with a quirk of his mouth, "I was already here when I called. That's how I knew they weren't jammed up yet."

She lifted a brow at him. Managed a light tone. "That certain, were you?"

"That I was going to call you? Yes. That you'd come? No."

She wasn't at all sure how to take that, so she said nothing as he opened the door and held it. They threaded their way between tables to the back doors that led out onto the small patio, which had only a half-dozen small tables but a great view of the marina, the cove and, on clear days, Mt. Rainier in the distance. The day's heat lingered, but she knew that, since summer was over, it would be cooling off more quickly once the sun went down completely.

But they wouldn't be here that long, she thought. That was the point of the place, wasn't it? In and out quickly?

They took the only empty table, next to the railing. He didn't, she noticed, even look at the expansive menu of local brews.

"No beer at the end of a long day?" she asked lightly.

"No, but feel free." He lowered his voice to a whisper. "Don't tell anyone, but I actually come here for the frozen lemonade."

She let out a laugh. While most came here for the alcoholic menu to numb the long waits in the summer—when you had an hour or two to kill, that was the only thing to do for some people—kids usually preferred the frozen lemonade spiked with various in-season fruits, the restaurant's most popular summer drink.

"For somebody who was upset at herself, you sound cheerful."

"I…feel better," she admitted. *And more in control, thank goodness.* "Maybe I needed to get out, get some fresh air."

"Clear out the cobwebs, my mom always says."

"Exactly like that," she said, still smiling. "Do you see them often? Your parents?"

"Whenever I can. They started taking on foster kids after my youngest sister left home, and that and the dogs they raise are a lot of work, so I like to check on things now and then. I was just back there last month." His mouth quirked again. She found she liked the expression. "And learned I have definitely acclimated. Texas in August didn't used to faze me at all, but, after all this time here, it was a little hard to take."

"I've heard the heat is formidable."

"That's one word for it," he said with a laugh. She liked that, too. His laugh.

Admit it, there's not much you don't like about him.

"So," she said when two strawberry lemonades and a

plate of luscious-smelling crab-stuffed mushrooms had arrived, "what did you want to bounce off me?"

He froze in the act of reaching for one of the mushrooms. For an instant she would have sworn a shiver went through his hand. She played back what she'd said in her mind. Had to reach for a connotation that might cause that reaction. Almost blushed when she got there.

But when he spoke his voice was even, almost flat, and she knew she must have imagined it.

"You met Dylan's mother, right?"

"Yes, I met with her several times, and with both her and her husband a few. Good?" she asked, indicating the appetizer he'd taken a bite of as she answered.

"Very. What was she like?"

"Nice. Involved, which I liked. She was determined Dylan would do well at the Cove."

"She was young. When she died."

"Yes. I remember thinking, when the news reports came out, that she was young to have a sixteen-year-old."

"Maybe that's why they got married," Liam said with a wry smile. "My dad would still grab his shotgun if one of us put the kid before the wedding, as it were."

She lifted an eyebrow at him. "Even you and your brothers, or just the girls?"

"Don't push me into that minefield," he said with a laugh. "They divided that one up. My mother can guilt the best of us boys with a look."

His voice hadn't really changed, but something in his face did. "I gather she's done that to you?"

"Oh, yeah," he said softly. And then his eyes widened as he seemed to realize that what he'd said could be taken the wrong way. "Not for that reason," he said hastily. "I never got a girl—I mean—" He took a breath and finally ended it simply. "No."

She smiled widely at him, indicating she hadn't taken

it that way. "I gather you mean your...questionable computer activities?"

He shifted as if he were uncomfortable, as if he'd had no intention of going here. "Yeah." He grimaced. "Ask Quinn. He talked to her. She thought he was letting me off too easy when he offered me a job instead of pressing charges and sending me to jail."

Ria blinked. "Wow. Tough love."

"Yeah." He smiled then. "I didn't think so at the time, but it was love. Best thing they could have done to make sure I stayed on the right path."

"It must have been hard for them. To see you in trouble and not step in."

"Quinn told me later—much later—that my mother chewed him out pretty hard, made him swear he'd make me keep my nose clean. Said half the reason he pushed me so hard was to make sure he didn't let her down."

"Your mother must be quite something."

"She is. So's the old man. Raised five kids with practically nothing and we've all turned out okay." He grinned then. "Dad says they were just investing in their own future, since we can all help to take care of them now. We updated the house last year. This year we're doing the kennels."

She smiled. "I'm glad." Obviously whomever he'd lost in his life, whoever had died to put that understanding of Dylan's situation in him, it wasn't a parent or a sibling.

He looked at her for a moment. "Mom always wanted to be a teacher."

"Sounds to me like she is."

He smiled widely at that. "Yes. She is." He studied her for a moment, glancing at her earrings before saying, "Your family is Connelly Hardware."

She nodded, not surprised that he knew. That was Foxworth thoroughness. "That's us. Our slogan, 'We help people who build and fix things,' was my grandfather's motto. My great-grandfather built the first store, Grandpa expanded it and now my parents run the chain."

"But you never had the urge?"

"To go into the family business? No. One of my brothers is the accountant, so he's holding up the family honor for the next gen. And Grandpa's always available for advice."

"He's still…with you?"

She smiled. "Alive and kicking in the literal sense. I'm very lucky." She looked up from her lemonade, met his gaze. "That's one reason I'm glad you're on this. You understand. I've never lost anyone close to me, so it's still… theoretical for me."

She hadn't really meant it to encourage him to talk about who had taught him that harsh lesson. Which was a good thing, since he was suddenly concentrating on the last stuffed mushroom, neatly cutting it in half as if the fate of the world depended on getting it exactly even. So whatever it was, it was buried deep, and she told herself he had every right to keep it there. With an effort she made herself go back to what she assumed was the matter at hand.

"What has you wondering about Dylan's mother?"

"Her social media accounts."

"Ah. I know she wasn't the technophobe he says his father is, because he talked about how excited she was about a new phone. It had a better camera."

"That's exactly what I meant. She posted a lot of pictures. And apparently did a lot of hiking."

Ria nodded. "She loved to go out and look for wildlife, especially eagles. Dylan said she used to take him a lot, when he was little, before Kevin was born. That kind of curtailed those expeditions."

"Except that day."

"Yes." She sighed. "It's so sad—she gets back to what she loves, and it kills her."

He gave her a look she couldn't quite interpret. "She was with her husband that day, but her photo captions seem to indicate she usually went with friends."

Ria nodded again. "A group of three. I remember Dylan laughing about her calling them her girlfriends. You know, like kids do when they think their parents are way too old to use the word." Her smile faded. "I wonder if Dylan realizes how young she really was."

"Probably not. The thirties seem old at sixteen. But when he hits them himself, it's liable to come down on him like a thousand-pound bronc."

She leaned back in her chair and looked at him. "You're very wise."

"Thanks for not adding 'for my age.'" His tone was dry.

"I'll bet looking young comes in handy sometimes, with your work."

He shrugged. "Sometimes."

"And when you hit thirty, maybe you'll be glad."

He eyed her for a moment before saying neutrally, "Two years, if you're asking."

She managed not to blush. Or show the relief she didn't want to even feel that he wasn't as young as she'd feared. That he was, in fact, only a year younger than her. Not that it mattered, she told herself firmly. They were merely working together for a common goal, not starting a relationship.

Images blasted through her mind, visions of what that might be like. They took her breath away, and she seriously considered taking her frozen-lemonade-chilled hands and clapping them over her cheeks as the blush she'd beaten down at first finally won.

It took Liam a tenth of a second to decide he would give a great deal to know what had brought on the rise of pink in her face. A bit longer to fight down his own reaction, to quash the hope that she'd been curious for a private reason. He was not going there. He couldn't. He had no right to even think about it. How could he even consider risking it, for her sake?

No, this was business, and business it would stay. And it was time he took this back there, right now.

"Did Dylan ever mention them all going hiking, the whole family?"

She looked thoughtful for a moment and then shook her head. "Not recently, as far as I remember. Just trips when he was a kid."

"What about his mother and father going hiking without him and his brother?"

"He talked about that last day, of course, but it was upsetting, obviously, so we didn't talk about it all that much." She frowned. "Does it matter?"

He shrugged. He thought it might, but he wasn't ready to go there yet. "Just putting together the picture. The more I know, the better. So Dylan wasn't a hiker?"

"It wasn't his favorite thing, no."

He finished the last of his lemonade. Looking at the empty glass made him realize that on some level he was wishing this could go on. She was easy to talk to, as long as he kept his baser urges under control. True, he was having to work harder at that than he had in a long time, but it seemed worth it to look across the table and see that smile.

She looked at him curiously. "How long does Foxworth pursue something before giving up?"

"Foxworth doesn't give up," he said. "Unless the person we're working for calls us off."

"What if you don't find an answer?"

"Then it's still open. Quinn's got things whirlin' in his head that are from years ago. He hates loose ends. And he gets what he wants. Eventually."

She smiled then. "Like he got Hayley?"

He grinned. "Just like that. Although one of those loose

ends is still dangling from the case they met on. And it's one Quinn will be relentless on."

"More than others?"

He nodded. "This one's personal to him. I don't envy his target when he finds him."

He remembered the conversation he and Rafe had had about the time when—and it would be when, not if—Quinn finally nailed down the mole that had almost cost them that mission and more. The mole that could have cost all of them their lives, including Hayley. They'd covertly investigated two FBI agents, a senatorial chief of staff and the senator himself. On the latter two, they'd found enough dirt to disgust them but nothing to do with their quarry. So Quinn had quietly turned the info over to one of the rarest beasts in DC, an honest politician, closed that trail and continued the hunt.

He snapped back to the present, belatedly tuning in to Ria's comment on Foxworth.

"—have built a remarkable thing."

"Yes."

"Out of tragedy, hope," she said.

"Who said that?"

"Countless, I'm sure. I think it's human nature or the two sides of it, anyway. How we deal with tragedy, I mean. The optimist looks for some kind of hope."

"And the pessimist...what? Says, 'See, I told ya so'?"

She laughed again. And he still liked the sound of it. "Exactly that."

He realized suddenly they had strayed far from the reason he'd wanted to meet with her. Or, at least, the reason he'd told himself.

He also realized he was enjoying this, more than he'd enjoyed anything in a while. And he only now noticed the place was filling up as the late-nighters began to arrive.

They should clear out. And he didn't want to. He wanted

this night, this conversation, to go on. And on. Blaming Cutter for planting this damned idea in his head wasn't helping it go away.

"Dang dog," he muttered, barely aware of saying it out loud until she looked at him oddly.

"Need to get back to him?"

That easily she handed him an out. And that quickly, he was at war internally, one part of him demanding escape, the other tempted—oh, so tempted—to stretch this out as long as he could.

Regarding the case, he already had what he'd come for. And he thought he'd managed to do it without setting off any warning bells in Ria. He didn't want her to inadvertently let something slip to Dylan, not before he had a chance to dig further.

So if he had that, why was he still sitting here? For that matter, why had he felt the need to do this in person anyway? He could have asked her over the phone about the hiking.

"Liam? What's wrong?"

"My daddy would say my ox is in the ditch."

She blinked. "Translation, please? My Texan's not up to par."

"You're better off not knowing," he said, letting her think it was something off-color, rather than explaining it simply meant he couldn't do what he wanted to do.

He got to his feet, taking the out they'd stumbled into. When she pointed out where she'd parked three blocks down, he wondered if situtations like this were half the reason men had invented gentlemanly manners. Because if he should walk her to her car, it also meant another few minutes spent with her.

There was enough traffic headed for the ferry that he noticed it as he walked to the driver's door with her. He stood by as she opened it, turning to look down the road to see if it was safe to pull it open.

He turned back. She'd taken a step to be clear of the door. They collided.

He expected her to jump back. Break the contact. She didn't. Maybe she couldn't. The car. The traffic. *Damn it. Don't do this. Don't...*

He was still thinking it as he kissed her.

Chapter 20

The sound of the ferry traffic faded into nothing, inaudible over the pounding of her heart. She'd known he was going to do it. Or was that hoped? Did she, really?

And then even thought faded away, crowded out by new and vivid sensations, the feel of his mouth on hers, the feel of his body against hers, the overwhelming heat that seemed to swirl out from every point of contact.

He didn't crush her lips with his—this was more of a tasting, testing, as if he were as curious as she was. But the heat grew and, with it, the urgency, so quickly she only realized when her head started to spin that she'd forgotten to breathe. Or maybe it was the effect of the kiss itself; she didn't know. She didn't know anything, except she'd never felt this way in her life over a simple kiss.

Simple? You call this simple?

The same voice in her head that had been mocking her efforts to keep Liam Burnett out of her thoughts was sounding annoyingly triumphant now.

He broke the kiss, pulling back sharply. She felt bereft, and that in itself was disquieting. The only saving grace was that he looked as unsettled as she did.

"I—" He swallowed, tried again. "I'm sorry. I shouldn't have done that."

"Why?" It came out faintly, breathlessly, because he'd stolen what air she had.

She could almost feel him drawing himself up, steadying himself. She liked that he had to but not that he was doing it. Which fit perfectly her own tangled state.

"You're a smart lady, Ria. You don't want anything to do with me, that way."

That kicked her breathing back into gear. She honestly did not understand. It wasn't like he was a cop and she a... witness or something. They might be working on this, but they normally didn't work together.

Maybe that was it. He had this exciting, sometimes dangerous—how could it not be if they had a sniper, for God's sake—job, and she was...well, what she was.

"Is a teacher too boring for you?" she asked.

He pulled back slightly. "You? Boring? When I have to work just to keep up with you?"

She smiled inwardly at the compliment, but she didn't want to get sidetracked and said only, "Some men find that...annoying."

He reached out then, brushed the back of his fingers over her cheek. "Darlin'," he said, the drawl suddenly leaping to the fore, "I find you a whole lotta things, and boring isn't even in the footnote to the list."

She wasn't sure if it was the accent or the way he put it, but she was charmed all over again.

"Then why?" she asked again.

He sucked in an audible breath. "There are things you don't know."

"I know you got in trouble as a kid, went to jail. How much worse can it get?"

He went very still. It was a moment before he said flatly, "Much."

He meant it. The shadow she'd seen before, that told her he was one of those who knew grief firsthand, was there in his eyes again. Only this time it wasn't merely a flicker; it stayed.

"Go home, Ria," he said. He sounded weary, in that too-much-of-the-world way she'd seen in police and military personnel. Too weary for his age and far too weary for the age he looked. And yet he spent his time helping people and clearly loved what he did, what Foxworth stood for. It was a puzzle she couldn't seem to let go of.

But she sensed this was not the time.

How much worse can it get?

Much.

It wasn't until she was pulling into the garage of her condo that she remembered something else he'd said, about working for Foxworth.

Some days it's the only thing that gets me through, knowing what we do.

So there had to be something, other than relatively minor hacking offenses, that ate at him, that he couldn't get past. She wondered what it would take to turn a normally laid-back, easygoing guy like Liam into someone who couldn't let go.

But more than that, she wondered if that's how he felt, why he'd kissed her in the first place.

If he went up in flames the way you did, then you know why he did it.

That, she thought as she went inside and tossed her keys and purse down with more emphasis than usual, was what she should have asked him. Not why he shouldn't have done it but why he had.

* * *

Cutter nudged at his hand. Liam absently stroked the dog's head as he stared at the screen of what Rafe called his industrial-grade laptop. He wasn't even sure what he was looking for; he was just following tangents and connections hoping something would hit. Or as Rafe also called it, falling down the rabbit hole.

Now there was a guy with a past, one worth warning someone off for. But Rafe never had to warn anyone off, because he never let anyone get close. Outside of Foxworth, he was a loner and seemed to prefer it that way. You'd never catch Rafe doing something stupid like…like…

And just like that there he was, back in the moment on the street, next to her car, when he'd made one of the more stupid decisions in recent memory and kissed her.

Stupid. Definitely the word.

But, damn, it was sweet. She made him feel like the first burst of bluebonnets in spring did. Like the way the smell of his mother's pecan pie baking always made his stomach growl, Ria made every carnal sense he had leap to life. As if it were inbred, instinctive, not just a response but some deep, intrinsic part of him.

He'd never had that kind of reaction before, and it unsettled him. While Ria had all the things that attracted him, there was so much more to her, what his mother called still waters that ran deep, that he knew better than to even think what he was thinking. She was not the sort of woman who kept things light and easy, the *easy* part—as in *easy to walk away*—being the operative word there. No, she was the kind who lured you in simply by not trying, by just being who she is, so that you knew there were no phony fronts, that she was utterly genuine.

Cutter nudged him again. And again, until he shifted his gaze from the distraction of the screen and looked at the animal. The dog's steady and sometimes unnerving gaze was fastened on him intently.

"Don't think I don't know what you're up to, hound," he muttered at him.

The dog never wavered, just stared up at him.

"It's not happening. I've got my reasons, and you'd better get used to it."

The dog shifted then, but only to stretch out and nudge his cell phone with his nose.

"I'm not calling her."

The dog nudged the phone again.

"No."

And again, only this time Liam had to grab it to keep it from sliding off the table. He set it back down, this time well out of the dog's reach. And practically the moment he let go of it, it rang.

Startled, he looked at the screen. His gaze shot back to the dog.

"Is that all that was? You knew your mom was going to call?" He felt silly, thinking the dog had been urging him to call Ria. Which told him where his brain was at, no matter how much he denied it.

He grabbed the cell and answered.

"Hey, how are two of my favorite boys?" Hayley asked.

"We're good. He knew you were going to call. Practically knocked my phone off the table right before. I swear, it must ring at a doggy sound level before we can hear it."

Hayley laughed. "Just checking in. I know it's late, but I figured you'd still be awake."

"Yeah." *Like I've been sleeping much lately anyway.* "How are Walker and Amy?"

"Busy. Her boss had a big case coming up and she's researching like mad. And Walker's got the office under control. In fact, he just wound up another case."

"Not bad for only being in operation since May."

"No, he's doing well."

Liam smiled. Hayley and Walker's relationship hadn't been the best when he'd had secrets to keep. But now his actions had been explained, he was an out-and-out hero and the two were very close. Even more so because her brother just happened to be flat-out in love with her best friend Amy.

Another of Cutter's successful matchups.

He wondered if the dog had ever failed on one of those before.

"Liam?"

He snapped back to the conversation. "What?"

"I asked how it was going on your end."

Other than your dog trying to pull his matchmaker routine on me? "Early days still. Got a few threads peeking out, but nothing that's unraveled yet."

"How's Dylan?"

"Stressed out, that boy is. Met his father this afternoon, so I can see why."

"He one of those threads?" Hayley asked.

"Yes. I know anger's part of grief, but he's one touchy guy. Heard anything from Quinn?"

"He thinks he's onto something, but he's not committing yet."

"He'll find that mole, you know he will."

"Yes," she said simply, "I do."

The utter faith and confidence in her voice gave him an odd feeling. What must it be like for Quinn, to know the woman you loved had such trust in you? To know she never, ever doubted you would get the job done? That you would do the right thing? He wondered which came first, the trust or the love? Or did they have to come together before you had a rock-solid relationship like the Foxworths had? How did you even start building a thing like that?

You start with being the kind of man Quinn is and al-

ways was, not a dumb-as-a-fence-post kid who makes stu-pid choices that other people pay for.

He grabbed for something else to talk about.

"I've been looking at the pictures Melissa Oakley posted online that last day, and I read the report again. It's thorough, and it's clear that the edge of the trail had gotten undercut by water and wind erosion and just collapsed."

"But?"

"I don't know. Just seems like an experienced hiker would have... I don't know, noticed something."

"Not everybody's as eagle-eyed as you, Mr. I-could-track-a-fly-through-a-tornado."

He laughed. "Thanks. I think."

"Now what else is bothering you?"

He was tempted to tell her that her dog was at it again, but he was afraid she'd just tell him to stop fighting and go with it. And *that* he would not do. Ever. He couldn't risk it. Not again. He had no right.

"Just trying to figure out why Oakley had such a conniption over Ria suggesting counseling."

"Some people are like that. They think it's weakness. Or don't believe it's any use."

"My daddy used to say counseling might help you handle it, but you're going to go through the grief no matter what, one way or another."

"Your daddy is a wise man," Hayley said.

Liam smiled. "He's a tough ol' bird, but he knows things."

When they'd disconnected, he sat for a moment, looking at Cutter. He knew he was imagining things, but something in the dog's gaze reminded him of Ria's quiet steadiness. The dog even tilted his head in the way she did when she was thinking. But he'd always done that. Hadn't he?

"Focus," he reminded himself, for all the good it would do. Even knowing that sometimes the cases that seemed the most straightforward could get complicated fast. Complicated, and dangerous.

"You need a distraction," he said finally. "And," he added ruefully, "so do I."

He changed clothes, trading jeans for sweatpants and his boots for running shoes. He didn't do this often, just enough to keep his cardio and wind up, but this seemed like a good time to run himself—and his persistent companion—into quieter minds.

"I'm no Brett Dunbar," he told the dog, "but I'll give you a couple of miles. You just leave me out of your plans, okay?"

Cutter gave him a happy bark and his most innocent look.

Liam didn't buy it for an instant.

Chapter 21

"You can do better, Dylan. But you know that."

Ria watched her student dodge her gaze. He focused on the graded essay she'd handed back to him. While a B- wasn't a horrible grade, it was less than his best, and she knew he knew it.

"It read as if you were having trouble concentrating."

He shrugged.

"Dylan—"

"Look, I was thinking about other things, okay? Sorry."

"Like your brother?" she suggested gently, not taking issue with his sharp tone.

The way his gaze darted back to her face told her she'd hit a nerve. Whether or not it was the one causing the problem, she didn't know.

"Your father seemed pretty angry last week. Is he over it now?"

Dylan let out a compressed breath. "He's never over it. Not since Mom died."

"So he's still upset with you?"

"Kevin more than me. Which I don't get. Kevin never does anything bad." He grimaced. "Well, at least he didn't until he started cutting school and falling off things."

"And you do?"

He gave her a sideways look. "Sometimes I don't do exactly what he wants."

"You're a teenager," she said dryly. "That's in your job description."

She got a smile for that. Small victories, she thought. "Is he unfair about it?"

"Not about that," Dylan said then stopped. About something, then, she thought.

"What is he unfair about?"

"Kevin," Dylan said after a moment. "He gets in trouble for…nothing."

"More than you do?" He nodded. "Could it be that he's home more, because he's younger? Simply more chances to get in trouble?"

"Maybe."

But the boy didn't sound convinced.

"I gotta go," he said, getting to his feet.

"Yes," she said neutrally, knowing it was time for his session with Liam.

"Sorry about the essay. I'll do better next time."

"I'm not worried about it. And I'm always here if you want to talk, Dylan. Even if it's about nothing."

"Yeah. Thanks."

He left her feeling as if she'd failed him utterly. She could only hope Liam had better luck.

"That Brazilian stuff…could you stop a guy without hurting him?"

Liam looked up from putting his boots back on to face Dylan. They'd just finished their session, and it hadn't been pretty. To be honest, he'd been almost as distracted as Dylan had been, from the moment Ria had appeared in the upper gallery. Just his luck Dylan's free period coincided with hers.

He straightened and turned to the boy, made himself focus. He saw more than just idle curiosity in Dylan's eyes. This was specific.

"Depends on how rabid he is," Liam said. "But any time there's contact, somebody could get hurt."

"You stopped Alan without hurting him."

"Except maybe his pride," Liam said. Dylan's mouth seemed to try for a grin, but it faded almost instantly. "Calculated risk," Liam said with a shrug. "I figured he'd rush me. His kind usually do. And there was a mat, which you won't have in the real world."

"Could a kid stop a big guy?"

Was he the kid? Had Alan been giving him trouble? Was he taking out his public embarrassment last week on Dylan? Liam had thought he'd ameliorated the situation by pretending the bully had been in on it all along, but maybe not.

"Up to a point, yes. Although if the size difference is too great or the kid too small, he's not going to win."

Dylan let out a sigh, as if he'd feared that answer.

"What the kid can do is get himself a chance to escape," Liam said, wondering if Dylan was talking about himself or his brother.

Dylan's mouth curved downward in a sour expression. "No escaping this." The boy's jaw tightened. Liam saw the moment when he decided. "Never mind. Doesn't matter."

"It does if somebody's trying to hurt you."

"I'm not helpless!"

The exclamation came out with such force that Liam guessed it was because the boy felt exactly that—helpless.

"Dylan—"

The school chimes pealed out, and Dylan seized on the chance to say hastily, "Gotta go."

As Dylan gathered his things, including the tablet computer in its case, Liam asked the boy casually, "You or your dad have a computer at home? Something bigger than your tablet?"

Seemingly glad of the subject change, the boy answered normally. "Dad's got Mom's old one, but he only uses it for email. I use it for homework sometimes, but mostly I just use my phone and tablet. Why?"

"I want to send you some sites to check out, and it would be easier to see on a bigger screen. Some photos you should study for positioning and stuff."

"Oh. Okay. I think he'll let me use it for that, but it's really slow."

"Maybe just leave it turned on and online tonight? Not sure when I'll get it sent."

"Okay."

"See you Thursday," Liam said. The boy didn't respond, just kept walking, as if he were afraid Liam would bring up things he didn't want to talk about again.

The moment Dylan was out of sight Liam realized he was tensed up. And he reluctantly had to admit why. Ria was already on her way down. He could hear her light, steady footsteps on the metal stairs.

He hadn't spoken to her since Saturday night. Not that he hadn't had the urge, but he'd fought it down. Maybe a thousand or so times. He knew it was pretty insensitive to kiss a woman and then vanish—his sisters had certainly whined about it enough growing up—but every time he'd reached for the phone he'd stopped himself. Tried to tell himself it was because this was just proximity, and he'd been without too long. Tried to tell himself he was just falling prey to believing in Cutter's machinations. Tried to tell himself any number of things, all of which fell short of the memory of that kiss.

It couldn't have been that...much. That hot. That fierce. That instantaneous. He didn't have that kind of feeling in him—not anymore, anyway. He'd successfully quashed that long ago, when he'd had to face the price of not thinking and the cost to others for caring about him. No, he was ol' easygoing, never-ruffled, never-serious Liam Burnett, and that was what he would stay.

Steady now, he turned as she stepped out onto the polished wood floor.

And forgot how to breathe.

She was wearing a dress. A red dress. A red dress that somehow made her dark hair gleam even more. A red dress that hugged her curves and flared at the bottom, which hit a couple of inches above her knees and hinted maddeningly at the rest of her long, shapely legs, curved even more by a pair of simple black heels. He'd never thought of red and black as a favorite combination before, but right now he could be persuaded.

Some old lyrics, from a song he'd heard back in Texas, about what happened to a man every time his woman wore that little red dress, ran through his head. Back then, he'd always thought of some super short, low-cut sexy thing. This was none of that. Except sexy. It came up to her neck and almost to her knees, yet it was the sexiest thing he'd ever seen.

"You...you're dressed up." *Well, that was lame.*

"Teacher's meeting with the board."

"Oh." *Lamer still.* Then he frowned. "Why?"

"Monthly assessments. We go over all the students to identify anything that needs attention."

"Oh." *Again.* "You going to bring up Dylan?"

"Dr. Halvorson will ask for a report, I'm sure. But she's reasonable. She won't expect results this soon."

"Oh." *Damn.* "Well, you look…great," he finally managed.

She smiled, and appeared genuinely pleased. "Thank you. How did it go?"

He took a breath, the first one he'd been conscious of since she'd come into view. "I…okay. One little blip. Don't know yet if it means anything."

"What?"

"He brought up self-defense again. Asked if it was possible to stop an attacker without hurting him."

"Like you did Alan?"

"That's the example he used. But then he asked if a kid could stop a big guy. He bailed before I could get any more. Like if he was talking about himself or his brother."

Her frown deepened. And she wasn't just pondering. She was thinking about something specific. He wasn't sure how he knew that, but he did.

"What?"

"I had a talk with him after class today, about his essay. It wasn't up to the standard of his usual work."

"He said he had a discussion with you. That that's why he was late."

She nodded. "I asked how things were, if his father was still mad, like he was the day he came here. He said his father has been mad ever since his mother died."

"Understandable."

"Yes. But he said something else that bothers me."

"What?"

"That he treats him and Kevin differently."

Liam smiled crookedly. "Sometimes it's necessary. My dad chewed on me all the time, more than my brothers and sisters. But I was the black sheep, the one always in trouble."

She smiled, as if the image amused her. He wasn't sure how he felt about that. But when she spoke, she stayed on the subject at hand.

"That's just it. He said Kevin gets in trouble for nothing. Implied that he does things that are worse and doesn't get in trouble. That his father is unfair about some things."

Liam frowned. "Favoritism?"

"Sounds like it."

"Has it always been like that?"

"I'm not sure. I get the feeling it's all since their mother died, but he didn't say that in so many words." She looked thoughtful. "I do not like the juxtaposition of three of those things."

"You mean Oakley's anger, the boys being treated differently and Dylan asking if a kid could hold off a big guy?"

"Exactly."

"Throw in Kevin suddenly turning up with scrapes and bruises and I really don't like it."

"Exactly," she said. "I should report this. He's not our student, but—"

Liam held up a hand. "Give me tonight. I want to… check something out."

"Something?"

"Just a hunch."

"What are you going to do?"

"What I do best," he said. "Track."

He didn't explain that he meant in the cyber world, not the real one. He had the feeling Ria wouldn't approve, since it involved his old hacking skills and Barton Oakley's old, hopefully vulnerable computer.

Chapter 22

Ria was sitting curled up in her favorite chair, trying to read—for pleasure this time—and having trouble. There was a fine hum of tension just beneath the surface, and it had Kevin Oakley's name on it. She trusted Liam, enough to give him the time he'd asked for, but the thought that that little boy might be being abused ate at her.

In the morning she would take the proper steps, she told herself. She wasn't comfortable with waiting any longer than that. As a teacher she knew well what needed to be done, and while the fact that Kevin was not her student took it out of her realm of direct responsibility legally, morally she had no doubts.

That Dylan might be angry at her, since he was so clearly torn between protecting his brother and his love for his father, was just a consequence she might have to take. He—

Her cell phone text alert went off. She smiled at the notes of *The Yellow Rose of Texas*. She'd assigned the famous folk song to Liam's number, telling herself that, as long as they were working on this, he might text or call. And somewhere under the logic was the emotional reason: she wanted a warning if it was him. Time to get her pulse under control, if nothing else.

She picked up the phone and tapped to open the messaging app.

Still up?

She took a moment and a breath, and then she nearly laughed at herself. It was only a text, after all.

Yes. Reading. Or trying to.

The answer came back quickly.

New info. Changes everything. Meet?

Her breath caught. What had happened? Obviously it wasn't something urgent, something happening right now or he'd be taking action, not just wanting to meet. And she doubted he would consult her first; for all his laid-back demeanor, once stirred he moved fast. Hadn't she seen that in the way he'd uncoiled on Alan, going from that easy grace to swift, efficient action?

The fact that for a split second she considered texting back *Your place or mine?* steadied her. Where? she sent instead.

She had a sudden image of him having the same thought, of suggesting they meet here or at his place. Telling herself not to be a bigger fool than she'd already been, she waited. Then the reply came.

I'm at Foxworth. Can you get here?

On my way in 5.

Thx.

She was glad she hadn't changed out of her jeans and sweater yet. Even though she'd thought about it after shedding the dress and kicking off those damned heels, she hadn't surrendered to the lure of pajamas at eight o'clock. She found herself smiling as she remembered Liam's reaction to that dress. She'd found it on the sale rack at a high-end store, a place she could never afford normally. It had looked rather plain on the hanger, but she'd liked the cut of it and tried it on.

She would have bought it then, even if it meant she had to live on rice for a month. And Liam's stunned stare had made it worth every penny.

She told herself that she would have felt pleased if any man reacted like that. And that little voice that had been so much more active lately merely laughed.

She ran a brush through her hair, grateful as always for the sleek bob's simplicity. Checked her makeup, brushed away a flake of mascara, did a quick swipe with tinted lip gloss and decided that was enough. She was not trying to impress him, she told herself firmly.

She grabbed the soda she'd been drinking in the hope that the caffeine would help her focus on her reading. It hadn't, but she might need the alertness to deal with whatever it was that Liam had discovered.

As she drove, she found herself hoping fiercely it wasn't anything negative about Dylan, that Liam hadn't found proof somehow that Cutter had been wrong, that it really had been Dylan causing his brother's so-called accidents. Then she wondered how Liam had found out whatever this was. Had he perhaps gone to Dylan's home? Followed him?

Her thoughts kept tumbling. Cutter hadn't liked Dylan's

father when he'd shown up. But that could have just been the man's angry mood. It would be silly to read any more into it than a dog's instinct to protect against a threat. No matter how clever Liam said he was.

In fact, Cutter was outside to greet her when she arrived. She bent to pet him, guessing he'd heard her car on the gravel drive long before she'd actually wound her way through the trees to the clearing. She straightened just as Liam followed the dog out the door.

"Thanks for coming," he said when he reached her.

There was something different in his voice. Not something added but rather something missing—that undertone she often noticed, that always made her wonder what he was thinking that he wasn't saying. Even his demeanor was different. Gone was the casual, almost lazy-seeming stroll and posture.

"How bad is it?" she asked instinctively.

"It's big" was all he said as they walked toward the green building. Cutter ran ahead to paw the automatic door pad, and the heavy door swung open. "Upstairs."

The lights were already on in the big upstairs meeting room and office, so apparently that was where he'd been when Cutter had announced her arrival. He led the way to the large cubicle in the back corner, which had several computer stations with large monitors she'd noticed before.

"Your bailiwick?" she asked, looking at the array.

"Everybody's got access but, yeah, my turf."

"Why so many?"

"Different purposes. General inquiries, probability analysis, graphics, that kind of thing. Oh, and Bathys over there."

He gestured with a thumb at an apparently separate machine in the corner.

"Bathys?" she asked.

"Like in *bathyscaphe* or *bathysphere*."

She knew what the words meant, but what vessels designed for extreme ocean depths had to do with computers she didn't—

Depths. They went deep. Deeper than anything else could. Down to where creatures never seen before lived and light was just a memory.

"Let me guess," she said, looking at the computer as if it had a malevolence all its own. "The infamous dark web?"

"You are quick," Liam said with a smile that made her forget for a moment why they were here. But then the reality flooded back.

"You have occasion to…use that?"

"Sometimes. It's where some people hide. And *dark* can be a misnomer, in some cases. Sometimes *deep* is more fitting. As in having to hide deep."

"But isn't it where bad guys hide out on the internet, to put it generically?"

"Yes. But, then, so do some good guys. Dissidents fighting totalitarian regimes. Underground railroads, trying to save exploited or endangered innocent people. People who don't dare show up on the surface web."

From the way he was talking, it clearly didn't have anything to do with why she was here, but it was scarily fascinating.

"But don't the people looking for them know that and use it, too?" she asked.

"Yes." He shrugged. "The routing protocol—they call it onion routing—where your search is sent to random other computers before it gets to the site you want, making it nearly impossible to backtrack, was originally developed for the US Navy. Gone way beyond that now."

"Anonymous?" she asked, thinking of the hacking group with the famous mask symbol.

"Probably," he said. "Gotta admire their skills, even though I left that game behind years ago."

"Thank goodness."

He gave her a sideways glance. Seemed to hesitate slightly before saying, "Quinn hired me in part for those skills."

"You mean you still hack but for a good cause?"

He nodded. "All white hat now."

Belatedly it hit her. "You found something?" A memory flashed through her mind, of him asking Dylan about a computer and telling him to leave it on so he could send him something. "You hacked his father's computer."

He nodded. And waited. For her to react, she realized. She thought about asking if he didn't need a warrant for that, but two things stopped her. A little boy was getting hurt, and a student she very much liked was getting sucked down into a dark place.

And she trusted Liam. *All white hat now.*

In the end all she asked was, "Was it worth it?"

"I think so. It explains everything."

After a moment she nodded. "I guess it's good that his father's a technophobe, then."

She thought he smiled, briefly, as he turned back to the main bank of computers. He hit a couple of keys, and the image of a document popped up on the largest monitor, above the others. It was page with a column of letters and numbers next to two columns of hyphenated numbers.

"I have no idea what I'm looking at," she admitted.

"It's a DNA comparison."

She blinked, drew back slightly. Shifted her gaze to his face.

"Bottom line?" he suggested.

"Please."

His mouth tightened for an instant. Then he said bluntly, "It's 97.8 percent certain that Kevin Oakley is not Barton Oakley's son."

Chapter 23

She was more devastated than he'd expected. He doubted she could be much more upset had she found such evidence on herself.

"Those poor boys," she said as he handed her a mug of the coffee he'd had going since he'd gotten here.

"Makes sense of some things. Like why Cutter reacted the way he did the first time he saw the boys together at the park."

"You think...he knew? That they weren't...full brothers?"

"Sounds crazy, I know, but that dog knows things. And this would explain the way Oakley talked at the gym that day. It wasn't 'He's *my* son'; it was '*He's* my son'."

"As Kevin isn't."

They'd moved down into the living room area. She'd been pacing at first, and when he noticed she was rubbing at her arms as if they were cold, he turned on the gas fireplace, even though it wasn't really cold in the room. He doubted the extra warmth would ease the kind of chill she was feeling, but it couldn't hurt. And finally she'd taken a seat on the sofa, still shaking her head as if in shock.

"It's stronger than you like," he warned her before she took her first sip of the coffee he'd given her.

"I'll take it," she said with a grimace. "Not like I'll be sleeping tonight anyway, not after this."

Cutter nudged him with a head butt behind his knees. He knew immediately what the dog wanted; he'd seen him pull this move before. But then he looked at Ria's face, saw the tangled combination of emotions there and decided there might be a different reason for the Foxworth inveterate matchmaker to be urging him her way. She might just need the moral support to deal with the powder keg they'd just pried the lid off of.

Then Cutter went to her and sat at her feet, his chin resting on her knee. She smiled at the dog as she stroked the fur between his ears. "You," she crooned, "would make a wonderful therapy or hospital-visiting dog, you know?"

"Hayley's working on that," he said. "He's got his certification, breezed through it. Now she's working on places for him to go visit."

"He'll be great at it." She leaned over the dog and planted a kiss on his nose. "You have such a way of making me feel better."

Liam hesitated before saying, "You're taking this a bit personally, aren't you?"

She gave him a surprised look. "Of course I am. I started this."

"Well, you and Emily."

"But I could have talked her out of it."

"I don't doubt that, but that doesn't make you responsible. Besides, this makes sense of it, and now we know Kevin could really be in danger."

He'd wondered if she'd made the final leap, but saw

in her eyes that she indeed had. "From his…" Her voice trailed away.

"Non-father."

"Yes." She shook her head slowly, rubbed at her forehead as if there were a pounding ache behind it. "Do you really believe he would take this out on Kevin?"

"The guy I met? Absolutely."

"I know, but he's not usually like that."

"But Dylan says his dad's been like that since his mother died."

"I've only met with him one other time since she was killed. He was pretty quiet then but not angry. Nothing unexpected, given the circumstances."

Again she rubbed at her forehead. And again he felt the urge to sit beside her, put his arm around her. In comfort, not as a sexual overture. And that unsettled him. Not that he hadn't comforted people in stress before; it was part of this job. But he'd never had that urge tangled up with all sorts of other urges before.

It's part of the job.

But she's not the client.

But she's part of the case.

He felt an itchy sense that made him shift his gaze. Cutter was staring at him. The dog looked utterly disgusted. If an animal could roll his eyes, Cutter was doing it. Then the dog made a low sound that sounded for all the world like "Well?"

He felt a rising inclination to resist the animal. But there was enough on the other side that he gave in. It was, after all, his job to keep all aspects of the case going.

You win this round, hound. But only this round.

Satisfied, the dog retreated to his bed and curled up contentedly.

The moment Liam sat down beside her, the moment he felt her warmth and caught that light, lovely scent he already associated with her, he wasn't so sure. He schooled himself to businesslike comforting.

"Don't worry."

"How can I not worry?" It seemed she wasn't suffering from his own kind of distraction. Or her worry overpowered it. His ego preferred the latter, he admitted silently. Which only further confused the matter. He didn't want her feeling like this, did he? Because if it was mutual…

"I only meant we'll figure it out."

"If there's even a chance Kevin is being abused, we have report it. Immediately."

"Already did," he said.

She blinked, drew back. "What?"

"I called Brett Dunbar as soon as I saw that DNA report. He's a friend of ours, a sheriff's detective. First thing in the morning he'll talk to one of their juvenile detectives, who will take it from there."

The look of relief that flooded her face made his doubts about the skimpy suspicions that were all he'd had to tell Brett vanish. It was the right thing to do if only for that.

"Maybe we should go get Kevin and Dylan right now," she said.

"We have no standing in this," he pointed out. "Besides, Oakley doesn't know we know. Kevin won't be in any more danger than he was."

She frowned. "I suppose us confronting him wouldn't help. He already thinks I'm interfering."

He nodded. "It might just set him off. Better that it be someone with the weight of a badge behind them."

She let out a breath. "I hadn't thought of it like that. You're right."

One of the things he liked about her—one of the many things—was her levelheadedness when something made sense. Along with everything else she was.

"The legal wheels are turning now," he said quickly, before his mind could veer down that path again. "Let them. Dunbar's a good guy. He'll see to this."

She let out a long breath. "Thank you, Liam."

The way she said his name sent a shiver through him. He told himself he should get up, get away. She was better now, now that she knew the boys she cared about would be okay and the matter put to rest one way or the other. She didn't need comforting anymore.

And what he needed probably wasn't even on her radar.

Her expression changed. "What were you thinking, just now?"

He dodged her gaze. "Things I shouldn't be thinking."

She was silent for a moment. He stole a glance at her. Her lips were parted. His body knotted as she bit at the full, lower one. "Funny. I was thinking things, too. Are you saying I shouldn't be?"

He could barely get the word out. "Yes."

"Why?"

He looked away again. "A lot of reasons. One, you're a client."

"Actually the client is Dylan, isn't it? Or if not him, then Emily."

"We're still involved on the same case."

"Foxworth has a rule about that?"

He laughed, even though it blew away his argument. "If they did, Hayley and Quinn wouldn't be together."

"They met on a case?"

"Actually, Quinn kidnapped her. And Cutter."

Her eyes widened. "What?"

He relaxed a little as he told her the story. Surely a tale of black helicopters and a midnight mission would divert them both, her from questions he didn't want to answer and him from feelings he didn't want to feel.

He underestimated her, not for the first time.

"I see," she said, shaking her head in wonder at the

fantastical account but quickly went back to where they'd begun. "So it would be hard for Quinn to enforce a no-fraternization rule when that's how he met the love of his life."

"Hayley is that," he said.

"So you believe in soul mates?"

"I believe Hayley's his." That was nothing less than the truth. He did believe it; he had to. He had evidence of it every day.

What he didn't believe was that everyone had one. After all, hadn't Amanda thought he was hers?

"I'm sorry," she said unexpectedly.

He blinked, snapped back to the present, thankfully before his mind could wander down that old, worn, never-changing path.

"What?"

"I'm sorry for whatever you thought just now. It obviously wasn't a happy memory."

"No. No, it wasn't."

"Is it the real reason?"

He didn't pretend not to understand. Somehow he couldn't, not with those vivid blue eyes staring at him.

"Yes."

"Is it who you lost?"

He blinked. "What?"

"The person you lost, who gave you that understanding of grief—is that what you were thinking about?"

And you thought Cutter was perceptive. Ria Connelly was on a whole 'nuther level.

"I'm so sorry, Liam. That you have that knowledge."

Her words, the soft gentleness of her voice made him hungry for more from her, even as it soothed the old pain in a way nothing ever had. And in that moment he wanted to kiss her more than he could remember wanting anything in his life. And no amount of telling himself that he was footloose, unencumbered and intended to stay that way for everyone's sake, stopped it.

He knew the moment he gave in that he would regret it. But he could no more stop himself than he could match Rafe's skill as a sniper.

And then he was kissing her, and it wasn't like he'd remembered from that night on the street. It wasn't as hot, as sweet, as consuming.

It was more.

More, because she was answering in the same way, as if she couldn't get enough. As if she were as hungry for the unexpected fire as he was. Just feeling that response, sensing it, sent him over the edge and he was tasting her, sweeping his tongue past her lips, reaching for the sweetness that was unlike anything he'd ever known.

She made a tiny, awed sound. It made his entire body clench with a fierceness that took his breath away entirely. He pressed her back on the couch as he deepened the kiss. She went willingly, and he lost all semblance of thought as she clutched at his shoulders as if to pull him even closer. That sign that she wanted this too, that she might just be as hungry for this as he was, shattered him. He was nothing but fierce, driving need now, as if all the years of denying he was capable of this had burst forth to show him the lie.

He felt every curve of her, felt the press of her breasts against his chest, the length of her legs tangled with his. He'd been painfully aroused before but not like this, never like this. He couldn't stop himself from moving, pressing harder against her and feeling his pulse hammer in his ears when she arched upward to him, increasing the pressure on his aching body.

He wanted her more than he'd ever wanted anything in his life.

The images slammed into his mind, the only things powerful enough to break this spell. Yes, he wanted her more than anything he'd ever wanted. Except to erase those pictures in his head. To erase the guilt. To erase the accusing glares of grieving families. To erase the memory of the hurt, disillusioned look in his mother's eyes.

He broke the kiss.

He was aware, vaguely, of harsh breathing. His own? Hers? He wasn't sure. She was staring up at him, looking a little stunned. That he'd kissed her? That he'd let it go so far? That he'd stopped?

"Liam..." She whispered it, her voice tinged with a wonder that stabbed at him.

He scrambled off of her, stood up abruptly. He couldn't take this anymore. He didn't have the strength to resist Ria on his own. He was going to need her help. And there was only one way he could see to get it.

"You should be more careful who you kiss," he said, making his voice as cold as he could, a difficult task when his mind and body were so full of her warmth, when the need hadn't even begun to ebb.

He'd startled her with that. It was in her face when she said, "If you mean you, I seem to remember it was you who kissed me."

"But you didn't stop me."

"And I should have?"

"Yes."

"Again, why?"

He drew in a breath, held it for a moment and then said the words.

"Because you're the kind of woman who would mind kissing a killer."

Chapter 24

Of all the things she might have expected, that hadn't even made the list. And yet he was serious, she couldn't doubt that, not when his eyes, normally that warm amber color, had darkened so.

Odd, she thought. She hadn't even felt a chill, either at his words or at the fact that she was here, alone, in this isolated place with a man who had just told her he was a killer.

Killer.

Not murderer.

Her brow furrowed, and she realized she was more concerned with what he meant than what he'd actually said. Because somehow she knew that no matter what he said, the truth of it was much more complex.

"I don't believe that. At least, not in the way you're implying."

He ran a hand over his sandy hair, tousling it even further. Only then did she remember she'd done that herself, in the moments before he'd broken the kiss and pulled away, leaving her feeling strangely cold.

"You're smart," he said, his tone sharp. "Don't be stupid."

"Thank you, and I'm not," she said, earning her a sideways glance that nearly stopped her heart. He looked… desperate. She couldn't think of any other word that described his expression.

"That person you lost," she began slowly, "are you saying you killed them?"

"Might as well have." His voice was tight, the words spoken with his jaw clenched.

Ah. There it is.

"Who was she?"

"What makes you think it was a she?"

"You have close male friends. It's me you're pulling away from, hence…"

"Clever."

"Who was she?"

He whirled on her then. And there was a world of bitter sarcasm in his voice when he asked, "Which one?"

For the first time Ria felt a qualm. Not that she believed he was a killer, not for an instant, but something had obviously made him feel that way. Based on his words, more than once. She hesitated long enough that his expression became grim.

"You think I'd feel this way if it was only one?"

Suddenly she didn't want to hear this. Didn't want to know what could make cheerful, happy-go-lucky Liam Burnett look and sound like this. But she also knew that, as much as she didn't want to hear it, he needed to say it. Because it was eating him alive.

"Tell me."

"No."

"You've gone this far," she pointed out.

"I'm not talking about this."

She ignored the words and listened to the pain. "Who was the first one?"

"You're too damn stubborn for your own good."

"If you mean I refuse to go away and leave someone hurting, then yes. Who was she?"

He turned away, staring at the fireplace, into the flames. She wondered if he felt as if they were licking at him. Finally, without turning back, he said, "My best friend's kid sister."

Ouch. More than one layer there.

She waited. He didn't turn. Shifted restlessly on his feet. But after a moment he kept going. "Jessica…had a crush on me in high school. Matt—my friend—told me, because he thought it was funny, the way she followed me around. I liked her, but she was just a kid."

She tried to imagine him at that age. He looked so young now that it was hard to picture him even younger. But she could certainly see why a girl would have a crush on him. Empathize, even. Wasn't she sliding down the same slope?

"What happened?"

She heard him take in a deep breath. "One spring, Matt and I went out to the Guadalupe River. It had been raining hard for a couple of days, and it was running high and fast. We were playing a stupid game of chicken, where you tied a rope onto a tree, hung on and jumped in."

Ria's stomach turned over. "She followed you?"

He nodded. Still without turning, as if he couldn't look at her and tell her. "We told her to go home. She wouldn't. By my last go it was getting rougher, and I had a little trouble pulling myself out. She tried to help."

She knew where this was going now. "She drowned?"

He turned then, sharply. "Yes. Trying to help me, she lost her footing and went in. They didn't find her for two days."

She opened her mouth to ask why the girl's decision was his fault, then stopped. She didn't want to derail this, not now that he was talking. She worked to put all the calm she could manage into her voice.

"Next?"

He glanced at her then, and she saw surprise in his expression. She looked at him steadily. He turned back to the fire.

"Heather. College girlfriend. Cancer. I wasn't there when she died."

Well, that was concise, she thought, trying not to think of everything that kind of death entailed.

"Is there more?"

She thought she heard a low, bitter chuckle. "Oh, the prize of them all. Girl I planned to marry. I was crazy about Amanda. She wanted me to quit the hacking thing. Told her I would, but I had to finish something first."

He lifted his hands to brace them on the mantel above the hearth. Inner pain seemed visible to her in every line of his body. He who was so casually strong, so quick and graceful, who usually moved with such ease, was wire-tight with tension.

"I was making some side money, hacking into school records and tweaking grade reports. I wanted to finish because when I did I'd have enough to get us started. Bad call."

"That's when you got caught?"

He nodded. He fell silent then, just looking at her. "Aren't you going to ask?" he finally said.

"I figured you were rolling now; you'd finish it on your own."

Something different flashed in his eyes then, something that she couldn't put a name to. And when he did go on, his words were blunt, his voice harsh.

"When she found out I'd been arrested, she drove to the jail to see me. Her sister said she was mad and crying at the same time." He took a deep breath and finished it.

"She was going fast, lost control on a turn and hit a lamp post. Died instantly."

She stared at him. She had no words for this. All she had was an aching heart and the tears that had welled up in her eyes.

"No answer for that one, is there?" His voice was still harsh, and she realized then what she'd seen in his eyes before. Hatred. Directed inward. He hated himself for this. "You have no idea. You've had this perfect life, always knowing what you wanted, your family's still intact, you said yourself you've never lost anyone."

She fought not to feel painfully stung, but she knew he was right—she had been lucky. Hadn't she told him that, as well? But what she'd told him didn't matter. Right at this moment her feelings didn't matter.

"I'm so sorry," she managed to get out.

"That night taught me that *sorry* doesn't mean much, after it's too late."

She knew he didn't mean that to be a jab. Not at her, anyway. He was too busy castigating himself. She wanted to go to him, hug him, but she knew he wouldn't accept it, not now, not when he was so deep into feeling the guilt. She tried to keep her voice even.

"I won't say you shouldn't blame yourself. Because if you hadn't, at least a little, you probably wouldn't be where you are now."

"That's thanks to Quinn."

She caught a movement on the edge of her vision. Cutter, watching, listening. She guessed he had been, but, bless the canny dog, he hadn't intruded. As if he somehow knew the slightest interruption would stop the flow of something that simply had to come out.

"So Foxworth's guy found you'd been into their system?" she asked, both wanting to know and guessing he could use a breather. And she thought, when he turned to face her and spoke in a more even tone, that she'd been right.

"The cops confiscated my computer. Eventually, they found where I'd gotten into the Foxworth system, but since I didn't do anything but look, it was way down on their list. So all they did was notify Quinn." His mouth quirked upward, but the effort faded quickly. "Never expected him to show up."

"I'll bet. What did he say?"

"Just that his guy—Ty—was one of the very best, and he wanted to know how I'd gotten in. I figured I couldn't be in any more trouble than I was, so I told him. He went and talked to my family. All of them. I didn't know that until later. But he came back and asked me if I wanted to straighten my life out."

"I gather your answer was yes."

He grimaced. "I was twenty, sitting in a jail cell, my fiancée dead because of me, kicked out of college, with everything my parents had ever warned about proven true. Yeah, I said yes."

"What did he do?" she asked, genuinely curious.

"He paid my fine, got them to release me to him on probation—Foxworth has an unmatched reputation in a lot of places—and gave me a plane ticket here. Told me if I showed up as promised, I'd have a job doing good things. If I didn't, he'd hunt me down and make sure I ended up worse than where I started. I believed him."

"I would have, too," she said. Quinn Foxworth was not a man who made idle threats. "I'm glad he gave you the chance to redeem yourself."

"There's no redemption. Don't try to defend me."

"I'm not. I'm just looking at it with the benefit of a step back and years later."

He laughed, the harshest sound yet. "Do you think

Amanda's family or Jessica's family or even Heather's have taken a step back just because some time has passed?"

"No. But—"

"There are no buts, Ria. You didn't know them, know me, or you'd realize that."

She stood up. She searched for the right words, sensing that they could be the most important ones she ever said.

"No, I didn't know them. Any of them, or their families. I understand that means you think I have no right to an opinion."

"I didn't say—"

She cut him off. "So I'm not going to give you opinions. Just facts. Truth. That's what Foxworth does, isn't it?"

He was staring at her now, his brow furrowed. She steadied herself and began, determined to get it all out quickly.

"One, yes, playing in a flooding river was stupid, but your friend was just as responsible. More, in fact—she was his sister, and he should have been watching her. Two, you did not give that girl cancer, and it's known that sometimes people wait until they're alone to go. Three, while you were partially responsible for your fiancée's emotional state, you were not responsible for her choice to drive in that state. So, yes, you should have some guilt. Some. But just as you're responsible for some of it, you're not responsible for all of it. And you've done the only thing it is humanly possible to do to make amends. You've changed your life, and you spend it now helping people who have nowhere else to turn. Maybe you can't make it up to those people whose lives were changed for the worse, but you're changing other lives for the better. That's the best that can be done, and not many people do it. I won't say, don't feel guilty. I will say, keep using that guilt as fuel to do what you do—help. It's the only thing that can help you live with what you can't change."

For a long moment after her outpouring, he just stared at her. Then, slowly, he shook his head. Judging by his expression, it was in wonder as much as negation.

"Why does it matter to you so much?" The wonder echoed in his voice, which was barely above a whisper.

"Because..." She hesitated and then plunged ahead. "Because I care about you."

He went pale. And when he spoke, his voice was the coldest thing she'd ever heard.

"Don't. Don't ever. Didn't you hear me? Every female who's ever risked really caring about me like that is dead. I don't want you to join them."

He turned his back on her, strode to the door leading to the clearing and walked out.

Chapter 25

He felt scoured out, utterly hollow inside. He took long, deep breaths of air tinged with the chill of fall coming. Normally it invigorated him, but there was nothing normal about this.

He felt a shiver go through him. Held out a hand in front of him, saw in the moonlight that his fingers were trembling. Wasn't surprised. Not after what he'd just done.

Something he had never done before.

He'd never told anyone all of it. His parents knew a lot of it, by necessity, but not because he'd told them. Nor had he ever told his siblings. Quinn knew most of the facts, but only because his research was thorough and Liam hadn't denied anything.

But he'd never, not since Amanda died, put it into words all at once. Or admitted how he felt about it all. And now that he had, he felt...

He wasn't sure how he felt.

Cutter nudged at his hand. He should have been startled—

and worried—since he hadn't heard or been aware of the dog's approach. But he wasn't. He wasn't sure he could feel anything at the moment.

Another nudge. He knew the dog had an almost miraculous way of comforting people in distress; he'd seen it in action enough times. But he doubted it would work for him. *If* it was distress he was feeling. He wasn't even sure of that. But it was second nature for him to pet a dog who asked for it, so he did.

After a moment he looked down at Cutter, his brow furrowed. His hand was resting on the statue-still dog's head. Those amber-flecked dark eyes were fixed on him. Then the animal tilted his head and flicked his tongue over Liam's fingers.

He felt it. Not just the dog version of a kiss but more. Felt something, anyway. Not warmth, exactly, but an odd sort of comfort, an easing, a lessening of the pain. Enough to let his mind start to work again, albeit slowly, foggily.

"So that's what you do," he murmured.

He realized belatedly the animal had come out the same door he had. And that there was no opener on it.

Ria. She must have let him out.

Ria. He sucked in a breath. She would have been easier to dismiss if she'd absolved him of everything, but she hadn't. She'd admitted—was too honest not to—that he should feel guilty.

I won't say, don't feel guilty. I will say, keep using that guilt as fuel to do what you do—help. It's the only thing that can help you live with what you can't change.

He stared out at the trees, dark sentinels against a sky lit by a nearly full moon. Over there was the barely discernable trail the deer used to slip in and out of the clearing where they frequently grazed. No doubt the local raccoons were out in force tonight, foraging. Out there in those woods, just beyond the low, wet spot that sprouted alder in a thick grove, was the eagle's nest. He traversed those acres of trees regularly, keeping his tracking skills sharp, challenging himself on the terrain and vegetation that was so different than his native Texas.

Images slammed through his mind again. Jessica's sodden, river-battered body. Heather, wasted away to nearly nothing. And Amanda, mangled by steel and glass and concrete.

What would happen to Ria? Sure, in his saner moments he told himself it was just circumstances, mere chance that had taken those three who had cared about him. Logic told him his mother and sisters were fine, weren't they? But they were blood. Nothing had ever budged that sense of doom those deaths had instilled in him.

Then Ria was there, beside him, and he hadn't heard her coming either. She didn't speak, just stopped beside him. Looked out into the night as he was doing. After a moment, she took his other hand. Still without speaking she simply held it, not even looking at him but still out at the trees. His mind ordered his hand to pull away, but he must have been foggy because it didn't happen. And so he stood there, a dog with an eerie way of comforting on one side and a woman who apparently had the same knack on the other. He couldn't deny what he was feeling. As if the burden was still there, but he wasn't carrying it alone anymore.

He wished he could freeze this moment. That he could freeze it and walk away, leaving it forever intact, never changing, never marred by some tragedy later on.

Time and life didn't work that way. At least his didn't. Maybe Ria was right and Matt should have been watching his sister better, but he was the one who'd gotten in trouble and needed help. Maybe he hadn't given Heather cancer, but he'd been off at some movie, desperate for a break, when she'd died. And Amanda…

He might look young, might hide behind a carefree facade, but his heart and mind were old before their time and he had left fantasies far behind the day they'd told him Amanda was dead, killed rushing to his side as he sat stewing in a pot of trouble of his own making.

Ria's fingers tightened around his, as if somehow she'd realized he was still battering himself. As if she had that same kind of instinctive understanding that Cutter had, sensing pain. And the same urge to ease it.

Unable to stop himself, he squeezed her hand in response. He owed her that much, he thought.

I care about you...

He hadn't wanted that. He'd been trying to avoid it. But she'd said it, and if there was one thing he'd learned about Ria Connelly in the last couple of weeks—God, was it only two?—it was that she didn't lie. She meant it. She cared about him.

A shudder born of long-carried guilt went through him. Another woman who cared about him. What would happen to this one?

He pulled his hand free. "Don't," he said again, hearing the near-hoarseness of his own voice.

"Don't what? Try and comfort someone in pain? Sorry, it's hard-wired."

"You know what I meant."

"Don't care about you? Too late. That ship already sailed."

Something about her light, almost cavalier tone made him look at her. "Ria—"

"There's only one thing you can say to call that ship back."

"What?" he asked, determined to do whatever it took to get out of this.

She turned, looked at him straight on. "You have to kiss me again first."

Heat shot through him, driving away any touch of chill from the night air. On its heels came a spurt of anger. "Don't play with this, Ria."

"Oh, I'm not playing, not in the least. But that has to come first."

"First?"

"Then I'll tell you how to make me go away."

His eyebrows lowered. He didn't like the sound of that. Which was crazy, because it was exactly what he wanted. Wasn't it?

No, what he wanted was to do what she'd asked for. Kiss her. And suddenly he wanted that more than his next breath. He tried to step back, away from her, but Cutter was in his way and the stubborn dog refused to move. In fact, he almost seemed to be leaning against his legs, pushing him closer to her.

She was just looking up at him, silently, waiting. Those eyes focused on him, gleaming in the moonlight.

That ship already sailed.

If she cared, then it was already too late, wasn't it? He could kiss her, and it wouldn't matter, wouldn't make any difference. Except to him. If he kissed her and it seared him like it had before, he was going to be the one finding it hard to walk away. But maybe he deserved that. Maybe it would serve him right to…to…

He was having trouble thinking again. She just kept looking at him, like…like that. And then it was too much. He just had to taste her once more. He had to know if that incredible sensation would rocket through him again, making this woman and the feel of her lips the only thing that mattered in a crazy world.

With the sense of a man on a ship—that ship of hers?—sailing toward the edge of the world, he lowered his mouth to hers.

* * *

She was no child, no starry-eyed girl just discovering what could happen between a man and a woman when it was right, yet that's what she felt like. As if she'd discovered some whole new landscape of untold beauty, something she had never known existed. And at this moment, that landscape was made up solely of the blasting heat of his mouth on hers, and the solid, strong feel of his shoulders beneath her hands.

She hadn't even been aware of grasping him like that, but she vaguely realized that she'd likely be in a puddle on the ground if she hadn't. Because he was making not just her knees weak but turning every part of her to some molten, fluid thing she didn't recognize.

She felt the touch of his tongue over her lips. She never hesitated to part them; she wanted more. Much more. When his tongue brushed hers, she heard a low moan, a split second later realizing with a little shock it had been her. It seemed to inspire him for he drove deeper, probing, tasting as if he were starving. For her.

The thought sent fire licking along every nerve as her body responded. She'd wanted proof, some sign that this was different, was somehow…more. Her heart wanted to believe she'd gotten it, but that part of her mind that was still functioning—barely—would only acknowledge that this was a physical sensation she'd never known before.

And perhaps it was only physical, for him at least. It was women, wasn't it, who kept insisting on building it into more? As she had with Chad? But Chad had never made her feel like this. Ever, especially with just a kiss.

When at last he pulled back, she nearly staggered. She felt almost dizzy, as if the blaze they'd kindled had eaten up all the air in the room. But she was pressed so tight against him—when had that happened?—his arms so wrapped around her she was in no danger of falling. She may have been rocked to the soles of her feet, but Liam was still standing. Had it not been like that for him? Was that even possible, for such a fierce, swift fire to be one-way?

She stole a glance at his face. The shock in his expression, the surprise in his eyes and the slight, wondering shake of his head told her he was as stunned as she was, and she could breathe again.

"You want that answer now?" Her voice came as barely a whisper, but they were so close it didn't matter.

He stared at her, as if it were an effort to process her words. He sucked in an audible breath, as if he'd found the oxygen in short supply, as well, before saying rather confusedly, "What?"

"What will make me go away."

His nostrils flared and she felt his fingers clench on her back. As if he were expecting her to bolt at any second.

And wanted to stop her. Keep her.

"It's easy, Liam," she said, her voice just slightly stronger now. "All you have to do is look me in the eyes, straight on, and tell me you don't feel anything in return. That this is nothing more than a kiss, that you can walk away with no regret and never question what you might have missed."

"You should let me do just that. For your own good."

"I don't believe you're jinxed or whatever it is you think. Some bad choices, and matching luck, yes. But no more than that."

"Ria—"

"Look me in the eye and say it, Liam. And I'll go."

"Aren't you afraid I'll lie?"

She looked at him steadily. "No," she said simply.

"You have reason to be," he pointed out, his breathing sounding steadier now. "Given whatshisname."

She nearly smiled at the way he said it. But she realized he'd just given her the best argument she could have.

"And yet I'm not. Perhaps you might do the same? Not let the past determine the present?"

"You're the one taking the risk."

Yes, but not the kind you mean. I don't believe I'm risking my life. But definitely my heart.

She felt a qualm. Because she knew what this was. More important, she knew what it wasn't. Or so she told herself. And yet she wanted this as she had wanted few things in her life.

She wanted him. In a way she'd never wanted anyone before. And that alone was not something she wanted to walk away from. She might regret this. She'd known him such a short time. And yet she knew what was important about him, to her at least.

He would probably run himself, if he knew the way she was thinking. Not because she was picturing some kind of glossy, unrealistic future with him, but because of the reasons she wanted him—his kindness, his strength, the work he so believed in and, oddly, the simple fact that, despite trying to hold himself apart, he cared enough about others to still blame himself years later for the deaths of three who had dared care about him.

She wasn't sure she could explain it anyway.

So she kept her tone light as she said, "More than one risk, unless you have a condom handy."

It was as clear as she could make her decision without blushing. And now it was up to him.

Liam felt as if Blue, his dad's old plow horse, had kicked him in the stomach. Did the woman have no sense?

He knew the answer to that. Ria was whip smart. And yet still kind, and caring. Too caring.

His mind recoiled from the very word. At the same time he had this roiling sensation deep in his gut that it wasn't the right word. It wasn't strong enough for what he was feeling.

He told himself he was crazy. He was hot for her, just as Dylan had teased him; he could admit that. Hell, he was way beyond hot for her. And if she was willing, then what was stopping him? It wasn't the lack of a condom, although he wasn't sure of the condition of the one he lugged around in his wallet since it had been there a while. Funny, he hadn't been interested for some time in the occasional no-strings hookups that had been his sex life since Amanda had died.

Then came Ria Connelly, who could send him into overdrive with a look from those bright blue eyes.

This was nuts. And yet there she stood, waiting. He knew her well enough to know that this was not her normal approach. That she wanted this—him—enough to make the choice first. That alone almost put him on his knees.

He swallowed tightly, managed to speak. It came out sounding harsh, almost hoarse. "You'd better be damned sure. I can't handle morning-after regrets." *Not from you. Anybody else, but not you.*

Somewhere in the back of his mind an alarm bell went off at his own thought, but then she answered him and it was blasted away.

"No regrets."

She said it simply, easily. And he had no doubt that she meant it, that there would be no recriminations, no blame. She would take responsibility for her decision, because that's who she was.

He couldn't fight it. Not any longer. With her standing there looking at him, her lips still looking freshly kissed, he didn't even want to.

And then he was kissing her again, fiercely, and the heat that blasted through him told him the fire they'd started had only been banked while he tried—halfheartedly—to talk sense into her. Now he didn't care about sense anymore. He didn't care about anything except this woman in his arms.

He picked her up easily, since she was already half hanging on him anyway. He treasured every sign that this was what she wanted, kissed her again as he walked back to the door. He never lifted his mouth as he turned sideways to edge through the door. He only looked up when Ria reached out to push the door closed behind them. The certainty he'd seen in her eyes was still there, relieving his fear she would change her mind once they were inside.

The ever-vigilant Cutter headed for his bed without a command. The phrase *my work here is done* went through Liam's head, but out just as quickly when Ria raised her head to press a kiss to his throat. For a moment he forgot how to breathe.

He managed to remember which way to go, and then he was kicking open the door to the bedroom with his heel. He couldn't remember ever having been so…frantic before. He pulled at her clothes, barely taking time to savor every revealed curve and hollow. He muttered something about wanting to go slow, but she merely whispered, "Next time," and it sent the flames even higher.

He tried to unhook the lacy bra that was the color of her eyes, but his fingers were suddenly thick and uncooperative. She reached back and did it herself, the movement thrusting her breasts toward him, and his breath jammed up in his throat. And then the lace fell away, revealing silken, ripe curves tipped with a luscious, berry pink, and he groaned aloud.

He cupped her breasts in his hands, gently, loving the weight of them and how the soft flesh molded to his hands as if made for them. That the nipples were already tight was a temptation too luscious to ignore, and he ran his thumbs over them reverently. The tiny sound she made then sent an arrow of heat through him, tightening his body to an exquisite ache.

She tugged at the button of his jeans, and it was more than he could take. He shed his clothes hastily, kicking everything aside before taking them both down to the bed in a rush. He barely managed the condom in his haste. He couldn't touch enough, kiss enough, he wanted to lick every lovely inch of her but he couldn't wait, he just couldn't.

"Then don't wait," she whispered, and only then did he realize he'd said it aloud.

Her response sent him to a fever pitch he couldn't fight down. He slipped a hand between them, fingers stroking, probing. The heat of her made him groan again, but when he found her wet and slick and ready, he nearly shattered right then. Never had the proof that a woman really wanted him been so powerful, and in the last part of his mind still functioning he knew it was because it was this woman.

When she reached for him, the feel of her fingers on his painfully erect flesh sent the words *at last* hammering through his head.

And then, as he began to slide into her, he couldn't think at all, couldn't do anything but feel, savor the hot, honeyed embrace of her body around him, the heat, the wetness, the tightness. He began to move because he had no choice, not when he was in her deep and hard, not when she'd welcomed him with an upward thrust of her hips and a cry of his name.

Stroke after stroke the blaze grew, expanded, until he was gasping in disbelief at something he'd never experienced. He slammed into her until he was afraid he might be hurting her and yet she clung to him, urging him on with those little sounds she made, eager, reaching…

And then he felt it begin for her, felt the fierce clenching of those inner muscles around him as she cried out his name one last time in the sweetest voice he'd ever heard. He felt her nails dig into his shoulders, and the tiny spark of urgent pain sent him over the edge and he let go, uttering her name and a heartfelt oath as the explosion of sensation overtook him.

And again it echoed in his head.

At last.

Chapter 26

"We should probably get up," Liam said, sounding reluctant.

She was feeling reluctant to move herself, so she asked lazily, "Why?"

"Don't you have to get to school?"

"Not until nine. It's barely six thirty."

He sat up. Ran a hand over his hair. Ria watched, quietly enjoying the way the muscles in his arm and shoulder moved. Remembering the way every part of him had moved last night.

Each time they had come together she learned something new about him and, unexpectedly, about herself. Once the decision was made they had both cast aside doubts and fears and it had been the night she'd hoped for, full of fierce sensation, tender moments and even some laughter as they fumbled their way to that new knowledge of each other's bodies.

And what a body his was, she thought with an inward

sigh. Just as she'd imagined. Leanly muscular, beautifully put together and strong. Oh, yes, very strong.

Somewhere in her mind a warning clanged, that if just that enthralled her, she was well down the road she hadn't meant to travel.

The road Liam had as much as warned her not to travel.

"Teague's due back today. I don't know when he's liable to show up here."

She wasn't sure what to say to that. True, they were in his workplace, but the other implications stung a little. "So…we're a secret?"

"I didn't mean—" He broke off, tried again. "It's just that…"

He stopped, getting no further this time.

"Or is it just that we're not a 'we'?"

"Ria," he began and stopped yet again.

Well, now I understand about the proverbial awkward morning after.

She shook off the thought. She was a big girl, and despite her lack of experience with one-night stands, she'd known that was probably what she was getting into. Reminding herself of her promise last night, she sat up, as well, belatedly grabbing the sheet and wrapping it around her body. He reached out and curled his fingers around her arm. Even that contact sent heat rocketing through her. As did the way his gaze slid over her.

"It doesn't matter," he said softly, putting a hand on the crisp white cloth over her breasts. "I remember every inch, every curve."

She stared at him. She felt utterly lost, not knowing how to take his words or the way he'd just sounded. And the way he was looking at her. When he finally spoke again, she realized that what she'd heard—that undertone in his voice—was fear.

Every female who's ever risked really caring about me is dead. I don't want you to join them.

It was still there when he spoke again. "I don't know what we are, Ria. Except not the same as before."

Those were not the words, nor was that the voice of a man who didn't care. It wasn't a romantic declaration, that admission he'd been changed by what had happened between them, but, all things considered, for now it would have to do.

She stood up and quickly pulled on her sweater. It was long enough to cover the essentials while she retreated to the bathroom. But when her head popped through the neckline, she found him watching her with a hunger he either couldn't or didn't even try to hide. Either way it soothed her unsettled emotions, and she was able to speak normally.

"You'll let me know what your detective friend or the juvenile officer does?"

A trace of a furrow creased his brow, but he made the shift to businesslike tones quickly. "Of course."

"Will they really dig into this?"

"Brett Dunbar said so, and he doesn't lie or say anything he doesn't mean."

She told herself she should trust his faith in the detective. He'd said Foxworth had worked with the man several times. But she hated to think of little Kevin or even Dylan—although it seemed his father limited his cruelty to the younger boy—stuck there any longer than necessary.

Liam seemed to sense her doubt. "If it helps any, Quinn says he'd hire Dunbar in a split second, if he ever wanted to leave law enforcement."

"That says a lot." She already had a solid respect for Quinn Foxworth.

Liam glanced at his phone screen. "He gets an early

start. He'll probably be rounding up help within the hour. They'll be there before the morning's out."

She had to be content with that, she supposed.

"I was also thinking," he said, "that maybe we should keep Dylan from going home until we know what Dunbar finds."

She hadn't thought of that but saw his point and nodded. "It might be best if he wasn't around while…whatever happens happens."

"Yes."

She looked at him for a moment. "Could you just keep him busy until we know?"

"I could ask him for another session. Maybe say I can't be there Thursday. Something like that."

"That would work." She hesitated and then added, "I could be there, just in case. If it turns out your friend has to take some action, it might be better if both of us were with Dylan."

"Agreed," he said. Without hesitation, she noticed. Whatever his feelings, he wasn't letting them interfere with looking out for Dylan. Which, in an odd way, comforted her.

I wonder," she asked, thinking she should have before, "why did Dylan's father have a DNA test done in the first place?"

His grim smile told her he had thought of this already. "Now that's the real question, isn't it?"

"No answer?"

He ran a hand over his hair—the hair she'd tousled with her own eager fingers not long ago—as if thinking. Was he still debating what to tell her?

"Only speculation," he said finally. "Or, as Teague calls it, a wag."

"A what?"

"Wild-ass guess."

She grinned at that. "I love English," she said, earning a fleeting smile back. "A wag based on?"

"The date of that report."

Her brow furrowed. "I didn't even notice. When was it?"

"Two weeks after Melissa Oakley fell to her death."

Ria stared at him. Felt a sudden chill. "You think… they're connected?"

"I don't know."

"But you suspect."

"Obviously she had an affair." Ria nodded, thinking she now understood why her suggestion of grief counseling had failed—he hadn't been grieving. No wonder he was angry when Dylan asked where Kevin was. He must hate the child for being daily evidence of his wife's unfaithfulness.

"If he found out," Liam continued, "let's just say I don't believe in that much coincidence."

"'A trout in the milk,'" she murmured.

He blinked. "What?"

"Thoreau," she explained. "He once said, 'Some circumstantial evidence is very strong, as when you find a trout in the milk.'"

"Sorry, teach, that one goes over my head."

"It comes from the days when dairy farmers used to water down the milk they sold."

He got there quickly. "With water from the nearest trout stream?"

"Exactly."

"That timing is a pretty big trout. That alone would never hold up in court, but…"

She frowned as something else occurred to her. "Wait… did he only have Kevin tested?"

"No, both of them." Liam mouth twisted. "Although with Dylan, the relationship's pretty clear."

"He does look like his father," she agreed. "But that he had both of them tested… That could be evidence either way, couldn't it? I mean, couldn't that mean it was innocent, just an ancestry-check kind of thing?"

"Exactly what Brett said. Maybe you should be a detective." His mouth twisted upward at one corner. "He probably would have gotten the Thoreau quote right off the bat. He reads a lot."

"You don't?" The automatic question was out before she could stop it. Reading was so intrinsic to her life she couldn't help it.

"I do. Just not usually Thoreau." He gave her a look then that disconcerted her even more than the fact that this discussion seemed out of place in the midst of her concern for the Oakley boys. "Thinking you should have found that out before last night?"

Her breath stopped and her brain seemed to seize up. Was he implying that a "no" would have been a deal breaker for her? That she wouldn't have slept with him if that had been the answer? Or did he mean something else? She'd misjudged Chad so badly she had little faith in her ability to correctly interpret the workings of the male mind. Hence her reaction earlier.

And yet…

Memories of last night, of the incredible sweetness they'd found together, flooded her. Memories of his strong, lean body moving over hers, his hands touching, caressing, and his mouth…

Heat flooded her at the memory of what that mouth had done to her. The images made her blush. And the thought of what she'd done to him, how eagerly, and the way he'd responded, only added to the heat.

"Well, now," he drawled, "didn't that question just send your clever mind racing."

It could have been a dig; she might have taken it that

way if she hadn't been looking at him when he said it. But she was, and she saw an echoing heat in his gaze, as if the same series of images had just played back in his head.

"I was just thinking," she said steadily enough, "that no matter what you want to do—or not do—now, last night was worth it just to learn that feeling like that is possible."

She heard him make a sound, something low and sharp as if his throat had locked up. Then he swore under his breath.

"Nothing like getting your guts ripped out by a compliment," he muttered.

Her heart skipped a beat and then raced to catch up. He might not want to admit it—yet—but he'd been as affected by their night together as she had. He stared at her. She thought he looked a little pale.

"And by the way," she added gently, "nothing's going to happen to me."

She saw the narrowing of his gaze. And a trace of that fear again. But it wasn't as strong as it had been, and she hoped that simply talking about it had eased it a little.

She left him there, staring after her.

As she drove, Ria contemplated the kind of man who would blame himself so deeply, three times over, for things he'd had little control over. So deeply that years later, he still carried it.

By the time she reached the turn for her condo, she was wondering if what Quinn had seen in the young hacker he'd taken on was an ingrained need to make things right. That—from what she'd seen—would make him a perfect fit for Foxworth.

She sat at the stop sign where the narrow road met the state route, watching the cross traffic. It was building as the hour for many to go to work neared. But she had plenty of time to get home and get ready to head to school. She needed to bring in the first exams for her first-period class and the notes she'd made for the upcoming track for the first years.

The last car to pass going east was a state patrol vehicle. It made her remember Dylan's house was not far from here, in that direction. Her pulse kicked, until she remembered the detective Liam had called was with the sheriff's office. The state trooper seemed in no particular hurry and he turned south, heading away from Dylan's house.

She told herself not to be silly; it was going to take a little time for Liam's friend to organize things, and it wasn't even eight o'clock yet.

She saw a break in the cross traffic coming. Got ready.

But when she turned, it wasn't toward home. At the last second, driven by a gut-level impulse, she turned the opposite direction. Toward Dylan's house.

She wouldn't stop, she told herself. She would just drive by, make sure everything was all right. Maybe give Dylan a ride, if he'd let her. They could talk, maybe she could find out more to tell Liam's detective, to hurry things along and get Kevin at least out of there.

And she wondered if she was as driven as Liam by the need to make things right.

Chapter 27

For a split second when he heard the tires on gravel, Liam thought she might have come back. The way his stomach knotted and his heart kicked up his pulse told him the painful truth about what he'd done last night. He'd gotten himself in way too deep. He was in trouble.

Big trouble.

At the same time his body was remembering last night, the most amazing experience of his life, and clamoring for more. Surely that impossible sweetness, that breathless soaring, was worth any price?

Except you won't be the one to pay it.

The grim words echoed in his head as Cutter abandoned their game of fetch and loped off toward the drive. His ears and tail were up in the way that signaled someone familiar. The minute he rounded the back of the building, Liam saw Teague's car slowing to park. He let out a breath of relief. Half an hour ago and he really would have walked in on them. Ten minutes ago and he would have caught Liam changing the sheets on the bed. When he'd been doing it, he'd figured if Teague arrived he'd just tell him he crashed here after a late night; it wouldn't be the first time for any of them. But every time he tried to phrase it in his mind, he heard instead Ria's quiet question.

So we're a secret?

An unmistakable trace of hurt had colored her words, and it had stabbed at him. He'd thought of saying he just hadn't wanted to face the teasing he would inevitably get, but that seemed a damned weak reason to have put that sound in her voice.

But the real reason, the gut-level fear, was even worse. Fear that she, like every other woman outside of family who'd ever cared about him, would end up paying far too high a price for that caring. And saying it out loud, saying that they were that "we" she'd spoken of, would somehow make it real. Too real. Crazy though the feeling might be, some part of him was furiously hoping if he didn't acknowledge it, she'd stay safe.

"Hey, Texas!" Teague called out as he got out of his car. The former marine was smiling widely as he slung his familiar, battered leather jacket over his shoulder.

But then he always seemed to be smiling since he and Laney had met last year about this time.

As he waved a greeting it hit Liam that Teague had been in a similar situation. It had been Laney who had had a friend in trouble, and Foxworth had stepped in. The immediate attraction had been obvious to everyone—except Teague and Laney.

His gaze snapped back to Cutter, who had been instrumental in that matchup, who had finally taken action of his own to make them get it together. Liam had even laughed about it himself, at the time. But all of a sudden it didn't seem so funny. Not from this side.

"Coffee's on," he said, jerking a thumb toward the building. "How'd it go up in Bellingham?"

"Good, in the end. Got word out what was going on, the locals got mad enough and noisy enough that they dropped the criminal charges. Guess there's hope for common sense yet."

Liam grimaced as he pulled open the door and they went inside, Cutter at their heels. "Well, arresting a ten-year-old boy for saving the life of a bird was pretty stupid."

"And since when has stupid stopped anything?" Teague asked.

"Point taken," Liam agreed. "Hell, I didn't even know there was a Migratory Bird Treaty Act, let alone that taking an injured bird home to nurse it could land you in prison."

"Well, it didn't, this time." Teague grinned as he filled a mug with Liam's strong brew, which he also preferred. "He's a cute, big-eyed, innocent-looking kid, and by the time the image of him and that goose got around the internet, there were some pretty angry people gathering at half the Fish and Wildlife Service offices in the state."

"Nice to see social media used for something good," Liam said.

"Yeah. I wanted to keep going, push to get rid of the fine, too, but the kid was pretty upset already and his parents wanted it over."

"Their call," Liam said. "We paying the fine?"

Teague nodded. "Saddest part is, that kid probably won't ever try to help again."

"Unintended consequences," Liam muttered as he poured himself a cup.

"Yeah. How about you? Quinn—he's on his way back, by the way, left before dawn cracked and has an ETA of about ten local. But he texted me you're onto something?"

They walked out and sat on the patio as Liam gave him the digest version of what Emily and Ria had said.

"The actual locket girl?" Teague asked.

"Yep. She's quite a kid." *And her teacher is quite a woman.*

"Anything to it?"

"Something," he said and explained about what he'd found last night. At least, what he'd found on Barton Oakley's computer. The rest of what he'd found last night, in Ria's arms, he kept to himself, even though it seemed so huge it was putting pressure on every part of him.

"I see what you mean about the suspicious timing, but that could get dicey," Teague said. "Pretty circumstantial."

Trout in the milk. Liam nearly smiled.

"You think the kid's being physically abused because Dad found out he's not his?" Teague asked. "That's ugly."

"It's enough of a possibility that I called Dunbar. He's going to round up a juvie detective and check it out."

Teague nodded. "Good. He'll sort it out. What about the older kid, the one they came about in the first place?"

"I'm heading over to his school in a bit. We're going to keep him there while Brett does his thing."

"We?"

Oops. He thought fast. "Cutter and me. The kid likes him."

So we're a secret?

Remorse jabbed at him again. Damn. Why wouldn't she get out of his head?

"What's up with you, Burnett? You're acting like a cat on a hot stove."

Liam studied him for a moment. Decided to risk it. Decided he had to, because he was going to explode if he didn't let some of this pressure off. And even if talking about it, admitting it, would make it real, too real to deny.

"Can I ask you something without you getting on my case?"

"Me?" Teague asked with exaggerated innocence.

"Yeah."

He saw his friend and colleague register his flat, non-joking tone. Teague's expression shifted, became serious.

"Ask."

"You and Laney," he began and then hesitated.

"Best thing that ever happened to me."

"But…it almost didn't, right?"

Teague didn't hesitate, and Liam knew he'd sensed the importance of this. "Almost. If she wasn't the gutsiest woman I've ever met, it might not have."

"Why?"

"I didn't believe it. I didn't trust it because of how we met. The case. Thought I'd taken advantage of her worry about her friend, that she'd only…wanted solace and I let it get out of hand. So I tried to end it. But she and he—" he nodded toward Cutter "—wouldn't let it happen."

Liam let out a long breath. Considered his friend's words.

"Bottom line," Teague said after another sip of coffee, "she faced me down, told me not to walk away without even giving it—us—a chance, just because of how we met."

Yes, gutsy, Liam agreed. But the problem with the correlation was that Teague didn't have his history. And no matter how reasonable, logical and valid Ria's answer to that had been, he couldn't shake the conviction that somehow, someway, the deaths of three had been his fault. That he was a jinx or had been cursed or any number of things he didn't really believe in, yet seemed the only explanation.

Or maybe it was that he couldn't believe in that much coincidence. He was the only common denominator in all three deaths.

"I gather you're not going to tell me why you asked? Or would asking that constitute 'getting on your case'?"

He looked up. Teague was watching him steadily over

the rim of his coffee mug. Liam shook his head, at a loss for words.

"All right," Teague said. And thankfully left it at that before saying, "You need me to do anything?"

Knock some sense into me, maybe. Not that I'm sure what that would be right now. "No," he said, "not now anyway."

Teague nodded. "I'll go finish up my report for Quinn, then." He rose and headed inside. At the door he stopped, looked back. "You want a woman's view, Laney's in the shop today." He grinned. "You need a trim anyway."

Liam watched him go, thinking it was just like Teague to make the offer and then make it a joke. But he knew it had been sincere. He also knew Laney would help if she could. They'd gotten to know each other a bit while she'd been working on him with her clippers.

He just wasn't sure anyone could help him with this particular problem.

He went back inside, Cutter following. The dog went over to the kitchen and sat expectantly in front of the fridge. He looked back at Liam with his head at a silly angle that made him laugh.

"You'd better hope your mom didn't forget to stock up before she left," he told the dog before he pulled open the door. In the crisper drawer he found what the dog was waiting for. He pulled out a handful of the peeled baby carrots and occupied himself for a few minutes tossing them to the animal, who caught them easily and crunched them happily.

He glanced at the clock on the wall. He knew Dylan had a math class first thing this morning, in the time period that Ria had first years for English. He planned to be there when that class was over. Which gave him about half an hour to get there.

In the truck, he pondered what exactly he would say to

Dylan, how they would explain. Ria would make sure it was tactful, gentle, instead of the blunt way he'd probably blurt it out. He didn't relish the thought that the boy might be seriously angry that he'd lied about who he was and why he was there, but the safety of Dylan and his brother was more important. He'd just have to—

The ring of his cell phone cut off his thoughts. It was the generic ring, so he half expected—hoped?—it might be Ria. He hadn't assigned her a ringtone. Told himself he couldn't decide on one, although he knew on some deeper level that it smacked of a permanency he couldn't allow himself to think about, as if not doing it could somehow protect her.

But a glance at the screen surprised him. Emily Parker.

He tapped the button on the Foxworth interface they all had in their vehicles.

"Burnett."

"Mr. Burnett, it's Emily. Emily Parker. You know, from—"

"Of course, Emily. What's up?"

"I wasn't sure what I should do, but it's just so unusual I thought you should know." The girl sounded worried, and Liam sat up a little straighter.

"What is it? Dylan?"

"No, he's fine. He got here early in fact, I saw him well before first period. It's Ms. Connelly."

Liam's heart sank. The kind of morning-after they'd had, and now Emily's worried enough about Ria to call him? Maybe she hadn't been as calm about the whole thing as she'd seemed when she'd left. Maybe he'd hurt her even more than he'd thought. Guilt slammed through him anew, harsher, sharper. He'd never meant to hurt her, at all, yet he had. Like always. He never, ever should have let last night happen, for so many reasons.

"Hang on." He was encountering traffic rushing for the

next ferry, so he pulled over to the side and stopped before asking, reluctantly. "What about her?"

"She's not here."

He frowned. He hadn't expected that. "What?"

"She just didn't show up for first period. We can't find her."

Chapter 28

Liam swallowed, but it didn't budge the sudden lump in his throat. "What do you mean, you can't find her?"

"She's never missed a day we didn't know about in advance, not in the two years I've been here."

"She must have called in," he said.

"I talked to some of the staff, including Dr. Halvorson. Nobody knew anything. She didn't call in sick or late, nothing. Mr. Burnett, she would never do that."

Unless some callous jerk hurt her so badly she couldn't bear to face anyone.

"Did they call her?"

"Yes. So did I. No answer. It went to voice mail. I tried texting her, too, and nothing."

Liam's mind was racing, turning over possibilities.

"I'm worried," Emily said. "Honestly, she would never just not show up, without a word."

"I believe you," Liam said, all the while thinking that Emily didn't have two key pieces of information: how

Ria had spent last night and the reason she might have to be upset.

Upset enough to desert her post, as it were? That didn't fit with what he knew of her. She was dedicated, and it would take more than a jerk like him being a jerk like him to make her do that.

He was torn. The plan was to see to Dylan, make sure that he was safely at school and that he stayed there until they could explain to him what was happening. Dylan was the job, and his first responsibility. But at the same time, that was all the more reason Ria wouldn't fail to show; she cared about the boy, she'd been part of this from the get-go and it had been her idea to be with him just in case things went haywire at his house.

"Do you know where Dylan is now?"

"I saw him go into the library right before I called you."

His mind raced. He needed to keep Dylan away from home. But it wasn't likely, if he didn't suspect anything, that the boy would go home in the middle of the day, was it? Unless Kevin somehow managed to call him. Which he might do, when Dunbar's friend showed up.

"Can you keep an eye on him until I can get there?"

"You're coming here? To Cove? What about Ms. Connelly?"

He hated this. It was most likely she was just upset about last night. Wasn't it? And his first priority was Dylan; that was his job right now. Ria would get that. But, by the same token, since she'd been in on the start of this, she'd feel it was her job, too, and she just wouldn't drop out without a word. He was certain of that. She cared too much.

Yeah, and about you, too. And you know what happens to women who care about you.

He told himself he was being crazy, that she was right—none of it had been completely his fault; Jessica and Heather and Amanda hadn't died solely because of him. But when he threw her into the equation, logic seemed to fly out the window. How could he risk it? Risk her?

But Dylan was his job, and he couldn't be in two places at once.

From the cab's backseat Cutter woofed sharply.

"Of course," he murmured.

"What?" Emily said over the speaker.

"I'll be there in five," he said, as he pulled back onto the road, calculating how fast he could get there the back way, avoiding the ferry traffic. "Keep track of Dylan for me. If he starts to leave, tell him to wait, that I'm looking for him."

"Okay, but—"

"Trust me," he said. "Or at least trust Foxworth."

"I do. Completely."

He made it in four minutes. He and Cutter left the parking lot at a run, heading for the library building. About a hundred feet away, Cutter suddenly shifted direction. Liam started to call him back, then saw the two people standing to one side of the building, where the dog was headed. Dylan and Emily. She'd done exactly as he'd asked.

"Hey," Dylan said calmly when he got there some seconds after Cutter. It was clear by the easy way he spoke, and how he was smiling at the dog as he scratched his ears, that there was nothing amiss on his radar. Liam relaxed a little. "Emily said you were looking for me?"

"Yeah. You okay?"

The boy frowned. "Yeah. Why?"

"Emily said you got here early."

He shrugged. "I was ready, so I took an earlier bus. Dad was in a mood. Seemed best to just get out of there."

Dad was in a mood. "What about your brother?"

Dylan's mouth twisted. "That's why he was in a mood, I guess. He said Kevin's got the flu or something, and he had to find somebody to watch him."

"He didn't ask you to do it?"

The boy shook his head. "He's big on me not missing school. Paying a lot for it, as he reminds me all the time."

Liam pondered for a moment telling the boy right now. He had the feeling Emily would be a good one to help get him through it. She obviously cared about her classmate. Maybe more than cared about him, from the way she was watching him. But it didn't feel right, not now. Not without Ria.

But, then, none of this felt quite right without her.

"You free for a while?" he asked the boy.

Dylan looked puzzled but nodded. "I've got about forty-five until biology."

"Can you do me a favor and watch Cutter for me?"

"Sure." The boy glanced at Emily and then looked back at Liam. "You going to check on Ms. Connelly?"

Liam was a little startled at how quickly the boy had put it together. It must have shown—that lousy poker face of his—because Dylan explained.

"Emily told me she didn't show up for classes this morning, and you're her friend, so I figured."

Oh, yeah, he was a really great friend, Liam thought sourly, but he only nodded.

"What if you're not back in time?"

"I can watch him while you're in biology," Emily said quickly. "It's my study period." She looked at Liam. "If that will work?"

It would give him extra time if necessary. Emily was, as Quinn had said, a very smart girl.

"He'll be fine. He likes both of you. Call me if she turns up or if either of you hear from her, okay?"

"Sure," Dylan said as Emily nodded.

"Thanks." He bent down to the dog as if saying good-bye but instead whispered, "Guard. Keep."

Cutter woofed an acknowledgment of the orders. Not

only would the dog watch Dylan like a hawk, he would do everything in his considerable power to keep the boy right here.

"Tell her we're worried about her," Emily said.

Liam nodded. *No more than I am*, he thought as he ran back to his truck. While he knew what street her condo was on, he didn't know the exact address, but it only took him a moment of searching on his phone to find it via her phone number. He drove a little faster than he should have, but his gut was starting to scream at him. Whether it was with self-blame for this morning's clumsiness with her or fear that there was something else wrong, he wasn't sure and didn't dwell on it since it didn't change anything.

On the way he tried to call her himself and got the same result: voice mail. He would have assumed she just didn't want to talk to him if Emily hadn't had the same result. Ria would never turn down a call from her.

Him, on the other hand, she'd likely be avoiding like the plague.

As well she should. He had the track record to prove that.

I care about you.

Every female who's ever risked really caring about me like that is dead.

The simple truth of it hammered at him. While she could argue cause and guilt with him, nothing could change the concrete numbers. He never should have let her get so close. But he had. And if anything happened to her, it was going to be his fault.

And this one he wasn't sure he could live with.

His anxiety—and his instincts—were at a high hum when he turned onto her street. He slowed in front of the row of six tidy, two-story connected duplexes. They were all painted different colors that still seemed to go together, and each one had a covered porch in front with neatly cared-for yards and a single-space garage on the lowest level.

He confirmed the location by checking the mailboxes in a bank outside. Her name was on the third box in, but the development had wisely not correlated that to the house numbers, so no one could read the box and know the name of the resident of a particular unit. He parked and started down the sidewalk. He could have guessed the cheerful red unit was hers even without the address, from the wood carving on the front wall, in the shelter of the porch. An orca.

She didn't answer the doorbell. Or his knock. He called out her name, although he wasn't sure if hearing it was him would make her more or less likely to answer. Still nothing.

He walked around back. Each unit had a small, fenced backyard. He grabbed the top cross rail and pulled himself up. Ria's was filled with lush greenery, some lingering flowers and a comfortable-looking seating area with a small table. A tree with foliage starting to turn a brilliant red was in one corner, no doubt having provided a nice, shady spot during the heat of summer. It was all tidy, pretty and inviting. Like the woman herself, he thought, then shoved those thoughts ruthlessly back in a cage.

There was a large, glass sliding door into the house, but the drapes were closed. Through a smaller window to one side he could see partially into the kitchen. The counters looked clear of any breakfast debris and the coffeemaker he could just see the edge of looked clean and empty. And there were no lights on inside that he could see, upstairs or down.

It had the look of an empty house, he thought as he lowered himself back to the ground. He walked back around to the front. The garage door had a strip of windows in one panel, to let in light. He'd never liked the idea because it gave away not just whatever a person might keep there but also whether or not they were home. At least they'd put this one high enough up that the casual passerby wouldn't see anything. But he was able to get enough of a grip on the rim with his fingertips to pull up and hang on for a couple of seconds. Long enough to see that her car wasn't there.

He pondered his next move. He was aware he was treading a very fine line. Ria the teacher who was involved in what could become an abuse case was on one side, but Ria the woman who had driven him wild last night, who hadn't just snuck in under his guard but had blasted it to bits, was on the other, and he suspected they would have very different views on him breaking into their home.

It was the missing Ria that drove him, and moments later he was over the fence and on her back patio. He hoped the neighborhood was as quiet as it seemed; he didn't relish having to call Dunbar for yet more help if somebody called the local police on him. He checked the glass slider first. The latch was typical and easily broken. She had the standard burglar bar stopping it from sliding open, but it was easy enough to bend the metal track and simply lift the heavy door out of place. He'd have to make sure she installed one of the more secure pins that ran through both the moving and fixed door, preventing just this action.

He made a silent apology as he stepped inside. The kitchen was dim with the drapes closed, and he left it that way. He verified that the coffeemaker was clean and empty but thought she just might have skipped it this morning. He would have thought she might need it after last night, though. Again he fought down the heated memories. Who would ever have thought there would be such a fiery, sexy woman beneath that calm, almost prim exterior? And yet she'd burned him to the ground last night.

He made himself focus, moved into the next room, a light, open living area with tall ceilings that made it feel bigger than it actually was. The furnishings looked chosen for comfort more than style but still managed to look like everything belonged. Gray and a dark, bluish green were the main colors, and he liked the feel of it. He liked the feel of the whole place.

And he wondered, had they met here instead of at Foxworth, if last night would have even happened. Would she have invited him into her home, her bed? A sudden image of his apartment flashed into his mind. His own rather spartan apartment, utilitarian rather than pleasing, since he was the only one ever there. The closest it came to any kind of style were the photos, mostly from back home in Texas, that graced the walls. And he couldn't even start to imagine inviting her to stay with him there.

No, this felt like a home, not just a place to crash. Warm, welcoming, like Ria herself. A chill went through him, and he was grimly aware it was at what he lacked, what his life outside of Foxworth had become.

Sometimes you don't know how cold you are until you step up to the fire.

His father had been speaking literally at the time, on a camping trip they'd taken, but the words rang with a different kind of truth in his head now.

Again he fought to separate the task at hand from his tangled thoughts. He walked through the rest of the place. The den off the living area apparently served as an office. He could see where she docked a laptop for working at home. Here at least he found a bit more chaos, which wasn't saying much: a stack of papers here and there and a few books stacked on the desk. A small bathroom was next to it, accessible from the whole ground floor. It was cheerful, with more of the dark blue-green and a pen and ink drawing of a pod of orcas frolicking.

Steeling himself, he headed upstairs, knowing he was going to see that bedroom. A smaller room came first, set up as a cozy guest room apparently, with a tray of things a visitor might need on the small dresser. He peeked into the bathroom next door, and it had the same kind of feel— welcoming, thoughtful for guests.

He sucked in a breath and walked to the last door, which was partly open. *Focus on business*, he ordered himself.

He stepped inside, scanned the room. Bed was made. More of the gray and blue-green, but this time with a splash of red added that somehow made it seem more cheerful. Pillows in those colors piled on the bed in that way that looked nice but always made him wonder what a pain it must be to deal with them every night and morning.

Nothing jumped out at him. It just seemed a pleasant, soothing, cheerful room. He noted the stack of books here on the nightstand, beside a docking station for her phone and what was apparently a backup alarm clock. The reliable, trustworthy Ms. Connelly would never be late if she could help it. Phone in her pocket so she was always in touch but put on vibrate only if she was driving. Responsible, too.

Another door was slightly ajar, drawing his attention. The closet, he realized as he pulled it open. And smiled to see a bit of casualness, a couple of things tossed heedlessly. At least, he did until he caught sight of a pair of black heels on the floor. The heels she'd been wearing with that damned little red dress.

Heat blasted through him. He backed out of the closet hastily, closed the door, but the image of those shoes, and the impossibly sexy curve of her legs when she wore them, curves he'd touched and traced and kissed last night...

He swore, and it echoed crudely in the calm, quiet room. He didn't belong here, and he should get the hell out. Out of her home and out of her life. He'd been crazy to let it go this far, but it needed to stop. Maybe if it stopped now, she'd be safe.

Or maybe it was already too late.

He spun on his heel, finally doing what he should have done before he'd ever come in here, would have done if he hadn't been so curious. He shoved all the memories, the vivid images, the thoughts into a cage and slammed the door. His jaw set with determination he headed for the last thing to check, the last and most personal, her bathroom. The roomy space held double sinks, but it was clear she used the one closest to the door; a toothbrush in a holder, a tube of mascara and a couple of other makeup-looking things in a basket beside it and a hairbrush were close at hand. Towels in the same colors of gray and blue-green hung on the rack beside the large tub. He glanced at it, not allowing through any of the images his imagination was clamoring to let loose. He looked at the shower, a large space tiled in those same colors, gray with a strip of the blue-green in what looked like sea glass.

It was dry. He checked the gray towel hanging on a hook just outside the shower door, a glass affair etched with one of her beloved orcas. Also dry.

Absolutely nothing in the entire place looked amiss. But he would have expected her to take a shower when she got home. Especially after...

Not going there.

He turned and headed back downstairs. Looked into the garage once more, but other than a row of shelves with various things stacked neatly, it was empty. He came back in, saw a folder of papers on the table just inside the garage door. He flicked open the cover. He grimaced instinctively and then felt as amused as he could be under the circumstances when he understood he was reacting to the fact that the papers were exams for one of her classes. The amusement faded when he saw they were dated for a class today. It was not like her to forget something like this.

Now he was restless, unease building. Feeling the need to move, he set about putting the slider back in the track, regretting that he wouldn't be able to lock the door again. He'd have to make sure she knew and locked it again as soon as she got home.

A last minute thought occurred to him. He turned, walked back into the kitchen. Pulled open the refrigerator door.

And found himself staring at the insulated zipper bag on the top shelf. The one she'd told him she always brought her lunch in, prepared the evening before so she didn't have to do it in the morning.

She would have fixed today's lunch likely before he'd texted her last night.

But it was still here.

The dry shower.

The exam papers.

The lunch.

His gut knotted, and the cage door in his mind blasted open. Because there was only one explanation.

She had never even made it home.

Chapter 29

He'd knocked on every door in the row of condos and then on those across the street. Found only two people home on a Wednesday morning, neither of whom had seen anything unusual. Only this one, from right across the street, said that she'd heard Ria's car leave last night, which was odd for her.

"I was hoping that she had a hot date," the older woman with the stylish haircut and nice smile said as she eyed him with interest.

"I'm working with her on something," he said quickly, as if it mattered to this total stranger.

So we're a secret?

He winced inwardly as his mind jabbed him anew with the sharp edge of that memory.

"Too bad," the woman said. "She's a sweet girl, a genuinely good person. They're not thick on the ground these days."

"No," he'd muttered, staring at said ground.

"Lots of thick-headed men around, though."

His gaze shot back to her face. He summoned up the manners his mother had taught him. "Yes, ma'am, there are a lot of us. My mother says it's the nature of the beast."

The woman laughed. "I'd like your mother—she raised a polite son. And now I really mean it when I say too bad. You'd be a lucky man." Liam felt another jab, though he completely agreed with the woman's assessment. Whoever ended up with Ria in his life would be a very, very lucky man.

And as long as it wasn't him, she'd stay alive.

Her expression changed then, became serious. "You let me know if there's anything I can do. Ria's always been a good neighbor and a good friend, and if she needs any help…"

"I will," he promised and handed her his Foxworth card, figuring that even if Ria wanted to avoid any contact with him, at least her pleasant neighbor would let him know when she came home. "And if you see her, please call me. Or have her call me. No matter what," he added, knowing Ria might well want to avoid any contact with him at all.

He started back down the street, shaking his head at the tangle he'd made of things. He just had to hope she would put Dylan's case before her own feelings. And he realized in some surprise that he didn't really have to hope, because he knew she would do just that. Because of who she was. She cared, deeply.

And there it was again. She cared. His effort to keep this in the confines of work-related matters failed miserably, because all the way back to his truck he was inwardly telling himself Ria was all right. She had to be all right.

He kept silently chanting it as he got in, feeling as if he were trying to build a dam with the words to hold back an oncoming flash flood. It took him a moment to recognize the emotion; it had been so long since he'd felt it. Not

because he wasn't capable of it or was too well trained—
Foxworth-trained—to let it in, but because he'd not let
anyone close enough to generate it in a very long time.

Panic.

He sat in his truck outside Ria's place, noticing that the
knuckles on the hand clenched around the steering wheel
were white.

She's a sweet girl, a good person. You'd be a lucky man.
Last night was worth it just to learn that feeling like
that is possible.

She won't think that in the end, he thought, fighting
down the roiling emotion that churned him up in a way
he'd never felt before. She won't think it was worth it when
feeling like that about him cost her everything.

He couldn't let that happen. There had to be a logical
reason for her vanishing like this. Even if it was just to
go off somewhere and castigate herself for being foolish
enough to go to bed with him. Even if she hated him, he
could live with it as long as she was all right. He could—

His cell rang, triggering the Foxworth system. He hit
the button on the overhead console instantly, hoping to
hear Ria's voice.

He didn't.

"Liam? Dunbar."

His hopes sank. "Yeah. What's the status?" He knew
the veteran detective wouldn't take the lack of small talk
personally.

"We're out at the Oakley house. No one here."

Liam's first thought was to be thankful Dunbar had
made the effort to involve himself in this, since anything
involving juveniles was not his jurisdiction, as it were.
The man had gone over and above time and again for Foxworth. But they'd returned the favor a time or two, as well.

Then what Dylan had said came back to him.

"Wait, no one's there? I just talked to Dylan an hour ago and he said his brother was home sick with the flu."

"No sign of anyone home, and there's a vehicle in the garage. But a neighbor says he saw them leaving about an hour ago. Hold on a sec," Dunbar said, and Liam could hear him talking to someone else. Then he was back. "Detective Devon just made a call to the boy's school. Kevin didn't show up there today."

"If he's really sick, maybe his father took him to the doctor."

"Could be," Dunbar said. "But the school says he didn't call in that the boy would be absent today. And he didn't answer the number they have on file for him."

"Maybe he didn't think about it if the kid was sick enough."

"Or maybe he's not sick at all."

Liam had been half hoping not to hear those words, because they'd been tumbling around in his head from Dunbar's first report of no one there. But that he'd gotten there so fast told Liam the same thoughts were sparking in his mind, and Dunbar was a very, very good detective.

"Guy says Oakley slapped the kid around a little."

Liam's jaw clenched. "Bastard."

"So it seems. You know anything about a new, younger girlfriend for Dad?"

Dunbar's query caught him off guard. "No. Something Dylan would have mentioned at some point, I think. Why?"

"Just something a neighbor said. The one who saw them leave."

"Them?"

"Yeah. Dad, the boy and a woman he didn't recognize. In a car he didn't recognize. And none of them seemed very happy, he said."

An unlikely, even impossible thought slammed into

Liam's mind. But it wouldn't go away and had hit with such force he couldn't shrug it off.

"Did he say what she looked like?"

"Younger than Oakley. Dark hair. Pretty."

Liam's heart jammed up into his throat.

"And," Dunbar added, "the wit said the kid seemed to know her. Which is why he thought girlfriend."

An image flashed through his mind, that day in the park at the swings, when Kevin had talked to Ria, told her things he hadn't told even his brother.

"The car the guy didn't recognize…was it a small red coupe?"

"No." Liam breathed again. "It was an old, banged-up hatchback. Oakley shoved the kid in back. And the woman in front. He was rough with her, too, the guy said. Who's the red coupe belong to? Because there is one here, right across the street. Driver door's not closed, and there's a big bag on the passenger seat."

Liam's breath stopped again as an image of a big, black leather purse shot into his mind. "Is there a Cove Academy parking sticker on it? Back window?"

"Hang on," Dunbar said, and he could hear the faint sound of movement. Then the answer came, and the last hope it was someone else was blasted away. "Yes, it's there."

Ria.

Nothing's going to happen to me.

She was wrong.

It was happening.

"Shut up, kid, or I'll give you a real reason to cry."

Ria had been listening to Kevin's quiet sobbing from the back of the car for ten minutes now. It was quieter after Barton Oakley had ordered him to get down on the floor in the back. Ria thought perhaps he felt safer back there in the cargo area, curled up in a ball that seemed smaller than he could possibly be. How he could even breathe was beyond her; the entire vehicle reeked of cigarette smoke.

"I said, shut up!" Oakley shouted.

"That's a sure way to get him to be quiet—scream at him," Ria snapped.

Oakley glared at her. "Nobody asked you, teacher. But then you seem to make a habit of butting in where you don't belong."

"If you mean looking out for my students, then yes, I do."

"He's not your student."

"But Dylan is. And since he loves his brother," she said pointedly, projecting her voice toward the back toward Kevin, "what affects him affects Dylan."

"His brother," Oakley snorted. But Kevin, she noticed, reacted to her saying Dylan loved him. She heard his tiny whimper the moment she said it.

Ria's mind was racing. How to play this? Should she let on that she knew that Kevin wasn't his? She could empathize with him, perhaps get him to talk. But that would raise the question of how she knew, and she doubted explaining that would calm things down.

Besides, she didn't know what his plan was. She only knew that just as she had been deciding she had to leave or she'd be late for her first class, the man had emerged from the house dragging a protesting, weeping Kevin toward this car. She had faced a dilemma. Liam's sheriff friend might be on the way, but if she let Oakley get the boy into the car they'd be gone before he got here.

Then Oakley had backhanded the boy across the face when he tried to pull free, and it had been more than she could let pass. She had called 911, given a hasty report, stuffed her phone in her back pocket ready to call again and gotten out of her car. She'd hurried across the street, calling Kevin's name.

The look on the child's face when he spotted her almost brought her to tears. But her anger was uppermost, anger at a man who looked three times the boy's weight. She broke into a run toward them.

"Mr. Oakley, stop. Do *not* hit that child again."

He stopped, which had been the goal. But he turned on her as she reached the driveway, and his frown was deeper. Out of context and in her jeans and sweater, he clearly didn't recognize her. But Kevin had. And the hope that had flared in the child's eyes was enough for her. She was doing the right thing.

"Wait," Oakley muttered, his brow still furrowed. "I know you." She saw his expression clear a little as he recognized her.

"You're that damned teacher. What the hell are you doing here?"

"Call it a welfare check," she said, holding out a hand to Kevin, who reached for it eagerly. Oakley yanked the child back. Kevin yelped in obvious pain.

"Get the hell out of here. This is none of your business."

"You are abusing a terrified child. That makes it everyone's business."

"Abusing?" He snorted with harsh, unamused laughter. "I haven't even come close."

Yet.

The man didn't say it, but Ria heard it hovering anyway. Whatever he had planned for Kevin, it wasn't going to be pleasant. She had to stop this, had to stall and pray Liam's Dunbar or his colleague would get here. Fast.

"He's just a little boy, Mr. Oakley. Whatever is bothering you, it is not his fault."

"The hell it's not. He ruined everything."

It happened fast then. He grabbed at her. She yanked

her arm back, jamming a knee into his stomach at the same time. She connected, and he let go. But he was not as stupid as she'd thought. Or maybe hoped. Because he quickly shifted tactics.

"Bitch," he said, grabbing up a screaming, struggling Kevin and lifting him off the ground. Ria got hold of the boy's leg and tugged, hoping to free him. Oakley just tightened his grip, making Kevin cry out again.

And then she realized Oakley had pulled out a knife. It looked like the kind of blade her father used for fishing, not huge but long enough to easily do serious damage to a child. He rather clumsily held it near Kevin's head. She had to let go before the boy was truly hurt.

"This is a big mistake," she said as she tried to wedge herself between Kevin and the car-door opening.

"No, it's the first right thing that's happened. I'll teach you to mind your own business. Get in," Oakley ordered.

Her? Ria stared at him. "Not likely."

"Oh? How about get in the car or I'll do some real damage?"

Kevin whimpered as she stared at Oakley in disbelief. She saw the fury, the hatred in his eyes, his expression, the tight line of his mouth.

"Whatever you're thinking, you're only compounding the trouble you're in. The authorities are already on their way here."

He let out a disdainful laugh. "Sure they are."

"There were already investigators on the way, but I also just called 911. If you're hurting or threatening Kevin when they get here, it will only make things worse for you."

The man didn't answer. But in a way Kevin did. He let out a scream as his father—or rather the man he'd been raised to think was his father—shifted the knife to his throat. Ria stared at the thick, heavy fingers on the thin, delicate-seeming neck and the tiny trickle of blood that had already started beneath the filleting blade.

Looking back at Barton Oakley's face, she now had no doubt that he would do it.

She couldn't leave Kevin alone with the clearly deranged man. She just couldn't. Part of her was screaming to get away, to run. She kept her gaze fastened on the one thing that overwhelmed that urge—Kevin's terrified face.

So she had gotten into the car.

So now, terrified as they drove, she sat here telling herself she had had no choice. And trying not to visibly shake as she acknowledged she'd gone along with her own kidnapping.

Chapter 30

It hadn't been a good choice, but it had been the only one left to her, Ria told herself. She'd suggested he let her drive, thinking she could somehow use the car as a weapon, but the man would have none of it. He'd ordered her into the passenger seat, only releasing his threatening hold on the child and shoving him in the back of the battered, brown hatchback when she'd complied.

So now here they were, heading west to a destination only Barton Oakley knew.

She pondered it all as she sat helplessly two feet from a man clearly far beyond thinking clearly. To blame an innocent child for what was his mother's infidelity made little sense to her. She tried to put herself in his shoes, reminded herself of what she knew of the male ego, of how he must feel—not only had she been unfaithful but she had lied and let him believe this boy was his. Had, in his view, perhaps, tricked him into raising the child, providing for him. Maybe he felt as if she'd made a fool out of him, because he'd believed it, treated Kevin as his own, raised him as his own.

She thought she could understand, at least how he felt, but taking it out physically and emotionally on a ten-year-old blasted it out of the realm of comprehensibility for her. Anger, yes; she could understand that. She could even understand not wanting the boy around as a constant reminder. But battering a helpless child?

She yanked her mind off fruitless wonderings. This was no time for a quiet, thorough analysis of the situation. She needed to deal with what was actually happening. Time enough to figure out the why of it once Kevin was safe. Right now she needed to figure out what to do at this moment.

She needed to have taken some lessons from Liam. But she'd never thought that, in her quiet life, she'd ever need that kind of skill. Even if she had it, to protect herself while simultaneously keeping a terrified child safe was something else.

Liam could do it without even breathing hard. He would do it, were he here. He would and could do what was necessary to keep Kevin safe. And her, for that matter. No matter what he felt about her. She believed that down to her core, because she knew with an unwavering certainty what kind of man Liam Burnett really was. He would not leave someone in trouble if he could help. He would do the right thing. He might walk away afterward, dodging the personal aspects of what had grown between them, but he would never free himself from entanglement at the cost of danger to her. He would not want yet another death he would no doubt lay at his own door. And there was Kevin, too. He wouldn't abandon the child to his fate.

Her breath caught in her throat as Oakley made a turn. A turn she recognized. She knew where this road led. In another five or so miles, they would come to the Hood

Canal Bridge. The mile-and-a-quarter-long floating bridge, that wonder of modern engineering that let traffic cross the deep fjord, led to the much wilder and less populated Olympic Peninsula. Was that his goal? The thought gave her a chill. She took a deep breath to steady her nerves, sternly telling herself panic would accomplish nothing.

Right now, this was up to her. Because no matter how much she trusted Liam to do the right thing, regardless of how he might feel, he wasn't here to do it. And he had no idea she or Kevin were even in trouble. She tried to stay calm, to work it out in her head. Eventually he'd learn she hadn't shown up at work. Dylan would tell him, if nothing else. But that could be tomorrow, at their next session. She had a gnawing gut feeling that would be too late for her. And for Kevin.

Everyone at Cove would know it today. She glanced at the clock on the dash. If it was right, first period would be ending about now. She tried to picture the scene, predict what would happen. Emily, bless her, was in that class, so she would obviously know right away. And being Emily she would ask and learn that she had not called in, had just not shown up.

So what would the girl do?

And what would Dylan do when he arrived home to find both his father and brother missing? Surely he would call Liam?

Almost on the thought she felt the vibration of the phone in her back pocket again. Emily? Dylan? Or even Liam himself? She didn't dare try to answer; she was even afraid Oakley might be able to hear the faint sound of the vibration.

She just had to hope that eventually Liam would figure it out. Maybe even figure out that she had her phone on her, or find out that she hadn't left it in her purse in her car. If they even found her car. At the least he would know she hadn't gone to work, when it clearly had been her intention when she'd left him.

Of course, she hadn't left under the best of circumstances. But Liam was not the kind of man who would let his personal feelings interfere. In fact, given the painful history he'd shared with her, he would likely move the entire planet if he had to to stop it from happening again.

They made the turn. They were headed for the bridge. And on the other side lay wild places, including a national park spanning nearly a million acres, with more surrounding it. Including massive mountains, cold-running rivers, deep forests and a windswept ocean.

Including the place where Kevin's mother had died.

She told herself her imagination was running riot. That all the wild possibilities that were occurring to her were crazy. *Stick with what you know*, she ordered silently.

She clung to the rock-solid certainty that Liam would do what had to be done. He would be coming for her. He would find her.

She just had to keep herself and Kevin alive until then.

Brett Dunbar looked up from the screen of his phone. He had come to Foxworth from the Oakley house. Liam knew he realized from prior cases he'd worked with them on that he'd be able to access whatever he needed from here, and it was a lot closer than the main sheriff's office. Carly Devon, the juvenile detective, was still at the house, working up her own reports and making the call to children's services. Teague had gone to pick Quinn up at the local airport an hour ago and would fill him in on the way back.

"We got lucky," Dunbar said. "Devon found another neighbor who remembered the car Oakley brought home last night. Gave us a good description. Including that it has some pretty noticeable damage to the left rear."

"Last night? Bought for just this, then?"

"Maybe," Dunbar said, registering the ramifications. But before he said anything more his phone rang again. He answered, listened, saying little, and then thanked the person.

Liam took one look at Brett Dunbar's face as he disconnected from the call and knew it wasn't good news.

"Two things. Oakley didn't show up at work today. And your friend Ria called 911. Oakley was slapping the boy around."

Liam let out a compressed breath. "And she confronted him," he said flatly. "She'd be incapable of letting that go."

"Looks likely, when taken with our witness statement of Oakley forcing a woman answering her description into the car with the boy."

"I should have known, damn it." Liam slammed a fist down on the table in the Foxworth meeting room. "She wanted to go get Kevin out of there the moment we put it together, and I told her to wait, let the law handle it."

Something hot and corrosive boiled up inside him. If anything happened to her, it would be his fault. Again. His jaw was so tight even his teeth were hurting.

Dunbar's expression didn't change, but Liam belatedly heard how his own words had sounded.

"That wasn't aimed at you," Liam said. "I know you guys got there as fast as you could. Hell, you didn't have to go personally at all. It's not your thing. I just…"

He ran a hand over his hair, trying not to think of how Ria had done the same thing just hours ago. Trying not to think of how intense it had been and how the thought that had kept echoing in his mind as he held her against him was *at last*.

He felt as if his bones would snap under the tension of every muscle in his body. It was all he could do not to unleash a chant of *number four, number four* in his head.

"Interesting," Dunbar murmured.

"What is?" Liam turned, thinking he'd found something in whatever search he'd been doing. Hoping. Seizing on the distraction to regain a little control.

"You."

Liam drew back. "What?"

The tall, lean detective with the touch of gray at his temples was studying him with every evidence of just that—interest. "I've never seen you like this."

"It's a kidnapping," he muttered.

"I don't seem to recall you being quite so tightly wound on the Kiley kidnapping," Dunbar said, referring to the case of six-year-old Luke Kiley that he'd worked with them last winter.

"This is different," Liam said, aware it sounded a bit lame but also aware he'd gotten a bit of a grip on his emotions.

"Oh."

"It is," he insisted. "That was coercion. Leverage. This is some crazy guy who found out his whole life has been a lie."

"Point taken," Dunbar said, "but you're still a bit revved up. And it's not your fault. Anybody would have made that call."

A lot of people telling him what wasn't his fault lately. Liam was thankful when the big screen blinked to life and saved him from having to deny the obvious. Or, worse, explain it. Hard to do when he couldn't even explain it to himself.

"Hey," Ty said over the speakers. "Got it strung together. Ready?"

Dunbar had gotten them access to the back feeds of DOT traffic cams, and Ty had put those together with a couple of weather cams that showed various sections of local roads either directly or in the background. Liam had given him time and probable route parameters, starting from the time Ria had left here. He supposed that was what had triggered Dunbar's suspicions, when he'd said she'd left here a little after seven in the morning. Thankfully it didn't seem to occur to Ty to even ask, but then Ty wasn't the detective Dunbar was.

"Run it," he said. Ty's image vanished, to be replaced with the familiar camera views. Ty had warned them it would be rough, since speed was uppermost, but it was easy enough to follow the red car through the frames, even with the tendency toward washed-out colors. In the frame time-stamped 7:47, the car made the turn into the residential area and vanished, out of reach of any camera. Liam had known it was true, but somehow seeing her car heading for Dylan's house made it real. His gut was churning, adrenaline spiking and he felt like he was about to jump out of his skin.

"That fits," Dunbar said. "Wit said he first noticed her car parked across the street at zero seven-fifty hours."

"Observant guy," Liam muttered.

"Lucky for us, between the two neighbors we've got solid info."

Ty's voice came out of the speakers. "I picked up the other car leaving about a half hour later, on a weather cam aimed at water, somewhere. Here."

A new image popped up. Liam studied it for a moment. The nondescript, brown hatchback was made recognizable by accident damage. "That's the camera on the marine supply place, above the harbor. So they're headed west."

The parade of images continued. Liam pictured the route in his mind, filling in the gaps between cameras as he followed the progress of the hatchback. His nerves strung tighter and tighter as they went, as the suspicion grew in his mind as to where Oakley was headed.

Not there, not there, he chanted silently. And then the

car rounded the last turn, dropped out of range and then reappeared. And made the final turn that committed them to the Hood Canal bridge.

"Son of a bitch," he said.

Two sets of footsteps spun him around. Quinn and Teague strode into the room, Quinn already focused on the image of a damaged car heading down the access road to the long span of the bridge in a series of stop-action frames Ty had pulled from the camera. Liam had updated them via phone on the way, so they both knew what was happening. If Quinn had learned anything worthwhile on their mole, it was shoved aside for now.

"Never a submarine going by when you need one," Teague said.

Liam knew he was joking, but he couldn't deny that having the bridge open for a sub on its way to Bangor would have been a big help, trapping Oakley in the backup.

Phone in hand, Quinn leaned in to look at the time stamp on the last image of the car on the screen. "Damn," he muttered, "too late." He slipped his phone back into his pocket.

It took Liam a moment to realize he'd been checking how far behind real time they were. And the next set of photos Ty put up showed the car out on the bridge itself, the last one showing it already down on the floating section. Thinking of Teague's joke, Liam wondered for a moment if Quinn really had that much pull, if he could have had the bridge opened with a phone call. It wouldn't surprise him in the least.

"I'm guessing, from the age, no GPS on the car?" Quinn asked.

Liam shook his head. "I checked on that model. No nav system even available."

"You sure this guy doesn't have a smartphone?" Ty asked.

"Yeah," Liam said. "He's a bit of a Luddite."

"Too bad. It gets sketchy once they get over the bridge. Some of the cameras on the state route are out, but if they head for the Port Townsend ferry dock I should get them or, if they go straight, catch them on the camera at Sequim."

No one in the room bothered to correct Ty's pronunciation of the town as See-quim—not now. Liam was too busy calming a gut that churned at the thought of the ferry that ran from Port Townsend to Whidbey Island. Too easy to get from there to other points north. Way north. Like Canada.

"They haven't yet?" Quinn asked.

"Not within view," Ty said.

"Judging by that last time stamp, they haven't had time to get to Townsend yet," Dunbar said.

"Sequim's farther," Quinn said, dropping the *e* from the name, "but they'd be on the highway and it's faster. Should be about a wash."

"Assuming," Liam said grimly, "he doesn't take any of the million or so little side roads that vanish into damn near nowhere."

Quinn shifted his gaze to Liam. Then he exchanged a glance with Teague, who shrugged in a way that made Liam wonder what else they'd been talking about on the way here from the airport.

"Then it's a good thing," Quinn said, "that we have the best tracker around. You'd better get going."

The casual words snapped Liam out of the haze he seemed to have been in. And he took the fact that it had taken Quinn's order to wake him up as further proof that he was in way over his head. If he hadn't been so tangled up, if Ria hadn't had him so upside down, he would have been on this the moment Ty had provided their direction of travel.

"We'll fire up the bird for air support," Quinn said. "We

can get there a lot faster than anybody else at this point. Maybe we can pick them up. Teague, you'd better fly, I'm still in fixed-wing mode."

"On it," Teague said, heading out to the large metal warehouse that served not only as storage for various pieces of equipment but as a hangar for Quinn's other favorite toy, the black helicopter that still bore the scars of the mission on which he'd met Hayley: two bullet holes—one patched, one left alone on Quinn's order. Only Quinn Foxworth, Liam thought, could get sentimental over a bullet hole.

"Thanks for stepping up, Brett," Quinn said.

The detective was looking thoughtfully at the screen. "I think I'll make a call to the Park Service," he said slowly. "Have the rangers keep their eyes open."

Liam's stomach turned over as he thought of the national park where Melissa Oakley had died.

"Dylan," he said suddenly.

"You know where he is?" Quinn asked.

"School. I left Cutter to keep him there until I found out what was happening. And Emily's keeping an eye on him, too."

"You may need Cutter."

"Yes." His mind was racing. "I'll go get him on my way. But what the hell do I tell Dylan? That his dad kidnapped his little brother and Ria?"

"I'll call Devon. She wanted to talk to him anyway. I'll tell her to do it now," Dunbar said. "She's really good with kids. She'll find the best way to deal with it. He doesn't need to know all of it until he needs to."

Liam nodded. He turned on his heel and headed out. Went down the stairs three at a time. Headed to the warehouse at a run. Teague already had the helicopter out on the pad. If only he'd been so quick. He'd already wasted too much time, lost in that damned fog of worry. That's what happened when you got too personally involved.

Now he shoved all those feelings aside, summoning up all control he had in him. He hit his equipment locker and grabbed the gear he wanted.

He was the Foxworth tracker, and it was time—past time—for him to do what he did.

Chapter 31

They had been riding in total silence since Kevin had managed to smother his sobs. Ria knew conventional wisdom said to try to get a kidnapper to talk to you, try to make them see you as a person, not just a means to an end. But she was at a total loss for what to say. Oakley was already angry at her for getting involved at all, and it seemed to her that meant he wouldn't care at all about anything personal she might say. Besides, what was there?

Please, I can't die now, because I finally met The Guy?

Too bad The Guy didn't feel the same. Too bad he was so full of guilt that he wouldn't let any woman get close. And she wasn't egotistical enough to think that she was the one who could change that, after he'd carried it around for years.

Maybe I should tell Oakley the martial arts guy will be coming after us.

No matter what else she had doubts about she didn't question that for a moment. Once he figured out what had happened—and he would—Liam would be on their trail. And he wouldn't quit.

Liam never quits once he's on the scent.

Foxworth doesn't give up.

She only wished it would be because of her as well as the Foxworth creed. But he'd made it pretty clear.

I don't know what we are, Ria. Except not the same as before.

And that could as easily mean they were done as anything else.

She gave herself an inward shake. This was not helping. She tried to focus. She had the sense that talking about Kevin would only enrage him more. The boy had been painfully quiet for some time now, huddled on the floor of the cargo area of the hatchback. He was probably hoping the man he still thought was his father had forgotten about him, at least for now.

So what to say? What on earth could she say to the man who had essentially kidnapped her? She stared out the windshield, barely noticing the cloud bank headed in from the ocean. After all, it was hardly the time to start jabbering about the weather. Not when—

Wait, she thought. Maybe that was it. Talk about something…ordinary. As if nothing extraordinary was going on.

She took a deep breath and then the plunge. "I hope Dylan does well on his exam today."

Barton Oakley's head snapped around. She'd startled him, if nothing else.

Trying to put even more casualness into her voice, she continued. "If he keeps these kinds of grades, he should have no trouble getting into U-Dub."

She used the local nickname for the University of Washington intentionally. As she had picked the words. She knew the man had gone to the Seattle-based school himself.

He was back to looking at the road ahead, but she sensed she still had his attention.

"I think it's wonderful that he wants to go there because you did," she said.

His head came around again. He stared at her, long enough that she got worried about the road ahead.

"He said that?" he asked.

"He did."

He looked forward again, correcting for the slight veer the car had taken, and she breathed again. She tried to decide what to say next, since this had at least gotten him talking. Should she tell him Dylan loved him? Admired him? She thought about what the man had been through. Thought she might know what would get to him the most.

"He respects you very much," she said.

Although she couldn't be sure, she thought she saw a shudder go through him. Maybe she'd hit upon the key word. And she felt a rush of relief as it occurred to her that, had she not been forewarned by Liam's foray into the man's computer, she might have brought up his dead, unfaithful wife. Hardly likely to endear Ria to him.

And then he went cold again. "Whatever you're trying to pull, it won't work, so shut up."

"I just thought you'd want to know how Dylan feels about you."

"I said, shut up."

"He's a good kid. He's got a bright future."

Oakley snorted. "As long as some slut doesn't get hold of him."

And there it was. The bitterness, the rage, the betrayal. She didn't blame him for feeling that way. His response to it was something else entirely.

Again she weighed the possible gain from bringing up his wife against the possible disaster it could become. She had to keep him talking, get him to interact with her, see her as a person, not just an impediment. She simply didn't know which way to go, which might work, which was the greater risk.

In fact, there were only two things she was certain of right now. That she could never, ever forgive this man for what he was doing to the little boy cowering barely a foot behind her.

And that Liam was coming for them.

She drew in a deep breath and chose.

"They haven't hit Sequim or Port Townsend that we could find," Ty said.

"Copy," Liam said as he turned past the former mill town turned picturesque tourist attraction. Cutter shifted restlessly, nudging at Liam's cell phone atop the center console, even though Liam had activated the earpiece that put him in constant, live contact with the Foxworth system. He supposed the dog could still hear the familiar voice.

He glanced at the animal. He'd tried to play it as if he were just retrieving his dog before continuing to search for Ria, but both Emily and Dylan were smart kids, and they'd sensed something was up. They were both worried about their teacher, but he hoped they didn't realize Dylan's father had anything to do with it. Not yet, anyway, at least until the juvenile officer showed up.

There was a crackle of static and then Quinn's voice in his earpiece, less clear over the sound of the helicopter. "We're overhead. Nothing yet."

Cutter nudged his phone again, oddly no differently when it was Quinn than Ty. This time Liam had to grab the device to keep it from hitting the floor. But he was focused on the road ahead as they neared the bridge.

"Copy," he said to Quinn.

"We'll keep looking."

Liam acknowledged the words, but he had little hope.

The thickness of the trees that gave this part of the northwest much of its beauty also made tracking anything from the air hit or miss at best. The only thing they had going for them was that the damaged car would stand out if they spotted it in the breaks in the trees. And the fact that Teague had become a damned good chopper pilot, nearly as good as Quinn.

They stopped at the light at the turn for the bridge. Cutter yet again nudged the phone with his nose.

"What's with you, hound?" He glanced at the dog and found those amber-flecked dark eyes fastened on him in that intense way that signaled this was not some casual distraction. Very pointedly the dog nudged the phone again and then looked at him.

Halfway across the floating span and far too belatedly it hit him. Barton Oakley might be a technophobe with a decade-old flip phone, but Ria was not. A series of images flashed through his mind, of her in jeans, slipping her phone into her back pocket rather than into the slot on her big purse. At the time he'd been more focused on the sweet curve of her backside than the phone.

Your friend called 911.

Could she have? Could she have made that call and put her phone in her pocket, not back in her bag, which was in her abandoned car?

He swore but followed it with a fervent "thanks, buddy" to Cutter, whose tail wagged faintly.

"Ty!" He knew the tech genius was also monitoring their channel in real time, and the answer came back quickly.

"Here."

"Ria might have her phone on her."

He rattled off the number, knowing he wouldn't have to tell Ty to ping it.

"Copy." It was all Ty said, but Liam knew he was on it.

Dunbar could get them the clearance they needed to do it, since Ria had in fact called 911.

"Thought they had her car and purse," Quinn said over the speaker.

"A lot of times she puts it in a pocket."

Under the circumstances, he knew he wouldn't have to explain why he hadn't thought of it before, or how he knew her phone habits or how her number had been etched into his memory from the moment she'd first given it to him. Foxworth knew when things had to be all business, and they damned sure had to be now.

"Worth a shot," was all Quinn said.

They were across the bridge now and coming up the hill on the other side. He had a couple of minutes before he hit the first turn that would head north to Port Townsend, which also meant the ferry that had likely left ten minutes ago, with the next not for at least a half an hour, putting him even farther behind them. He was tempted to entreat God, fate and the world at large that they hadn't gone that way, but the other direction wasn't much better given the suspicions that were eating at him. The thought that Oakley might be headed to the same area where his wife had died was even more unsettling.

He resisted the urge to push harder. Ty was the best and already going as fast as was possible on both tasks before him—tracking the car and finding Ria's phone. There was a second, more frequently used road that was a bit faster another eight or so miles along; Liam could take that if the answer was north, but he had a gut feeling that if Oakley was going that way, he'd want off the main highway as soon as possible. Teague was already following that road overhead, and there were several open spaces where the car might be spotted but only if the timing was exactly right.

"Got the signal. Don't turn!" Ty yelped.

Liam didn't know if he felt better or worse. "Where?"

"Midway between Sequim—" he pronounced it right this time because Ty was a quick learner "—and Port Angeles. And he's slowing."

Damn. He was going there. He was really going there.

The tension built in him until his knuckles whitened as he gripped the steering wheel. Rafe had talked once, on one of those very rare occasions when he was feeling expansive, about human ties and how they could blind you to what needed to be done. Liam had understood, but he'd never really experienced it until now. Because he'd never had that kind of tie to anyone, except his family.

But somehow Ria had done it, snuck past his defenses and wrapped herself around him in a way he'd never known before. And now she was in deep trouble, life-endangering trouble, because he couldn't keep his head in the game. And some part of him—that scared, illogical part of him that had been born the day Jessica had drowned—was screaming.

She was going to die, like the others had, because of him.

"You're sure?" Liam asked before he got out of the truck.

"Positive," Ty said. "It's held steady since I told you it stopped. That phone isn't moving."

Liam didn't need to look around. He already knew he was in one of the wildest areas near the border of the Olympic National Park. Thanks to Dunbar, he also now knew that the car he was tracking had been purchased just yesterday, with cash, from a private seller who hadn't had time yet to change the registration out of his name. The buyer, who answered Oakley's description, had paid more than the car was worth, so the guy hadn't asked many questions. He'd also told him there was no rush on the paperwork; he'd be working on it for a while.

He buys an anonymous car without any GPS, tells the guy to take his time on the paperwork because he won't be driving it and then drives it—after forcing Kevin and Ria into it—to a place all too near where his wife died.

He didn't like any of this. Every instinct he had was screaming at him.

Once Ty told him he was practically on the location, Liam parked the truck. He turned to the dog, who was watching him intently.

"Okay, hound, it's up to us now. Both of them are depending on us." His throat tightened as he remembered other times and how they had ended. "Maybe you can make the difference, this time."

Cutter whuffed softly and nosed at him, swiping his tongue over Liam's knuckles. It was oddly steadying.

"Let's roll, buddy."

He slid out of the truck, grabbed his Colt M1911 from the truck's door holster and slipped it into the clip holster he fastened on his belt. He took the smaller go bag and slung it over his shoulders. It wouldn't interfere with his draw and if he needed more than what was in it, then he had really lost control of the situation. And lastly he added his classic Remington .243 rifle, the weapon he'd been shooting since he was twelve. It wasn't as powerful as some, but he was deadly accurate with it. If it came down to keeping Ria safe, he wanted the weapon he knew as well as his own hands. He wanted it to be so instinctive he didn't even have to think. He wouldn't trust her life to anything less.

It didn't take him long to find the set of tracks in the soft ground on the west side of the road. Cutter apparently agreed, because he took off along the faint trail eagerly. Liam barely had time to wonder if he somehow knew what track they were on, which seemed impossible, or if he'd caught some scent on the breeze—maybe that sweet touch of roses that meant Ria.

He slammed the door in his mind, closing up the box that held all things Ria. If he let them out, he'd lose focus again, and he had to maintain it. Everything depended on it.

He'd barely gotten out of sight of the paved road when he heard a single bark from Cutter. The bark that was his signal he'd found something. Liam picked up the pace and pushed through the ranks of trees, knowing that if anyone was around, Cutter would have told him with a different bark.

The car he'd watched so intently on screen sat slightly cockeyed and at an angle, as if it had skidded to its current position half off the narrow track. It seemed slightly odd to see it in person, in three dimensions.

"Got the vehicle. Empty," he said.

"Copy," Quinn's voice said in his ear. "En route."

He'd known the car was empty long before he got up to it, both by the way Cutter was acting and his own gut instincts. Ria was not here, and yet her phone signal was stationary. Had she left it? Had Oakley found it? Had he hurt her in the process?

Again he had to clamp down; his imagination had never run wild like this before and he was having trouble corralling it. He focused on Cutter, who was circling the vehicle like a wolf circling prey, his nose to the ground. When he reached the passenger side, the dog stopped, sat and gave an urgent whine.

Liam gave up his own visual inspection of the car, which so far had yielded little, and went to where the dog was. There was a scrabble of tracks and marks all over the ground on the passenger side of the car. He studied them, ignoring for the moment what Cutter had found, that Ria's phone lay in the dirt. Those tracks told a story, and he needed at least the gist of it before he proceeded.

"Hold," he ordered Cutter, who was clearly anxious to be off. This alone told Liam they had a trail. But he had to assess this first.

Two main sets of marks, adjacent to the front passenger door and back near the hatch. Smaller, tighter arcs and sprays near the back. Kevin had fought. He must know now something was very wrong with the man he'd thought of as his father.

Near the front passenger door, the ground was less disturbed. Enough so that he saw at least one clear footprint. Saw the pattern of the shoe tread. The simple leather slip-on mocs Ria had had on. The ones she had kicked off so easily last night.

He managed to quash the rising boil more easily this time. He was on the hunt now, and instinct and experience were giving him that half step back he needed.

Less disturbed here. She hadn't fought? He glanced at the other, more roiled pattern. No. Oakley had used the boy against her. Threatened him, to gain her cooperation.

He turned to where Cutter was sitting, practically trembling with his eagerness to get moving, yet held by Liam's command as surely as if he were chained to that spot. A prince of a dog, as his father would say.

He studied the object near Cutter's front paws. The screen was broken, dented, as if someone had dropped or thrown it down and then stomped it. Sounds like something the tech-averse Oakley might do, underestimating what it took to put a device designed to withstand a lot of abuse out of commission. It had brought him this far, but it was of no further use now.

"Phone's here, broken," he said into the live connection. "We're on our own now."

He left the phone untouched. He wasn't sure what Oakley had planned, only that, whatever it was, he didn't want to or couldn't do it here. Still, if Oakley happened to come back to the car, Liam wanted no sign anyone had been there, didn't want him to know he was after him. He sent Cutter a few feet up the trail, ordered him to wait and then took ten seconds to brush out what he could of the dog's prints. He doubted Oakley would notice them or think they were anything other than local wildlife, but he was taking no chances when Ria's and Kevin's lives could be at stake.

He started toward the dog, who was again trembling with eagerness. But then Liam noticed something else, something completely unexpected. A couple of feet away, there were two more sets of scratches and furrows in the dirt, in the softer, damper ground off the path, under the trees. One looked similar to those at the back of the car. The other was very different. They weren't random.

They were a sign.

A dollar sign.

He frowned, puzzled. It had to be Ria, but what was she trying to say? That Oakley had done this for money? He knew her family was successful but doubted they ran to the kind of money a kidnapper was usually after. Besides, Oakley wouldn't know anything about her, other than that she was Dylan's teacher. And why drag along his own son?

Except... Kevin wasn't his own son.

He stared at the markings in the dirt. Realizations slammed into him, one after the other.

Kevin had started to struggle again.

Oakley had had to stop to deal with him.

Ria had taken advantage.

She had left him a clue.

He found himself smiling. "That's my girl," he whispered, completely forgetting about the three men who could hear every word.

And then, for a brief moment, he forgot about everything as the impact of two last things hit him.

She'd known he would come for her.

And he'd meant it. She was his.

The old panic tried to rise, but this simple evidence of her nerve, her trust, wiped it out.

This was not going to end that way.

"Find her, Cutter. Find Ria."

Chapter 32

Ria hung back, dragging her feet as if she were exhausted. Oakley snapped at her yet again, although she noticed sweat beading up on his forehead. Probably, she thought, from having to wrestle with the stubborn Kevin, who might not understand exactly what was going on but wanted no part of this trek. Maybe he instinctively realized what was happening.

She wondered if the boy knew this was near the place where his mother had fallen to her death. Hoped he didn't; he'd be even more scared. Liam had told her the police and ranger reports had seemed pretty cut-and-dried, there had been no sign of foul play and there was that witness who had been talking to Oakley several yards up the mountain when his wife had screamed as the trail had given way under her feet. Ria no longer cared what the reports said, hadn't from the moment Oakley had made that slight, small slip back in the car that had made the situation clear to her.

Amazing what a difference three little words could make.

When I collect.

It was all she'd heard, in the middle of a tirade when Kevin once again had begun to struggle, but it was enough.

When I collect I'll be out of here the next day.

Collect.

Was there any context in this where that didn't mean money? So he thought he was going to get money out of kidnapping them? She had news for him—her family didn't have that kind of money. Yes, they owned a few hardware stores, but almost everything they made over costs went back into the business. And Kevin…it would have to be his mother's family, and Dylan had told her long ago she had no family but an elderly uncle somewhere.

But he'd said *I*. Not *we*. Did that mean he was going to abandon Dylan, as well?

It didn't matter, she told herself. Why he was doing this didn't matter; she had to deal with the simple fact that he was. She didn't want to believe any of this was happening. But she had no choice. She had to believe it. And act accordingly.

They reached a nexus of three trails, one going straight and level, one veering to the right and up, one to the left and steeper still. Oakley never hesitated in choosing the left. He clearly knew where he was going.

She looked around for something, anything, to mark the trail with. She'd dropped her car key, the only thing she had left in her pockets after he'd found her phone, at the first fork in the trail. Here she couldn't see anything handy that would make it look different than the other two, at least not that she could do without drawing Oakley's attention. He was focused on Kevin, assuming—correctly—that as long as he had the power to hurt the boy, she would stay with them.

She needed something that would look wrong, out of place, and she had nothing. She—

She did have something. It wasn't much, but it was something.

She prayed she was right in believing Liam—and Cutter—were as good as Quinn said they were.

Cutter never wavered. He went up the trail at a steady trot, Liam imagined as quickly as he could go and not overrun the scent.

They were moving steadily upward. At the first fork in the trail Cutter hadn't hesitated; he kept going straight. Liam had found Ria's car key—he was certain because of the carabiner-style holder she used, which she'd said had come from the flagship Connelly hardware store— a few feet farther on, far enough to make it clear which path they'd taken.

Always thinking—that's my girl.

He didn't even react to the phrase this time. Whether he'd accepted the truth of it or was too focused on the pursuit for it to really register, he didn't know or care. All that mattered was finding her and Kevin, and breaking the hideous pattern that had marred—and controlled— his life for so long.

Early in his time at Foxworth, he had asked Rafe about it once, without revealing why he wanted to know. Had asked how he lived with all the death. The man had simply stared at him for a very long time, with those eyes that could make any man wish himself elsewhere. Liam wished he hadn't started it, but he had, and he made himself hold that gaze, despite the urge to run.

Liam had already known that Rafe was not the sort to talk about himself or his past, but he hadn't realized yet how deep it went. But apparently the taciturn man had somehow sensed this was more than casual or morbid curiosity. Or he appreciated that Liam hadn't turned tail and

scampered away like a scared rabbit, even though that's
what he wanted to do.

"Every kill," Rafe had said, his voice inflectionless,
"saved many more."

And that, Liam thought, was the difference. Rafe might
have more—probably much more—death to his credit, but
there had been reason.

The deaths to Liam's account were cruel, pointless,
senseless.

He was not going to let it happen again. He would die
himself first. Because if it did happen again, if he had to
add yet another name to the list, he was dead anyway. All
that would remain was the formality.

That grim determination carried him along the ever-
rising trail, behind the ever-watchful Cutter, who made
sure his partner didn't get too far behind. A couple of times
he stopped just to listen, knowing how sound could carry
in the still of a forested mountain. Cutter would stop and
sit, waiting. Liam wondered if the dog would do the same
if he stopped because he was tired. Somehow he doubted
it; the dog was on a mission and, while tactical decisions
were accepted, lack of resolve or strength would not be.

He caught up with the dog when he reached a three-
direction option on the trail. Cutter had run ahead a little on the trail they'd been on and then stopped, sniffing
deeply as he cast around on the dirt path. His tail had
dropped, and his ears were back. Liam knew this body
language, the dog's signal he'd lost the scent. Taking this
as a sign their quarry might have turned off, Liam checked
the other two trail options while the dog cast around. This
trail was obviously used often enough to keep the actual
track clear of growth but not the sides. At least not used
enough by humans, less at home here than the deer and
other creatures he guessed used it. He studied a branch

that was bent at an unnatural angle, trying to determine if it was recent.

That was when he saw the glint.

Not much sunlight made it through the thick canopy of the trees, but this spot, where a tree had come down and now lay at an angle alongside the even narrower path, allowed a single beam through. He moved and saw the glint again, bright silver and unmistakable in that tiny beam of light.

A moment later he had it in his hand. A small earring, a rendering of a crossed saw and hammer. The Connelly Hardware logo.

We help people who build and fix things.

Well, he would fix this. His resolve expanded, until there was no room for doubt. And then Cutter was there, nose down, that ever-reliable detector searching. The moment he started down the trail where Liam had found the earring his demeanor changed, his tail went up and he began to trot in the same way as before, back on the scent.

Cutter would have found the trail again anyway, but Ria didn't know that. And that earring told him something even more important anyway.

Ria was alive.

She was alive and thinking, although Liam figured with her the one followed the other.

He tucked the earring carefully into the watch pocket of his jeans as he followed Cutter up the trail. He would return it to her once she was safe. And she would be safe. He would see to it.

What would happen after that, he didn't know, nor did he allow himself to think about it. Because right now nothing else mattered but that she be alive and well. Not even the fact that the feelings that had once been so tangled were now as clear and bright as the glint of that earring.

The trees began to thin, whether from natural arrangement or because the area had once been logged he didn't know. Or care, actually; his entire being was focused on Ria and Kevin.

"Three minutes out."

"Copy," Liam said softly in response to Quinn's terse report. He knew Ty had been reporting on Liam's own position via the GPS built into his Foxworth phone, but he had tuned it out to concentrate on tracking. Not that it was taking much, not with Cutter along. He had a sudden boyhood memory of how his father had always sent him out without the dogs, saying he needed to learn to track himself so he could learn to understand what the dogs were saying with their body language when on a scent. There'd not been much of a learning curve with Cutter; despite the legion of animals that Liam had known and grown up with, he'd never seen a more expressive, able-to-communicate dog.

Even as he thought it, the dog's demeanor shifted again. His head came up, although his nose was still working fast. Testing the air now, sucking it in over those millions of scent receptors, his sides moving like a bellows.

The air.

He was no longer following the trail on the ground. They were close enough that he was getting the scent by air, carried by the faint breeze Liam could barely feel.

"Cutter's on the wind," he said, knowing Quinn would understand what that meant, in all senses.

"Copy," Quinn said.

"Easy, boy," he said to Cutter. "Slow."

He didn't want to startle Oakley into anything. A panicked predator was a more dangerous one. He didn't know what kind of predator Oakley was, natural or situational, but he suspected the latter since the man had apparently lived a law-abiding life.

Until now.

Cutter whined but obeyed the command to proceed

slowly. Liam hoped the rest of his training held. He and Quinn had worked together to get the dog to wait for his human companions to assess a situation before following his instinct to rush in. Liam hadn't been sure the lesson had taken, because it had been so easy. But the dog had yet to fail, so Liam had to assume it had. This was not the time to start second-guessing his partner.

The trees got thinner still. Light dappled the ground in large patches, where the ferns also gave way to plants suited to the sunnier spots. The path curved to the right, along the flank of the mountain. He could tell by the way the trees stood on his left that they were on the rim of a steeper section, with the drop-off more severe. And then the trees became sparse, the trail curved back left and he caught a glimpse of what was ahead.

Severe drop wasn't the word. Only a few trees clung to the rocky outcropping the path topped out on. A jutting outcropping that no doubt made for a great overlook of the park and the Olympic range. An outcropping that perhaps was even the reason the trail existed at all.

An outcropping that was also potentially dangerous if you didn't watch your step, with a sheer drop at least seventy-five-feet high.

And there was only one reason he could think of that Oakley would drag a child and a woman up here.

Someone could lie at the bottom, undiscovered for decades; it was hardly unheard of.

At that instant the dog let out a low growl. And Liam saw Oakley, half dragging, half carrying Kevin out onto the rocky point. His eyes darted until he spotted Ria, limping but whole, a few feet back.

He was already operating at a high pitch, but a new burst of adrenaline shot through him. He felt his pulse kick up, and it took everything he had to make his approach quietly. He appreciated even more that Cutter obeyed that command to go slow, because he himself wanted to charge in gun blazing. He tried to channel that tension into moving quietly. Surprise was his chief advantage here. With luck Oakley had no idea he was being followed, but Liam wasn't about to trust Ria's life, or Kevin's, to luck.

He skirted the edge of the rocks, using what trees there were and the thicker underbrush for cover. Cutter moved like a wolf, low, silently but with deadly focus on the pair ahead.

Liam was at the side edge of the outcropping now. He stayed there; he didn't want to approach Oakley head-on, maybe startle the guy into going over while he still had the kid. He gauged the distance. Calculated the time it would take him to cross the sixty-or-so feet. Too long. Oakley said something, but Liam couldn't make out the words. Ria took another step forward, gingerly. But this time she put the leg she'd been limping on down solidly. She'd been faking, he realized. Stalling.

That's my girl, he thought for a third time. And meant it more than ever. He was going to break this damned curse, here and now. Or die trying.

He unslung the rifle, the feel and balance of it long familiar. He readied the weapon and his mind. It could come down to split seconds now. Cutter growled, low and deep. His gaze was fastened on Liam, waiting, begging for the signal to go. Would the hurtling dog be distraction enough? He had to hope so.

And then Oakley pulled Kevin to the edge. The boy screamed. The terror in it echoed off the rocks. Liam saw the gleam of a blade at the boy's throat.

There was no doubting his intent now. No denying it was murder.

He let Cutter loose. The dog charged Oakley.

But in the same instant so did Ria.

Chapter 33

She had to do something. Anything.

Ria knew it in the moment Oakley dragged Kevin to the edge of that horrifying drop. The boy was so terrified it made her heart ache beyond bearing. The man was likely going to kill them both anyway, but she'd be damned if she'd make it easy for him. And maybe, just maybe if she could make him worry more about her, Kevin could break free.

She dug one foot in against a small ridge in the rock. Kevin struggled, screaming. Oakley screamed back at him to shut up.

She launched, running toward him. Oakley whirled, yelling at her. She kept going. Readied herself to lunge. She'd hit him at the knees. Hope she could put him on the ground, so Kevin could run.

She caught movement, low and fast, on the edge of her vision. It was a split second before she realized. Cutter!

Liam was here. She'd been right. And in that instant she

made the hardest decision she'd ever made in her adult, independent life. She stopped. Skidded, slipped, fell. Her left knee screeched a protest, but she never took her eyes off Oakley.

She could see his eyes dart from her to the dog and back, rapidly. Confused. More important, frozen in place.

That's it—keep looking at us. You have no idea what's really coming at you.

She looked toward the spot to her right where Cutter had emerged. Saw Liam, solid, steady and armed. Startlingly close, which told her how silently he could move. Their gazes locked. He gave a short, sharp nod. She took it to mean stay where she was. She could only hope she was right. He pointed upward. She had no idea what he meant by that.

"Give it up, Oakley," he called out as he moved forward, out onto the rock, in full view.

Oakley wheeled to face him. The man's side was to the drop now, although he could still get there easily. He was wild-eyed, and Ria was afraid he'd lost all grip on reality. He—and Kevin—were still perilously close to the edge. He shifted, bringing the knife he'd lowered in his shock at being charged on two fronts—now three—back to Kevin's throat. If the sight of Liam's weapon gave him pause, it didn't show.

"Last chance, Oakley. Let the boy go."

"I'll cut his throat and toss him over," Oakley warned. Kevin looked as if he were afraid to breathe.

"You don't want to do that."

"You don't know anything. Back off."

Oakley inched toward the edge. Ria wanted to scream herself, barely managed to stifle it. Another couple of steps and he would be close enough to turn and throw Kevin over without much effort. The boy's eyes were closed now and he had gone limp, as if he'd passed out or his ten-year-old brain had simply been overloaded with fear and shut down.

Liam, on the other hand, was utterly cool. A true alpha male. She heard him speak but quietly, too quiet for Oakley to hear. "Buzz him."

She heard it then. The powerful sound of an engine above. And getting closer. The helicopter. Foxworth. That's what he'd meant by pointing up. He'd brought the air force with him.

To Oakley it must have seemed like the helicopter had dropped out of nowhere. Against the clear blue sky it was an ominous, gleaming-black machine, coming straight at him. From the corner of her vision she saw Liam raise the rifle to his shoulder. Oakley looked upward, stunned. Kevin slipped downward. For just an instant the hand with the knife drifted as Oakley gaped.

For that instant, he was a clear target.

Liam shot.

Oakley went down. Kevin scrambled free. Cutter ran to the boy, who threw his arms around the dog, weeping.

"Guard!" Liam tossed the order at the dog as he ran. To her.

She reacted to him as Kevin had the dog. She threw her arms around to him and clung, weeping in reaction. He held her, strong and steady, assuring her again and again it was over.

In a spot she wouldn't have thought big enough, the black helicopter touched down. And then Foxworth was there in force, and she buried her face against Liam's shoulder.

Ria sat in the Foxworth living room, contemplating the hole in her jeans and the bandage on her knee that she could see through it. She studied it as if it were some great work of art, because it was the only thing that kept

her from staring at Liam, who was deep in conversation
with Quinn and the other Foxworth operative she'd only
met briefly and who had been piloting the helicopter. She'd
been told his name was Teague, but she'd forgotten the last
name, too puzzled by the way he'd looked at her and then
at Liam and said softly, "Now I understand."

"Ms. Connelly?"

Her head snapped up, and she looked into the steady
gray eyes of the detective Liam had promised was a good
guy. And he was; she could sense that. Liam hadn't mentioned he was also a very attractive man, tall, rangy, with
a touch of gray at his temples. But, then, Liam wouldn't.

Belatedly she realized he'd asked her a question. She'd
thought they'd finished; she'd given him a detailed statement at the hospital some hours ago. "I'm sorry?"

He crouched down beside her chair. "I was just asking
if you'd be able to meet with Detective Devon some time
tomorrow and give her what you know on the boy's situation at home before—" he made a room-encompassing
gesture with his hand "—all this. For her report to CPS."

"Of course. I'm done at school by three."

Detective Dunbar smiled at her. "You don't have to
work tomorrow."

She blinked. "What?"

"Liam called them to explain. You're off through the
weekend with Dr. Halvorson's best wishes."

She didn't know whether to be glad or upset at Liam's
presumption.

"Trust me," Dunbar said gently. "You're running on
what's left of adrenaline in your system now. It will all
hit you hard soon."

She guessed, as a cop, he would know. She sank back
in her chair and let out a sigh.

"Liam knows it, too. That's why he called them."

Her mouth twisted slightly. "I won't take his head off, if that's what you're worried about."

He studied her for a moment before saying, "I always suspected there was more under that good old Texas-boy manner than we knew. Something darker, less charming. I'm guessing you found it?"

She thought of the harrowing story he'd told her. "Yes."

"He's a good guy, Ria," Dunbar said, dispensing with the formality, as if he wanted her to know this was his personal opinion. His gaze flicked to Liam and then back to her. "If I've learned anything in the last few months, it's that things like that are easier to carry if shared with... someone."

Ria wondered what his story was, was sure there was one, but this didn't seem the time to ask. But she did want to ask something else. "Foxworth," she began and then floundered.

"Is unique," Dunbar said with a smile. "They skirt the edges sometimes, and I don't always appreciate untangling those situations, but there is one thing I am solidly sure of and that is that they are utterly honest and completely true to their mission."

And then Liam was there. "Ty found the last piece of the puzzle, I think."

Dunbar lifted a brow at him. Liam glanced at Ria. Dunbar gave a one-shouldered shrug. "I think she's earned the right to know, don't you?"

Liam didn't even answer, just went ahead as if she weren't even sitting there. "A couple of months after his wife's death, Oakley took out a sizeable life insurance policy on Kevin."

Ria's breath caught. Dunbar asked the question that had leapt to her mind. "Just Kevin?"

"He took one out on Dylan, too, but not until a month

later. Maybe he figured out it was too suspicious to only cover Kevin."

Dunbar nodded. "I'd say reopening Melissa Oakley's case would be wise at this point. I'll make a call." Dunbar walked away, phone in hand.

Clearly she wasn't needed here anymore, Ria thought almost numbly. The two men had carried on that entire exchange as if she weren't even here. She should just gather her things and go. Except she didn't have anything. Even if she had her keys, she didn't have a car. It was still parked at the Oakley house. Unless it had been stolen by now. She had left it not only unlocked but, she suspected, with the door open. And her purse inside. And her keys were lying in the dirt on that mountain somewhere and—

"Ria!"

The way Liam said it told her he'd said it before. She looked at him.

"You're shivering," he said, sounding a bit alarmed.

"I—Am I?"

He turned, did something with a control on the wall, and the fireplace leapt to life with dancing flames. Then he vanished into the compact kitchen. She stared at the fire, wondering why she was shivering when it wasn't cold. And then he was back, pressing a mug of warm liquid into her cold hands. She stared at it for a moment, vaguely surprised it wasn't coffee.

"Hot chocolate?"

"The last thing you need right now is a hit of caffeine," he said.

She looked from the cup to his face. "You're doing a lot of deciding for me."

"Right now, yes," he said. "Drink. You can chew me out later."

She took a sip. Couldn't deny the warmth and sweetness were exactly right just now. She felt warmer in general, whether from the fire or the fact that Liam had sat down next to her on the couch.

Fire was fire.

On that inanity, she gave up trying to think for the moment and took another sip of the warm, luscious drink. As she did she noticed the fading light through the windows.

"It's getting dark," she said with some surprise.

"Yes," Liam said gently. "It's been a long day."

"Kevin," she began and then stopped. "I'm sorry," she said. "The last few hours are kind of blurry."

"I'm not surprised. Kevin's fine, physically, but still at the hospital. They're going to keep him overnight, as much to keep him away from the furor as anything." He smiled. "He was so excited by the helicopter ride out of there that I think the horror has faded, at least for now. And Cutter's with him, and that helps. Dog's got a way."

"I know," she said. "Dylan?"

"Also still with him. He'll probably stay the night in that chair."

She remembered the moment when Dylan had arrived, with Emily and her adoptive parents. Good people, she'd thought at the time, coming without question when there was need. And that Dylan had been so worried about his brother, almost frantic, had warmed her.

Her brow furrowed as she tried to think. "Does he... know now? That his father isn't Kevin's?"

"Yes."

Something in the way he said it registered. "You told him?"

"Had to. It's the only thing that would make sense of it for him. Dunbar offered—he's used to doing that kind of thing—but I thought it might be easier coming from somebody he knew."

Something stirred in her, a different kind of warmth.

Whatever else he was, Liam Burnett was a good man. Despite his own doubts on the matter.

"How did he take it?"

"Like a man. He's a stand-up kid. He'll be there for Kevin."

She was glad to hear it, but her heart was hurting for those two boys. "What will happen to them? They have nobody now."

He gave her a puzzled look. "They're going to go stay with my folks until the trial, remember?"

She did, then, vaguely. Funny, she remembered clearly him telling her a week ago about his parents and the foster kids they'd begun taking in from the time their youngest had been out of the house, but the memory of this today was foggy at best.

"I'm sorry," she said again, shaking her head as if it would clear away the fuzziness. "I don't know why I don't remember all this."

"Ria," he said gently, "you were kidnapped, dragged up a mountain, nearly thrown off a cliff."

"But he didn't have the knife at my throat."

"Exactly," Liam said. "You could have run, saved yourself."

She stared at him. "And left Kevin to die?"

He smiled, and this time it warmed her to the bone. "And that's why you're who you are, Ria. You didn't run. You kept it together enough to fight back. You saved Kevin."

"*You* did that. And you did it without killing Dylan's father."

"That was luck. Situation like that, you take the shot you've got."

"But you gave him a chance to give up."

"Foxworth policy. You have to give them a chance to do the right thing."

She managed a smile at that; she was coming to quite like Foxworth. "And you did."

"I never would have had the chance if you hadn't distracted him. It's amazing you're even upright. You're amazing."

The words were sincere—she didn't doubt that. What she did doubt was that he meant them the way she wished he did. And suddenly the fog in her brain that was lifting now seemed preferable. Maybe it had been self-protection, at least in part. But it was lifting, and she had to deal.

"I'm still glad he didn't die," she said.

"So am I. Dylan's got enough on his plate, not just that his dad tried to kill his brother and maybe did kill his mother but that his mother cheated, as well."

"And lied," she said in agreement. "Yes, all that, but I meant I'm glad for you."

He blinked. "Me?"

"Yes. Not another death on your overactive conscience."

He looked surprised and then shook his head. "This is different. They were innocents. He wasn't."

She was relieved that he wasn't blaming himself, not when he'd had no other choice. And she was together enough now to ask something that had occurred to her at the time. "Why didn't you tell him what we knew?"

"Thought about it," Liam said. "Thought he might give up. But he had Kevin too close to the edge, and I couldn't risk him reacting with despair and jumping, taking Kevin with him."

Her eyes widened. "I hadn't thought of that."

"My turn," he said. "When you charged him…you stopped."

She nodded, instinctively flexing the knee that had taken the brunt of that sudden cessation of movement. "I'd always known you would come, and the moment I saw Cutter I knew you were there. I thought I'd best leave it to you."

"You trusted me."

She lifted her gaze back to his face. Looked into his eyes steadily. And did something that took more courage than anything today had.

"I will always trust you."

"Ria—"

"I know you said not to care about you," she said. "But you broke that jinx today, didn't you?"

She would have sworn she saw hope flare in his eyes. But then his gaze darted away. And without a word, he got up and walked away.

Chapter 34

Ria pulled her new cell phone out of her pocket. She was faintly proud of the fact that she no longer jumped when it rang, thinking it might be Liam. It never was. In the two weeks since that day on the cliff, she hadn't heard a word from him. She'd heard from Foxworth several times, and Hayley in particular had been wonderful helping her deal with the aftereffects of being kidnapped—she had been there herself—and nearly thrown off a cliff.

But not a single word from the man who had been there every step of the way. That was only to be expected, she lectured herself severely every time she thought of him, which was far too often. He'd been a man on a job, she'd been part of that job and if she'd been foolish enough to fall for him, that was nobody's fault but her own.

The call was Hayley this time.

"You between classes?" she asked.

"Yes. I've got about ten minutes."

"Good. I just wanted to let you know Oakley finally broke."

She went still. "What?"

"Brett's good." She could hear the smile in Hayley's voice. "Oakley was still denying everything, saying he only bought the insurance because his wife's accidental death had scared him into it. But Brett kept at him. In the end he got him to confess to it all, including setting up his wife's death. Even his lawyer couldn't shut him up once he got going."

"Setting up her death?"

"Crime of opportunity. He saw from below the trail was iffy after a big storm. So he grabbed the chance, used her love of the eagles to urge her to the edge by saying he'd seen a courting pair, knowing she'd be focused on searching the sky, not on the ground beneath her feet, while he went ahead to be in view of the witness."

"My God, that's cold."

"Yes. He just couldn't handle that she'd cheated on him."

"And took it out on an innocent child." No motivation was forgivable for that, for her.

She was slipping her phone back into her pocket as students began to arrive. One of the first was Emily, who came straight to her.

"I talked to Dylan this morning," she said, smiling.

Ria returned the smile. And found herself wondering how much of the girl's loving, caring nature was founded on the fact that, when she'd been about Kevin's age, Foxworth had shown her that despite her own tragedy there really were good people, people who cared about doing the right thing.

"How is he?" she asked.

Emily's smile widened. "He sounded really good. Said he and Kevin are having some fun, even. Mr. Burnett's parents are very kind, and Kevin loves the dogs. And Dylan's not mad at me, for going to Foxworth. I was afraid he would hate me, but I didn't care, as long as he was safe."

"It was the right thing to do, Emily. And I'm glad they're doing well."

"I'm glad Mr. Foxworth was able to get it worked out." Ria knew the complications of an out-of-state foster placement had been largely facilitated through Foxworth. "And when they have to come back for the trial, my folks are going to see if they can stay with us."

"Dylan," Ria said, "is very lucky to have a friend like you."

"I just remember how I felt when I lost my dad and then my mom," Emily said simply, as if using what she'd gone through to help someone else was something anyone would do.

Ria was writing the homework assignment on the board when the chimes sounded, signaling the end of class. Yet not a single student moved.

She heard a sudden buzz of whispers rippling around the room behind her. She turned. Froze. Stared.

Liam.

He was walking up the aisle of her classroom, Cutter at his heels. He paused beside Emily, who reached out to pet Cutter. He put a hand on the girl's shoulder for a brief moment before continuing. His gaze was fixed on Ria, who knew she was probably gaping but couldn't help it.

He came to a halt in front of her. Close. Too close. She could feel his heat. He looked a little tired and his jaw was stubbled, but all she cared about was that he was here. Even if she didn't know exactly why.

"Dylan says thank you again," he said.

Apparently, Emily hadn't been the only one the boy had talked to. Ria would be concerned about him airing the boy's private situation in front of the entire class, if she wasn't certain they all already knew anyway. News traveled fast in the tight-knit world of Cove, and these kids were as active on social media as anyone.

"He'd like to call you later, if it's all right," Liam said, as if his only reason for being here was to relay that message. Which it might well be, she warned herself.

"Of course. I'm glad he's doing all right."

Liam nodded. "They both are. And my folks are enjoying having them. Kevin is helping with the dogs. And it's easy to see that's helping him."

It hit her then. "You've been there?"

He frowned. "Yes. I took them, to get them settled in. I just got back—" he glanced at his watch "—an hour ago."

And he'd come straight here? She tried not to read anything into that. Obviously he was just relaying information. Which she appreciated, because her worrying about the boys hadn't stopped when they were safe.

"Dylan's a good kid. When he turns eighteen, he wants to get custody of Kevin."

She hadn't known that. "Will he be able to?"

"Hopefully. Foxworth will help him with that. And with getting their lives set up after that."

She managed a smile, but it was difficult. This was all good news, but it wasn't making her as happy as it should. "Foxworth really follows through to the end."

"Yes." He smiled back. "That's Hayley's doing. She brought that philosophy with her."

"I believe that," she said. "She's been wonderful to me, checking up on me, talking whenever I need to."

Something flashed in his eyes then. Concern? "I kind of assumed that because you were back to work you were okay."

"I am," she said. "Or at least, I will be." *Even without you.*

She was suddenly aware once more that they had an audience. Liam, on the other hand, didn't seem to care. Not to mention Cutter, who seemed to be ignoring everyone else as he stood barely a foot to one side, watching as if he were waiting for something.

"I went back home for three reasons, Ria."

Something had changed in his voice. The tone of merely

updating her had gone, to be replaced by something deeper, more personal.

"Three?"

"To get the boys settled, yes. But also to get my head straight. I had some long talks with my folks. About the past and…guilt."

She thought of that night, when he'd poured it all out to her. And she couldn't say anything except "I'm glad."

"So were they. I'd never told them all of it before."

"What did they say?"

"Pretty much the same thing you did."

The smile was easier this time. "I like them already."

And suddenly he wasn't just looking at her, he was watching her with an intensity that reminded her of a certain dog. And she knew he had enough respect for Cutter that he wouldn't be insulted by the comparison.

"Good," he said, and his voice echoed what she'd seen in his eyes. "You'll like them even more when you meet them."

She blinked, drew back slightly. Meet them?

"I talked to them about some other things, too. Like what they have together. Still in love after forty years."

Her breath caught. She stopped her careening mind, forbidding it to go where it wanted to go.

"Asked them how to get past…being scared."

"Scared?" she whispered.

"I couldn't see how, if just…caring scared me so much, how could I get to actually loving somebody. Real love, like they have."

Her heart was beginning to hammer in her chest; she could almost hear her own pulse in her ears.

"What…" She had to stop, swallow, try again. "What did they say?"

"That you start with trust and build from there."

You trusted me.

I will always trust you.

The last words they'd spoken echoed in her head. Liam kept his gaze fastened on her as he went on.

"That third reason I went home? It was to give you time. Time to get past the trauma of what happened. Time to get yourself back. So you could…answer me with a clear heart and head."

"Answer you?" It was all she could manage to say.

"I meant to give you longer, but… I missed you too much."

The spirit in her that had been stunned by his sudden appearance and afraid to believe what he seemed to be saying rallied at last. "Phone?" she suggested, rather dryly.

He shook his head. "I couldn't pressure you. Not about this."

Usually she'd argue that a mere hello on the phone wasn't pressure, but there was nothing usual about this. And she'd swear the entire watching class was holding their breath, because she'd never heard such silence in an occupied classroom before.

"You needed time to be thinking logically again, so you didn't make any…rash decisions." He reached out then, clasped her shoulders with his hands. "I know it's corny—the one-time delinquent falling for teacher—but here I am. I love your caring, your wit, your sanity, your laughter. I want it in my life. I need it in my life. I need you in my life."

There were a couple of hoots from the students, but Ria never took her eyes off of him. She couldn't. Joy was flooding her, erasing the misery of the past couple of weeks as if it had never been. He held her gaze as he said the words she most wanted to hear.

"I love you. If you trust the jinx is broken or never existed, if you really do trust me, will you risk it?"

She let everything she was feeling show, in her eyes, in the width and fierceness of her smile. "I trust you, Liam Burnett." He waited, and she had the feeling he was the one holding his breath now. She gave in because she couldn't not. "And I love you."

In the instant before he pulled her into an ardent hug, the joy in his face echoed what she was feeling inside, and she barely managed not to laugh aloud at the sheer pleasure of it. And then she did laugh, because Cutter had let out a satisfied "woof" and gone to sit by Emily. As if he'd orchestrated it all.

As, perhaps, he had, she thought.

Then she said with mock sternness, in her best teacher voice, "I didn't need that two weeks. You're going to have to make up for that."

"Oh, I intend to."

He started in the next instant bringing his mouth down on hers with an eagerness that told her the truth about how much he'd missed her.

She barely heard the raucous cheer that went up from every kid in the room.

* * * * *

And if you loved this novel, don't miss other suspenseful titles by Justine Davis:

OPERATION SOLDIER NEXT DOOR
OPERATION HOMECOMING
OPERATION POWER PLAY
OPERATION UNLEASHED
OPERATION BLIND DATE
OPERATION REUNION

Available now from Harlequin Romantic Suspense!

COMING NEXT MONTH FROM

⊕ HARLEQUIN®

ROMANTIC suspense

Available April 4, 2017

#1939 COLTON UNDERCOVER
The Coltons of Shadow Creek • by Marie Ferrarella
Betrayed by her ex-lover, Leonor Colton, the daughter of a
notorious escaped serial killer, returns home to Shadow Creek
to lick her wounds. She catches the eye of Josh Howard, an
undercover FBI agent investigating her mother's jailbreak by
keeping tabs on her children. But a hit man may force Josh to
reveal himself—if Leonor doesn't end up a victim first!

#1940 THE TEXAN'S RETURN
by Karen Whiddon
Mac Morrison returns to his small hometown in Texas
determined to clear his ill father's name of murder and
reconnect with Hailey Green, his high school sweetheart. When
evidence begins to implicate him, will he be able to save the
woman he loves from a vicious killer *and* convince her they
belong together?

#1941 SECRET AGENT UNDER FIRE
Silver Valley P.D. • by Geri Krotow
The True Believers are still wreaking havoc in Silver Valley
when a string of fires are found to be linked to the cult. Fire
chief Keith Paruso is mesmerized by Trail Hiker secret agent
Abi Redland, but with an arsonist on the loose and Abi's own
secrets between them, their love might turn to ash before it can
even catch fire...

#1942 COVERT KISSES
Sons of Stillwater • by Jane Godman
Undercover cop Laurie Carter discovers two things when she
starts investigating Cameron Delaney: that he is *very* attractive
and that his girlfriend was murdered—by a serial killer! Cut off
from the FBI, Laurie must turn to Cameron—a man she's not
sure she can trust—to uncover the killer before he makes her
his next victim.

HRSCNM0317

"Back at the club, when we were dancing, you told me that I
was too perfect." *If you only knew*, he couldn't help thinking.
"But I'm not. I'm not perfect at all."

So far she hadn't seen anything to contradict her
impression. "Let me guess, you use the wrong fork when
you eat salad."

"I'm serious," Josh told her, pulling his vehicle into the
parking lot.

"Okay, I'll bite. How are you not perfect?" Leonor asked,
turning to look at him as she got out.

"Sometimes," Josh said as they walked into the B and B,
"I find that my courage fails me."

She strongly doubted that, but maybe they weren't talking
about the same thing, Leonor thought.

"You're going to have to give me more of an explanation
than that," she told him.

Making their way through the lobby, they went straight
to the elevator.

The car was waiting for them, opening its doors the
second he pressed the up button.

He'd already said too much and he knew that the more he talked, the greater the likelihood that he would say something to give himself away. But knowing he had to say something, he kept it vague.

"Let's just say that I don't always follow through and do what I really want to do," Josh said vaguely.

That didn't sound like much of a flaw to her, Leonor thought.

After getting off the elevator, they walked to her suite. She used her key and opened her door, then turned toward him.

Her heart was hammering so hard in her throat, she found it difficult to talk.

"And just what is it that you really want to do—but don't?" she asked him in a voice that had mysteriously gone down to just above a whisper.

As it was, her voice sounded very close to husky—and he found it hopelessly seductive.

Standing just inside her suite, Leonor waited for him to answer while her heart continued to imitate the rhythm of a spontaneous drumroll that only grew louder by the moment.

Josh weighed his options for a moment. Damned if he did and damned if he didn't, he couldn't help thinking. And then he answered her.

"Kiss you," he told Leonor, saying the words softly, his breath caressing her face.

She felt her stomach muscles quickening.

"Maybe you should go ahead and do that," she told him. "I promise I won't stop you."

Get 2 Free Books,
Plus 2 Free Gifts—
just for trying the Reader Service!

HARLEQUIN®
ROMANTIC suspense

"No," Billy replied, shaking his head. "It's not a matter of revenge."

"Then . . ."

Billy steepled his fingers and, after a long pause, said, "I never told you that I had a kid sister—not a real blood sister but a close kin, lived right near us. We protected little Nellie as one of the family, pretended she was part of the family, just like a kid sister. I never mentioned Nellie because she was a worry, always a troubled child and young adult."

Longarm set his cup of coffee down on the side table and leaned forward with interest. "Why don't you just start from the beginning and then tell me why you asked me here to talk about a sister that you've never before mentioned."

"All right, I will. You see, Nellie was difficult from the start. As a baby, she never stopped crying and was always angry. When she was a little older, she was obstinate and prone to having temper tantrums."

"A lot of little kids have temper tantrums."

"Not like the ones that Nellie threw. Her temper tantrums were really . . ." Billy paused, carefully choosing his next words. "Nellie's temper tantrums were violent."

"Oh."

"And when my kid sister became a teenager, she quickly began to run with a rough crowd. She had always been beautiful, and when she became a teenager she attracted a lot of attention . . . but mostly from the wrong kind of men and boys."

"She was wild and promiscuous."

"Exactly. And being her only sibling, I felt responsible and I tried hard to make her understand that she was going down a dark path that might one day lead to prison or death."

"What *exactly* did she do that was so violent?" Longarm prompted.

"She wasn't completely violent. In fact, she was very kind to animals, but Nellie grew to hate older boys and men. One time when she came upon four older boys tying a bean can to a dog's tail and whipping the poor animal into a run; Nellie grabbed a brick and attacked the boys. She actually managed to knock two of them out cold and sent them to the hospital."

"You should have been proud of her," Longarm offered. "You and I both care enough about animals never to mistreat them."

"I was proud of her, but Nellie . . . Nellie wasn't trying to just hurt the boys . . . she was trying to *kill* them."

Longarm's jaw dropped. "You can't be sure of that."

"I saw it happen, and it was clear that my sister was out of her mind with rage. If there hadn't been four boys and two of them beating on her to stop, I'm positive that she'd have bludgeoned them all to death."

Billy took a sip of his coffee and made a face. "Dammit, I keep telling Mildred that she needs to double the dose of coffee or cut the amount of water. This stuff is terrible!"

"I know."

Billy set his cup down and folded his hands on the desktop. "I watched Nellie grow into a beautiful but very troubled young woman. She used men, and it seemed to be her greatest delight to break their hearts. To actually trick them into thinking that she loved them . . . then jilt them out of spite, or revenge, or whatever it was that drove her to such meanness. I called her Naughty Nellie, and the name stuck. She actually seemed to *like* it."

"So your kid sister, Miss Naughty Nellie Vail is a real man-hater, huh?"

"I thought so for many years. Then she left Denver and moved west searching for . . . I'm not sure what. I worried

about her constantly. My father had died by then and my mother, as you know, was afflicted with a crippling dementia. I worried that my sister was already a victim of the same kind of dementia at a very young age."

"So what finally happened to Nellie?" Longarm asked.

"About five years ago I received a newspaper from Virginia City, Nevada. It was the *Territorial Enterprise*, the very same paper where Samuel Clemens had worked under his pen name of Mark Twain before becoming famous. And do you know what article was circled on the front page of that newspaper?"

"Nellie had finally killed a man?"

"No. Actually, she had married a very rich man. His name was John Bolton and he owned a mansion, a mine, and a part of the Virginia and Truckee Railroad."

"Well, well," Longarm mused. "So Naughty Nellie Vail becomes wealthy Mrs. Nellie Bolton."

"That's right. The article also said that Nellie was an artist of great talent. Can you imagine that?"

"Did your kid sister show any early artistic talent?"

"As a matter of fact Nellie did. She used to draw animals of every description. She would go through this big book of animals and sketch monkeys, an elephant, crocodiles, birds, and they would be excellent. But you know that a child sketching animals isn't especially uncommon. Once, I asked Nellie if she ever sketched the faces of people."

"Had she?"

"She had, and my kid sister showed me some of her work." Billy shivered. "I can't exactly tell you what it was about those human faces . . . all of older boys or men . . . but they were, for lack of a better word, scary."

"So you never asked her again about sketching people's faces?"

"Of course not. But she continued to sketch animals, trees, buildings, or whatever struck her fancy, and she was very good. She even sold some of her sketches, although she gave most of them to our parents."

"So what happened after the wedding up on the famous Comstock Lode?"

"I don't know. I immediately sent her a congratulatory telegram and a wedding gift. Its receipt was never acknowledged and she never wrote me again."

"Why didn't you go and see your sister and meet her new husband?"

Billy shrugged. "You know. Life sweeps you up. I have my family, and this job takes up a lot of my time."

"Not really an excuse."

"No, I'm aware of that. I'm ashamed to admit that the true reason that I never went to visit Nellie Bolton was . . ."

"Let me guess," Longarm interrupted. "You were afraid that something very bad was going to happen?"

"Exactly."

"And now it has."

"You are perceptive, my friend."

"How bad?"

Billy heaved a deep sigh. "As bad as it could possibly be. My kid sister has been arrested for the murder of her rich husband and is right now in the state prison in Carson City almost certainly awaiting the gallows."

Longarm saw the deep pain and misery in Billy's eyes. "What do you know about the case?"

"Almost nothing except what is printed as the headline story of a recent copy of the *Territorial Enterprise*."

"Did your sister send it to you?"

"I'm sure that she did."

"How?" Longarm asked. "If she was arrested for murder, how could she have mailed you a copy?"

"I . . . I don't know," Billy whispered brokenly.

"Can I see the paper and read of the account?"

"Of course. But it is sensationalistic journalism at its worst. The article seems to revel in the account, and somehow it got ahold of the old nickname I had given my sister many years ago. Naughty Nellie"

"Show me the paper."

Billy opened one of his desk drawers and drew out the paper whose headlines read, NAUGHTY NELLIE MURDERS RICH HUSBAND!!!!!

As he read the article printed only ten days earlier, Longarm's jaw muscles began to tighten like iron bands and his eyes darkened with outrage at the literary sensationalism. He finished the paper and tossed it back on Billy's desk. "You're right, it tells almost nothing of the murder but condemns the woman as being a wanton murderess after her older husband's considerable wealth."

"She could have done what they're saying, Custis. Nellie always hated men, and with her mother losing her mind . . ."

"I've met your mother, Billy. She's a very sweet old lady in her eighties now, and you told me she was always kind and never spiteful or vicious."

"That's true, but . . ."

"Why did you call me in to tell me about your secret sister and show me that newspaper?"

"You're the only one that I can trust to go to Nevada and find out the truth."

"Why don't *you* go?"

"I can't."

Longarm folded his arms across his chest. "You mean you won't."

"All right. I won't, but . . . but I must know if she really murdered her rich husband."

"Burned him alive tied up in his bed."

"Yes," Billy said and choked.

Longarm came to his feet and began to pace restlessly back and forth. "I don't have much vacation time, Billy."

"You do now."

"What if I find out that Naughty Nellie really is a murderess who burned her husband to death?"

"I absolutely *have* to know."

"Based on what you've just told me, I'd say the odds are very good that she is guilty as charged."

"Make sure of it. Make sure that . . ."

Billy tried to say more but was so overcome with grief he bowed his head and wept into his hands.

"I'll leave on the train this afternoon," Longarm promised. "But I'm a little short of funds and . . ."

Billy extracted a large manila envelope filled with cash and the only picture he had of his sister, who was very beautiful.

Longarm didn't need to count the money, because he could see that there was more than enough to buy a round-trip ticket to Reno, where he could either rent a horse or take a short-hop stage to Carson City.

"Custis, if she is going to hang . . . "

"They don't often hang women," Longarm reminded his boss.

"Look again at the headlines," Billy responded. "Can't you just see the passion and realize that this heinous, horrible murder will require my sister's death-dancing at the end of a noose?"

Longarm wanted to argue the point, but he knew Billy was right. Naughty Nellie was most likely going to hang before an excited, vengeful crowd of thousands.

"So long, Billy."

"Do whatever you can," he pleaded. "If she is guilty as

charged, just leave and don't watch the spectacle. But . . .
but if by some miracle there has been deception and Nellie is really innocent . . . then please try to save her."

Longarm looked his boss straight in the eye. "By *any*
and *all* means?"

"Do whatever you must."

"In that case," Longarm said, removing his badge from
his vest, "I had better leave this here with you."

Billy stared at Longarm's badge for a moment, and then
he snatched it and the newspaper article from Virginia City
up in his hand and put them into his desk drawer. "Thank
you, Custis. No matter the outcome, thank you!"

"You're welcome," Longarm grimly replied as he
headed out of the door and gently closed it behind him.

Chapter 2

Longarm wasted no time in heading off to make his arrangements. His first stop was to get a shave and a haircut, and then he walked over to the general store to buy some things he figured he would need for the long train ride to Nevada. He was not in a big hurry, because the Denver Pacific Railroad that he would take up didn't leave until five o'clock. That 106-mile ride would get him to Cheyenne, where he would board the Union Pacific and travel on to Reno, where stages left every day for both Carson City and Virginia City.

"You must be going on another assignment," the clerk at the general store said as he filled Longarm's order.

"I am," Longarm replied. "Leaving this afternoon."

The clerk's name was Joe Polk. He was an intelligent lad obviously bored or unhappy with his dull, repetitive job. Longarm noted that Joe had a pleasing and outgoing personality and seemed to be good at his work and helpful to customers.

"Marshal, do you mind telling me what this one is

about? I always enjoy hearing what you're up to and wish I could have a job as important and exciting as yours."

"I'm afraid this one is secret, Joe. Maybe I can tell you something after I return."

"Did you put in a good word with your boss like you promised?" Joe Polk asked, lowering his voice so as not to be overheard. "I've been practicing with my pistol and Winchester and I'm getting more accurate with both weapons every week."

"I'll get around to speaking to him," Longarm said. "How old are you?"

"Almost twenty," Joe said brightly. "I'm ready to do a real man's work instead of standing here all day in an apron waiting on cranky and sometimes difficult customers."

"Nothing wrong with doing that," Longarm told the lad. "But I told you that your best chance of breaking into law enforcement work would be with the local sheriff."

"I keep asking him to give me a chance," Joe said with a sigh. "But I don't think Sheriff Green likes me."

Longarm's eyebrows lifted. "And why would that be?"

"Well," Joe admitted, "I did get into some trouble about six months back. Got into a fight and broke up some furniture and stuff and then knocked the sheriff's deputy out cold and they threw me in jail for three nights."

"Hmmm," Longarm mused. "That would sort of kill any chance you have with our Denver sheriff all right."

"The deputy that I knocked out is related to the sheriff. A cousin or something and he's a real horse's ass. He comes around with this swagger and cocky attitude and he mocks me in my apron."

"That would be Billy McFee?"

"Yeah, that's the one." Joe raised a clenched fist. "I just set my feet and drove an uppercut to his jaw that lifted that

strutting peacock completely off the ground. He hit the floor and lay there quivering."

"I'm sure that felt good, but it won't get you a job as a deputy in this town."

"I know that," Joe said quietly. "I been thinking that, if I really want to be a lawman, I'm going to have to leave town."

"Tell you what, Joe. I'm pretty good friends with some of the lawmen that I'll meet on my journey this next week, and if I hear of one willing to take on a kid like you, I'll let you know. In fact, I have a layover tonight in Cheyenne, and I might be able to stop by the marshal's office up there and put in a good word for you."

Joe Polk's eyes lit up. "Thanks, Marshal Long!"

"You just have to remember that being a law officer means low pay and high personal risk."

"I'm not looking to get rich."

"Good to hear that, because you won't. And the first few years wearing a badge are the hardest and most dangerous. A lot of inexperienced young men get killed in the line of duty before they know how to look for the warning signs and read men with murder or mayhem in their hearts and minds."

"I'd sure like to work with you for a few months . . . even weeks. I'll bet you could teach me plenty."

"Maybe I could," Longarm agreed.

Joe leaned a little closer on the counter and whispered, "I have some money saved up, and if you just say the word, I'd quit this job right now and come along with you to wherever you're going. I'd do whatever it took to help out and I'd be happy to work for free."

"I appreciate the offer, but I'm afraid that's not going to happen on this assignment."

Joe tried to hide his disappointment but didn't do a

very good job of it. He was a tall kid with sandy-blond hair and blue eyes. He looked like a choirboy, but Longarm sensed that Joe had not only big ambitions but also a lot of grit and determination. The owner of this general store had a well-earned reputation for hard daytime drinking and being extremely difficult and physically abusive to his employees. To his credit, Joe Polk had lasted longer than anyone under the iron hand and cutting tongue of that man.

"Marshal Long, can you at least tell me what state or territory you're going to?"

What could be the harm in that? Longarm thought.

"All right, I'm going to Reno, Nevada."

Joe's eyes lit up. "I've heard that Reno is quite the place! And that the Comstock Lode is wilder than a wet weasel! I'd sure like to go there with you and maybe I could get a job working for the sheriff in Virginia City!"

"Kid," Longarm said, "first of all, the Comstock Lode has seen its best and wildest days come and go. And second off, the mines that are still operating up there hire tough, hard men that would eat a brave but inexperienced greenhorn like you for breakfast."

"But . . ."

Longarm decided that he had to be firm and clear with his message. "Hear me out, Joe."

"Yes, sir."

"If you really want to become a law officer, your best option would be to go with a big department, like the one here in Denver, where they'd pair you up with a veteran. On the opposite side of the coin, I'd suggest a small town where the worst thing that happens is a drunken fistfight or two on Saturday nights."

Joe drew himself up to his full height, which almost matched Longarm's six foot, three inches. "Marshal, I'm

not the bragging kind, but you need to understand that I'm not afraid of trouble. I won't cut and run in a tough spot and I can already whip most older men. Not someone like you, of course . . . but most."

Longarm couldn't help but admire the kid's confidence. "So you think you're pretty tough, huh?"

"I'm tough enough and won't back down when I know I'm in the right. And one more thing, Marshal Long."

"What's that?" he asked as he started to gather up his purchases and leave.

"If I promise to do something or set my mind to it . . . it's going to happen."

Longarm had to smile. "I like you, Joe. I think you would make a fine lawman someday. And I will ask my friend up in Cheyenne if he'd give you a chance."

"Really?"

"Yes, but don't get your hopes up."

"I'd be willin' to work almost for room and board. Maybe a few dollars for ammunition and a beer now and then. But I'd work awful cheap and I wouldn't be cocky and pushy like Billy McFee."

"I'll do what I can for you, Joe."

"Thanks!"

Longarm left with his purchases and headed for his room over near Cherry Creek. He lived on the second floor of a brick building and liked it well enough. The rent was reasonable and people in the six-unit rooming house generally minded their own business.

Except for the new waitress, Miss Jenny Coddington.

"Well, hello, handsome!" Jenny said as Longarm was fumbling with his key. "Got some groceries for dinner?"

"No," Longarm replied. "I'm leaving this town for a while and needed some things for the trip."

Jenny Coddington was probably in her late twenties and

pretty good-looking. A little heavy in the hips, though, and her voice was loud and grating, with a laugh like that of a donkey. But otherwise, she seemed to be a nice enough girl. Longarm had invited her into his apartment a few times, but mostly Jenny was at work in the evening, and from the look of her clothing and the furniture in her room, Longarm guessed that the former farm girl from Missouri made pretty good money with tips earned from men because of her warm smile and voluptuous figure.

"How soon are you leaving?" Jenny asked. "And do you want to leave me a key so that if anything happened in your room, I could get in and help."

"Help with what?" Longarm asked out of idle curiosity as he finally got the key into the door lock and barged inside.

"Well, you know," Jenny said.

"No, I don't." He placed his packages on his only table. "How come you're not at work?"

"I go in later," Jenny said. "The evening crowd is drinking, and the tips are a whole hell of a lot better than they are from the breakfast or lunch crowd. Why, do you know how much I made in tips last evening?"

"I have no idea."

"Eight dollars and forty-five cents!"

"That's a lot of money for one evening."

"Well, I really put the flirt on with a couple of older gentlemen that I could tell were admiring my . . ." She cupped her hands under her large breasts, leaving no doubt about what the "older gentlemen" had so much admired. Not that Longarm hadn't also been admiring them.

"I'm glad to hear that you are doing well."

"Sure beats shoveling shit in a cow barn twice a day at the family farm."

"I'm sure it does."

"Marshal, do you like me?"

The question was not only very direct but a complete surprise. "Sure, Jenny. We don't know each other very well, but you seem to be a nice person."

"I'm glad you think so. Do you find me attractive?"

"In what way?" Longarm asked, closing the door.

"You know, like how I look."

"You're a very . . . desirable woman. Why do you ask?"

"Because you haven't tried to you know . . . get me into your bed yet."

Longarm laughed. "I've been sort of busy, Jenny. And now I've got to pack and go away."

"On the five o'clock train?"

"As a matter of fact, yes."

"It's still early in the day, Custis. I don't have to go to work until four o'clock and you don't have to board the train until five o'clock. So what do you think might be a fun thing to do until then?"

Longarm grinned. "I could think of something fun that would pass a few hours."

"So could I," Jenny said, unbuttoning her blouse and then more.

Longarm just stood and stared at the big melons that were being presented in such an easy, casual way.

"Do you really want to do this now?"

"You're going away for a while, and what you do is dangerous, right?"

"Usually."

"That means you could be killed and not come back. Right?"

"That's right, I suppose, but . . ."

"Then why take the chance we might never have the chance again to make love?"

Longarm threw up his hands. "I like your reasoning, Jenny."

"You're going to like a whole lot more than my reasoning before you and I head off to work," she said, beginning to undress completely. "I have been imagining you have a dong as big as that of a pony."

"Bigger."

Jenny giggled and slipped out of the last of her undergarments. She walked over to Longarm's unmade bed and flopped down on it with her legs spread wide apart. "Take 'em off and show me what you have for Jenny."

What the hell?

Longarm undressed and saw that he was already starting to get a huge erection. He playfully slapped his manhood back and forth and then walked over to the bed. "How would you like it the first time?"

"Hard and fast!"

"That's the way I like it too," Longarm said, climbing in between Jenny's legs and wagging his manhood tantalizingly across her public hairs.

"Don't tease me . . . just *please* me," Jenny scolded, thrusting her hips upward and reaching around to grab his butt cheeks. "Come on and let's make some sucking sounds!"

Longarm buried his tool into Jenny, and she wrapped her pretty legs around his hips and they began slowly.

"Oh," Jenny whispered, "this is gonna be good."

"First time is going to be hard and fast, remember?"

"Yeah! How about the second and third times?"

"Slow and juicy."

Jenny laughed that damned donkey laugh, but by then Longarm didn't care, as he was moving deep inside her with power and a growling, urgent desire.

Chapter 3

Joe Polk stood waiting on a crotchety old woman named Maude Landers, who was trying make up her mind as to whether to buy two yards of calico . . . or three yards. She had been trying to decide for nearly fifty minutes, and Joe was about to go crazy over her dithering. And all *he* could think about was that Marshal Custis Long was heading off to Cheyenne and then all the way to Reno, Nevada, to do something very important and no doubt dangerous. And he . . . Joe Polk . . . was being driven mad by this old woman who could not make up her mind about a piddling extra yard of calico.

"I just don't know," Maude said, shaking her head. "If I buy three yards, I might be wasting my money."

"Then buy two," Joe said, hearing desperation in his voice as he repeated the advice he'd been giving the old woman over and over. "You can always come back and buy another yard if you are short."

"Oh, I suppose that's true, but what if someone came in and bought the last of that bolt? Then I'd have a dress that I couldn't finish!"

"We could probably order more of the exact same pattern," Joe offered, hoping to get her to decide one way or the other.

Maude clucked her tongue and nervously chewed her lower lip as if this was the most important decision of her long, uneventful life. "But what if the pattern has been discontinued? And I'd not want to wait so long for it to come all the way from . . . Where does that pattern come from, Joe? Chicago? Or maybe even New York City."

"I have no earthly idea."

"Well perhaps you should find Mr. Eli Hamm, and then we could get a straight answer to my question."

"Mr. Hamm is not available," Joe said, knowing his boss had already finished off his first pint of whiskey and was taking a nap.

"Oh, but I think I saw him go right back into that room," the woman insisted. "I'm *sure* he's in his office."

"Mrs. Landers, I . . . I'm sure that Mr. Hamm is kind of busy right now. Maybe . . ."

She stomped her foot on the wooden floor with outrage. "Boy, if you are too lazy to go back and summon him on this very important matter, then I will! Really, you have not been your usual self today and I'm not very happy with you."

What the hell, Joe thought, let her go back and find Eli starting to get hog drunk at four o'clock in the afternoon and maybe lying on a filthy cot in his underwear. Might be fun!

"Mr. Hamm's office is that door right straight down the aisle," Joe Polk said, giving the tedious old bag his most sincere smile.

"I know where it is. And I'm going to tell Mr. Hamm that you have not been as cooperative as usual. That's right; I'm going to tell your boss that you have been *far* less than helpful."

"I'm very sorry you feel that way," Joe said, trying to look contrite. "But . . ."

"Save your breath because my mind is made up."

"Yes, ma'am."

Joe looked up at the big clock on the wall. It was a quarter past four, and he knew the northbound train was taking on coal and water, knew that the marshal would be on his way to the train station and that he would board and then disappear, perhaps never to return if he were shot down by Nevada outlaws.

Gawd, Joe thought, I hope he doesn't forget to talk to that marshal up in Cheyenne about me wanting to be a lawman.

Joe forced his attention back to what was about to happen at the rear of the store. He came around the counter, hand untying the apron at his waist and letting it fall. He knew that he really should have found a way to keep Mrs. Landers from opening the door and interrupting his boss's afternoon nap.

Mrs. Landers didn't even knock on the door. She just turned the knob and barged inside complaining. But then she froze. Joe could see her standing in the open doorway and he heard her let out a scream of outrage. "Oh my Lord!"

Joe was grinning from ear to ear because he could well imagine the disgusting sight of his stinking boss lying in his dirty underwear snoring away like some filthy hibernating bear.

"Oh my gawd!" Maude wailed, backing up rapidly out of the door, then almost falling before she turned and came charging back up to the front of the store. "He was . . . he was almost *naked*!"

"Really?"

"Yes! And, and he stunk of whiskey and his pants were . . . Oh my gawd!"

Mrs. Landers lurched for the front door yelling, "I'll never set foot in this horrid establishment again. And neither will anyone in my church if I can help it!"

Joe Polk doubled over on the counter and started laughing so hard that tears filled his eyes. And he would have laughed for quite some time if he hadn't heard Eli Hamm's roar and then saw the big man come charging up the aisle knocking things off the shelves as he bounced from side to side wearing nothing but his soiled red-flannel long johns.

"Damn you, Joe Polk, I'm going to wring your neck!"

Joe had time to escape out the front door. But he was owed twenty-three dollars in wages and he knew he'd never get them if he ran. So he vaulted over the counter, punched the cash register, and coolly counted out his earnings.

"Eli, I'm collecting my back pay right now."

"You've ruined me and now you're *robbin'* me!"

"Just taking what I'm owed," Joe said as Eli Hamm rounded the counter grabbing a brand-new hammer off a shelf.

He raised the hammer and hissed, "Put my money back and get out of my store or I'll bust your head wide open!"

"I *need* this money," Joe said, standing his ground. "I earned it and it's mine to keep."

"Boy, you probably just cost me my business, damn you!"

Joe stuffed the money into his pants. He could try to vault the counter, but Hamm would still be between him and the front door. There was no choice but to face and fight the larger man. Joe was taller than Eli Hamm, but a good sixty pounds lighter.

"I'm quittin' and going to Nevada, Mr. Hamm. Now, I know you've been hitting the bottle pretty hard already, but you have to let me go."

"Put the money back in my cash register!" Hamm's meaty face was red and blotched with rage and he was spewing spittle with each word. He took a few steps forward. "I'll cave your head in, boy! You've got my money in your pocket and the law doesn't like you around here. They'll believe you were stealing from me and then that I was attacked."

"That'd be a lie," Joe said, knowing it was a lie that would be believed.

"Lie or not, I'll be pissin' on your grave two days from now," Eli Hamm said, licking his lips and then grinning wickedly.

"You'll be pissin' blood is what you'll be doin'," Joe hissed as he kicked his right foot straight up as hard and fast as he was able and caught his boss in the crotch.

"Ahhhh!" Hamm screamed as he lurched forward, driving the hammer at Joe's skull. But he was drunk and slow, and Joe ducked sideways then punched the heavier man twice . . . once in the nose, breaking it, and then just below where his ribs met.

Eli Hamm crashed like a big tree, while knocking over his cash register along with several jars of licorice and candy, which shattered across the floor. He struggled to push himself erect, and then he even managed to grab Joe's ankle.

"You ain't goin' anywhere!"

"Oh, yes I am, and now it's back to sleep for you," Joe Polk said calmly as he picked up the fallen hammer and gave Eli Hamm a sharp rap on the forehead that knocked him out cold yet was not hard enough to crack the man's thick skull.

Joe walked across Hamm's broad back and out from behind the counter a free man. He had just enough time to get to his room and collect his few belongings, his rifle and pistol, and almost a hundred dollars in hard-earned cash he had stashed under a floorboard.

Fifteen minutes later, Joe Polk was bounding up the street in his long-legged stride, hair flopping and breath coming fast. He was certain that he was going to have enough money to buy a one-way ticket to Reno and that the train would be well gone before the local Denver lawmen were able to arrest him and put him behind bars.

Chapter 4

"What the hell are you doing here?" Longarm growled as Joe Polk charged up the aisle and took a seat across from him with a big grin on his boyish mug.

"I'm going to Reno with you, Marshal!"

"Like hell you are. What about your job and . . ."

"I don't think Mr. Hamm wants me to stay and work for him any longer."

Longarm's gaze narrowed suspiciously. "Something you need to tell me?"

"I don't think so."

"Well, you still can't go to Reno with me."

"Last I heard this was a free country." Joe held up his one-way ticket. "I bought this with my hard-earned wages and I believe I can go all the way to Reno, Nevada."

Longarm snatched the ticket from the kid's hand and looked it over closely before he gave it back. "What did you go and do that for?"

"Why not? I'm young and free. I've always wanted to see the Comstock Lode and Virginia City. I thought you might even be glad to have some company."

"I'm not," Longarm said bluntly.

Joe was disappointed but tried not to show it. "Then maybe you and I can meet that Cheyenne marshal so that he can see for himself what a fine and upstanding lawman I will become."

Despite himself, Longarm had to smile. "I'll give it this much for you . . . You're not lacking in confidence."

"I mean to be a lawman come hell or high water. A federal lawman even someday, and I know you could help me."

"Maybe."

"I'll take that as a yes."

"Take it any way you want, Joe. You're correct about having the right to go where you want, but I'm right about not wanting to put your life in danger."

Joe folded his arms across his chest, mind working furiously. "Can't I just sort of tag along at a distance and watch?"

"No."

Joe's shoulders slumped. "Well, you're not being very encouraging, Marshal. But I guess I can understand how an older man might not want to take on a younger man and get upstaged."

" 'Upstaged'? Ha!" Longarm laughed out loud and shook his head in amazement. "Joe, how'd you get those knuckles all skinned up on your right hand?"

"Guess I bumped something, maybe when I was stocking the shelves."

"Your knuckles weren't skinned when I saw you a few hours ago. What *really* happened?"

"I'd rather not talk about it."

"Then I guess I'd rather not put in a good word for you with the marshal up in Cheyenne. Lawmen like to be honest with one another, Joe. And you're not being honest with me. Are you?"

Joe hung his head. "I popped Eli Hamm a pretty good one in the nose. Broke it and hit him a couple of times more."

"How come?" Longarm asked, eyes growing hard.

"He came at me with a hammer. I had just taken twenty-three dollars out of his cash register, which is the amount I had coming for back pay. Mr. Hamm threatened to call in the locals and say I had robbed him, and I knew they'd believe him over me and I'd go to jail again."

"Yep," Longarm agreed, "maybe even to prison."

Joe looked straight up into Longarm's eyes. "I swear that I didn't rob the man and was owed exactly what I took. And he was drunk and was trying to smash in my skull with a hammer. I only defended myself, Marshal."

"How bad did you leave him?"

"I . . ."

"How bad!"

"I kicked him in the balls and put him down. Then I took the hammer he was wanting to use on my head and I conked him a pretty good one on his thick skull. He was out cold when I left to get my things and rushed over to buy my ticket."

Longarm clucked his tongue. "Joe, if he doesn't live, I'll have to arrest you for murder."

"It was self-defense!"

The train whistle blasted, and they both felt the coach lurch forward and begin to roll. Longarm scowled. "Well, kid, I guess we're on our way to Cheyenne."

"You're not going to arrest me?"

"I haven't got time for it now," Longarm admitted. He pointed out the window. "Looks like a couple of the local lawmen are running this way."

Joe Polk ducked as the men rushed up onto the passenger platform, peering into the windows of the now moving

train. "Please, Marshal, if they look right at you, just smile and wave."

Longarm considered it for a moment, and sure enough two deputies did run up to his moving window and tried to look through it. But Longarm smiled and waved, and then the train was outrunning the deputies.

"Joe, you sure are a pain in the ass."

"I know."

"You can sit up now because we're almost clear of Denver."

"Hot damn! On my way to a new life filled with thrilling adventures!"

"You've been reading dime novels, haven't you?"

"Yes, sir."

"You should stop that right now if you have any intention of ever becoming a real lawman."

"Why?"

"Because they're written by people who don't know the first thing about being a lawman, and they make us seem like we can't be killed. I'm afraid that I've known a few young men like you who, after reading a dime novel, just went haywire and got themselves shot to death. Do you understand what I'm trying to tell you?"

"Yes, and I won't read them anymore."

"Good, because they're nothing but pages of foolishness."

Longarm drew a cheroot from his coat pocket and bit off the tip. He lit the cigar and turned his attention to the landscape that was rolling by at a nice, leisurely clip. He wasn't sure if he'd talk to his friend the marshal up in Cheyenne about hiring Joe Polk. The kid was basically good but too headstrong, and Longarm did not want to inflict that kind of grief on a good fellow lawman.

It was dark when their train arrived in Cheyenne.

Longarm and Joe disembarked, and Longarm struck out for the Pronghorn Hotel with Joe right on his heels.

"How much does it cost to stay here overnight?"

"Two dollars."

"That come with breakfast?"

"Yes it does, and it's a good one."

"Then I'll stay here too. Maybe we could share—"

"No. Get your own room."

"Yes, sir. Just thinkin' we could split the cost and save us a few dollars."

"I demand my privacy."

"Sure, and so do I. When are we going to see the marshal of Cheyenne about giving me a deputy job?"

"Maybe in the morning."

"*Maybe?*" Joe asked, looking pained.

"Maybe. We don't board the westbound until around noon. Gives us some time to sort this all out."

"I already told you that I was just defending myself when Mr. Hamm tried to smash my skull with a new hammer."

"Yeah, you did."

"Well then?"

"I'll sleep on it," Longarm said as they stepped up on the hotel's porch. "And you had better have told me the truth."

"Swear to god I did!"

Longarm went up to the registration desk, where a clerk was waiting. The man grinned, showing a fine set of teeth. "Good to see you again so soon, Marshal Long. Staying just one night as usual?"

"That's right."

The clerk glanced over at Joe Polk, who was standing close behind Longarm. "Come with a friend?"

"Nope."

"But I'm staying, too," Joe gushed. "I'm going to be a lawman. Maybe a new lawman right here in Cheyenne."

"How very fortunate for Cheyenne," the clerk said dryly as his eyes surveyed the tall, shabbily dressed, and gangly young man.

"Well," Joe said, missing the sarcasm, "I mean to make my mark, and I suppose this is as good a place as any."

"That's one way of looking at it."

"Are there a lot of pretty young and unmarried women in Cheyenne?"

The desk clerk rolled his eyes and didn't even bother to respond.

"Tell you what," Joe said, looking excited, "I would like a room and then I'm going to take a look around and sort of get the lay of the land, so to speak. If I get hired here, I'll need to get to know everyone. Even you."

The clerk's cheeks colored and his lips pursed in a tight bud. "I doubt that Marshal Blanding is looking to employ someone like you."

"Oh, don't be so sure of that," Joe said, not the least bit fazed by the remark. "I come with Marshal Long's high recommendation. Isn't that right?"

Longarm and the registration desk clerk exchanged a look, and then Longarm was given his room key and headed up the stairs.

"I'd like a room next to the marshal's," Joe said. "He might have some enemies here, and I want to be close to help out if that should be required."

The desk clerk was by now wearing a pained expression as he shoved the registration book at Joe Polk and told him to fork over some money.

Chapter 5

Longarm went to bed earlier than usual, still trying to decide if he should dare visit Marshal Blanding in the morning and recommend Joe Polk as a possible new deputy. He and Blanding had always gotten along just fine, and Longarm wanted to keep the relationship that way and not foul it up by recommending someone who would cause the Cheyenne lawman endless problems.

When Longarm awoke in the morning, he dressed and went down to breakfast and saw Joe babbling away while all the other hotel guests were trying to gobble down their meals and beat a hasty retreat.

"Marshal Long!" Joe cried, grinning from ear to ear, with a biscuit laden with strawberry jam lifted halfway to his mouth. "I've been telling these nice people about you and that I might be staying here in Cheyenne instead of going on to Reno."

"Have you now," Longarm remarked, sitting down and signaling for a cup of coffee.

"I sure have!"

Longarm smiled at the others: two middle-aged women, their husbands, an attractive teenage daughter with auburn locks and a dash of freckles on her rosy cheeks, and three others who didn't even bother to acknowledge his presence.

"Well, Joe," Longarm said, tasting the coffee and finding it to be excellent, "I'm sure that everyone here was very interested in your plans for a career in law enforcement, but they might want to enjoy their breakfasts in silence."

"You think so?"

"I found what he had to say very interesting," the teenage girl gushed, smiling warmly at Joe. "And I think he must be very brave to want to help good people by arresting and even killing bad ones. Joe, have you shot a man to death yet?"

"Rebecca!" her mother cried. "Really! Why on earth would you ask such a ridiculous question? Can't you see that this is just a boy filled up with himself?"

"I just think he is really . . . gallant to want to be a lawman, that's all, Mother."

"Well, never you mind about that kind of business," the girl's father snapped. "We are boarding the train for Reno and whatever happens here is none of our concern."

"You're going to *Reno*! Why, if Cheyenne's marshal isn't smart enough to offer me a job this morning, then that's where I'm bound too."

"Then let's hope he *does* offer you a job," the mother said, giving her daughter a stern look of disapproval.

"Well," Joe said, jamming the rest of the biscuit into his mouth while strawberry jam ran down his stubbly chin, "if I don't get the job, then I'll at least get to know you folks better on the train to Nevada."

The mother muttered something under her breath and

the father stood up from the table leaving most of his food on his plate. "Rebecca, Mother, I think we have things to do now to get ready for our journey."

Longarm could see what was going on. Everyone at the table except Joe knew that Rebecca's parents were desperate to get their daughter far away from the handsome and enthusiastic young man from Denver.

"But I'm not finished with my breakfast yet," Rebecca complained as she was hauled out of her chair. "I'm still hungry."

"You can eat later," the father growled, pulling his daughter toward the door.

"Bye, Joe Polk!" Rebecca called as she was being dragged out the door by her parents. "Hope you *don't* get the job here and come to Reno!"

"I probably will," Joe called back. "Sure a pleasure to meet you, Rebecca!"

When the girl and her parents were gone, Joe turned to Longarm and said, "She was a real pretty girl, wasn't she, Marshal?"

"Yes, she was, Joe."

"And I think she kinda took a shine to me, wouldn't you say?"

"I'd say you're right."

Joe laughed and dug into his biscuits and gravy with gusto.

An hour later, they were standing in front of Marshal Blanding's office and Longarm was giving the excited kid one final piece of advice. "Don't go in there and brag or talk too much. Let me do the talking for you."

"Yes, sir."

"Just keep quiet and only speak when spoken to."

"How come you're telling me all this?" Joe asked. "Is Marshal Blanding a bully and a jackass like Mr. Hamm?"

"No. But he's a quiet man, and he wouldn't hire a jabber box, so you need to stop your constant jabbering."

"I'll do my best," Joe promised. He patted the gun strapped to his side. "Is Marshal Blanding a *good* lawman?"

"He is."

"Has he killed some outlaws and murderers?"

"I'm sure that he has."

"I can hardly wait to meet him."

Longarm squared his shoulders. "Joe?"

"Yeah?"

"Wipe the strawberry jam off your chin before we go inside."

Joe wiped furiously, and Longarm opened the door and stepped through the office door. Marshal Blanding was reading the morning paper, boots up on his desk and a cup of coffee in one hand. When he saw Longarm filling his doorway, he smiled and dropped his boots to the floor. "Well, Custis, good to see you again!"

"You too, Orville. I'd like you to meet my friend, Joe Polk. Joe here is bound and determined to become a lawman, and he was hoping you might have an opening here."

Blanding came to his feet, sipped his coffee, and looked Joe up and down. "How old are you, son?"

"Almost twenty."

"That's younger than I like to hire my deputies."

"Well," Joe countered, "don't let my youthful good looks fool you. I've been watching Marshal Long, and I've been practicing with both my pistol and my rifle. I'm a good shot, honest, brave, and ready to toe the line no matter how dangerous the circumstances."

" 'Toe the line'?" Blanding asked, shooting a questioning glance at Longarm. "I thought that was what they did in bare-knuckle boxing."

"Well, yes sir, it is. But I figure it also could mean to say that I won't back down from a fight no matter what the odds. If I was wearing a badge and a sworn deputy marshal, I'd face a dozen men, if that was what it took to do my job and be a credit to your office."

"Hmmm," Blanding said, turning away. "Would you fellas like me to make a new pot of coffee?"

"I've had my fill," Longarm said. "Joe?"

"Well, the truth of it is that I drank so much coffee at breakfast that I'm about bustin' to take a piss."

"Go out the door you walked in and circle down between this building and the one next to it. You'll see some outhouses. None of 'em clean, but they'll do you in a pinch."

"Yes, sir," Joe said, hurrying outside.

Herman Blanding looked at Longarm and shook his head. "What are you trying to do to me with that boy?"

"I'm sorry," Longarm replied. "But some of what the kid said is true. I realize Joe kinda lets his enthusiasm get in his way, but he does have grit and he wouldn't back down in a tight spot on you or any of your men."

"He's wild-eyed and clueless as to what we do in the line of duty."

"That's true enough," Longarm admitted, "but he kept badgering me about getting an introduction, so I had to at least try."

"Well," Blanding drawled, "you tried and the answer is *no*. If that kid doesn't get killed before he's twenty-five, then he can come back and we'll talk about a job in Cheyenne. But there's something about him that tells me he is probably going to get himself shot to death or stabbed first."

"I like Joe," Longarm argued.

"Then you take care of him, because I've had a few young ones like him get killed working my streets, and I'll never forgive myself for being the one that pinned on their badges. Besides, the city council has cut my budget again this year, and I can barely keep the men that I already have working for me."

"I understand."

"Where is Marshal Vail sending you this time?"

"To Reno and then on to Carson City and Virginia City."

Marshal Blanding smiled. "I hear that country is still hell on wheels, even though I understand that the Comstock Lode is petering out just like all boom towns eventually do. Hell, if it weren't for the railroad supporting half the town, Cheyenne wouldn't be much more than a little ranching community."

"When he comes back from the shitter, let Joe down easy," Longarm said. "Give him a little encouragement because I've never met anyone that wanted to be a lawman as bad."

"Why?"

Longarm shrugged. "He just does. Joe Polk is a good kid. I don't know much about his upbringing, and he never talks about that, but I do know he's basically good, and if he stays on the right road, he'll become a fine man."

"Did he try to get hired on with the Denver people?"

"Joe got into a little trouble with the law in Denver, and they've sort of got a bad attitude toward him."

"And you wanted *me* to hire him?" Blanding asked with disbelief.

"Naw," Longarm said, turning for the door. "It would be a bad match."

"Then why the deuce did you . . ."

"See you another time, Herman," Longarm said over his shoulder as he stepped outside, closed the door, and waited for Joe Polk to return from the back-alley crapper.

Moments later, Joe hurried back around the corner of the building furiously buttoning his fly. "Well, Marshal Blanding really liked me, didn't he?"

"He did."

"Then I got the job!"

Longarm really didn't want to crush the young man's spirit, so he cleared his throat and said, "Marshal Blanding is under a lot of pressure from the town's city council over money. They're cutting his budget to the bone and he just can't afford to take on a new deputy right now, but he said he might hire you someday."

Joe's shoulders slumped with disappointment. "No chance of my changing his mind by telling him I'd work for almost nothing but room and board?"

"Afraid not."

"Then I guess we're both on our way to Reno."

"Are you sure you want to go there?"

"Why not? I'd like to get to know Rebecca better, and this way we'll have a lot of time to get acquainted on the train."

"Makes sense to me, but it might not to her parents."

"Aw," Joe said, swatting away the comment with his hand, "they just don't know me yet. Once they do, everything will be fine."

"I'd like to think so," Longarm replied.

"We've got an hour or two before the train leaves," Joe said, patting the gun on his narrow hip. I thought maybe you and I could do a little target practice with our pistols. You could give me some shooting tips."

"I expect we could do that," Longarm decided, not wanting to hand the kid any more disappointment. "Let's walk to the north end of town and out on the prairie a ways. Maybe we can find a few empty cans to shoot."

"That would be great! I've wanted to show you how much better I'm getting."

Longarm nodded and they walked through Cheyenne. He liked the way that Joe Polk got over his disappointments so quickly and didn't sulk. And he also liked it that Joe was so enthusiastic about whatever he undertook to accomplish in his life.

A quarter mile outside of town Joe took several of the tin cans they'd collected and set them up on the open ground. "You want to shoot first, or should I?"

"Doesn't matter to me."

"Then you go first," Joe offered. "And why don't we draw and fire from the hip real fast."

"I don't shoot from the hip," Longarm told the kid as he drew his Colt and took aim. "I purposefully try to shoot straight rather than fast and hurried."

"Why, that could get you killed if you came up against an outlaw who was both fast and accurate."

"Yeah," Longarm agreed, "I guess it could at that."

"Then . . ."

"Joe," Longarm said as he began steady firing and making the cans kick up into the sky, "focus on being accurate and you'll never go wrong. I've been up against men who were faster than me, but they were so intent on trying to be fast that they couldn't have hit the side of a livery barn."

Joe watched all the cans skitter to a halt. "Nice shootin', Marshal. Now it's my turn."

"Go at it."

Joe drew his pistol and fired much faster than Longarm

had, and of the six rusty cans that they were using as targets, he drilled three.

"Dang," Joe swore, "I usually do better than that. I guess I'm a little nervous having someone like you watching."

Longarm reloaded his revolver and reholstered his gun. He spread his legs a little apart, and his hand flashed down to his gun and came up quick, his shots so closely spaced that they blended together into a rolling thunder. But he missed two cans.

"See what I mean, Joe? I hurried myself and missed two."

"That's still mighty fine shooting, Marshal."

"Not bad. Better than most. The thing of it is that you should work on not missing at all. You move fast, but smooth and not jerky."

"I'll work on that."

"Go ahead and shoot again, only this time slow down and aim."

Joe reloaded, drew his pistol, and took his time hitting five of the six cans. He looked pleased. "I still missed one, but they were farther out this time around."

"You're already far better than most with that six-gun, Joe. Just keep practicing."

"I will." Joe reloaded and holstered his gun. "Marshal?"

"Yeah?"

"How old do you think Rebecca might be?"

He damn near laughed. "I dunno. Maybe eighteen."

"Old enough," Joe said, grinning.

"For what?"

The kid blushed. "You know."

"No, tell me."

Joe blushed even deeper. "For kissin' and huggin'."

Longarm chuckled. "Well, you're going to have to find a way to get her out of sight of her parents and then find some privacy on that train."

"Shoot," Joe said, toeing the ground. "That ain't goin' to be much of a challenge at all."

"No," Longarm said, "for an enterprising and determined young man like yourself, I don't believe it will."

They fired a few more rounds and Longarm offered some professional tips to the kid, and then they headed back to town.

"I sure am excited about seeing the Comstock Lode and Virginia City."

"Joe, I hope you're not going to be disappointed."

"I won't be. I've read all about those deep mines and how they get hotter the farther down you go into Sun Mountain."

"Maybe you'd like to be a hard-rock miner," Longarm suggested.

"Nope. They lower those poor miners down in wire cages hundreds of feet, and they're constantly having accidents. Sometimes a miner will be working and he'll send his pick through a wall and hit a whole cavern of boiling water. Scalds them like a stewed chicken. Awful way to die, Marshal."

"Yeah, I'd much rather take a bullet than be boiled alive."

"Me too!"

Longarm pulled his railroad watch from his vest pocket. "Joe, we've got to get back to the hotel and get our things and move a little smartly, or we're going to miss the train to Reno."

"Can't do that!" Joe said, breaking into a run.

Longarm shook his head and broke into a jog. The more

he was around the kid the more he liked him . . . but he sure didn't think that would be the case with pretty Rebecca's parents.

Too bad for them.

Chapter 6

Longarm and Joe Polk left Cheyenne and rode the train over mountains and then down through Laramie in the dark, through Rawlins, Rock Springs, and Green River. They rolled past Evanston and into Utah the next day. As the long miles passed and the country grew increasingly arid, Joe could hardly contain his mounting excitement.

"I never saw so much desert country in my life!" he exclaimed. "How in the world do people make a living out here?"

"Cattle and sheep, some mining," Longarm replied. "But mostly I think the little towns we're going through depend almost completely on this railroad."

"Will we pass through Salt Lake City, where Brigham Young has his big temple?"

"No, we'll skirt north of the Great Salt Lake and stop for coal and water in Ogden. Not long after we'll rumble through Promontory, where the Union and Central Pacific Railroads met in 1869 and a golden spike was put into the track to commemorate the historic event."

Joe's eyes lit up. "Is the golden spike still imbedded in a railroad tie? I'd sure like to see it."

"Naw," Longarm told the kid. "They just did it for the publicity. But there is no way you can overstate the importance of the transcontinental railroad. It linked the West with the East and made travel across this country fast and affordable."

"I heard that the Chinese who laid track for the Central Pacific outworked the Irish tracklayers going west with the Union Pacific."

"I wouldn't say that was true," Longarm replied thoughtfully. "The Chinese were extremely hard and sober workers, and their greatest accomplishment was laying track over the high Sierra Nevada Mountains. But once they topped that range, they had pretty easy going through Reno and across Nevada into Utah. The Irish had their own set of problems that mostly had to do with the Plains Indians wiping out their forward surveying and bridge-building crews. Also, the Union Pacific had to contend with blizzards and huge prairie wildfires."

"So you'd say that the railroad companies and their workers each faced different obstacles?"

"No doubt about it," Longarm answered. "From Cheyenne to Promontory we're riding the rails put down mostly by the Irish and a lot of Civil War veterans of every nationality. After Promontory and heading west all the way to Reno we'll be riding rails put down in large part by imported Chinese laborers."

"What happened to everyone after the rails were joined at Promontory?"

"The crews just scattered like tumbleweeds in a high wind. A lot of men stayed in the small towns that the railroad created, and some became quite wealthy, although

most of the boom towns died. Other men went home to the South or other parts of the country."

"What about the Central Pacific's army of Chinamen?"

"Most of them came for the money and returned to China, but many remained in America. They were hired through San Francisco, and they went back there to form a huge Chinatown."

"You ever seen it?"

"Yeah, and it's quite a place. I've heard that it looks and smells just like the big cities in China. They're pretty smart and industrious people, Joe. They work hard and have prospered in our country."

"I met some in Denver's Chinatown. They seem friendly enough, but they look, smell, and act a whole lot different and pretty much stay to themselves."

"They're a clannish people," Longarm agreed. "But so are many other nationalities."

"What is there to see as we cross Nevada?"

"Lots of sagebrush, rocks, barren mountains, and whatever else can survive in the high desert."

"Is Reno dry and parched?"

"No," Longarm told his traveling companion. "Reno is right at the base of the eastern slope of the Sierra Nevada Mountains. It's a handsome place with the Truckee River running through its downtown. You'll find that Reno is a very pleasant place to be, although its climate can be harsh . . . hot in the summer, with lots of snow in the wintertime."

"And Virginia City up on the Comstock?"

Longarm scoffed. "Virginia City is about as inhospitable a spot as ever you'd expect to find. It's on a sun-blasted mountain with very little water, and the miners long ago cut down its trees so they'd have firewood and timbering for the deep mines."

Joe started to ask another question, but his thoughts were diverted when he saw Rebecca enter their car and beckon him with a fetching smile and a crooked finger.

"I'd better see what she wants," Joe said. "I won't be long."

"Take your time and enjoy yourself," Longarm advised. "I'm sure not going anywhere, and we've a long way still to travel on this train."

"Yeah," Joe said with a wink. "Two more nights!"

Longarm couldn't think of a gentlemanly reply as Joe hurried off to join pretty Rebecca.

Joe didn't return to the car until well after midnight, and Longarm was asleep. "Marshal?"

"Yeah?"

"I just wanted to make sure that you weren't worrying about me."

Longarm stretched and yawned. He looked through the window but it was as dark as a cave. "You have a good time, Joe?"

"Heck yes I did!"

Longarm studied the kid in the faint light. Joe's hair was all mussed up, his shirt was half-unbuttoned, and most incriminating of all, his fly was open. "What did you do?"

"Oh, we found a hiding place and had some fun getting to know one another better."

"From the looks of you, I'd say that you got to know one another a whole lot better."

"I'm going to marry Rebecca when I get settled in with a good and steady job," Joe declared. "We . . . we just need to get married as soon as we can."

Longarm was wide awake now. "What do you mean when you say that you 'need to get married' right away?"

Joe gulped. "Well, we got carried away some and did a whole lot more than kiss and hug."

Longarm groaned. "Damn, Joe! You and that girl have to be careful, but just because you . . . you know, that doesn't mean you have to marry the girl."

"Even if she isn't pregnant, I want to marry her! I love Rebecca and she loves me."

"You move even faster with women than I do," Longarm said, shaking his head. "You just need to slow it down a little, Joe."

"We're meeting together again tomorrow night," Joe confessed. "It'll be our last night together on the train and we got to make the most of it."

"What about Rebecca's parents? How did she get away from them?"

"They fell asleep real early."

"Button up your pants and take a seat," Longarm told the kid. "It sounds like you're going to need all your strength and stamina tomorrow night."

"Well," Joe said, "it does take something out of a man, doesn't it?"

"It sure does," Longarm replied, yawning and then going back to sleep.

Chapter 7

Longarm stepped off the train in Reno, Nevada, and looked around for a few minutes noting the changes that the town had undergone since he'd last visited. It was clear that Reno had experienced a sharp growth spurt, and the main street was all filled in with hotels and other businesses. Down at the south end he could see the bridge that crossed the Truckee River and all the big cottonwood trees that shaded the fine riverside walk.

Joe Polk stepped off the train and grinned. "My gosh, this is sure a pretty town with those big mountains in the background. Kinda reminds me of a little Denver."

"Lot of similarities," Longarm said. "Reno started out as just a little jumping off point for people heading over the mountains to California during the gold rush. The big strike up on the Comstock Lode gave its economy a huge boost just like the strikes up in the Rockies did for Denver."

Joe nodded. "I sure am excited about—"

He was interrupted by Rebecca, who came flying off

the train to throw her arms around his neck and hug him tightly. "Joe, let's just run away right now!"

"What?"

"Let's run!"

Joe looked to Longarm, who just shrugged. And before he could think of anything else to say, Rebecca's father charged down the steps and grabbed Joe by the arm, shouting, "Get away from her! Let go of my daughter!"

"Well," Joe stammered, "she's got hold of *me*!"

Rebecca's father was a heavyset man, and he was so enraged that he grabbed his daughter, tore her away, and hurled her into the side of the train. Longarm and everyone else heard the crack as Rebecca's head struck the metal side of the passenger car, and they all gasped with shock as she crumpled unconscious beside the tracks.

"Oh my God!" Rebecca's mother screamed. "You've killed our baby!"

Longarm and Joe were the first to reach the unconscious girl. Rebecca was breathing, but blood was leaking from her nose, mouth, and ears, and that was a very bad sign.

Longarm scooped her up in his arms and shouted at the crowd who had just arrived and those that had come to greet them. "We need a doctor!"

A man in his forties rushed forward. "I'm a doctor. What happened!"

"She struck her head against the train," Longarm replied. "I think she's hurt pretty bad, Doc."

The doctor took one look at Rebecca and nodded. He took her pulse as Longarm cradled her in his arms. "We need to get her to my office right now!"

"Lead the way!"

"Oh, God, what have I done!" Rebecca's father wailed, throwing his hands to the sky.

"Damn you!" Joe shouted at the man. "I ought to beat the hell out of you right now!"

"Leave him be!" Longarm yelled. "Come along, Joe!"

The crowd at the train depot parted to make way for their rush to get into town and to the doctor's office. Longarm was running as hard as he could while carrying the girl, and she felt like a rag doll in his arms. He glanced down at her face, and her fair complexion was slightly bluish. He'd seen before men who had been struck with a pistol or had other types of head injuries, and he knew that this one was very bad.

"In here!" the doctor cried. "Bring her in and put her on that examining table!"

Joe crowded in close. There were tears streaming down his cheeks. "Is she dying?"

"I don't know," the doctor admitted. "And to be honest, there isn't much that I can do for the kind of head injury I'm seeing."

"But you must be able to do something!"

"I can keep her stabilized and I have some options. Mostly, I have to make sure that she doesn't swallow her tongue or aspirate and fill her lungs with vomit and suffocate."

Joe Polk looked as if he was about to pass out. "I'm going to marry her, Doc. As soon as I find work, we're getting married! She can't die. She's too young and . . ."

"Get him out of here," the doctor ordered. "Just wait outside. If we can keep this girl breathing, she stands a good chance, but I don't need hysterics right now."

Longarm grabbed Joe and forced him out of the room, closing the door behind them. "Calm down, Joe. This doctor seems like he knows a thing or two about medicine and isn't just some tooth puller. Let's just . . . just leave him to

what he does best, and you can pray or just keep Rebecca in your thoughts."

"I ain't usually a praying man," Joe said brokenly, "but I think I'll try to do it right now."

"That's a good idea," Longarm said. "You stay here while I go back to the train station and get our things. Rebecca's parents need to know where we went, and I'll bring them back here directly."

"Keep him away from me," Joe warned, wiping the tears from his face. "I'm just not sure that I can stop myself from killing him on sight."

"You can't do that," Longarm told the kid. "Her father loves her and he just lost his temper and did a very stupid thing. Joe, you have to know that he didn't mean to hurt his daughter."

"His time of taking care of Rebecca is gone and my time has come," Joe said. "And if he can't see that plain, I'll have to put him out of his blindness and stupidity."

Longarm laid a hand on Joe's shoulder. "If you mean it when you say you want to become a lawman, then you'll have to learn to use your head and do the right thing in times like this instead of blowing up and making matters even worse than they are. If . . . When Rebecca comes around . . . she won't want to find you in jail and her father either dead or beat up. She won't want that, Joe. So get a hold of yourself right now!"

Joe took a deep breath and nodded his head up and down. "You're right, Marshal. Rebecca has enough to handle without me adding to her misery pile."

"I'm glad that you see it clearly," Longarm said with relief. "Now, go get our things and bring back Rebecca's parents, without incident, mind you, because they're probably going clean out of their minds."

Joe hitched up his pants and headed for the door. "I sure never thought things were going to come to this," he said as he left.

"Me neither," Longarm said, starting to pace back and forth across the waiting room floor.

Ten minutes later, Joe Polk arrived hauling their belongings from the train and with Rebecca's distraught parents in tow. When Longarm looked at her father, he thought he was seeing a stranger. Rebecca's father had aged years in just minutes.

"I'll never forgive myself for this," he kept saying over and over. "What have I done? Oh, God, what have I *done!*"

"My name is Mrs. Mildred Butler," the mother said. "And this is Orville. My husband is a very good man and father. He's never struck Rebecca before in her life, and he doesn't know what overcame him back at the depot. As you can see, my husband is nearly out of his mind."

Longarm could see the suffering and anguish on their faces, and he felt sorry for Mildred, but he had very little sympathy for Orville Butler.

"If she dies, you could go to prison for murder," Longarm told the man, not caring if he did make Orville Butler feel even worse. "There is no excuse for what you did to your daughter today."

"I know," Butler whispered. "And as God is my judge, if Rebecca dies because of what I did, then I will gladly go to the gallows, because I wouldn't be able to live with myself."

"The doctor," Longarm said, softening his tone, "thinks that if he can keep your daughter alive for the next few hours, she has a good chance."

"But will her brain be damaged permanently!" Mildred Butler cried.

"I don't know," Longarm told the couple, "and I doubt if the doctor does either."

"If she lives," Joe Polk said, stepping right up close to Orville, "I'm going to marry her even if her brain is ruined. You understand that, Mr. Butler? You try to stop us again and I'll . . ."

"Easy," Longarm said, not wanting his young friend to say something that he would later regret.

"All right," Joe agreed. "But I want this man to know that Rebecca and I have pledged our hearts to each other, and we'll be married with or without his damned blessings!"

"Okay—" Orville choked. "I won't oppose that any longer if my daughter lives. I swear that I will give you my full blessing and a beautiful wedding and honeymoon together."

"I've no money and no prospects yet," Joe said, "but I'll hold you to your promise, and of that you can be sure."

Mildred Butler came over and hugged the young man. "We've been too harsh in our judgment of you, Joe. If our daughter has given you her heart, then there must be things inside you that we didn't see."

Joe blinked, not sure what to say to that.

The door opened and the doctor stepped out to join them. "Good news. The young woman's eyes opened and she spoke to me."

"Praise the Lord!" Mildred cried.

Longarm stepped back and let the three of them stampede inside the other room. He heard crying and more praising of the Lord, and he figured that everything was going to be all right after all.

Longarm waited another ten minutes before deciding to grab his bags and go get a hotel room.

"Marshal?"

He turned to see Joe filling the doorway with a smile on his tear-streaked face.

"Yeah?"

"She's going to be fine, and we're getting married tomorrow if she's strong enough to stand. You heard what her father said about that wedding and honeymoon."

"Yes, I did."

"So we'll hold it to him, right? I mean, it's only fair."

"It is," Longarm agreed. "But I thought you were going to wait until you had a steady job."

"What just happened made me realize that none of us knows when our time is up, so we shouldn't wait to do what we want to do most."

"And that would be marrying Rebecca, not get a lawman's badge?"

Joe Polk looked him square in the eyes. "I want and will have *both*."

"There's no doubt in my mind of that," Longarm said. "I'll be getting us a couple of rooms at the Riverfront Hotel just down by the Truckee. We can talk about things, if you want, over a nice dinner overlooking the river."

"I'd like that plenty," Joe said. "And maybe if Rebecca is feeling a whole lot better by then, she could come along?"

"Hell yes."

Joe was beaming as Longarm grabbed his bags and headed out the door.

Chapter 8

Longarm had waited until nine o'clock for Joe to come and join him, and when the chef announced last call for orders, he ordered a steak, medium rare. Moments later, Joe rushed into the Riverfront's restaurant and sat down at the table.

"Sorry I'm so late," he said apologetically.

"That's okay. I just ordered a steak. You want the same?"

"How much do they cost?"

"Never mind that," Longarm told the young man. "I'm buying in celebration of your wedding. How is Rebecca feeling?"

"A lot better, but the doctor says that she's not out of the woods yet."

"What does that mean?"

"Doc says that she has a bad concussion and that there's always a chance of a blood clot in the brain. If that happens, it could be fatal."

"Oh." Longarm signaled for the waiter and ordered another steak. "How do you like it?"

"Rare," Joe said. "But not too bloody."

"Make his the same as mine. And bring us a couple of whiskies and then when the steak arrives a good bottle of red wine. Not too expensive, but nothing cheap, either. Two glasses, please."

"We have an excellent selection of California wines. May I suggest a merlot?"

"How much?"

"Only two dollars, and it is outstanding."

"That will be fine."

"Very good, sir."

When the waiter was gone, Longarm leaned back in his chair. "Gonna be kinda tough on you and Rebecca's family waiting to see if she's going to make a full recovery."

"I know. Rebecca's father said the same thing. He also said that he wouldn't go back on his word, but he's real worried about how I'm going to support his daughter."

Longarm nodded. "Seems like a reasonable concern to me. What did you tell him?"

"He knows that I intend to be a lawman like you. But . . ."

"But what, Joe?"

"He says that I ought to be doing something until I can land a job with a badge, and I had to agree. I mean, what are we going to live on as a husband and wife and what happens if she gets pregnant?"

"You'd have to find something to make money at, Joe. And you'd have to take whatever you could to make money fast. A wife and a baby aren't cheap to support."

"No, I suppose not. I was thinking . . ." The waiter appeared with their whiskey in two generous tumblers. "What's it called?"

"Old Mellow."

Longarm took a sip. "It'll make a fellow mellow, that's for sure."

The waiter smiled and left, and then Joe took up the conversation where he'd left off. "Marshal, this afternoon I already went over to the Reno department, and they said they couldn't use me, so I was wondering if you thought I could get hired by either the Carson City or Virginia City law offices?"

"I don't know."

"Could I tag along with you tomorrow to Carson City and maybe you could put a good word in for me there?"

Longarm frowned. "I don't know who the marshal is in Carson City so . . ."

"But you being a federal marshal, I thought maybe . . ."

"Joe, I have something I need to tell you. I am out here as a special favor for a friend whose sister has been convicted of murdering her husband. This friend is a lawman . . . in fact . . . he is my boss and so I'm here on *unofficial* business."

"What does that mean?" Joe asked with confusion.

"It means that I left my badge in Denver and I'm just a private citizen like you."

"You have no federal authority?"

Longarm raised his glass of whiskey. "To better days, Joe. And to the speedy and complete recovery of your future wife."

They drank, and then Longarm knew that he had to make a further explanation for his young friend. "Joe, I'm on vacation and a personal mission. I suppose, if push came to shove, I could use my federal authority, but I'd have to have someone send a telegram to Denver confirming that I'm a United States marshal. And given the situation that I may face in Carson City, that could be a real complication."

"How do you mean?"

"I mean that I can probably help my friend's sister . . . if

I think she's innocent . . . better as an ordinary citizen . . . if things get dicey."

Joe was smart, and he figured it out quick enough. "What you're saying is that if you had to step over the legal line, you could do it easier and with fewer problems than if you were a federal marshal."

"Couldn't have put it better myself, Joe."

"I'd still like to go to Carson City with you. You've helped me a lot, and maybe there is some way that I can repay you the favor."

"You don't owe me a thing, Joe."

"Maybe not, but I'd like to see if you could use my help, and I will want to talk to the marshal in Carson City about a job."

"All right," Longarm said. "There is a stage that leaves here at nine tomorrow morning."

"How much would . . ."

"It's cheap. Only two dollars, and I'll buy you a round-trip ticket back here to Reno."

"That would be swell," Joe said. "You want to tell me what this woman is supposed to have done to her husband?"

"It's too gruesome to talk about at the end of a long day. I'll tell you when we get to Carson City tomorrow. Oh, but what about Rebecca?'

"Soon as we're done eating, I'll drop by and see her again and tell her our plans."

"I don't have a real *plan*, Joe. I'm just going to go to Carson City, visit the prison, and find out what I can."

"Prison has to hire guards," Joe mused. "Maybe if I can't start out as a deputy, I could get hired on at the prison."

"Prisons are tough, dangerous places to work. You ever been inside one?"

"Of course not. But I was in that Denver jail."

"Not the same. Nothing like prison. In jail you get tossed in mostly among thieves, drunks, brawlers, pick-pockets, and crooked gamblers. In prison . . . well, Joe, in prison you have a much more dangerous and hardened criminal population. There are men in prison who would cut their own mother's throat for a dollar."

"I expect that is true, but I need a job, and if it's a prison where I have to get my start in law enforcement, then by gawd I'll do it!"

Longarm nodded, but just the same he sure hoped that Joe would never have to work in a hellhole prison. The worst one he'd ever spent even a little time in was down in Yuma, Arizona Territory, but he sure had heard stories about other prisons nearly as infamous. And one of them was the Nevada State Prison in Carson City.

Chapter 9

The stagecoach ride from Reno to Carson City took them over a short but scenic wagon track. They saw many large, steaming pools of hot water south of Reno and then entered a beautiful valley flanked by the high Sierra Mountains to their west.

"What happened up there on those slopes?" Joe asked, craning his neck out the stage's window to look up at the denuded mountainside.

Longarm had a ready answer. "Well, Joe, during the peak mining years of the Comstock Lode, loggers almost wiped out the eastern slope of the Sierra pine forests in their need to supply millions of running feet of timbering for the deep mines."

"They sure did!"

Longarm pointed in the opposite and eastern direction. "That's Sun Mountain up there on the Comstock Lode, and you'll find almost no trees still standing there. The Sierras trap the moisture, and so the country just to the east is very dry. What trees that existed before the gold and silver rush were either cut down for square-set timber-

ing in the mines or they were used as firewood in the mining camps."

"It looks like they were mostly piñon and juniper trees
and not many of them are left," Joe said.

"That's right. On one side of this Washoe Valley, the
Sierras are green and high. On the other side you have a
lot of barren rock and not much of any vegetation, because
it hardly ever rains out there in the summer. I always found
it interesting that only this valley separates such very
different-looking landscapes."

"I should say!" Joe shook his head and asked, "What's
Carson City look like?"

Longarm considered the question a moment before answering. "In my estimation it's not as handsome as Reno,
but it's still a fine little town. It's supported mostly by
ranching in the foothills of the Sierras and in valleys like
this that we're passing through. A little south of Carson
City is a very beautiful valley and a strictly Mormon settle-
ment said to be the oldest in Nevada, and it's named
Genoa."

"What's the prison in Carson City look like?"

"Tall stone walls. Pretty solemn-looking, Joe."

"Aren't *all* prisons?" a well-dressed fellow passenger
smugly asked.

"I guess they are," Longarm said. "Especially if you
happen to be an inmate."

"They're going to hang a woman in a week or two at
the prison," the man's wife offered, not making any attempt to hide her excitement. "My husband and I will be
invited guests, and it'll be my first hanging!"

"And how did you gain that privilege?" Longarm asked.

She beamed at her husband. "Mr. Harry Bodkin helped
get her the death sentence. My husband is one of the finest
and most respected prosecutors in Nevada."

"How wonderful," Longarm said dryly. "Was it a pretty open-and-shut case, Lawyer Bodkin?"

"Well, no murder trial is easy," the attorney said with a cavalier flick of his hand. "But I have been rather successful in my pursuit of justice, and you had better believe that there was an immense amount of publicity because of the heinous nature of the murder."

"What does that mean?" Joe blurted.

"Young man, it means that the woman who is going to be executed is nothing less than a monster. Surely you've heard of the circumstances. The trial was all that people talked about."

"We just arrived from Denver."

"Well then, allow me to enlighten you," Bodkin said. "This . . . this monster murdered her husband by setting him on fire while he was asleep in his own bed!"

Joe's jaw dropped, and he shot a glance sideways toward Longarm, who kept his focus on the outside scenery. Joe recovered quickly. "If the woman burned her husband in bed, then why didn't he jump up and try to save himself?"

"Good question, young man," Harry answered. "And the answer that was presented and the jury saw to be true is quite straightforward. The woman no doubt drugged her husband or plied him with too much liquor, then tied him up when he was incapacitated and poured kerosene over his body to light him up like a torch."

"My gawd," Joe exclaimed. "That's *awful*!"

"Oh," the woman said, looking a trifle faint, "it was an act of such depravity and lack of humanity that it nearly boggles the mind! The murderess on death row really deserves to be *strangled*, not hanged."

"And there is a difference?" Joe asked.

"Big difference," Bodkin solemnly replied. "Strangling takes a few minutes, and you can only try and imagine

how horrible it must be for the victim. But a hanging, properly executed, results in an almost instantaneous death. Breaks the neck and that's the end, except that the person's body kicks and jerks around on the end of the rope in a death dance."

"A death dance?"

"Yes, quite a spectacle to watch, which is why my wife is quite excited. A hanging is something that everyone who has ever thought of killing another human being ought to see. It really doesn't take more than a few minutes, but is highly entertaining and satisfying to watch."

"Let's talk about something else," Longarm said shortly, his anger coming to the surface.

"What's the matter?" Bodkin asked with surprise and a little amusement. "You're a big, strong- looking man, but are you squeamish?"

"No," Longarm snapped, "but I think given that it's a fine day and this is handsome country, we ought to think and talk about pleasanter things than someone kicking and jerking at the end of a rope. Especially if that someone is a woman."

"Woman or man, the law applies to both in equal fashion," Harry lectured. "If a woman murders someone, she should be shown no favors or given any special considerations."

Longarm jabbed his finger into Harry's chest. "I said I was tired of hearing this talk! So do you mind, or do I need to make my point a little more forcibly?"

Harry stared into Longarm's eyes and saw the threat and the danger. "Well," he stammered, trying to save face. "Your companion seemed curious about hangings, and so I thought to enlighten him."

"Enlighten someone else later," Longarm growled.

"Good gracious!" the man's wife exclaimed, huffing

with indignation. "You sure are a surly and combative fellow."

"Lady, if you and husband don't shut up and give me some peace, then you have no idea how combative things will get."

Joe blinked with surprise. It was the first time that he had seen Marshal Custis Long become upset and actually threaten someone, and it was pretty scary. He wondered if that was a part of being a lawman that you had to have inside to be effective.

"And do you see that ridge up ahead?" Longarm asked, changing the subject.

Joe leaned out the window. "Yep."

"Just beyond that ridge is Carson City."

"Be good to get there," Joe said, ducking back inside and then losing himself in thoughts about why Custis Long had come so far to try to help a woman who would drug, bind, and callously burn her husband to death. Someone who could do something that horrible to another person sure as hell *did* deserve to do a slow, strangling dance of death.

Chapter 10

After departing the stagecoach, Longarm and Joe checked into the Ormsby House and had an excellent lunch. Afterward, Longarm was very eager to get over to the territorial prison and meet Nellie, if that was possible. He had obtained a letter from Marshal Billy Vail requesting that visiting privileges be allowed and stating that Longarm was a deputy United States marshal on a *personal* assignment and that any consideration between fellow lawmen would be very much appreciated.

"Joe, I'm going to find someone that will drive me out to the prison, which is about a mile out of town. What are you going to do?"

"I'll pay a visit to the town marshal and see if I can hire on with him."

"Good luck."

"Sure would appreciate it if you could go there with me," Joe said as Longarm was turning to leave. "A good word from a famous federal marshal like you would be a big help."

"I doubt that very much."

"It would only take ten or fifteen minutes," Joe argued. "I sure do need a job, so I can marry and support Rebecca."

The kid looked so desperate that Longarm couldn't find it in his heart to refuse the request. "All right, let's go meet the marshal, which I was planning to do when I returned from the prison anyway."

"Gee, thanks!"

"Joe, you might want to wipe the mustard off your chin."

"Oh, you bet."

After leaving the restaurant and stopping at the hotel's registration desk, Longarm asked the clerk who the town marshal was and was told that the man's name was Marshal Dean Orton.

"Has he been the law in Carson City for a while?"

"About two years. Marshal before him was ambushed and killed chasing a horse thief. But the horse thief was captured a few days later and hanged right out there on the courthouse plaza."

"I'm glad that justice was served, but it sure didn't do much good for the dead marshal, did it?" Longarm said. He looked at Joe to make sure that the kid was listening. He wanted Joe to understand that being a lawman, even in a fine and relatively stable town like this, could be a fatal occupation.

"No, it didn't help our dead marshal, but we gave him one helluva fine funeral and felt a lot better about it after watching the hanging. Dean Orton was a deputy before his boss got killed, and they just promoted him up to being the new town marshal."

"How many deputies does Marshal Orton have in his office?" Joe asked.

"Two. Some folks say that they are a little rough on drunks and that they aren't above accepting favors from

businesses and whores when offered, but by and large, they seem to be doin' their jobs."

"Sounds to me like they're shaking down the townspeople," Longarm opined.

The clerk grinned, showing a large pair of buckteeth. "Yeah, but don't let them know I agreed with you. One of the deputies, Big Buck Toler, was real pushy about getting free rides on all the whores. But you know what?"

"What?" Joe asked.

"Buck came down with the French disease, and he ain't lookin' too healthy or happy these days. His wife left him and took his kids to Sacramento to live with her parents. Buck has sworn that if he ever learns for sure which whore gave him the French disease, he'll kill her with his bare hands. Trouble is, he was with most every one of the whores in Carson City and nobody is gonna let Buck him kill 'em all."

"He sounds like he deserves what he got," Longarm said.

"Sure he does! Rumor around town is that Deputy Buck Toler is in such bad medical straits that two town doctors said he needed to go to San Francisco and get a surgeon to cut his cock off."

The clerk giggled into his bony hands. He was a tall, thin fellow with a hooked nose. "Buck said that he'd rather die than be a cockless son of a bitch for the rest of his life. I hear that he's been dippin' his dick in everything from whiskey to axle grease to kerosene hoping they would give him a cure, but nothing has worked so far."

Longarm had heard more about Deputy Buck Toler than he wanted to. "Where is the marshal's office?

"Just two blocks west and you'll see it right across from the courthouse. Little sandstone building."

"Much obliged," Longarm told the man.

"This Deputy Buck Toler sounds like he might be on the way out of his job," Joe said hopefully as they marched down the street.

"Might be."

"Then that means that Marshal Orton would be looking to replace him."

"That's possible."

"Maybe I'm finally gonna get to wear a badge."

"Don't get your hopes up too high," Longarm warned. "If the town marshal is letting his deputies put the squeeze on businesses and whores, he can't be much of a marshal."

"I suppose that's true. But . . ."

"Joe, just let me size things up before you ask for a job in Carson City. Hiring on with a bad bunch sure as hell isn't how you want to start out your career as a lawman. You do that, and the next thing you know . . . you'll be expected to go along with doing things that aren't right. After that happens, you'll never be worthy of wearing a badge and holding up the oath of your office again."

"Sounds like you've seen it happen a time or two."

"I have," Longarm answered. "And it always ruins a good man."

They found the marshal's office and entered after knocking. The moment they stepped inside, Longarm had a bad feeling. The marshal's office was filthy and littered with the leavings of meals eaten long past as well as cigarette and cigar butts. Longarm was of the belief that if a man was too lazy or unprincipled to keep his own nest clean and orderly, then he was probably equally unprincipled in all his dealings and practices.

"What can I do for you fellas?" asked a chubby-cheeked man in his thirties with a long handlebar mustache and a gun on each hip, without the favor of a greeting or a smile.

"Are you Marshal Orton?"

"I am, and who might you fellas be?"

"I'm Custis Long and this is my friend Joe Polk. We've just arrived from Denver."

"Never been there and don't care to see it," Orton said. "Big cities are all filled with people trying to cheat or steal from other people."

"Denver is a good town," Longarm said defensively. "Safe, clean, and without a lot of lawlessness."

"I don't believe that for one damned minute," Orton said, looking over at a very large man with a full beard and deep-set little eyes. "Do you, Buck?"

"Nope."

Longarm studied Deputy Buck Toler, who was also sitting at a desk. He had to bite his tongue not to make a remark about the French disease, so he turned his attention back to the marshal.

"I've come to learn something about Mrs. Nellie Bolton."

"Ha!" Buck Toler roared. "You've come all the way from Denver to learn about a woman about to hang?"

"That's right."

Marshal Orton scowled. "Are you some kind of a news reporter or magazine feller?"

"Nope."

"Writin' a book on evil women that got hanged?"

"Nope."

"Well then why in hell do you want to learn about that woman?" Orton demanded.

"I have my reasons."

Both of the lawmen glared at Longarm and then at Joe. Orton broke the silence. "We got nothing to say about that murderin' bitch except that she's going to get what she deserves. If you want to find out about her and what she

did to her poor husband, there are men in every saloon in town that will tell you all kinds of stories for the price of a glass of whiskey or beer. Some of what they tell you might even be true."

Buck thought that was funny and laughed. Longarm didn't think it was in the least bit funny and decided that it was pointless to try and treat this pair with any kind of professional respect.

"Marshal, this office isn't fit for pigs."

Orton rolled out of his chair, looking insulted. "What did you just say?"

"You heard me right. You ought to be ashamed for being such a slovenly hog. And Buck, I hope the surgeon does cut off your diseased dick, because you aren't worthy to stick it in even the ugliest of whores."

Buck also came out of his chair, and started toward Longarm with menace in his dark eyes. "Nobody talks to me or Marshal Orton like that and . . ."

Longarm stood his ground and so did Joe. Orton yelled at Buck to hold up, but it didn't register. Buck was as tall as Longarm and heavier, but he looked soft and his face was a sickly, pasty-white with a yellowish cast, probably the effects of his venereal disease.

Buck shoved Longarm hard enough in the chest to push him back a step, and then he cocked his big fist. Longarm coolly shot an uppercut to the man's belly, and when Buck doubled over, he slammed a right cross to his heavy jaw, sending him cartwheeling over an empty desk to crash on the floor.

"I'm waiting for you," Longarm said softly. "Come on, Buck, let's see what else you got."

Marshal Orton lunged for a rifle that was leaning up against a nearby desk. Joe Polk's hand flashed down to the gun on his hip and Orton froze, face turning pale.

"Who the hell are you guys! Gawdamn you, this is my office and *I'm* the law in this town!"

Longarm ignored the question. "Joe, do you really think you want to be a part of this?"

"Nope."

"Then let's get out of this stinking shit hole of an office and get some fresh air."

Buck grabbed a desk and hauled himself unsteadily to his feet. "You bit off a whole lot more than you can chew . . . *both* of you. This isn't going to pass."

"Damn right it isn't!" Marshal Orton hissed. "I'll be getting a warrant for your arrest. Big Man, you are going to prison for this, and then you can see that murdering bitch face-to-face."

"I wouldn't bet on that," Longarm told the furious marshal. "Joe?"

They backed out of the office and slammed the door. After walking a few blocks, Longarm stopped and turned to Joe. "Maybe it would be a good idea if you had a look at Virginia City on the Comstock Lode for a few days. Might find a job there."

"I think that would be a fine idea," Joe agreed. "What about you?"

"I don't know yet," Longarm said honestly. "If at all possible, I'm going to visit Nellie Bolton at the prison, and after that I'll decide what I should do."

Joe frowned. "I just have to ask you something before we go our separate ways."

"Go ahead."

"Well," Joe said, "if Naughty Nellie Bolton is guilty as charged, are you still going to . . ."

"Try to break her out of the territorial prison?"

"Yeah."

Longarm shook his head. "I'll be able to tell in a very

short time if she really murdered her husband or not. If
she did, she'll hang, and I won't give her a second thought."

"But if you decide . . . despite what a judge and jury
decided . . . that she's innocent?"

"If that happens, you don't want to know about it,"
Longarm told his young friend. "Here," he said, giving the
kid some money. "It's the last I'm forking over to you, so
use it wisely. Get a job tomorrow come hell or high water."

"I will," Joe promised. "I'll go up to Virginia City and
take whatever I can find."

"Right," Longarm said. "And before I leave Nevada,
I'll look you and Rebecca up if I can."

"I want you to be my best man at the wedding," Joe said
earnestly. "I sure don't have or want anyone else standing
at my side when I take the marriage vows."

"I'm flattered, but let's just see what happens in the next
week or two."

"Don't let that marshal and his mean deputy catch you
by surprise," Joe warned.

"I'll give you the very same advice," Longarm replied
as he left the young man and hailed a buggy for hire that
was waiting by the courthouse.

"Take me to prison!" Longarm ordered.

The driver smiled. "Mister, I hope you ain't goin' there
to stay long."

It was obviously a well-worn local joke, but Longarm
was in no mood to laugh, and the remark did not warrant
a reply.

Chapter 11

"There she is," the driver said. "Pretty ugly, huh?"

Longarm stared up at the high stone walls, and his eyes went directly to the silent and solitary armed guard tower at each corner of the huge enclosure. He had been inside a lot of prisons, often to deliver prisoners or question them regarding unsolved federal cases assigned to him by Marshal Billy Vail, and he still found them intimidating. There was just something when they closed the iron gate behind a man that made a shiver go up and down his spine.

The guard at this iron gate was a large man with muttonchop whiskers and a shotgun in his beefy hands. "State your business."

"I'm come to visit one of your female inmates."

"Come back on Saturday between one and four. That's our visiting hours."

Through the heavy gate bars Longarm could see male inmates moving about the yard followed by armed guards. "I need to see Nellie Bolton."

"She's in maximum lockup, so it won't do you any good

to come back. Nobody in maximum lockup gets to see visitors."

"In that case I'd like to see your warden."

"No."

Longarm took a deep breath. Out of his inside vest pocket he pulled Billy's letter and silently handed it over to the guard. "Before you say anything more, you might want to read that."

The guard glanced down at the letter and saw the federal seal on the letterhead. "What's this about?"

"I'm a United States marshal working out of Denver, and I am here on an investigation that requires me to see Mrs. Bolton. It's a matter of the highest importance."

The guard frowned and his brow furrowed as he debated the implications of this new information. No doubt his foremost concern was his job security. He didn't know how important the man before him was, and he didn't want to know. All he wanted was for the visitor to go away.

Longarm was good at reading people, and he saw the objection even before it was spoken from the guard's mouth. "If I have to," he said, "I can go right to the top in Washington, D.C., but I doubt that your warden would want that to happen. He might even be pretty damned mad if it happened."

The guard's resistance broke. "Okay. You gotta leave your sidearm here at the gate along with any other weapons that you're carrying."

Longarm had a double-barreled derringer that was attached to his watch fob, and he momentarily considered trying to conceal that weapon and go in with at least one gun. However, after a moment's reflection, he decided that would be a foolish risk. If he started off breaking the prison rules and it was discovered, he would be the one in deep trouble.

"I have this derringer," he said, removing it along with his watch.

"Clever," the guard said with grudging admiration. "So when you are in a bad fix, you pretend to look at your watch and out comes the derringer."

"That's right. It has saved my bacon more than one time."

"I want to see your badge."

"I lost it on the way out from Denver."

"You lost it?" the guard asked.

"All right," Longarm said, trying his best to look embarrassed. "It was stolen while I was sleeping on the train, along with some other things."

The guard actually chuckled. "A thief stole your federal officer's badge?"

"Yeah," Longarm said. "But I'd rather you didn't tell the world about it."

The guard's chuckle turned into laughter. "That's rich!" he guffawed. "Someone stole your badge! Jaysus! They could pin it on and do all kinds of mischief."

"Yeah, I know. First time it ever happened, and I'll catch hell for it when I get back to Denver. That's another reason why I just have to see Nellie Bolton. It cost my department a lot of money to send me clear out here, and then I lose my badge. It's going to really go hard on me if I come up empty here."

"Sounds like you're in a world of shit right now, Marshal. But then, I'll bet that you make twice the money I do and don't have to put up with the daily bullshit they hand out here."

"It's a job," Longarm said. "Beats swamping out saloons or forking horse shit all day."

"Yeah, it does," the guard agreed. "All right. Follow me to the warden's office after I get a replacement here.

He may see you and he may not. Depends on how cheerful he's feeling today."

"I don't see how anybody could feel cheerful inside this place, even if they do get to leave at the end of their shift."

"You got that right." The guard turned back toward the yard. "Ernie! I need you to stand in for me."

Ernie was also a large man and he emerged out of the guard shack with the same kind of shotgun in his hands.

"This is a federal marshal from Denver and he's here to see Nellie Bolton."

"Yeah, and I'm here to visit the gawdamn tooth fairy," Ernie said cryptically.

"No," the guard argued. "This sounds legitimate and important, so I'm going to take him inside to the warden. You need to do the gate until I come back."

Ernie didn't look happy about becoming a gate guard. Longarm figured the man had probably been dozing in the guard shack or reading some lurid novel.

"Don't take all day," Ernie drawled. "And don't piss the warden off by bringing him somebody that he doesn't need to see."

"He'll be glad that he saw me," Longarm said.

"That your derringer attached to the watch and chain?"

"Yeah."

"Pretty clever."

Longarm nodded and followed the guard through the gate. The moment he heard the metallic clang of the gate behind him, he felt that icy tingle go up his spine. He was aware that dozens of eyes were instantly on him as they walked the short distance across a hard-packed dirt yard to another stone building.

"How many inmates are here?" Longarm asked.

"About sixty right now. We get the worst of the worst. You can't let your guard down for even a minute or you'll

get your throat cut or a knife stuck between your ribs. Lost two guards already this year."

"That's tough."

"Yeah," the guard said, knocking loudly on the door and shouting, "John Beal here! Permission to enter!"

Someone inside peered through a narrow slit in the steel door, saw Beal, and opened the door.

"This is a federal marshal from Denver, and he says that he has come on important federal business and needs to see Warden Slingerland."

"Not a good day."

"No day here is a good day," Beal replied. "Tell the warden that this sounds important."

The man disappeared up the hall, heels ringing loudly on the stone, while Longarm and Beal waited. The hall was poorly lit, low, and narrow. No rugs, no chairs or pictures, just more stone.

"What's the warden's name?"

"James S. Slingerland. He's a hard man but fair. He was appointed by the governor."

Longarm leaned up against the stone wall and closed his eyes trying to think what he was going to say that would get him permission to visit Nellie. And even if he did, so what? If she was guilty, she would soon hang. If she was somehow not guilty, then what was he to do about it? Breaking her out of this place would be impossible. Just standing here in this cold, hard corridor of stone was making him realize that he was on a fool's errand. And perhaps Billy Vail had known that all along but had just needed to make one futile effort to redeem something long lost. Maybe that was all that Longarm was here for . . . to salve Billy's conscience and free him of any possible doubts about his sister.

Ten minutes . . . or it might have been twenty minutes

passed without a word spoken between him and the guard. Finally, Beal asked, "How hard is it to get a job as a federal marshal?"

Longarm shrugged. "I don't know. I've been one for several years now."

"You get paid good, don't you." It wasn't a question, and there was some resentment in Beal's voice.

"I guess that depends on what you think is good pay."

"Anything over sixty a month."

"Then I'm paid well."

"I make forty-eight dollars and work six days a week ten hours a day, and you don't even want to know the names I get called."

"Maybe you should look for another job."

"Naw. I thought about that plenty at first. Then I found out that about the only job I could get was down in the mines or maybe some logging work that don't pay much and is just as dangerous. A man has to feed his family, and I manage to do that and still have enough left over to buy a bottle of bad whiskey every payday. I like to hunt on my days off."

"Hunt what?"

Beal shrugged his sloping shoulders. "I hunt jackrabbits mostly. They're stringy bastards and sometimes wormy, but if you boil them and know the right seasonings, they're tolerable. I hunt deer and elk in the fall. Ducks too. Once in a while I'll pop a coyote, skin it, and sell the pelt for a couple of dollars. There are mountain lions hereabouts, but they're hard to hunt unless you got a pack of good dogs. So mostly, I shoot gawdamn jackrabbits and sometimes a cottontail if I get lucky."

"Sounds okay."

"It's a life," Beal said grudgingly. "I've been stabbed twice, and once an inmate managed to get a belt around my neck and I nearly got strangled. But I'm pretty tough

and strong, so the inmates mostly leave me alone. They call me names, but I have my little ways of getting back at them. Everything in here is a game, you know."

"A game?"

"Yeah," Beal said. "It's like a poker game, and everyone is at the table and has a card up their sleeve. I've been here seven years and I've learned the game well. But some of the new guys that get hired here . . . well, they're walking on real thin ice and some fall through."

Longarm listened with interest. Beal was the first prison guard that had ever really opened up to him about his job. Nothing the man was saying came as a big surprise, but Longarm now had a better appreciation of how fortunate he was to be a deputy marshal and not a prison guard.

A door way down at the end of the corridor opened, and the guard emerged again to shout, "Bring him on down, Beal!"

"Will do."

They walked down the hallway and entered an office waiting room. There were two chairs, but Longarm stayed on his feet. The guard said, "Warden Slingerland will see you in five minutes."

"Thank you."

"Don't call him Mr. Slingerland," Beal whispered. "Just call him Warden."

"Okay."

"And don't ask him nothing about his family or what kind of a day he's having or any of that usual bullshit, or he gets mad. Just come right to the point and you'll have a chance. Oh, and one other thing," Beal added.

"What's that?"

"If what you told me was bullshit and the warden calls me into that office to climb up my fat ass, then I'll find a way to get even."

Longarm nodded. He understood, and he believed that Beal was a hard and tough man, but that was only inside these prison walls. Outside, well, if he came at Longarm, the man wouldn't stand a chance.

"Come on in now," the other guard said in a terse voice. "Warden will see you. Remove your hat first."

Longarm removed his gray hat with the flat brim and stepped inside. Warden Slingerland was seated behind a big desk shuffling paperwork. When he looked up, Longarm smiled, but Slingerland didn't return the smile.

"State your business, sir."

Longarm took a deep breath, and then he began to try to spin a tale that would finally allow him to stand face-to-face with Naughty Nellie Bolton . . . a convicted cold-blooded murderess who had only a short time to live before she did the dance of death.

Chapter 12

"I'm a deputy United States marshal from the Denver office, and I've come to speak with Mrs. Nellie Bolton about the murder that she has been convicted of and for which she has been sentenced to hang."

Warden Slingerland eyed Longarm closely for a moment before speaking. "My guard said that there was something of a *federal* involvement?"

"That's right, Nellie Bolton is my boss's sister and he wants to make sure she's really guilty," Longarm explained, deciding to just spell it out and let the chips fall where they may.

"That's *it*?" the warden asked with amazement. "You came all the way from Denver just because she's related to your boss?"

"That's it, but I'm not being paid to do this and I'm on vacation time."

Slingerland leaned back in his chair. "Sit down, Marshal."

Longarm took a seat.

"I can't believe that you are here for that reason alone."

Longarm shrugged. "My boss says that his sister was called 'Naughty Nellie' when they were kids, but that she really doesn't have it in her to murder anyone."

"How long has it been since your boss has seen his sister?"

"Many years."

"People can change dramatically over a period of time." Warden Slingerland frowned. "The evidence against Mrs. Bolton seemed pretty clear-cut to almost everyone."

"Did Mrs. Bolton ever admit to the murder of her husband?"

"No, and . . ."

Longarm pounced on the hesitation in the warden's voice. "And what, Warden?"

"Well, her late husband, John Bolton, was a rich and successful man up on the Comstock Lode. But he was a womanizer even at his advanced age, and over the years he'd ruined a lot of people financially and in other ways. The defense attorney did his best to bring that out, but he was young and inexperienced, while the prosecuting attorney was exactly the opposite."

"I met the lead prosecutor, Attorney Orville Butler."

"Orville has a nice family, but they've been through some very difficult times, and part of that was directly because of John Bolton."

"Is that right?"

"Yes. Orville Butler had a successful practice up in Virginia City, and he sometimes represented Mr. Bolton in some large monetary settlements."

"He never mentioned that to me."

"Not surprising," the warden said. "They had a terrible falling out over matters which were never made public. All that is known is that Orville Butler, his wife Mildred, and their daughter Rebecca were evicted from their home

on the Comstock Lode and sent packing without so much as their household furnishings."

"So Attorney Butler must have taken a great deal of satisfaction in the murder case and Nellie Bolton's murder conviction."

"Oh, he most certainly did. That conviction put his name on the map again, so to speak. Last I've heard, he's doing very well because of his successful prosecution."

"That's interesting."

"Yes it is, but hating a man and his wife who was charged with murdering him is not grounds for dismissal from the case, and I heard that Orville was tireless in his desire to see Nellie hanged."

"You would have thought," Longarm mused aloud, "that if he hated John Bolton so much, he would have preferred to see the man's wife go *free*."

"I would think so, but one can only speculate as to people's secrets and dark motives. And there is something else I should tell you."

"I'm listening."

"There were people who stood to gain a great deal from the death of Mr. Bolton, and I don't mean just financially."

"You mean those whom he cheated in business dealings and who hated his guts."

"Exactly. John Bolton was quite the lecher. He seduced several young women and ruined their marriages and lives. One pathetic creature actually committed suicide over the scandal."

"But despite his unsavory history, the jury still found Mrs. Bolton guilty and sentenced her to hang."

"True. And, to be honest, this hanging is one that really troubles me, although like you I'm sworn to uphold the law and my duty. But unlike many, I'll not be celebrating the occasion."

"Can I visit her?"

Warden Slingerland steepled his fingers and studied Longarm. "What possible good would come of it?"

"If I'm swayed to believe she might be innocent, I'd make sure that the conviction was appealed and try to see that she was retried."

"There is very little time and it would be expensive. Perhaps even impossible."

Longarm was dogged in his determination. He'd come too far to walk away now. "I'd still very much like to see Nellie Bolton."

"All right. I'll have her brought to us in chains from the small cell block where we keep our rare women inmates."

"Will you allow me to speak to her privately?"

"No," Slingerland decided with an adamant shake of his head. "If Mrs. Bolton has something to say in her behalf that was not already brought out in the courtroom, I'd be most interested in hearing it."

Longarm could see that the man was not going to change his mind on this point, so he nodded. "Thank you."

Fifteen minutes later, manacled both hand and foot, Nellie Bolton was prodded through the doorway. She had dark circles under her eyes and her black hair was in disarray, but she was still quite attractive in a sullen sort of way. She stood only a few inches over five feet tall and she was thin, almost frail-looking, with a sallow complexion. She stared right at Longarm, and he could read no dislike, friendliness, or curiosity in her brown eyes.

"Mrs. Bolton, this is a deputy marshal who was sent here from Denver by your brother to see you. Will you speak to him?"

"Billy sent you?" she asked, suddenly coming alive. "My brother?"

"That's right."

"How is he?"

"He is very well. I work for him and he is in good health and has a fine career and family."

"I'm glad to hear that," Nellie said. "Billy always was a good and obedient boy who minded his manners and studied hard in school. But as for him sending you all the way out here . . . well, what good would anything I have to say do me now? So why the hell did you really come?"

Longarm took a deep breath. "I came to visit you because Billy said that even though you had some violence in you, he knows you have a good heart, and although you were tough, he doesn't really think you did this."

Something in Nellie's eyes softened just a little. She swallowed hard. "What else did Billy say?"

"He said you loved underdogs and would fight to the death to protect helpless animals."

A tear slid from the corner of her eye, and Nellie rudely brushed it away with her sleeve, chains whispering.

"Nellie," Longarm said, "your brother just wanted me to hear you say that you are innocent."

She looked away for a moment and then lifted her chin. "All right, Marshal whatever your name is, I'm completely innocent, but nobody gives a good gawdamn."

"Did you tell the judge or the jury you were innocent?" Longarm asked.

"Sure. And it didn't matter. I was tried and sentenced the moment I was arrested up in Virginia City. I knew that I was a walking dead person, and so I didn't see much point in trying to defend myself, and it was obvious that my defense attorney didn't either."

"Words are cheap," Slingerland interrupted. "*Evidence* is what counts in a courtroom."

"Yeah, and it was all rigged against me," Nellie whispered. "I was the obvious patsy, and it is I who will drop through the trapdoor on your gallows."

Longarm came out of his chair and moved closer to Nellie. "Billy would want me to help you if I believe you're innocent."

"This is not something that my brother can undo," Nellie said. "Not unless he's the governor of this territory and grants me a full pardon."

"Who can I talk to about your defense?" Longarm said urgently.

"My court-appointed defense attorney was Matt Kelly. But the one that really knows what happened is Stella."

"Stella?"

"That's right. Stella, who owns and manages the Bucket of Blood Saloon up in Virginia City. She knows who set me up for this murder . . . but she's not going to spill her guts to a lawman and end up getting her throat cut."

"We'll see about that."

"Lawman," Nellie said quietly, "you seem like a good and well-meaning person, and I am grateful that Billy believes that I couldn't have committed the murder. But, if you get involved, it'll be a waste of your time and my brother's money."

"Like I told the warden, I'm on vacation and as for money . . . well, I've very little, and Billy probably doesn't have a whole lot, either. But I've come this far and I'll not quit until I have some facts."

"You'd better hurry then," Nellie said, "because a hanging doesn't wait for any man or woman."

"I know," Longarm said.

"Guard," Warden Slingerland said, "take Mrs. Bolton back to her cell."

"Yes, sir."

When they were alone, Slingerland asked, "What do you make of that?"

"She sounded sincere."

"They all do," the warden told him.

"Let me ask you a question, Warden. Why do I get the feeling that you also think that Nellie Bolton might be innocent?"

"Good question. I've only carried out five hangings in my time here as warden, but each one took a piece out of my soul. And hanging a woman that I think was poorly represented and very well may have been framed is going to take the largest piece of all."

"I see."

"Yes, I think you do," Warden Slingerland offered. "And if you can find anything concrete . . . something that really will influence the court . . . I will do what I can to obtain a stay of execution pending a new and *fair* trial for Mrs. Bolton."

"Thank you, Warden."

"You don't have much time. I think you'd better get up to Virginia City. Perhaps the local marshal can . . ."

"Uh . . ." Longarm hedged, not wanting to get into his altercation with the local authorities, "I like to work alone."

"Just as well, I suppose," the warden said. "Our marshal is inept and his deputies are corrupt."

"It sounds like I may need to go up to Virginia City and find this Stella person who runs the Bucket of Blood Saloon."

"Be cautious and discreet," the warden advised. "Virginia City doesn't even have a town marshal anymore

now that the mines are shutting down and money is tight. Also, the people up there are devious and desperate. If they learn that you are a federal marshal, no one will offer you any information or help."

"I understand." Longarm started to leave. "Oh, by the way. I have a young friend who is looking to get into law enforcement work. I was wondering if . . ."

"If he could work here?"

"Yeah."

Warden Slingerland shook his head. "I'd be willing to interview him on your recommendation, but you know that prison work is difficult and dangerous."

"All lawmen constantly face difficult and dangerous situations."

"Not Carson City's lawmen."

"I concede your point."

"If your young friend is looking for a job tell him to come here and ask to see me. What is his name?"

"Joe Polk."

"And he's of sound mind and body? Has an honest heart and is intelligent and not easily discouraged?"

"Yes, Joe is all that and more. Also, and this may not be a favor in your eyes, Warden, he is going to marry Attorney Orville Butler's daughter Rebecca."

The warden grinned. "I've met the girl a time or two and thought that she would have aimed a little higher than being married to a prison guard."

"She . . . she loves him, and if you meet Joe, you'll understand why. He's handsome and charming."

"Hardly good attributes for becoming a prison guard."

"I agree, but he needs a job right away."

"Tell him to come to the gate and to tell the guard there that I have agreed to see him immediately."

"Thanks, Warden."

"You can thank me by getting Nellie Bolton a reprieve, so that I don't have to stand and watch her swing from a hangman's rope, wondering if she really was innocent and if the real killer of her husband is going free."

"I'll do my best."

"I'm sure that you will."

Longarm left then, and when he stepped through the iron gate of the Carson City Territorial Prison, he took a deep breath of clean, fresh air.

Chapter 13

Longarm boarded the V&T Railroad that chugged east out of Carson City into the desert and then struggled up the mountains onto the Comstock Lode. It was a barren landscape, but the train ride offered impressive vistas. What struck Longarm the most was all the abandoned mines evidenced by their piles of mine tailings. Longarm had heard that all the small, independent miners had pretty much abandoned their claims, and those that were fortunate now had jobs with the big mining operations working pockets of gold and silver hundreds of feet below the surface.

When he arrived at the train depot, he climbed the hill up to C Street and headed directly for the Bucket of Blood Saloon, which was in a large building and had an impressive mahogany bar and a view toward the eastern high desert that was unsurpassed.

Longarm hadn't visited the Bucket of Blood in the last few years, but he was pleased to see that it seemed to be doing a good business even in the early evening. Miners were just getting off shift, the piano player was pounding

his ivory keys, and there was a lot of laughter and boister-
ous talk.

"I'd like to see Stella," he told the bartender after or-
dering a beer.

"What for?"

"My business and none of your own."

"Ain't good enough. Stella is a busy woman and—"

Longarm reached across the bar, grabbed the bartender
by his starched shirtfront, and yanked him up on his toes.
"I'm a busy man and I want to see her. Is she working in
one of the back rooms?"

The bartender nodded and pointed toward a door.

"Thanks," Longarm said, taking his beer with him.

He knocked and a woman called, "I'm working. Go
away!"

Longarm pushed open the door and stepped inside,
closing it behind him. Stella was a buxom blonde in her
early thirties, attractive and all business. "Who the hell are
you?"

"I'm a friend of Nellie Bolton and we need to talk
about her."

"Get lost."

"I'm also a United States marshal."

Stella had been sitting at a desk working on a ledger.
She scowled. "Let's see your badge."

"I left it in Denver."

"Sure you did." Stella stood up and walked toward him.
"Now, mister, I don't know what you want and I don't really care. So I'll tell you what is going to happen next. You
either walk out of here on two good legs, or I'll have a
couple of my boys come in here and you can crawl out with
two broken legs. Which is it going to be?"

"I saw Nellie in the penitentiary, and she said you know

who really killed her husband and framed her for the murder. Is that right?"

Stella had been about to step around him and go outside to hail her bouncers, but now she paused. "What are you trying to do, mister?"

"I'm trying to see that the wrong person doesn't hang for tying up and then burning John Bolton to death."

Stella eyed him up and down. "There was a trial and a judge. Nellie was found guilty and that's the end of the story."

"Is it?"

"Yeah."

Longarm shook his head. "Not for me it isn't. And maybe not for you, either."

"Meaning?"

"Meaning that Nellie says you know who really murdered Nellie's husband, and what I want to know is why you didn't bring that out in the trial."

Stella shook her head. "I was about to pour myself a strong drink. Want to join me while we hash this out?"

"Sure."

"Are you really a federal marshal?"

Longarm showed her the letter he was carrying from Billy. After she read it, Stella handed it back and then poured them a drink. "Okay, Marshal Long, I don't know or really care what your angle is on this whole thing, but I will tell you as much as I can without putting my own neck on the chopping block."

They toasted, and Longarm settled down on an expensive silk couch. "I'm all ears, Stella."

"I'll bet you got a lot more than ears."

"Meaning?"

"You're probably hung like a horse."

"Let's not get sidetracked," Longarm told her.

"How much money do you make as a deputy United States marshal?"

"What does that have to do with anything?"

"I was thinking you might be someone I'd like to hire. I got plenty of muscle on the payroll. Things can get rough here, and I need big, strong men. But I sense that you're a big cut above the types I've hired and was just wondering if I could lure you into my employment and maybe . . . maybe even somewhere very nice and soft."

Longarm sipped his whiskey. "Sounds like you're propositioning me, Stella."

"Maybe I am."

"Maybe I'm trying to save Nellie's neck. Can we talk about that?"

Stella laughed, and it was a good, throaty laugh. She nodded. "All business, huh?"

"I don't have a lot of time to help save Nellie if she is innocent."

"How do I know you won't say or do something that will get me killed?"

"I'm a federal marshal and I keep my secrets. Is Nellie innocent?"

"What do you think?"

"I think she might be. Are you her friend . . . or on the other side of the fence? Maybe friends with . . ."

"The person who framed her and murdered John?"

"That's right."

Stella kicked off her shoes and put her feet up on her desk. Her dress was pulled up high, and Longarm thought he'd never seen a nicer pair of legs. "John Bolton was a man who had a lot of enemies, but I wasn't one of them. In fact, John and I had a little thing going a few years ago. And he sort of . . . well, he helped me over the hump."

"What 'hump' are you talking about?"

"I'll be honest with you, Marshal. I was a high-priced whore. I serviced only the wealthy on this bloody, barren mountaintop, and John was one of my best clients. After a while, he began to think that I was his exclusive girl and he paid me enough to make that a reality. He paid me very, very well."

"And he was married to Nellie at this time?"

"Yeah."

"And what did you think about that?"

"Nellie thanked me for servicing her husband!" Stella laughed. "She couldn't stand the son of a bitch, and after he got the fever for me he started leaving her alone in their bed. So you see, it worked for everyone all the way around."

"Sounds like a fine arrangement, I suppose. So you and Nellie weren't rivals or enemies?"

"Nah! Nellie and I would get drunk together. We even went to an opium den once in a while over in the Chinese section and saw visions and dreams. We became, I'd say, almost like sisters."

"Okay," Longarm told her. "I'll buy into that story because it's too far-fetched not to believe. So what happened then?"

"John Bolton set me up in business. I used his money to buy a part interest in this saloon and I paid John every month in money and flesh. We were happy."

"If someone murdered him, they sure as hell weren't happy."

"That's right. John saw that I was as good a manager and businessperson as I was a whore, and when the profits here began to grow, he decided that we should buy out the other partners."

"And did that work?"

"Almost."

"Meaning?"

"There were a few who didn't want to sell, even though Virginia City was on the decline. They knew that this town still had some pretty good years left in her, and they wanted to squeeze out the last dollar."

Longarm nodded and was just beginning to see the picture. "So these 'partners' who didn't want to sell were probably unhappy, and from what I've heard of John Bolton, he would have been more than insistent that they sell their share of the business."

"That's right."

"Are you telling me that you think it was these 'partners' who . . ."

"Yes."

Longarm tossed down his whiskey, which was excellent, and leaned forward on the sofa. "Want to tell me who they are?"

"If I do, I put myself in a lot of danger, Marshal."

"If you don't, then your friend Nellie hangs."

"She might hang anyway."

"And she might not. So how about it?"

Stella got up and refilled their glasses. "I wonder if you know what you're asking me to do."

"Tell the truth. Save an innocent woman."

"And by doing that probably get myself killed and lose this business."

"If you let Nellie hang, how will you feel the rest of your life about it?"

"I'm a hard woman, Marshal."

"I don't think you're *that* hard, Stella."

Stella looked away suddenly, and Longarm saw that her eyes were glistening with tears that she did not want him to see.

"I'll protect you and save Nellie," Longarm promised.

"But you have to help show me who really is behind the murder."

Stella drained her glass and refilled it. "Want some more?"

"I'm fine," he answered.

"I'm not. Can we go upstairs to my room and make love? Right now I'm feeling very bad, and this whiskey isn't going to help all that much."

"And getting laid by me might?"

"I don't know," she said, smiling and giving him a wink. "But it's worth a try, don't you think?"

"Yeah," Longarm decided, eyes on those lovely bare legs, "I think it might be worth a try at that."

Ten minutes later they were in Stella's upstairs room tearing off their clothes and falling into her big feather bed with pink silk sheets. "You *are* hung like a horse, Marshal."

"Call me Custis, but for now, let's just screw."

Stella raised her legs and spread them wide. "Come on in, Marshal Custis, I'm loose, wet, and ready for some hot action."

Longarm growled, and then he plunged his manhood into Stella. She was loose, but she was a professional and she was juicy.

Stella began to wiggle her hips, and then she groaned and slammed her hips upward, wanting all of him that she could get. Longarm bent and sucked on one of her nipples and then the other as he worked out on top of the beautiful blonde.

"How long has it been since you had a woman?" Stella panted. "I'll bet not very long."

"More than a week."

"Sorry, but I can't say the same."

"I don't care, Stella. What you're doing is just fine, and I like a woman with some miles on her."

"Oh, I've got miles and miles, but I still can make a man shiver and shake!"

"I'm a believer," Longarm told her as they began to fuck with growing intensity. "Come on!"

She grabbed his butt cheeks, dug in her fingernails, and after that Longarm lost himself in a whirlwind of soaring fire and desire.

Chapter 14

"So now that you've had me every way a man can have a woman, are you still going to ask me to risk my life and all I own?" Stella whispered late that night as they lay in her bed trying to catch their breath.

"I am," he said. "But I meant what I said about protecting you."

"I'm sure that you're as good with a six-gun as you are with your man-gun, but you are only human and there is more than one person who would have to account for John Bolton's death."

"Give me *names*, Stella. No one needs to know that it was you who gave them to me."

She laughed, only this time it wasn't pretty. "Don't you think that everyone in my saloon knows you are up here screwing me to the mattress? Don't you think that some people are going to know that it was me who fingered them about setting up Nellie for the death of a husband that I screwed and used?"

Longarm had no reply to that one, because it was prob-

ably the truth. They had been consumed with anticipation when they'd left her office downstairs and bolted upstairs to lock themselves into Nellie's bedroom. There would be little doubt in anyone's mind what had happened next behind their closed door.

"Stella, Nellie told me to see you, and she must have thought you were her only chance to escape the gallows. She is betting her life that you will not deny her a chance to live."

"I know that," Stella replied. "And it's killing me inside. I've used men like ass wipe since I was a teenager, tossing them in the shitter when they'd paid me and served my purpose. I used John Bolton that way, and I think I was the only whore who ever did get the best of that skinflint bastard. Nellie saw and appreciated that because she only married John Bolton for his money. She knew he was a son of a bitch through and through."

"All right, then. You both used the old man, but neither one of you killed him."

"No, we didn't. But given how everything went and how I got control of this saloon because he loved nothing more than to fuck me, I played a part in his death."

"Who did it?" Longarm whispered in her ear. "Who really murdered the lecherous old goat?"

Stella shuddered. "I can't say who actually did it . . . but I know who set it up, and if they didn't do it themselves, they paid somebody."

"Just tell me who," Longarm persisted.

"The two men who were my partners until John forced them to sell their shares to this saloon. And maybe . . ."

Stella shook her head. "I can't say anything more."

"You're still protecting someone."

"What if I am!" she cried, jumping up from the bed and

drinking straight from the bottle. "I've given you two men that almost certainly had a role in the murder. In fact, they probably are the only ones that are responsible for it."

"I'd like to believe that, but something tells me that you're holding back on a third name."

"Thomas Elton and Myles Firth." Stella took another pull on the bottle. "I'd bet anything they did it."

"And the third one who might have had a role?"

Stella glared at Longarm, and after a moment, she deflated with a sob. "Maybe . . . maybe Matt Kelly."

"Nellie's *attorney*?"

"Yes."

Longarm shook his head. "What . . ."

"I insisted to Nellie that she hire Kelly."

"But why?" Longarm asked. "I heard that he was young and inexperienced. What . . ."

"Matt was my *brother*."

"And you insisted that Nellie hire him when he might have been part of the murder?"

"I don't know if he was or not!" Stella cried. "All I know is that Matt was starving to death trying to get a law practice going down in Carson City. He begged me to represent Nellie, feeling that it would finally get his law career off the ground."

"But he wasn't ready for a murder trial, was he?" Longarm asked quietly. "He was up against a very experienced attorney in Orville Butler, and he got his head handed to him in court, and now Nellie is the one that is going to pay the price."

"Yes." Stella collapsed on her bed, put her head down, and wept. "My brother was *awful*. Not only did he lose the case, he was made to look like a fool. He couldn't stand the ridicule and the failure, and he shot himself to death two days after Nellie was sentenced to hang."

Whatever anger had started to build up in Longarm instantly washed out of him. "I'm sorry," he said, sitting down beside Stella and taking her hand in his own. "You were trying to do the right thing and it failed."

"If I hadn't talked Nellie into using my brother as her attorney, she might have had a chance."

"No," Longarm countered, "given the evidence against Nellie, even the finest and most experienced attorney would have lost the case. But I have to ask you one question regarding your late brother."

Stella nodded, scrubbing away tears.

"Did Matt have *anything* to do with the murder?"

"No," Stella whispered. "He was a studious man, quiet, introspective, and in way over his head. I spent the money to put him through law school, but he'd have been a better minister or schoolteacher than an attorney. There was a girl whose Carson City family has a lot of respect and money. Matt believed that he had to become financially successful in order to win her, and that's why he chose going into law."

"I see." Longarm thought of Joe Polk, who had made love to Rebecca. "Your brother should have seduced that wealthy girl, and then everyone would have gladly seen them go skipping up to the altar."

Stella managed a sad smile. "Matt was too prim and proper to compromise a virgin. He was quite religious, and it was hard on him to have a sister who had been a whore and was now running a saloon. He never told anyone about me unless he had to."

"Stella, he took your money and used it to become a lawyer, so I wouldn't feel too guilty if I were you."

"He wouldn't ever come up here to see me," Stella confessed. "And he didn't want to be seen in public with me, either. We would meet down in Gold Hill for dinner once

in a while. Or once in a while in Reno. I would listen to him talk of the girl he loved and a little about his law practice, which couldn't even cover his office, much less his living, expenses. At the end of the dinner, which I always bought, I'd give Matt a fat envelope of money to tide him over until our next meeting. He always promised that he'd pay me back someday. I knew that he wouldn't, but I didn't care. I *loved* Matt. He was good but naïve, and everyone took advantage of his generous nature. He was my only brother, and I always thought that someday we'd both go away and start over fresh with the money I'd make from the sale of this saloon."

"Where would you have gone?" Longarm asked.

"We both thought we'd like to live in Oregon. By then, my brother was beginning to realize that the girl he thought he loved was pretty shallow and that maybe he really didn't want to marry her after all." Stella looked up at Longarm. "Custis, have you ever been there? Have you ever seen a place called the Willamette Valley?"

"Yes. It's beautiful. The Oregon coast is wild, windy, and rainy, but go inland just a ways and there are beautiful towns by big rivers. It's really nice, Stella."

"I bought books on Oregon and talked to some people about real estate prices. I was just biding my time until I could get a fair offer for the Bucket of Blood. Nellie knew about my plans, and she thought she might like to go along with us. She was going to leave John Bolton because they didn't love each other. He only married her for her youth and beauty. Nellie was the old man's showpiece, his prize, and he thought that by bedding and being with her he would remain young. It was very pathetic, actually."

"I wish it had worked out for the three of you," Longarm said. "I really do. And I wish I'd have had some time to educate your late brother, Matt."

Stella almost managed a laugh. "Yeah, I'll bet you would have really opened his eyes."

Longarm took a deep breath. "Stella, first thing tomorrow morning I'm going to look up the two men that you named. But first, I need to know something about them and why you believe they conspired not only to burn John Bolton to death in his bed but also to frame Nellie for the horrible crime."

"All right."

"So tell me their names again and whatever else I need to know in order to get them to admit their guilt."

"They'll never do it," Stella said. "What on earth could make them admit to murdering John Bolton so they could take Nellie's place on the gallows?"

"I don't know. I'm sure that you're right about them not admitting anything, but there might be someone who would tell a judge in Carson City what really happened that night when John Bolton died in flames."

"What you're saying is that they might have used an accomplice?"

"Are they hard men? Have they killed before?"

Stella thought about that a moment. "They're both former gamblers, so they are hard . . . but are they capable of murdering an old man in his bed? I'm not sure. My bet is that they hired someone to actually do the murder."

"If that's true, we only have to find that man or someone that he's spoken to, and then I'll do what I've always done."

"And that is?"

"I'll get the truth out of them . . . one damned way or the other," Longarm vowed.

Stella nodded. "Yeah, I believe that."

"You and Nellie could still go to Oregon and start clean."

"I could sell this place," Stella mused. "Not for a fraction of what it was worth even five years ago, before the mines started to peter out. But I could sell it tomorrow for at least ten thousand."

"Ten thousand would buy a lot of land in the Willamette Valley, Stella. Buy you a farm and a house with barns and fences."

"A farm?" she repeated with astonishment. "Now, what would Nellie or I do with a damned farm?"

"I dunno. What were you thinking about?"

"A hotel. A real nice, respectable hotel. Two stories, brick, with a restaurant that people would talk about for miles. And it would have a wine cellar and a gift shop. Nellie is good with fashion. She would like to own a dress shop, and we'd put that in the hotel lobby."

"Sounds like it would have to be a pretty grand hotel for all that."

"That's my vision," Stella said. "Wherever I land, I want to have the best hotel in town, and I want people that I meet on the street to smile and greet me as Miss Kelly."

"No background on the Comstock Lode, I suppose?"

"Nope. When I leave here . . . hopefully with a freed Nellie as my best friend and fellow business owner . . . we want to change our names and start entirely new lives." Stella laughed. "You've been around more than I have, Custis. Can two wild and formerly wicked women do that if they go to a new place with money?"

"I don't know . . . but I'd say if they were smart and thought things out real well, they could probably pull it off."

"We could!" Stella clapped her hands together. "And by gawd if you can somehow get Nellie out of prison we *will*!"

Longarm almost had to laugh at how quickly the dark

mood had changed. "Okay, enough of the dreams," he said. "It's time to tell me everything you can about Thomas Elton and Myles Firth."

"Sure," Stella said. "But it's going to cost you something first."

"And what would that be?"

Stella reached for his flaccid manhood and giggled. "You get one guess, big man."

Longarm didn't have to guess. His manhood was already starting to stiffen, and he was ready to pay the pleasurable price.

Chapter 15

After being forced to sell out their interests in the Bucket of Blood Saloon, Thomas Elton and Myles Firth had bought a smaller saloon called the Crystal Palace. It was only a block down C Street, and when Longarm entered the saloon, he saw that it was much smaller and more modest than the Bucket of Blood. There was the usual long bar down one side of the room, the ornate crystal chandeliers, and the poker and faro tables, but there weren't a lot of customers at nine o'clock in the morning.

"What's your pleasure?" the bartender asked without much enthusiasm.

"I'm looking for Mr. Elton and Mr. Firth."

"What for?"

"Business."

The bartender was a round-shouldered man, bald on top, with long, red hair swept back over his big ears. He had a bent nose, scarred knuckles, and a pugnacious look about him that told Longarm he might have been a prize-fighter in younger days. He looked like the kind of a man who would quickly take offense.

"I'm Firth. State your business."

Longarm was caught off guard. He had expected someone who looked like a gambler, not a fighter. "I understand that you and Mr. Elton were partners with Stella over at the Bucket of Blood."

"Everybody in Virginia City knows that." Firth scowled. "Look, I'm busy. If you got something specific to ask, then quit screwin' around and ask it and stop wasting my time."

Longarm stared into the man's eyes. "Maybe I'd rather talk to Mr. Elton."

"He comes in here around noon. Who the hell are you?"

"Someone who is trying to right a serious wrong."

Firth blinked, grabbed a beer mug, and began to polish it with his apron. "What wrong?"

"The death sentence imposed on Nellie Bolton."

Myles Firth nearly dropped the mug. "That bitch deserves to hang for murdering her husband."

"I'm not convinced of that."

"And who the hell are you that anyone cares if you're convinced or not!"

Longarm hadn't really wanted to let it be known that he was a lawman, but his instincts told him that it might be a good thing just to get it out in the open and put some pressure on Firth and his partner.

"I'm a United States marshal," he said.

Firth glared at him from across the bar. "My partner and I have nothing to say to you."

"I'll decide that for myself."

Firth slammed the mug down hard enough to turn the heads of the few customers in his saloon. He raised his finger and pointed it into Longarm's face. "Mister, I don't know who sent you or what the hell you think you are tryin' to do, and I don't care. But there is something I can tell you."

"I'm listening."

"Get out of here!"

Longarm knew that the half dozen or so customers and the two gamblers at the tables were all ears now. "Tell me where I can find your partner. I don't have anything more to discuss with you . . . yet."

"Go straight to hell."

Longarm knew that he should leave, knew that there was nothing to be gained right now in getting into a fight with this man, but Nellie was fast running out of time.

"I think I'll have a beer."

"I think you'll leave."

Longarm glanced down at the mug that Firth had just finished polishing. It was clean and heavy. He picked it up and studied it for a moment, as if wishing it were full of beer and suds, and then with a lightning move he slammed it down hard across Firth's forehead. The man's eyes rolled upward, and Longarm smashed him a second time with the mug, just over his left ear. Myles Firth disappeared from sight.

Longarm surveyed the room and drawled, "He isn't very friendly, is he?"

No one said a word or moved a muscle. Longarm walked around the end of the bar to stand over the unconscious bartender. He picked up a clean glass on the back bar and poured himself a shot of whiskey.

"Not bad," he said, dropping a coin on Firth's chest. "Now, is someone going to tell me where I can find Thomas Elton right now or do I start kicking the hell out of you assholes one by one?"

They stared, and finally a small, older man silently pointed up to the row of rooms overlooking the interior of the saloon.

"Which door?" Longarm demanded, coming out from behind the bar and advancing on the man.

"Number two."

"Thanks."

Longarm climbed the stairs that were covered in worn, smelly carpet. He counted six rooms and knew that at least half of them were occupied by the saloon's whores. When he came to the second room, he tried the door, found it locked, and then leaned back and kicked it off its hinges.

"What the shit!" a man in bed with a skinny woman barely out of her youth shouted.

"You Thomas Elton?"

"You broke my door down!" Elton yelled, batting the skinny whore off the bed and reaching for a gun on his bedside table.

Longarm's own pistol was out and pointed at the man's head before Elton could even grip his pistol. "Better not do that," he warned.

"Who the hell are you!"

"I'm Deputy United States Marshal Custis Long, and I have some questions about the death of John Bolton. You want to talk now or after I beat the shit out of you in front of your woman?"

Thomas Elton did look like a gambler. He had long, black hair and he was handsome and well built.

The girl jumped up and screamed. "You can't do us this way!"

"I can and I am," Longarm said, eyes taking in her girlish naked body. "Grab some clothes and get out of here."

She looked at Elton, her own eyes wide with excitement. "I got a gun in my room, Mr. Elton. Want me to—"

"No," the man said, climbing out of bed and reaching for his underclothes, pants, and shirt. "Just . . . just leave us be."

"But . . ."

"Dammit, Milly, get the hell out of here!" Elton roared.

Milly rushed past Longarm, and he heard a door slam in the hallway. "How old is Milly? Fifteen? Maybe a year younger? Not too smart to be bedding your child whores, Thomas."

"What do you want?"

"I want to talk about John Bolton."

"I'm not interested in that conversation."

"Neither was your partner, Myles. But right now, he's out cold. You want some of what I gave him?"

Elton buckled his belt and moved past Longarm to grab the door that was loosely hanging on one hinge. He pushed the door into place so that it was closed tight and then turned back to Longarm.

"All right. Let's get this over with for now. What do you want to know?"

"I want to know if you or your partner murdered John Bolton or if you paid someone else to do it and frame Nellie Bolton."

Thomas Elton had started to reach for his shirt, but now his hand froze in space and he stared at Longarm. "Are you serious?"

"Dead serious."

"Then you must be insane."

"Answer my question," Longarm demanded.

Elton pulled on his shirt and slowly buttoned it to the collar. "Neither I nor my partner had anything to do with the death of John Bolton. The man's wife hated his guts and so she tied him up in his bed and put a match to him. End of story."

"Why would she do that knowing that she'd go to prison and probably the gallows?"

"Ask her, but you'd better hurry because she'll be hanging soon."

"I'm asking you."

"And I'm telling you that you are insane. Furthermore, I'm going to contact the authorities down in Carson City and file charges against you for breaking into my room, threatening me, and injuring my partner."

"You can do all that," Longarm said with a shrug, "but it doesn't matter. You're not going anywhere until you tell me who really killed John Bolton."

"I will when hell freezes over."

Longarm walked over to the gun that Thomas Elton had tried to grab. He picked it up and slipped it behind his cartridge belt, and then he holstered his pistol and moved in close to the half-dressed former gambler. "You still deal a deck of cards, Thomas?"

"What if I do?"

"And I'll bet you are real slick with a marked deck and a few cards up your sleeve, huh?"

Elton's face grew hard. "You're digging your own grave."

"Well," Longarm said, taking a step forward. "At least I'll have the hands to do it when this is over."

Before Thomas Elton could think to react, Longarm grabbed the man's fingers and snapped them backward breaking all but the thumb. Elton screamed and collapsed to his knees. Longarm was on him like a cougar on a fawn, and he grabbed the man's other hand and bent the fingers back until Elton was screaming and down on his knees, eyes wild with fear. "No!"

"The pinkie finger," Longarm said. "That's the one that you use the most when you deal from the bottom of the deck, isn't it?"

"Please!"

Longarm broke the man's pinkie finger, and the snap was sickening. "Next up the middle finger," he said casually. "That will leave me three more and maybe I'll just saw them off with my dull knife."

"Oh, Jesus! Oh, gawd no!" Elton begged, tears running down his cheeks.

"Who really killed John Bolton?"

Elton was sobbing and looking up at Longarm. "I didn't do it! I didn't do it!"

"Who did?" Longarm asked, starting to bend back the gambler's middle finger. "Who really killed John Bolton?"

"I don't—"

Longarm broke the heaviest of the man's fingers, and Elton shrieked. "It . . . it might have been Deke Hill!"

That was a name that had not been brought up before. "Who is he and why did he kill him and frame Nellie?"

"I don't know! I swear that I don't know!"

"Of course you do, Thomas. Just two fingers left to break."

"Deke hated old John Bolton and was in love with his wife. I'm sure that he did it!"

"If the man loved Nellie, why would he frame her for the murder?"

"Because she . . . she couldn't stand him anymore and that drove him *crazy*!"

"Where can I find him?"

"He's gone!" Elton sobbed. "He left the Comstock right after the fire."

"But you and your partner paid him to do the murder, didn't you!"

"We . . . we paid him to make the old man suffer . . . but not to murder him. Never to set him on fire!"

Longarm released Thomas Elton's hand, and the man

crumpled to the floor, sobbing and rocking back and forth in agony.

"All right," Longarm said, dragging the man to his feet and shoving him at the door. "We're going to tell everyone downstairs what you just told me."

"No! Please!"

Longarm grabbed the man by his hair and propelled him forward. Thomas Elton slammed into the unhinged door and it crashed outward. Everyone down on the saloon floor was staring upward.

"Tell them what you told me!"

"No!"

Longarm grabbed the man's unbroken thumbs and twisted them savagely. "I'm going to break them like chicken bones and then I'll cut the last of your fingers off unless you tell those people what you just told me!"

Elton gazed down at the small crowd. He was probably looking for his partner, Myles Firth, to come up with a gun or rifle, but Firth was still out cold behind the bar.

"Tell them now!" Longarm hissed.

"Deke Hill murdered John Bolton!"

"And you paid him to do it!"

"No! Myles and I just paid him to *hurt* the old bastard. We never meant for Deke to go crazy and burn him alive! Never!"

Longarm swung his eyes around and glared at the customers below. He studied them for a full minute. He saw the girl stick her head out from her door, and then several other whores did the same.

Longarm shouted, "I'm a deputy United States marshal, and by gawd I'll remember the face of every single one of you when this goes before a judge, and you'd better tell him what you just heard from this sick son of a bitch!"

"Leave him alone!" Milly cried, rushing to the side of

her boss and falling to her knees still naked. "Don't hurt him anymore!"

"He's old enough to be your father," Longarm said. "He doesn't love or care a good gawdamn about you, Milly. You're wasting yourself on a piece of shit that is going to prison. Wise up!"

Milly turned her face upward to Longarm. "I hate you for doing this!"

"Yeah, I can see that," Longarm said quietly. "But my advice is still good. This man and his partner are going to prison, so you'd better think about your future, because it's in for a change whether you like it or not."

Longarm turned his eyes back to the crowd still standing frozen below. "Nellie Bolton didn't murder her husband in his bed by putting a match and kerosene to him. You just learned that Thomas Elton and Myles Firth paid a man named Deke Hill to either kill or beat the hell out of that rich old man. Ain't that what you just heard?"

The men downstairs finally began nodding their heads up and down.

"Good," Longarm said, starting down the staircase. "I'll expect every last one of you to testify to what you just heard when the time comes. Until then, I want to know where I can find this Deke Hill."

"He's gone," a miner said. "He's long gone."

"Where to?"

"Dunno."

Longarm's eyes raked the crowd. "Is there anyone that knows where Deke Hill might have gone? Anyone with guts enough to try to save an innocent woman from being hanged for something she did not do!"

"He used to talk about his days cowboying near Elko. Said he had friends there that would hire him to bust broncs again if he gave up on these mines."

"Elko?"

"Yeah, it's about a hundred miles east of here. You just get on the train and it follows the Humboldt River . . ."

"I've come out here through Elko," Longarm said. He studied the faces. "Anyone else know for certain where Deke might have run to?"

"He always talked about Elko," a big miner offered. "Said it was real pretty country and he had a brother that owned a little ranch at the base of the Ruby Mountains."

Longarm shook his head. He sure as hell didn't want to go climb back on the train and roll all the way back to Elko and find out that Deke Hill was someplace else. If he did that and Hill wasn't to be found, then he'd have wasted too much time, and Nellie would be swinging by a rope before he could return to Carson City.

"Custis?"

The front door to the saloon burst open and there stood Joe Polk. "Hey, Custis! I just heard that you—"

"I'm leaving," Longarm said, cutting off his friend. "You find a job yet?"

"I'm going to be a stagecoach guard starting tomorrow. But . . ."

"How would you like me to deputize you right now?"

"You can do that?"

"I can," Longarm replied. "I need you to help me track down a murderer."

Joe Polk beamed. "Why, I can sure enough do *that*! You gonna help me get hired on as a federal marshal?"

Longarm couldn't help but smile. "Why, I can sure as hell help you do that, Joe."

"Then we're partners!"

"First job we have is to deliver the owners of this saloon down to the prison outside of Carson City, where I'm sure that a cell can be found for them by the warden."

"Just point 'em out to me and I'll get to work on it."

"One is unconscious and stretched out behind the bar.
I'll drag this other one down the stairs."

Thomas Elton shook his head. "You ain't taking us to
the penitentiary. When we get to Carson City, we'll just
see what Marshal Orton and Deputy Buck Toler has to say
about what you done to Myles and me. *You're* the ones that
are going to go to prison!"

"We'll just see about that," Longarm told the man, as
he shoved him headlong down the stairs, knowing that he
would not even consider taking this pair to the Carson
City jail, where Marshal Orton would immediately set
them free.

"You and you," Longarm said, pointing to the big miner
and the other miner who had been brave enough to speak
about Deke Hill and his connections to Elko. "You're both
coming with us."

"No sir," one miner protested. "We don't want any part
of this."

"You want to see an innocent woman get hanged after
what you heard just now?"

"No, but . . ."

"I'll buy your tickets, and the federal government will
pay your expenses and lost wages so you can testify."

"We're just miners, Marshal. We don't want no
trouble."

"You've already got trouble, and you can go with me
by choice . . . or I can force you. Which is it going to be?"

The pair exchanged glances. "We'll go along. Ain't
right to see a woman as pretty as Nellie Bolton swing for
something she didn't do."

"Glad to hear you say that," Longarm told them. "So
help my young friend carry Myles Firth down to the V&T
Railroad depot and let's get a move on."

And that was how it went. Longarm with a gun in his hand following the two witnesses, who were carrying the unconscious Firth and prodding his partner, Thomas Benton. And out in front was Joe, a gun in his fist and a smile on his face as wide as a quarter-moon.

Chapter 16

The bespectacled and out-of-breath telegraph operator burst into Marshal Dean Orton's Carson City office and skidded to a halt. "Marshal, I've got some important news for you!"

Marshal Orton and his deputy Buck Toler had been dozing in their office chairs, but now they jerked into wakefulness. "Simmer down," the marshal said with a relaxed smile. "Can't be anything important enough to burst your pipes."

The small man waved the telegram in his hands. "This is *damned* important, Marshal, and that's why I thought you ought to see it right away."

Orton slowly climbed out of his chair, yawned, and scratched at his privates, while Deputy Buck Toler scowled.

"Let's see," Orton said, "where the hell did I put my spectacles? Buck, you see 'em anywhere?"

"Nope."

Orton gazed around at the clutter then grumbled. "Paul, go ahead and read the damned thing for me."

"You're not going to like this," the telegraph operator warned. "Not like it even a little bit."

"Well read it to me and let me decide!" Orton said crossly.

"All right. Here it is just as it reads," he said, peering through his own eye glasses.

FEDERAL MARSHAL AND FRIEND JUST ARRESTED MYLES FIRTH AND THOMAS ELTON. **STOP**. EN ROUTE TO CARSON CITY BY RAILROAD. **STOP**. STATED DESTINATION IS THE PENITENTIARY. **STOP**.

Marshal Orton had been about to yawn again, but instead his mouth dropped open and his face turned red with fury. "Gawdammit! What the hell is going on!"

Buck Toler came to his feet. "You know what is going on. That federal marshal is going to try to stop the hanging."

"Well . . . well he can't do that!"

"He can if he's able to convince Judge Cross that there is a good enough reason and evidence to put it off."

Orton stormed. "I've staked my reelection chances on getting that woman hanged! We can't allow justice to be delayed."

Buck Toler reached for his gunbelt. "Well, we know what we have to do next."

"Stop them," Orton said, glancing over at the clock on his wall.

"And before they reach town."

Orton nodded. "Buck, how many men can we gather and deputize in the next hour?"

"I'd say that we can count on at least five or six that I know of. Everyone wants to see that woman hang, so it won't be hard to rally support."

"Then do it!" Orton snapped. "I'll deputize the lot of them and we'll stop the train a few miles out of town, and

then I'll arrest the marshal and his friend. We'll put the clamps on this in a big hurry."

"Might not be quite as easy as we'd like it to be," Buck said, still hurting from the whupping he'd received from the federal marshal. "We've got to be prepared to go the limit."

"Meaning?"

"Meaning," Buck said, "that you have to be ready to do whatever it takes to stop them from getting Elton and Firth into the penitentiary."

"I'm prepared to go to the wall on this."

Toler finished buckling on his gunbelt and headed for the door. "Glad to hear you say that, Marshal."

"Buck!"

The big deputy turned. "Yeah?"

"Make sure that the men you get to ride with us know that I'll pay them five dollars each but I expect them to be willing to fight. Tell 'em we want them all well armed. I'll deputize them in this office just before we ride out. If you find a man drunk, I don't want him with us. Understood?"

"Sure," Buck Toler answered with annoyance. "And I'll make dead certain that they understand that this could get dangerous in a hurry."

"Try to include old Wyatt Reese. In his younger days he killed a passel of men with that double-barreled shotgun he likes to carry around all the time."

"He'll be happy to earn a quick five dollars. They *all* will," Buck assured his boss as he closed the door.

"Don't bring me back more than ten, because I can't afford to pay that many."

"We won't need more than five," Deputy Toler promised. "But I'll find good ones."

"You'd better, because our lives will sure as hell count on it," the marshal warned as his man headed out the door.

Marshal Orton went straight for his own double-barreled shotgun and checked the loads. He turned and was surprised to see the telegraph operator still standing in his office.

"What the hell are you doin' still standing there?"

"I'd ride with you and Buck if I didn't have to go back to work," the man said, wringing his narrow hands. "I could use that extra five dollars to buy medicines."

"You're not man enough to be one of my deputies," the marshal said flatly. "Besides that, you got a sickly wife and two sickly daughters to worry about. Now, get out of here."

"I . . . I was kind of expecting that you'd give me a little reward for leaving my telegraph and rushing all the way over here," the telegraph operator whined. "Marshal, I wasn't expecting a lot, but . . ."

Orton shook his head and dug in his pants for some loose, small change. "Here," he said, dumping a few coins into the telegraph operator's outstretched hand. "Now git, and don't tell a soul what you read and heard."

"Oh, no sir! My lips are sealed, and I sure hope it all goes right for you and Buck. Our townsfolk are awful excited about watching Nellie Bolton swing. If that don't happen, it is going to be bad for the town's businesses . . . especially the saloons, but all the merchants are also going to be real upset with you."

"Yeah, I know," Orton growled. "Now, go on back to work. I've got some things to do in a hurry."

The telegraph operator dared to smile. "You know, Marshal, if there's a shoot-out, it'll make the *national* news. I'll be the first one to send out the message, and that—"

"Git!" Orton yelled impatiently.

The telegraph operator dropped his coins into his baggy pants and hurried out of the office. "Miserable little

bastard," Orton grumbled as he collected a little canvas bag with a half dozen cheap tin badges that he would be pinning on his new deputies in the next few minutes.

Thirty minutes later, Buck Toler led five of Carson City's toughest men into the office, and the marshal was pleased to see that every one of them was well armed.

"What's this about?" old Wyatt Reese rumbled, spitting tobacco juice on the floor and cradling his shotgun in his skinny arms.

Orton shot a look at Buck. "You didn't explain it to them?"

"Wasn't time to explain it five times. I figured you'd only need to do it once."

"All right," Orton said. "Here's the deal. A deputy United States marshal named Long, out of Denver, and some kid that he's paired up with have somehow gotten it into their heads that two innocent men should be arrested and brought to the prison. Not my jail, mind you. Not with my permission or even knowledge, but on their own accord they are going to go against our local law."

"I saw that big federal son of a bitch," one of the men growled. "He looked tough and mean. We ain't going to have to kill a federal marshal, are we?"

Orton had been expecting this question and had an answer. "My authority is greater than the federal authority once they enter the city limits. And as you know, those limits run for nearly a mile east. We're going to stop the train and demand that Marshal Long turn over his prisoners to me at once."

"And what if he and his friend won't do it?" Wyatt Reese demanded.

"Well," Orton said with a shrug meant to cut off any further discussion, "he'd have to be wanting to buy a

one-way to hell. The thing you boys have to remember is that we have the law on our side. If that marshal and his young friend choose to ignore my demand and the local law . . . none of us can be held responsible for whatever might happen."

"He didn't look stupid enough to brace seven of us," one of the men offered.

"No, he didn't," Orton said, "but you can never be sure. We have to be prepared to take this to the limit, and that means standing up for justice and our local law."

Wyatt Reese spat again on the floor. "Only thing I give a good gawdamn about is that five dollars we been promised. I'd prefer to take it right now, Marshal. If you and your deputy get shot to shit, I want to make sure we still get paid, instead of the undertaker. I reckon these other boys feel the same way as I do."

There was a heavy silence as everyone waited for the town marshal to give them an answer to Reese's blunt question.

"All right, dammit!" Orton snapped. "You men wait here, and I'll go over to the bank and get the money. But you get half now and half when we're done, and that's the way it's going to be if you want to get deputized and ride with Buck and me."

"Well," another man drawled, patting the butt of his gun. "I surely do need the money, and I sure do want to see that murderin' bitch hang next week, so I'm in."

"Me too," another said, looking at his grim companions, who all nodded in agreement.

Marshal Orton stormed back into his office five minutes later and paid the men two dollars and fifty cents. Then he quickly pinned on badges. "Buck, did you tell the stableman to have our horses saddled?"

"Yep."

"Then everybody follow me over to the stable and let's get moving!" Orton yelled.

Reese looked over at the clock. "The V and T usually pulls in here in less than an hour."

"I know," Orton said. "And that ought to give us plenty of time to get out there and block the railroad tracks. We'll cover both sides and make plain our intentions."

"When we get 'em, they'll have to walk back here to town," one man offered. "Maybe we ought to tell someone to bring out a wagon."

"Or a *hearse*," Buck Toler added with a tight smile and cold chuckle.

"Let's go 'cause time is a-wastin'," Orton snapped, gun strapped to his hip and shotgun in his hands. "And Reese?"

"Yeah?"

"You be damned sure if you pull the triggers on that scattergun that you ain't going to blow one of us all to pieces."

"I hit what I aim for," the old man hissed with contempt. "And I was just fixin' to warn you not to kill any of us and then call it an accident to save yourself a few dollars."

Marshal Orton couldn't believe what the old man had just told him, but there was no time to display his outrage. And, to be honest, old Wyatt Reese wouldn't have stood any of it anyway.

Chapter 17

"You're not going to get away with this," a surly Thomas Elton warned for about the tenth time. "Best thing you and that kid could do is to jump this train while you are still alive and beat it the hell out of this country."

"We'll see," Longarm answered, glancing at Joe and the two miners he'd ordered to come along as witnesses.

The train was still coming down off the barren Comstock Lode, traveling very slow around hairpin curves. Looking out the window, Longarm thought it was an amazing feat of engineering that had allowed the laying of these sidewinder snake tracks. On both sides of the train he saw groups of miners standing or laboring on their claims, and he marveled at the toughness of men who could camp out in this harsh wilderness with so little shade and water.

"How do they stand it?" Joe Polk asked as if he had read Longarm's dark musings. "Look at them. Most all the men are scarecrows and they're wearing little more than rags. Do you think *any* of those miners get rich?"

"I don't know, but I rather doubt it," Longarm answered.

"I guess some did at first in Six Mile Canyon and other places up through Gold Hill Canyon. But I'll bet all the shallow veins and pockets of gold and silver have long since been picked clean."

"Then why do they keep working like that?"

"Hope," Longarm said. "Hope and gold fever. I've seen it everywhere I've traveled. You ask any hardscrabble, beat-down miner, no matter if he's struggling to buy beans in the Rockies, or in the Bitterroots, or here on the Comstock Lode, and he'll say that he could get rich at the next swing of a pick or panning of gold out of a freezing mountain stream. You can see the gold fever burning in their eyes, and they lust for fortune just as surely as a gambler or the wildest of dreamers."

"I hope I never get gold fever," Joe said. "What I want is a good, steady paying job. One that I can count on from one week to the next. Rebecca and the kids we'll have deserve no less."

"I understand," Longarm told him. "But being a lawman can get ahold of you in a different way."

"How's that?"

"Well," Longarm reflected, "a man can get addicted to danger just as sure as he can to fame and fortune. When you pin on a badge and head off on a manhunt, or just walk down a dark and dangerous street in your town at night, you feel the hair on the back of your neck stand up because you know you are putting your life at risk."

"Do you still get that feeling?"

"Yeah, at times. And when I get through whatever danger it is that threatens my life and take a deep breath, I get a feeling of accomplishment and satisfaction that I can't imagine finding any other way."

"I never had a feeling like that. Oh, when I was . . . well, you know. Kissing and doing things with Rebecca on the

train out here, I had a pretty excited feeling, but it doesn't sound like it was anywhere near the same."

Despite the tension he felt inside, Longarm had to chuckle. "Joe," he offered, "you're going to do just fine no matter what line of work you follow."

"I hope so."

"You will." Longarm started to add to that, but suddenly the train's brakes squealed and he was nearly thrown forward out of his seat.

"What the hell!" Joe shouted, landing in the aisle several seats up.

Longarm jumped up and ran to end of the coach and then stepped out between the cars. He looked up ahead and recognized Marshal Orton and Deputy Buck Toler along with several heavily armed riders. They had dragged a boulder across the tracks and were stopping the train.

"Joe!"

Yeah?"

"We've got trouble just ahead. The Carson City marshal, his deputy, and some other hard cases have stopped the train and I don't think they're doing it to be sociable."

"Told you that you wouldn't get us to the penitentiary," Firth said with a triumphant sneer on his face. "Too late to run now." •

"I've no intention of running."

Longarm turned to the pair of miners he planned to use as witnesses, and one of them threw up his hands. "We're not gonna get shot up for you. This ain't worth dyin' for."

The miners weren't even armed . . . at least not that Longarm could see. They both might have been carrying knives or hide-out derringers, but he very much doubted it. "You two just take your seats and keep your mouths shut. We'll handle this."

"Against Marshal Orton, his big-assed deputy, and some other men they have?" one of the miners asked skeptically. "I think you'd better get out the back of this train and make a run for it into the sagebrush."

"That's not the way it works," Longarm replied. "You two just stay put, and when the smoke and dust clears, we'll continue on into town and then head out to the penitentiary."

The miners were scared and worried. You could see that in their rough, unshaven faces. Longarm didn't blame them, but he didn't have time to bolster their spirits just now.

"How do you want to handle this?" Joe Polk asked, pulling out his gun and swallowing hard.

"Let me go out and face them. You move up to where you can jump down and open fire if necessary."

"Pretty long odds, wouldn't you say?"

"If I'm forced to open fire, I'll be standing near the locomotive and I'll have a place to jump for cover. They'll be on nervous horses and that means I'll have a bit of an advantage."

Joe stuck his head out of the window and said, "The marshal and a couple of them have shotguns."

"I saw that."

"You don't have to be too accurate with a shotgun," Joe noted.

"You want out of this?"

Joe didn't hesitate. "I'm not chickening out on you. I'd just like to think that if the shooting starts, we'll have at least some chance."

"We'll do what needs to be done." He turned back to the miners. "You men only have one job and that is to keep our prisoners in their seats. I don't want Joe and me to have to worry about something coming at us from behind."

"We'll do that, but if . . ."

"If it goes bad for Joe and me, you can just move to another car and you're out of it entirely."

The pair exchanged glances and then both of them nodded with understanding. "Good luck," one said.

"It looks as if this will take a little luck," Longarm admitted. "Ready, Joe?"

"I'm ready. Sure wish I had a shotgun like a couple of those fellas."

"Stay out of the shotgun's range if you can. Your pistol will carry a whole lot farther and shoot with more accuracy. If I go down, find a place to run and hide and then get way the hell out of this part of the country, because I won't be able to help you."

"I'm not going to leave you."

"Leave me if I get shot to death," Longarm ordered. "Understand?"

Joe Polk, face waxen, dipped his chin and nodded. Longarm gave the kid a pat on the shoulder and said, "It'll work out."

"I sure hope so."

"If it doesn't, we'll have tried our best to do our lawful duties and save a likely innocent woman from the noose."

"If we get killed, I'd like to think that it counted."

"Whenever a man does the right thing, even in the face of short odds, it always counts for something," Longarm told the kid.

"I believe that," Joe said. "See you up the tracks."

"Count on it!"

And then Longarm was leaping from the train and striding forward toward the sheriff and his deputy along with three others. He knew that there were a couple of riders on the opposite side of the locomotive as well, but if he

could handle this bunch, the others would cut and run without the local law backing them.

Longarm felt the familiar hairs stand up on the back of his neck, and a cold smile formed on his lips, because this was about to get very interesting and all of their lives were now on the line.

Chapter 18

"Hello, Marshal Orton," Longarm said, walking toward the four mounted horsemen on his side of the railroad tracks. "Since this is a flat stretch, I take it that boulder blocking the tracks didn't roll there all by itself."

"You've way overstepped your authority," Orton answered in a hard tone of voice. "I'd been inclined to let you do whatever the hell it is that you came here to do and then leave. But I can't let this pass."

"What pass?" Longarm asked innocently as his eyes moved from one horseman to the next trying to judge which one he might have to kill first.

"You've arrested a couple of upstanding citizens of Virginia City."

"News travels fast in these parts. Telegraph lines must have been singing between Carson City and Virginia City."

"Doesn't matter. You've arrested two innocent men from up on the Comstock Lode."

Longarm smiled coldly. "Are you *also* the marshal of Virginia City?"

"No, I am not," Orton admitted. "But now that you've crossed into *my* jurisdiction, I'm the law."

"And that brings us back to the question I'm most curious about," Longarm said. "Why did you stop the train?"

"To arrest you and that kid with the big mouth."

"On what charges?"

"You assaulted Buck the other day, and he's my deputy. I reckon that's enough of a reason."

"Not for me it isn't. Your stupid deputy got what he asked for and then some. No, it seems to me that the real reason for us standing here is that you have strong ties to Thomas Elton and Myles Firth, or else you just want to see a woman hang for your own political gains. Which is it or is it both?"

"You're wrong all the way around," Orton answered, looking sideways at his big deputy. "But we'll let the judge sort it all out in his own good time. These riders with us have all been deputized."

"Yeah, I can see their cheap badges. How much are you paying them to put their lives on the line today?"

"That's none of your damned business. Now, are you going to let us put you under arrest peaceably . . . or not?"

Longarm stepped a few paces closer, and he noted the two riders on the other side of the locomotive and just out of his line of fire. Joe Polk would have to handle them. Marshal Orton was cradling a shotgun. Longarm didn't figure he had a snowball's chance in hell of surviving a gun battle.

"All right," he said, smiling. "I'll let you arrest me and Joe Polk. But I'd like to know what charges you think you have to bring against the kid."

"I'll come up with a few," Orton promised. "Buck, get down off that horse and cuff this big bastard. Cuff him and cuff him tight!"

"My pleasure," Buck said, dismounting and handing his reins to Orton. He had a pair of handcuffs in his saddle-bags, and he pulled them free with a big smile on his meaty face.

Longarm could feel his heart pounding as the huge deputy strutted over to face him and then hissed into his face, "*Federal* Marshal Long, I'm going to give you some payback when we get you locked behind bars."

"Yeah," Longarm replied. "That would be your style, all right. You got your ass whipped by me when it was a fair fight. Maybe you can whip me if I'm handcuffed, but don't count on it."

"Oh, I'll do one helluva lot more than that," Buck promised, his black eyes hard and merciless.

Longarm knew that if he was handcuffed, he was as good as dead. Once his hands were locked behind his back, Buck Toler was going to beat him savagely. He'd be dragged back to Carson City and then thrown in the jail and abused until he was senseless and dying. Marshal Toler wouldn't stop Buck's cruelty, and Joe Polk would also be punished.

Toler unlocked the cuffs with a little key and then said, "Stick your hands out here."

"Whatever you say, Buck," Longarm answered.

"Put 'em together!"

"Okay," Longarm replied, suddenly making fists and then smashing them into Buck's ears.

Buck staggered, and Longarm's right hand flashed across his body to his Colt, which he wore butt facing forward. His gun came out and the old man was already raising his shotgun and taking aim. Longarm ducked behind Buck just as the double-barreled weapon exploded.

Buck Toler took both rounds in his back, and Longarm felt the heat of the big man's flesh wash across his own body.

Marshal Orton's horse, a nervous bay mare, spun almost completely around at the huge explosion, and Orton was thrown hard to the ground, shotgun still clenched in his fists.

Longarm snapped off a shot at the Carson City marshal, and his bullet caught Orton in the thigh. Orton screamed and began to roll around in pain, still trying to bring the shotgun up. Longarm fired again and blew a hole in the marshal's forehead. The other mounted men were trying to grab their weapons and at the same time control their plunging horses.

Longarm dropped the dead deputy and staggered back toward the train. He dimly heard other shots and guessed that Joe Polk also had his hands more than full.

A skinny man on a bucking roan dropped his six-gun and grabbed for leather. Longarm took careful aim and pumped a slug into the man's chest. The last one that he faced got his horse under control and lit out for town. Longarm decided to let him get away alive.

Whirling around and knowing that he'd been struck by some buckshot that must have blown completely through Buck Toler's thick body, Longarm hurried toward the front of the locomotive just in time to see Joe Polk come running up the tracks toward a pair of dead men whose horses were now disappearing into the sagebrush.

"Holy crap!" Joe cried. "Marshal, you've been shot! You're *dyin'*!"

Longarm came to a halt and looked down at the front of his coat and shirt to see that he was covered with blood.

He holstered his gun and then leaned up against the locomotive and shook his head as he brushed bone, gristle, and gore away with disgust. "Buck Toler was a big son of a bitch," he said as much to himself as to the kid. "If he had been as thin as you, Joe, I'd already be a goner."

"Then that isn't your blood?" Joe asked.

"Not much of it," Longarm replied. "I'll be fine."

"Oh my gawd!" Joe whispered as he took in the bodies. "I can't believe what just happened!"

"We had some luck and we stayed calm. Nice work, Joe. I'm not sure that I could have taken down the two you shot."

Joe stared at the two dead men he'd brought down and then he shook his head. "I'm feeling numb. I never . . . never killed anyone before."

"You had no choice," Longarm said, removing his ruined coat and then his shirt. "They were going to handcuff us and take us to the town jail. Once we were behind bars, I'm sure that Buck Toler would have found an excuse to either beat us both to death or shoot us down and claim we were trying to stage a jailbreak. There are witnesses to what happened just now. We'll be fine."

"But we killed the town marshal and his deputy!"

"Yeah," Longarm agreed. "That means there's suddenly a couple of job openings for you in Carson City."

"Do you think that we'll be charged with murder?"

"Of course not. The engineer saw the whole thing, and my guess is that Marshal Orton and Deputy Toler were despised and feared by the people they were charged to protect. I think when everything comes out in front of a judge, we'll be exonerated of all charges and what happened will be ruled as nothing more or less than self-defense."

"I sure hope so."

"Don't worry," Longarm said. "We just did what we had to do. The people of Carson City . . . once the shock of all this wears off . . . are going to consider us heroes."

"Yeah, maybe so." Joe shook his head, and Longarm was sure the kid was in the grips of a mild state of shock. It had all happened fast, and the results were so final.

"But I'm not sure I want to be a lawman anymore," Joe said quietly.

"You'll have plenty of time to think it over," Longarm told the kid as he put a hand on his shoulder. "I know what you're feeling, and it always takes a little time to get things like this straight in your mind. Killing a man isn't something that you ever get used to, Joe. And killing *two* men is even worse."

"You killed four men."

"Yeah, I did."

Joe held his hand up and it shook. "Look."

"Joe, tell the conductor to get some of his crew to pack those bodies into an empty car and then roll that boulder away from the tracks. There is no point in standing here talking about what just happened."

"No," Joe whispered, "I guess not."

Longarm looked down at his torso and saw that he'd taken a few superficial wounds from the shotgun. He was bleeding, but not badly. As soon as he got into town, he'd see a doctor, but the one who was really going to be in demand was the mortician.

And then a question passed through his mind . . . *What would happen now without any law still standing in Carson City?*

Chapter 19

The people of Carson City came streaming east out of town, mostly on foot but some on horseback and others in carriages and buggies, to meet the arriving train. Some were furious, well armed, and prepared to shoot Longarm and Joe Polk on sight. But most were dumbfounded by the news that their town marshal, his deputy, and four other well-known if not popular citizens had died minutes earlier in a blazing gunfight. No doubt they had heard the staccato crack of gunfire, especially the booming shotgun blasts.

Longarm had anticipated a crowd, and he was neither disappointed nor especially alarmed. He and Joe were standing with their captives, Thomas Elton and Myles Firth. Longarm had already instructed the train's engineer and conductor to initially confront the crowd with the truth about what had happened just inside the city limits.

"You men saw who opened fire first," Longarm reminded the railroad men. "You clearly witnessed that old man open up with his shotgun, killing Deputy Toler and forcing me to return fire in order to defend my life."

"That's right," the conductor said. "You didn't fire the first shot and neither did your friend. We saw everything, and damned if it wasn't a show I swear I'll never forget if I live to be a hundred!"

"You need to make sure to keep telling the crowd that over and over," Longarm warned.

"They won't settle for what we have to say," the engineer argued. "They won't wait very long for you to face 'em."

"We'll do that," Longarm promised. "But before anyone out there in front of the train goes off half-cocked, I want you two men to tell the crowd exactly what happened."

"And what if they don't want to listen or they don't believe us?" the engineer dared to ask.

"Joe and I will step out, and we'll have Firth and Elton out in front of us," Longarm said. "They're going to repeat what everyone in the Bucket of Blood Saloon heard them say . . . that they hired a man named Deke Hill to settle a score with Nellie's husband and that he went way too far and murdered him."

"I ain't sayin' nothin'!" Elton swore, perhaps suddenly emboldened by the thought that the crowd might turn in his favor against the federal marshal.

"Then I'll blow a hole in your spine," Longarm said quietly. "So the choice is yours. Either tell the truth to the people of Carson City . . . or you'll both be dead in the next few minutes."

Myles Firth was perspiring heavily and his skin was chalky white. "Tom," he whispered. "This man isn't bluffing. I'm going to tell the truth and take my chances with a judge. I sure hope you see it that way too and don't get us both shot in the back. I can face some prison time, but I sure as hell don't want to die caught in a cross fire between the marshal and that crowd!"

"You'd do well to listen to your friend," Longarm advised. "That confused and upset crowd is like a keg of dynamite, and if you say the wrong things, they're going to explode. Someone is going to pull a gun and start shooting, and guess who is going to be dropped first?"

"All right," Elton reluctantly agreed.

"I was sure you'd see the sense of it," Longarm told the man. "Joe, are you ready?"

"I thought when we survived the gunfight it was all over."

"No," Longarm told him. "We're not out of the woods yet. Just stay calm and keep your gun pointed at their backs. And you two miners are coming with us."

"Marshal, do we have to?"

"You're witnesses to what you heard about Deke Hill. If what I have to say doesn't go down well, then you become my pair of aces in the hole."

"I just don't want to be put in a hole by some crazy bastard out there in that crowd!"

"You'll both be behind us," Longarm reminded the frightened miners. "But if you turn and run, I'll find you and it won't be pretty."

They grimly nodded with understanding.

The train rolled to a gentle stop, and the conductor and engineer were quickly on the track bed, hurrying toward the gathering crowd. The hiss of steam and the settling of iron made it hard to overhear what was being said by both men to the crowd, but Longarm figured that by carefully observing everyone he could pretty much tell if the two men were being listened to.

Minutes passed, and Longarm could see that several members of the crowd were extremely upset, but the conductor and engineer stood their ground. Sometimes they turned and pointed or gestured, trying to make clear their

explanations. Once the engineer actually used his thumb and index finger to point like a gun. The crowd seemed rapt with attention, and then the conductor turned and pointed back down the line.

"It's time for us to get off this train and face them," Longarm decided. "Ready?"

Joe nodded and shoved their prisoners forward. Moments later they were walking up the track bed toward the crowd, which had suddenly fallen dead silent.

"For the benefit of anyone who doesn't know who I am, my name is Deputy United States Marshal Custis Long, and I'm from Denver. I've come here to clean up what I'm certain is a grave injustice, and that has to do with the arrest and sentencing of Mrs. Nellie Bolton to hang for the murder of her late husband, John Bolton."

"She burned him *alive*!" a man in the crowd screamed. "And she'll by gawd hang for it!"

A rumble of agreement formed in the mass of people, and Longarm felt their hard and angry resistance rise up at him like a giant wave.

"No!" he shouted. "I've got two miners with me who will back up my words because they heard the truth spoken at the Bucket of Blood Saloon. I've also arrested a pair of men who have reluctantly agreed to set the record straight. Hear them out!"

Thomas Firth spoke first. His voice was low and his head was down, and Longarm knew that he could not be heard by most of the hostile crowd, so he leaned in on the man and growled, "Shout, damn you, or this situation is going to blow up and we're all going to die!"

Firth raised his head and spoke loudly. "Myles Firth and I hired a man named Deke Hill to settle a score for us against old man Bolton. Hill must have lost his temper and did something that we never wanted or expected . . . he

put a torch to the old man. Maybe Deke Hill didn't mean to do anything but burn the soles of Bolton's feet or blister his toes to make him suffer for his sins. We don't know. All we do know is that it somehow got out of hand and the old man was burned to death while tied to his bedposts."

"Are you sayin' his widow didn't have anything to do with it!" someone shouted.

"I'm saying that there ain't much doubt in our minds that Deke Hill is the real murderer. After the night of the fire, he came running to me and Myles and said he had to have money so that he could go on the run. He was half-drunk and talking crazy. He said that he . . . he'd done something so awful that he doubted he could even live with himself."

"Then why didn't you tell that to the judge!"

"We paid Deke Hill to do a job for us. And when he did more than we had intended, we knew we had to get him out of this country or the truth would come to light and we'd wind up in the penitentiary."

"And you were going to let an innocent woman hang?" a small man in a dirty brown business suit asked with a mixture of incredulity and contempt.

"Nellie Bolton had a lot to gain and damn little to lose by the death of her husband . . . but she had nothing to do with his murder."

There was a moment of silence as the crowd digested what they'd just heard, and then everyone started talking at once. Longarm let them talk for a minute or two, and he saw some heated arguments.

"All right," he yelled. "I'm the only law that stands now, and I'm taking these two men to the penitentiary instead of the town jail. I'm sure that you all know Warden Slingerland and that he is a fair and honest man. But just as important, he can keep these two locked up while my

deputy Joe Polk and I track down Deke Hill and bring him back for a trial charging him with murder."

There were some who tried to object, but fortunately most of the people understood the wisdom of this decision.

The conductor leaned in close to Longarm and asked, "How'd I do?"

"You did fine and so did your friend. They just needed a few minutes to get the facts straight before we showed our faces."

"I was scared half to death," the engineer admitted.

"You both prevented a lot of blood from being spilled out here today."

"I guess we did at that. You need us any longer, Marshal? If not, me and Bert would like to get back on board and finish this run. I can't speak for Bert, but I'm fixin' to get drunk fast so I'll stop shakin' inside."

"If I see you in a saloon tonight, I'll buy you drinks," Longarm promised.

"Same for me," Joe added. "Or I would if I had any money to spend."

"You will have soon," Longarm told his young friend. "From the moment I deputized you, you were on the government payroll."

"I am?"

"That's right. But I have a hunch that after the truth comes out and we bring Deke Hill back for a trial and save Nellie from a rope . . . you'll get hired on here in Carson City."

Joe stood taller. "We're headed for Elko as soon as we can, right?"

"Right."

"I need to find Rebecca and tell her right away."

"Joe, I got a strong suspicion that by tomorrow Rebecca

and her family, as well as everyone within a hundred miles of Carson City, will know your name."

"Whooo-wee!" Joe whooped.

Longarm shoved Firth and Elton back toward their car, and when they were all in their seats, he leaned over and said, "Myles, I see you have some cigars in your coat pocket."

"So what?"

"So I'd like a couple right now."

Myles Firth gave Longarm a dirty look, but he handed over the cigars. Longarm inspected them and said, "Cubans. You've got expensive tastes. Too bad that you're going to spend a long time in prison, where expensive tastes are nothing more than an everyday torment."

"Screw you, Marshal!"

"No," Longarm said with a satisfied smile as he nipped off the end of the cigar and gave one to Joe before lighting them both. "When you get turned loose among the general prison population, my bet is that *you're* going to be the one that gets screwed, and it won't be one bit pretty."

Chapter 20

Two days later Judge Hannibal Cross took the bench and glared out at the packed Carson City courtroom. Longarm and Joe Polk were in the front row, and they were the object of a judicial hearing regarding the shoot-out and death of Marshal Dean Orton, Deputy Buck Toler, and four other men that had been deputized.

The judge was in his sixties and of medium height and weight, with a silver beard and a stern bearing. In his many years on the bench he had seen and heard some terrible things, and his inclination was to believe that the West was being overrun with carpetbaggers, thieves, and murderers. His solution was to see that the scum of the West did not cost the taxpayers undue expense and that they be hanged with expediency. That said, he was also known to have a sharp intellect and was willing to listen to a defense and sometimes reverse his earlier rulings in the name of fairness and justice. He was, by all accounts, a fair and contemplative judge who put the law and justice above any personal feelings he might have for or against the accused.

"Your Honor," attorney Orville Butler said, approach-

ing the bench. "What happened just inside Carson City's legal limits two days ago constitutes nothing less than a slaughter. I concede that we have heard witness after witness state that Marshal Orton and his brave deputy precipitated the deadly gun battle, but I ask the court to see that justice is both swift and evenhanded. I believe that United States Marshal Custis Long and Joseph Polk ought to bear the responsibility of their guilt. They should be charged with manslaughter at the very least."

"No!" Rebecca Butler cried from the floor. "Joe and Marshal Long were just defending themselves. This is wrong!"

The bailiff hurried over to silence Rebecca, but when he tried to escort her out of the packed courtroom, she slapped his face. "I will not leave this courtroom, and Father, I have never been so ashamed to be your daughter as I am right now!"

Orville Butler passed a hand over his round, florid face. He looked to his wife for support, but she averted her eyes downward.

"This is all such a tragedy," Orville muttered. "A grave tragedy."

The judge turned to Longarm. "I understand that you have *not* retained an attorney and that Joseph Polk has elected to also forgo formal legal representation."

"Yes I have, Your Honor," Joe said. "I stand by Marshal Long. I was fired upon first, and because I was the better shot and on solid ground rather than horseback, I'm alive. The two men who would have killed me are themselves dead. Furthermore, I was deputized by this federal marshal."

"Yes," Judge Cross said, "we know that. Marshal Long, it is time to speak in your own behalf."

Longarm stood up, and the whispering in the courtroom

died. He looked over at Rebecca and then down at Joe, who sat straight in his seat. "Your Honor, as a federal marshal, my authority in this case prevails over that of the late Marshal Orton. However, I am the first to admit that this sad affair was *not* a federal matter. No, it was entirely a *personal* matter."

"How was it personal?"

Longarm quickly explained that he had taken vacation time to come from Denver to investigate the murder of John Bolton and to make sure that his wife, who was now facing a hangman in ten days, was indeed guilty of the crime.

"Your Honor, I have witnesses . . . Mr. Thomas Elton and Mr. Myles Firth . . . who have publicly stated that they hired one Deke Hill to exact revenge upon John Bolton. Furthermore, they have publicly stated and agreed to testify under oath that they did not hire one Deke Hill to murder John Bolton but that he lost his head and in some kind of crazed state of mind then tied John Bolton to his bed and lit a match to his person."

"Yes, I have read their signed and sworn testimony, and we will deal with those two at some future date," Judge Cross said. "Until then, given the unusual and dire circumstances of this entire affair, I agree that they should be imprisoned in our penitentiary until a hearing date can be set. Orville Butler has agreed to represent their plea to the court for mercy and a light sentence."

"That is correct," Butler said, jumping to his feet. "And may I remind the court that Mrs. Nellie Bolton has already been tried by this court and found guilty of murder and sentenced to hang. That being the case—"

The judge raised his hand for silence, cutting the attorney's words off. "What we have here is new and stunning revelations that bring Mrs. Bolton's innocence or guilt into

an entirely new perspective. I sentenced Mrs. Bolton to hang, but I can also reverse that sentence if I have indisputable evidence that she is indeed innocent."

"But Your Honor!" Butler objected. "That would be precedent setting by this court and . . ."

"Sit down, Orville," Judge Cross commanded. "It would indeed be a precedent, and I'm not entirely comfortable with it, but I'm damn sure a lot *more* uncomfortable having an innocent woman hang for a murder that it now seems possible she did not commit!"

The courtroom began to hum with hushed, arguing voices.

"Silence!" the judge shouted, banging his gavel.

He surveyed the courtroom, and his eyes came to rest on first Longarm and then Joe Polk. "This is a very difficult and unusual case. And it is very, very important that justice be evenhanded and administered fairly. Having said that, I am inclined to give United States Marshal Custis Long ten days in order to find and bring to this court one Mr. Deke Hill."

Longarm was on his feet. "Judge, I respect your decision here, but ten days is not nearly time enough to go to Elko, find and arrest Deke Hill, and then bring him back to this court."

"Oh?" the judge asked, raising his bushy eyebrows. "Elko is a one-day trip by train to and from Reno. I have ridden that train and, to be precise, the journey is exactly two hundred and eighty-nine miles."

"But Your Honor, what if Deke Hill isn't in Elko? That is big cattle country, with thousands of square miles, and Mr. Hill could be anywhere."

"All right, Marshal Long. I will extend that deadline and make it *two weeks*. If you bring back Mr. Deke Hill to stand before me and he confesses to the murder of John

Bolton, then I will free Nellie Bolton. If he does not appear and I do not have indisputable evidence that he was the one that murdered John Bolton, then I will have no choice but to allow the hanging to take place the next day."

"Judge," Longarm pleaded. "After the confessions by—"

"The written confessions by Mr. Elton and Mr. Firth stated that they are guilty of hiring Mr. Hill to *punish* the late Mr. Bolton. Given that fact and the fact that Mr. Hill has not admitted to murder or been tried for that act, I do not feel that I have enough proof to exonerate Mrs. Bolton and set her free."

"But to let her hang!" Longarm said loudly. "Judge, surely you can't—"

"Silence!" Judge Cross interrupted. "I've made my decision. Marshal Long, if you do not produce Mr. Hill or if he does not confess to the murder, I'll have no choice but to uphold my earlier sentencing of death by hanging in two weeks and one day from now."

Longarm bit his tongue in anger and frustration, but he knew that Judge Cross had made up his mind, no matter how unfair it seemed.

"All right, Your Honor. I understand that this town's citizens are in a state of high anticipation of seeing a woman hang, and I will do my damnedest to see that they are disappointed."

Judge Cross did not like the remark, and his lips formed a tight line under his silver mustache, but he said nothing to Longarm and banged his gavel. "This hearing is over!"

The courtroom seemed to be paralyzed with what they had just seen and heard. Almost everyone who had learned of the sworn testimonies of Thomas Elton and Myles Firth had assumed that the judge would reverse his hanging

sentence and reschedule another trial given this dramatic new evidence. But now, with a hanging date still in effect for a woman who might very well be innocent, the people of Carson City were confused and upset.

"It's not right," one woman said. "This is too rushed."

"Oh, I still think she's guilty," another added.

And so went the conversation back and forth among the crowd as they filed out of the courtroom, most believing that it would be a terrible injustice to hang Nellie Bolton without a new trial. Others, especially the local saloon owners and many businesses who had been counting on a financial windfall, were furious.

Longarm watched Joe Polk push through the crowd to join Rebecca. He saw the young couple embrace and watched them hold each other tightly. Rebecca's father had his head bowed and looked old and angry. Rebecca's mother stood off by herself crying into a silk handkerchief.

What Longarm wanted most in the world was to get out of the courtroom and on that train to Elko. He roughly bulled his way through the crowd outside and marched toward his hotel, where he intended to gather his things and then get to Reno, where he would buy a round-trip ticket on the first train to and back from Elko.

"Marshal Long!" Joe yelled, running hard up the street to overtake him. "I just learned that the next train out of Reno leaves in just a little over three hours!"

"We'll be on it," Longarm snapped.

"But the local stagecoach schedule—"

"The stagecoach stops too often and is too slow," Longarm said, cutting off his young friend. "We'll rent horses, but we've not a minute to waste!"

The first livery was an old and dusty barn with several corrals. A man smoking a pipe sat on a stump whittling,

and when he saw Longarm and Joe Polk running at him, he jumped to his feet in alarm and threw up both hands.

"I didn't do anything wrong, Marshal! Whatever—"

"We need two fast and saddled horses to get to Reno in time to catch the eastbound train."

The man nodded. "That's about thirty miles, so you need some fast horses."

"Find 'em and let's get them saddled, bridled, and running," Longarm told the man.

"If you kill 'em getting to the train I'll want . . . a *hundred dollars*."

"You'll have it," Longarm promised. "But I don't think that is going to be necessary as long as we don't stand here wasting precious time haggling over money. Now, let's get some horses saddled!"

"I got a fast pair in mind. Buckskin and a bay. Buckskin for you, Marshal, because he's bigger and stronger. Bay more for you, kid, because she's fast and has bottom."

"Don't call me 'kid,' " Joe said, taking offense. "I had to shoot down two men and I'm probably gonna be your next marshal . . . or at least your deputy."

"Sorry! No offense meant."

"Then none taken," Joe said. "Now, let's see those horses."

The horses looked sound and fast, and Longarm gave the liveryman fifty dollars in advance. "I'll put them up at a stable in Reno during our time on this hunt."

"I sure do hope you return," the liveryman said fretfully. "'Cause if you fellas get killed, then your fifty dollars will hardly pay the board in Reno and—"

"Shut up!" Joe ordered. "We aren't going to get killed."

"Sure hope not."

Longarm was already grabbing a saddle blanket, bit, and bridle. There were just some men that worried about

damn near everything and couldn't stop telling everyone how much they were worried. Such men were a bane to men who just *acted*.

"Are you a good rider?" Longarm asked as he tightened his cinch and saw Joe standing beside the bay mare looking a little confused.

"I never rode a horse before," Joe confessed with embarrassment.

"What!"

"You heard me. I . . . I always intended to learn how to ride, but I just never quite got around to it, and I was always buying bullets and so I was broke."

"Great," Longarm muttered. "This is going to be one helluva long ride to Reno."

"Don't you worry about me. I'll make it even if I have to tie myself in the saddle," Joe vowed.

"I believe that, but you're going to have so many saddle sores that you'll be bowlegged for weeks."

"Make me look seasoned," Joe muttered as the liveryman took over saddling and bridling the bay mare. Then Joe clumsily climbed up on his horse.

"Good luck and don't ruin my best horses!" the liveryman shouted.

Longarm reined his horse hard out of the barn, and although he didn't have spurs, he put his heels to the flanks of the buckskin and it damn near ran over an old dog sleeping under a tree. Longarm glanced back and saw a stricken-looking Joe Polk clinging to his saddle horn as his mare pounded up the street not far behind. There was a lot of daylight between Joe and his saddle.

"Hang on, Joe!"

"What the hell do you think I'm doin'!"

People in town parted on the street as they raced past. One of them was young Rebecca, with her parents.

Longarm thought he heard her cry out Joe's name, but he couldn't be sure because mostly what he could hear was just the pounding of his horse's hoofbeats and Joe Polk shouting at the top of his lungs.

Chapter 21

Longarm had to help Joe Polk off the bay mare and then half-carry him to a bench. "How are you doin', Joe?"

"Not so good."

"You'll have an easy ride on the train to Elko," Longarm promised.

"I'm not worried about the train ride," Joe said through clenched teeth. "It's what is going to happen *after* we get to Elko that is a worry."

"Let's just face that when we get there."

Longarm quickly made arrangements with the Reno liveryman to hold their horses until they returned.

"You've used these two good animals pretty hard," the man observed. "Looks like they could use a rubdown and some rest."

"I could use that myself."

"What's the matter with your young friend?"

"He doesn't know how to ride very well, and I think he's badly chafed inside his upper legs."

"I see that now and then with my customers who rent horses and ride farther and faster than they should have. I

keep a can of medicinal salve just for that reason. He want some?"

"Anything," Joe grimaced.

"All right," the liveryman said. "Only cost you two bits. Drop those pants and let's see what you got."

Joe unbuckled his gunbelt, then his regular belt, and slowly dropped his pants.

"Man, you really got some saddle sores there!" the liveryman exclaimed as he opened his can of salve. "Must burn like fire."

"They do," Joe said, staring down at the fiery sores and blisters. "What is that stuff that you have to put on 'em?"

"I got the medicine from a Paiute, and he never would tell me the exact ingredients. But it works. So just dip your fingers into the can and scoop out a gob and rub it on nice and easy."

Joe dipped two fingers into the can and held the salve to his nose. "Sure does stink."

"You worried about smellin' good or easin' your pain?"

"Okay," Joe said, seeing the liveryman's point. He gritted his teeth and rubbed the salve on heavily, then expelled a deep breath and hiked up his pants.

"Bet it feels better already, huh?"

Joe slowly buckled his belt and then his gunbelt. He took a few steps, and then he nodded and managed a smile. "As a matter of fact it does feel better already. Not burning nearly so bad."

The train blasted its steam whistle, telling everyone that it was leaving soon.

The liveryman took his payment from Longarm. "Those Indians have some fine medicine men who know what they're doin'. Now, I don't know if they ever get saddle sores or not, but . . ."

"We've got a train to catch," Longarm said, interrupt-

ing the liveryman's conjecture. "Joe, can you walk that far?"

"Damn right I can."

"Then let's do it!"

The train depot was only two blocks away up Virginia Street, but Longarm could tell it was a painful walk for his friend. Even so, they made it with minutes to spare. Longarm bought them tickets and they took their seats.

"Best get some rest," Longarm advised. "Don't know what we're going to come up against in Elko. I just hope that we can find Deke Hill in a hurry and get back to Carson City in time to save Nellie Bolton."

"Me too."

Joe eased back in his seat, closed his eyes, and almost immediately fell asleep. Longarm stayed awake long enough to see the pines and grass around Reno give way to the high desert sage, and then he also fell asleep.

They arrived in Elko at five o'clock the following morning. The stars were just beginning to fade and the air was crisp and invigorating. Longarm had never spent much time in Elko, but he did know that the town was almost entirely dependent on the railroad and cattle ranching. There were also quite a few sheep operators that were part of the livestock industry. Most of the shepherds were Basque, generally short, powerfully built men with dark complexions and big, friendly smiles.

"No sense in getting ourselves rooms," Longarm told his friend. "Let's find a café and have a good breakfast then pay a visit to the local marshal's office."

"Hope he's a lot more cooperative than the one you shot down in Carson City."

The irony of that remark did not escape Longarm. "Most of them are, Joe. We just fell in with a pair of bad

ones in Carson." He pointed up the street. "Looks like that café just up the street is open."

"I'm hungry enough to eat a whole sow, her five piglets, and the boar that fathered 'em!"

Longarm chuckled. "That's pretty hungry, all right."

The café was empty when they entered, and it was obvious that it had just opened a few minutes earlier. The woman who came out to greet them was in her thirties and quite good-looking, with brown hair and a nice figure.

"I haven't seen you men here before," she said. "And what would you like for breakfast?"

"What do you have to offer?" Longarm asked.

The woman studied him with a smile. "Oh, I could offer you probably more than you could eat . . . but how about you start off with coffee? I just fired up the stove and the coffee is fresh and hot."

"That would suit us fine," Longarm said. "And as for breakfast, I'd like a steak and some eggs on top of fried potatoes. Maybe some toast, and if you have any apple or strawberry jam, that would go well."

"You're hungry."

"I sure am," Longarm told her. "Joe, how did that sound to you?"

"Real good."

"All right," she said, giving Longarm a wink. "I'll bring you out the coffee and get started on the breakfast."

"Thank you, ma'am."

"*Miss*," she corrected. "My name is Lola and I had a husband once, but he died of lead poisoning. Got caught with another man's wife."

"Sorry to hear that."

"Earl had a roving eye and couldn't keep his cock in his pocket. I miss him sometimes, but not all that much."

"I see," Longarm replied, wondering why this woman would tell him such a thing about her late husband.

"I get lonesome for love at times. Are you married?"

"No."

"Gonna be around for a spell?"

"Probably not. I'm looking for a man."

"Too bad. You ought to be looking for a woman."

"I might do that later," Longarm told her. "Do you know a fella who lives in these parts named Deke Hill?"

"I sure do. He a friend of yours?"

"Not really. I just need to find him."

"What for?"

"I'd rather not say," Longarm answered. "But I sure would appreciate any information you might have as to his whereabouts."

"Deke Hill is a pretty sorry son of a bitch," Lola said. "He works for the Broken Bow Ranch, which is one of the biggest in this part of the country."

"Where is its headquarters?"

"Up in the Ruby Mountains about twenty-five miles southeast of town. Deke comes in here and eats when he's in town, which isn't very often. He tips me well and I think he has taken a shine to me."

"Not surprising," Longarm told the waitress. "You're a real handsome woman."

She beamed and brushed back her hair. "So you think so."

"I'm sure of it. My eyes are a little gritty from lack of sleep, but I can still see well enough to recognize beauty when it stands before me . . . even at this early hour."

"My oh my, but you are a sweet-talkin' man!"

"I've got to find Deke. I sure would appreciate some directions."

"If it's trouble that you're bringing him, then please don't mention my name," Lola warned. "Deke has a streak of meanness in him, and I don't want any trouble with that cowboy."

"I'm sure most people here in Elko know where he works, so there isn't any way he'd guess we'd had this conversation."

"All right, you'll see a pinnacle of stone that stands about seventy feet all by itself out on the high ground just this side of the Ruby Mountains. The Broken Bow Ranch sits at its base."

"Does Deke have any family or friends working there with him?"

"Two older brothers that worked a small cattle ranch of their own but lost it playing faro."

"They sound like kind of a hard-luck bunch," Longarm observed.

"They're shiftless except maybe as cowboys. They work for a few weeks and then gallop into Elko, where they quickly gamble, whore, and drink their money away, and then they ride out again until next payday."

Lola headed back to the kitchen and retrieved a pot of fresh and strong coffee. "I'm going to get the food to frying," she said, hurrying off again.

Fifteen minutes later she was serving them huge platters of hot meat, eggs, and potatoes. "That ought to fill you men up."

"You've got several livery stables around here," Longarm offered around a mouthful. "Which has the best reputation for honesty?"

"I'd go to see Nate Crenshaw if you are going to rent horses or a buggy."

"He'd rent a buggy?" Joe asked, suddenly all interest.

"Nate does it all the time."

Joe looked at Longarm with pleading eyes.

"All right, Joe, we'll go for a buggy."

Joe threw his hands upward. "Thank you, Lord!"

"He don't like to ride?" Lola asked.

"Nope," Longarm told her. "I doubt that he'll ever be much of a horseman."

"I like to ride," Lola said, giving Longarm a devilish wink. "And not just horses."

Longarm blushed. "I'll be sure and remember that."

"I hope you do."

A half hour later, Longarm and Joe entered the local marshal's office and had a short discussion with the lawman. Longarm ended up saying, "Marshal Tanner, we don't want to step on any toes and we don't want you to have a bad surprise, but we have to find and arrest Deke Hill and take him back to Carson City."

The marshal shook his head. "So you expect Deke to just admit that he put a match to that rich old man up on the Comstock Lode?"

"Well," Longarm said thoughtfully, "I don't think he'll do it willingly."

Tanner nodded. "This young fella goin' with you out to the Broken Bow?"

"He is. Joe Polk is my deputy, and he's a good man, so don't be fooled by his youthful good looks."

Marshal Tanner eyed Joe up and down. "I could use a deputy with a good head on his shoulders. My former deputy ran off to strike it rich in the Montana gold fields, but I didn't care because he was worthless anyway."

"I might consider taking that job," Joe said, not wanting to sound too eager.

"Can you ride and shoot? Hold your temper and take orders? I won't stand for any shaking down of the mer-

chants or our whores. I am honest, and I expect a man who wears the badge here and takes my orders to be the same."

"How much do you pay?"

"I don't pay anything, but the town of Elko pays forty dollars a month plus a nice little house and two beeves a year. Would that interest you?"

"It would."

"All right, if Deke Hill and his two brothers don't kill you and your big friend here, then let's talk when you come back from the Broken Bow Ranch."

"I'll be sure and do that."

"You're a single and generally sober young man, aren't you?"

"Yes, sir! But I would be bringing back a new wife."

"She'd probably fit right with the local women. And they're not all old biddies either. Some are young wives."

"We'll talk," Joe said, still trying not to sound too eager. "Just as soon as we return with Deke Hill."

"Best of luck. And you'd better be ready to take on Deke's two brothers and maybe some of the boys on the Broken Bow payroll. Deke won't go without a fight."

"Thanks for the advice!" Longarm called over his shoulder as they exited the man's office.

The sun was well into the eastern sky by the time they had bought a few supplies and rented a buggy and a tall sorrel gelding to pull it.

"The way to the Broken Bow is to just follow their dirt track right to the ranch," Nate Crenshaw told them. "They bring a wagon in here every couple of weeks for supplies, so it'll be easy to get there and find."

Longarm now had a second pair of directions that matched those he'd been given by the waitress. And even

as he was thinking about her, Lola stepped out of the café and waved him good-bye.

"Hurry back!"

"We'll do that," Longarm promised.

"I think she took a shine to you this morning," Joe said. "In fact, I know that she did."

"She's a *real* attractive woman," Longarm said, waving and smiling at Lola. "I got a feeling she is itchy."

"What's she itchy for? Did you see a rash on her or something?"

"Never you mind, Joe." Longarm turned around in his seat and put the buggy horse into an easy trot. "Let's just start thinking less about women and more about Deke Hill, his two brothers, and maybe a few Broken Bow cowboys that might not like us taking one of their own off to stand trial for murder."

Joe leaned back on the seat and tipped his hat far back on his head. "Do you think that marshal was serious when he said he'd hire me?"

"I sure do. Marshal Tanner didn't strike me as a man who just whistles into the wind."

"Do you think Rebecca would like living here with me in Elko?"

"If she loves you, she'll be happy." Longarm gave his friend a smile of encouragement. "The thing of it is, Joe, we'll have to do things the right way when we get to the Broken Bow Ranch. If we have to draw our guns, then maybe it wouldn't be real healthy for you to come back to live in Elko."

"Hadn't thought about that."

"It's something to think about."

"Sure is. How we going to handle this?"

Longarm shook his head. "I have no earthly idea, but the main thing to remember is that we have to take Deke Hill alive. He's no good to us or Nellie Bolton dead."

"I understand. That's going to make it hard if he's packing a gun and goes for it."

"That's right, it will. But one way or the other we'll either get Deke back to Carson City alive and willing to tell the truth . . . or die trying."

Joe grimly nodded with complete understanding. He had stood his ground back by the railroad tracks just outside of Carson City, and he'd do the same on the Broken Bow Ranch.

Chapter 22

"Nice ranch house," Joe observed as they started up the track toward a rambling log house with a porch that ran its complete length. "Big barn, bunkhouse, and plenty of outbuildings and corrals. Whoever owns this must have some money."

"I'm sure that they do," Longarm agreed, noting the cattle and horses they were passing and how they were in good flesh because there was plenty of grass and water. "Let's just hope that they also have some good sense."

They noted a man working with a fractious horse in a round corral, and Longarm figured he might be the ranch's bronc buster. Another hand was fixing a corral fence, and there were two older people with silver hair sitting in rocking chairs on that big front porch. All but the bronc buster stopped to watch their approach.

"Don't expect they get a lot of visitors this far from Elko," Longarm offered.

"Are you just going to tell them why we're here?" Joe asked.

"I expect that I will."

"And what if they tell us to get the hell off the ranch and not come back?"

"I'll emphasize again to them that there is an innocent woman facing the gallows and that the only one that can save her is Deke Hill."

Joe clucked his tongue nervously. "Not sure that is going to get us much cooperation."

"You never know," Longarm replied as he raised his hand to wave a friendly greeting.

The two older people pushed out of the rocking chairs to lean on a porch rail and watch their visitors come into the yard. The bronc buster was trying to saddle a wild horse, and it had his complete attention. The man who had been fixing the fence stopped his work and walked over to join the older couple with a hammer still in his hand but no gun on his hip.

"Hello, there!" Longarm said with a disarming smile. "Nice ranch you have here."

"We like it," the old woman said as what Longarm assumed was her husband simply nodded. "What's your business?"

"I'm a deputy United States marshal and I need to find Deke Hill."

"What for?"

Longarm whispered to Joe, "Just sit tight and keep quiet. Let me do all the talking."

"Yes, sir. This is going to be a good lesson for me."

Longarm climbed down from the buggy and walked over to stand before the porch. "My name is Custis Long."

"Never heard of you," the woman said.

Longarm could see that the man was drooling and that one of his arms dangled uselessly at his side. He obviously suffered from some kind of physical problem and might

well be brain damaged. So it was the old woman who was doing all his talking.

"Deke Hill left Virginia City a while back, and he's got some things with the law that need to be explained."

"What things?"

"There was a wealthy old man who lived in Virginia City. He was tied to his bed posts and set afire."

The woman opened her mouth, then clamped it shut, and Longarm saw a shadow pass across her eyes. His first impression was that Deke might have done something similar before . . . or maybe he'd just lost his head and torched an animal, or showed some twisted cruelty during a fit of temper.

"What's the rich old man that got burned to death have to do with anything?"

Longarm cleared his throat. "Deke might not be some–one that had anything to do with it, but I have to question him."

"And if I tell you to get back in that buggy and drive it straight to hell?"

"Then I'll ride back with an arrest warrant from a judge in Elko. And, I expect, Marshal Tanner will be with me. So it would sure make things a whole lot simpler if I could just see and speak to him now."

The old man's hand moved over to cover his wife's hand. Something passed between them indicating to Longarm that the man might be physically damaged but his hearing and reasoning were still working.

"Come on up here on the porch where I can get a little better look at you," the woman ordered. "And tell your young friend he can tie that buggy horse up at our hitching post and join us."

"Thank you."

Joe climbed stiffly out of the buggy and walked bow-legged up onto the porch. "What's the matter with you, boy?" the old woman asked. "You get kicked in the balls by a man or a beast?"

"No, ma'am!" Joe's face flushed with embarrassment. "I got saddle sores is all."

"Saddle sores?"

"Yes, ma'am."

"You can't even ride a horse?"

"Not yet, ma'am."

"That's a sorry state of affairs, I'll tell you. Why, me and the old man were raised on this ranch, and we could ride like Indians when we were knee high to a frog."

"I mean to learn to ride well someday," Joe said with a voice that sounded lame. "But I just haven't quite got around to it yet."

"You thirsty for some cool water?"

"That would be real nice."

The old woman turned and shouted at her open door. "Martha, bring out a pitcher of water and some glasses!"

"Yes, ma'am!"

An Indian woman in her fifties brought out the drinks and glasses a few minutes later on a silver serving tray. Each glass had a slice of lemon hooked over its rim and it sure tasted good.

"All right," the woman said, speaking again to Longarm. "I am asking you a straight question and I want a straight answer. I'll know if you're lying to me." She looked to her husband and added, "*Both* of us will."

"Then ask."

"Do you think that Deke is the one that put the fire to some rich old man tied to his bed?"

"Yes, I do," Longarm answered. "But it's going to be up to a court of law to make that determination."

The old woman looked at her husband and sadly said, "I told you that something terrible had happened with Deke when he was on the Comstock. He ain't been right since he got back here."

There was a barely perceptible nod of the old man's head in agreement.

"And," the woman added, "we found those dead animals burned out back."

Again, a slight nod.

"Ma'am," Longarm said, "if I can't get Deke to admit that he murdered John Bolton, then Bolton's wife is due to hang in less than two weeks."

"Is she a good person?"

"I don't know," Longarm admitted. "I only met her for a few minutes inside the penitentiary at Carson City. I came to find out if she was innocent or guilty because her brother is not only my boss but my best friend. He said Nellie Bolton was always wild, but I don't believe no one should have to hang for someone else's crime."

"And Deke'd surely hang if he's guilty?"

"Maybe not. The judge would set a new trial. A jury might decide that the act was done in a fit of crazed anger that Deke could not control. If that happened, he'd likely just be locked up for many years."

The old couple listened intently, and a silent decision passed between them. "I don't want the wrong person to hang," the woman said stubbornly. "And to be honest, the only reason we keep Deke and his two brothers on at our ranch is that they are my late brother's sons. They think that they'll inherit this ranch when we die . . . but I never intended for that to happen, and our wills make it plain that the ranch gets sold and the money parceled out to our favorite charities. There are a lot of people in Nevada that are half-starved."

"That's a fine thing to do, ma'am. But—"

She interrupted him. "If you and your friend who can't even ride a horse come up against Deke and his brothers, they'll try to kill you both."

"My friend may not be able to ride a horse, but he's very good with a six-gun."

"For a fact?" the woman asked with surprise as she peered at Joe Polk.

"Yes, ma'am. I'm nearly as good a shot as the marshal."

"Maybe you're not as worthless as I first thought."

"No, ma'am."

"Deke and his brothers are working on some of our fencing about five miles off to the north. When you come up to them, they might put your shooting to the test."

"We understand."

"But there's a better way to do this."

"How would that be?" Longarm asked.

"I could send our bronc buster, Stony, out to fetch them back here, and then I could ask Deke to come into my house."

"I'd rather not put you and your husband up to such a danger," Longarm told her.

"Well, it's going to be that way whether you like it or not," she said. "Because I won't let you take Deke off the ranch until I hear him say he did what you think he did with my own ears, and neither will my husband."

Longarm was not clear where this was going. "Are you telling me that *you* will ask him if he burned that man in Virginia City to death?"

"That's exactly what I'm telling you."

"But . . . but why would he admit it to someone like you?"

"Because he is afraid to get on my bad side and lose

what he thinks he'll eventually inherit. And because he knows I can tell if he's lying, and if he does lie to me, I'll toss his skinny ass and well as those of his brothers off this place quicker than a goose can squirt shit."

Longarm turned and looked out at the nearby Ruby Mountains for a moment before he pivoted back to face the old couple. "And I'm supposed to . . ."

"You and your friend who can't even ride a horse will be listening in an adjoining room, and we'll hide the buggy and wipe out its wheel tracks. If Deke admits to me that he murdered that rich man, you step out and arrest him. But if Deke swears he didn't do it and I believe him, you'll have to leave without him."

"I'm not sure that . . ."

"That's my one and only offer. Take it or get off our property."

"Take it," Joe urged.

"All right. It's a deal, but if Deke is armed, it might blow up in our faces, and you and your husband might get shot and killed."

"Oliver and I are old and we're failing anyway," she explained. "So a couple of quick bullets don't hold much of a threat to us."

"Then send your bronc buster out to get him. Tell him to ask Deke to come here alone. We don't need three of them pulling their guns."

"I understand."

She put her fingers into her toothless mouth and let out a long, shrill whistle. The man who had been repairing the fence came running, and after he'd been given instructions, he led the rented horse and buggy around behind the barn. Five minutes later, the bronc buster was on a horse and galloping north.

"Oliver," the woman said, giving her silent husband a nudge with her elbow into his ribs, "this is going to be the most interesting day we've had in years."

Oliver nodded slightly, and damned if Longarm didn't see just the hint of a smile form on his thin, bloodless lips.

Chapter 23

Deke Hill and the bronc buster named Stony galloped
into the ranch yard just as the sun was starting to disappear
on the western horizon. Longarm and Joe peered out
through the curtains of a bedroom and watched as Deke
handed his reins to Stony and walked purposefully toward
the house. Deke was tall and moved like a man who had
spent most of his time in the saddle. He was wearing a
sidearm and his face was narrow and unshaven.

"Here we go," Longarm said. "Unless I'm badly mistaken, Joe, that old woman is not going to waste any time
confronting Deke about what happened in Virginia City."

"Sure glad Deke's two older brothers didn't tag along."

Longarm and Joe moved to the bedroom door and listened. Sure enough, the old woman went right after Deke
with her hard questions.

"Deke, we've learned today that you might have something to do with a rich man in Virginia City who was set
afire and died."

"What!"

"You heard me."

"Mabel, you know that can't be true."

"You've cruelly burned live animals before. Oliver and I have spoken to you about this several times."

"I didn't do *anything* wrong."

"I think you did, Deke. And you know that if you lie to me I'll throw you and both your brothers off the Broken Bow and you'll never be allowed to come back. I can always tell when you're lying to me."

There was a long silence, and then Deke said, "All right. I . . . I killed that man, but I didn't tie him up and then light him up."

"How did you *know* he was tied up?" Mabel demanded.

Longarm and Joe looked at each other behind the door, amazed at how Mabel had gotten Deke to step into her clever trap.

Deke stammered, "Well . . . well how else could you burn someone alive unless they were tied up?"

Mabel was slow to answer. "Why did you do it? Just tell me why you did such a terrible thing, Deke."

"John Bolton was an evil old bastard that everyone hated. And he had a lot of money. More money even than you and Oliver. It wasn't any good to him after he was dead, was it?"

"No," she said, voice suddenly low and tired. "I suppose not."

Longarm figured they had heard all they needed to hear, and so he drew his gun and burst into the living room with Joe close on his heel.

"What the hell . . ." Deke shouted.

"You're under arrest!"

Deke's hand shot to his gun, and even before he could clear leather Joe Polk's gun came up and exploded. Deke howled, dropping his gun and clutching his hand. Joe's

bullet had gone right through it, and blood was spurting everywhere.

Longarm took two steps forward and smashed his fist into Deke's jaw, knocking him to the floor. He turned and looked at his friend. "Nice shooting."

Mabel dipped her chin in agreement. "You wasn't lying about being good with a gun, young fella."

"No, I wasn't," Joe said as Longarm grabbed Deke Hill by the collar and dragged him outside, where he was tied up and tossed into the ranch yard.

Joe came outside. "Will he bleed to death on the way back to Elko?"

"I'll bandage the hand so that don't happen." Longarm turned to the old couple standing on the porch. "I don't know what you are going to say to Deke's brothers, but . . ."

"We'll give you a good head start on them."

Longarm took that to mean that the brothers would be coming and that he, Joe, and their prisoner needed to be on the first westbound train and headed for Reno.

"Joe, get the buggy out from behind the barn and let's get moving."

"Learn to ride a horse and we'll hire you, young fella," Mabel shouted from the porch.

"I'll do that," Joe promised as he took off at a run.

"That young man is a fooler," Mabel told Longarm. "I can see now why you brought him along. Deke always said he was real fast with a gun, but that fella beat him to the draw. I doubt Deke will ever have the full use of his right hand again."

"Where Deke is going, he won't need the full use of anything," Longarm told the ranch woman as he dragged Deke to his feet and shoved him toward the buggy.

It was a tight fit on the buggy seat for the three of them,

and Deke was moaning and carrying on over his wounded hand until Longarm threatened to shoot a hole in the other one if he didn't shut up.

"What about his brothers?" Joe asked.

"With luck, we'll be rolling down the tracks before they even know we came and went," Longarm answered.

"But if the train isn't due to leave for a few days?"

"Then we'll just take care of Deke's brothers if they come looking to set him free."

"More killing?"

"Probably," Longarm said quietly. "The thing I know is that this isn't over yet. Not over by a long shot."

Chapter 24

When they reached Elko, darkness had fallen, and Longarm made a stop at Marshal Tanner's office, where they
put Deke behind bars.

"Hey!" their prisoner wailed at the top of his lungs. "I
need a gawdamn *doctor*! I've been shot!"

Marshal Tanner was not at all sympathetic. "The bullet
went cleanly through the back of your hand, so you'll
live . . . unless you keep yelling and carrying on enough
to drive me to shoot you."

"But my hand hurts like hell!"

"Too bad."

"We'll be taking him to Carson City on the next train,"
Longarm told the local marshal.

"Your timing is good because there's a train coming
through around midnight. It makes a quick stop here to
take on wood and water."

"Then we'll be at the depot waiting no later than eleven-
thirty," Longarm announced. "Joe, maybe you'd like to get
something to eat."

"My stomach is too knotted up to take on food, so I

thought I'd just sit around and jaw with Marshal Tanner awhile."

Longarm thought that was a fine idea. If Joe wanted to work for Marshal Tanner, this was his chance to get to know the man and the job.

"Suit yourself."

Longarm went over to the café, and Lola was just getting ready to close up. "Hi there," she said in greeting. "I was just about to leave, but I can stay on and cook you something."

"A thick slice of that apple pie would be just fine."

"Coming up. I saw you and your friend bring Deke Hill into town. He looked to be in pretty bad shape."

"He'll live to stand trial in Carson City," Longarm vowed as she cut him a big slab of apple pie, which he dug into immediately. "Hmmm . . . this is delicious!"

"I baked it myself. When are you leaving Elko?"

"About midnight."

"Dammit, I was hoping that you might stay a few days so that we could get to know each other better."

Longarm wiped pie crumbs out of his handlebar mustache. "I'm sorry, Lola. But the sooner we get Deke Hill to Carson City the better. There is a woman in the penitentiary awaiting a hangman's noose, and I won't rest until she's freed."

Lola cocked her head a little sideways. "Are you and her . . ."

"No," Longarm said, already guessing her question. "We've only met once briefly, behind bars."

Lola folded her apron and put a few things away. "There are still a few hours until midnight. Doing anything special until the train leaves?"

"As a matter of fact I am."

Lola's disappointment was written across her tired but pretty face. "Oh, well . . ."

"I thought it would be special if we got together for a couple of hours. Do you know a place where that could happen?"

"I sure do. My place."

"Then let's not waste time."

Lola kissed his mouth. "I don't know what it is about you that attracts me so strongly, Marshal Long."

Fifteen minutes later Lola was squealing with pleasure as Longarm drove his manhood into her warm wetness. She wrapped her legs around his hips and shook her bottom like a dog shaking off water.

"Oh," she breathed in his ear, "this is *nice*!"

"Very," he agreed, as his hips moved and their bodies found an easy but extremely pleasurable groove. "You're a fine-looking woman, Lola, and you feel real good."

"You just keep doing what you're doing and it's only going to feel even better."

Longarm growled low in his throat, bent his head down to lick her nipples, and then let himself tumble into a whirlwind of ecstasy.

Two hours later, Lola rolled off Longarm's stiff pole and breathlessly panted, "You *will* be coming back through here on the train, right?"

"Yep. And I'll hold over a couple of nights so we can spend more time together."

"I can't wait."

Longarm kissed her tenderly and dressed. He consulted his pocket watch and was surprised to see that it was a quarter after eleven. The train was due in and out of Elko during

the next forty-five minutes. "I've got to get over to the marshal's office and get Deke and Joe to the train station."

"Be careful."

"We'll be fine."

He kissed Lola once more and then headed for the jail. Longarm heard the train pulling into the depot, and then he saw it through some buildings and suddenly felt a sense of urgency.

Longarm's long stride carried him to the marshal's office, where Joe and Marshal Tanner were both nervously waiting.

"I was just about to send Joe after you," Tanner said. "You're cutting it pretty close."

"Sorry. I had something important to do."

"Yeah, I'll bet," Tanner said. "We saw you and Lola heading to her room."

Longarm turned to the jail cell. "Are we ready to go?"

"I don't want to go anywhere!" Deke Hill shouted as he backed up to the far wall of his cell. "I'm not leaving Elko."

"You're wrong about that," Longarm told the man. "Marshal, unlock that cell."

"I still need a doctor!"

"There are doctors in Carson City. Let's go."

Five minutes later they arrived at the train station. Longarm explained the situation to the conductor and asked for an empty car if one was available.

"We're almost full," the man said. "Sorry, Marshal."

"That's all right," Longarm assured the conductor. "How soon before we leave?"

"About fifteen minutes."

"Good. Joe, take Deke inside and put him in a seat next to you. Don't take your eyes off of him for even a minute."

"No, sir!"

Joe shoved Deke up the steps and into the coach car. Longarm peered up and down the empty train depot and then said to the conductor. "I'm going to stand here and watch until we start to roll and then I'll take a seat behind my prisoner."

"He a real bad one?"

"Not anymore."

"Just keep him under control," the conductor warned. "I sure don't want him upsetting my other passengers."

Longarm understood, and his eyes continued to rove restlessly back and forth across the dimly lit and empty train depot. Finally, the train began to move and he relaxed a little . . . until he saw two horsemen. They were riding hard and disappeared behind the caboose, but moments later Longarm saw their saddled but riderless horses galloping into town.

"Deke's brothers," Longarm swore to himself. "And they're into the caboose."

He rushed inside and down the aisle until he found Joe sitting beside their prisoner. "We've got *two* problems, Joe."

"Deke's older brothers?"

"I'm afraid so."

Deke had been bent over holding his wounded hand, but now his head shot up and he barked a laugh. "They've come to kill you and set me free!"

"If that's their intention, they're about to die or join you in prison. Joe, have your gun ready and wait while I go back and take care of this."

"But . . ."

"Do as I say," Longarm told his friend. "You're my deputy, and deputies follow orders."

"Yes, but . . ."

Before Joe could say another word, Longarm was

hurrying through the coach. He wanted to have this show-down between him and Deke's brothers before they got among the passengers. He collided with a fat man and sent him sprawling, then leapt over his body and tore through another passenger coach.

Longarm saw the two cowboys at exactly the same moment they saw him. They were just emerging from the ca-boose, and because the aisle was very narrow, only the one in front had a clean line of fire. He tried to get off a shot, but Longarm fired so quickly that the man died with two slugs buried in his chest. His fall knocked his brother off balance, and Longarm shot the man three times before he could regain his balance and return fire.

He reloaded and went to kneel by the second man, who was still breathing.

"Am I dyin'?"

"I might be able to save you, but I'm no doctor."

"Well . . . well maybe there's one on the train. I want to see my kid brother before I bleed to death!"

Longarm knew the badly wounded man wasn't going anywhere, so he collected guns and said, "I'll bring Deke. Hang on."

"I'm running out of time, Marshal."

"We all are," Longarm told him as he left to bring Deke back to his dead and dying brother. "But you brought this on yourself. You could have stayed on the Broken Bow and none of this would have happened."

Longarm hurried back up through the cars, got Deke and Joe, and returned to the dying man's side.

"Help me, Deke! Do something."

Deke looked down at his brothers and swiped tears from his cheeks. "Nick, I've been shot myself."

"Find a doctor! Please, Deke, make them find a doctor!"

Deke swung around to face Longarm. "Nick is bleed-

ing to death. There must be a doctor or somebody on this train who can save him."

Longarm had a sudden inspiration. "Deke, if I go to find help, first you're going to have to save Nellie Bolton."

Deke's eyes bulged, and his brother began to cough blood. "What . . ."

"Admit that it was you who killed John Bolton, and if there is a doctor or someone that can save your brother, I'll promise you that I'll find them."

Nick's hand shot out and grabbed his younger brother's pant leg, and he pulled on it with the last of his failing strength. "Deke. Deke! There's a darkness comin' over me. Hurry, please, Deke!"

Deke's frantic eyes shot back and forth between Longarm and his brother Nick. His lips trembled and his body started shaking as if he had the ague. "All right! I burned that rich old bastard! I did it, but I'm not the only one that should pay! Myles Firth and Thomas Elton paid me to get even with him."

"To beat him up," Longarm asked, "or did they pay you to *kill* him?"

"To *kill* the old son of a bitch! They paid me to kill John Bolton." He dropped down beside his brother and cradled his head in his hands. "I'm gonna get you help, Nick! I swear I'm gonna get you a doctor!"

"I'm a doctor!" a loud voice shouted. "What the hell is going on in here!"

Longarm shoved the doctor back a step and grabbed Deke by the shirtfront. "Admit what you did to John Bolton one more time or this doctor doesn't touch your brother!"

Deke screamed, "I killed John Bolton because Thomas Elton and Myles Firth *paid* me to do it!"

Longarm shoved Deke backward. "We all heard him, right, Doctor?"

"Yes, now let me see if I can save that man."

Longarm moved aside. The doctor yanked open his medical bag and began to grab bandaging.

But when a death rattle filled Nick's throat, they all knew it was too late.

The doctor shook his head. "There is nothing I can do for either of these men."

"No, but you can still save a life."

"What do you mean?" the doctor asked, shoving the bandages back into his bag and snapping it shut.

"I mean that you can tell a judge in Carson City that the woman they intend to hang is innocent of the death of her husband."

"I don't understand."

"Doctor, you will understand before this train gets to Reno."

Four days later Nellie Bolton spread her arms wide and turned her face to the bright Nevada sun. "I'm a free woman thanks to you, Marshal Long. And to you, Joe Polk, and finally to you, Dr. Hanson."

"I swore an oath to save lives," the doctor replied. "And by testifying about what I heard Deke Hill say just as his brother was dying, I did help save your life."

Longarm added, "And I swore an oath to uphold the law and to see that the guilty were punished and not the innocent."

"Thank you, Marshal. Thank all of you, and Joe, I understand that you are getting married tomorrow and then are leaving for Elko to take a job as a deputy."

"That's right," Joe said proudly. "Rebecca and I sure would like to have you come to our wedding."

But Nellie shook her head. "I'd love to, but I think it might cause some trouble. I'm sure that feelings are still

running high, and it will take the people of Carson City a while to come to terms with what really happened to my husband. So I believe the best thing that I can do is to leave for Oregon."

"Maybe someday you'll come back."

"Maybe," Nellie said.

Then she kissed all three of the men who had been instrumental in keeping her from being hanged and walked over to the carriage where a woman named Stella was waiting to drive her to a beautiful place called the Willamette Valley.

Watch for

**LONGARM AND
THE DEADLY DOUBLE-CROSS**

the 405th novel in the exciting LONGARM
series from Jove

Coming in August!

LONGARM

GIANT-SIZED ADVENTURE FROM
AVENGING ANGEL LONGARM.

BY TABOR EVANS

penguin.com/actionwesterns

M456AS0510

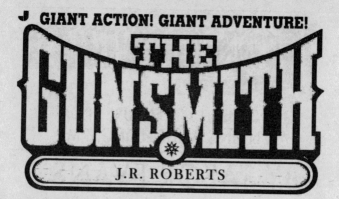

GIANT ACTION! GIANT ADVENTURE!

THE GUNSMITH

J.R. ROBERTS

penguin.com/actionwesterns

M455AS0510

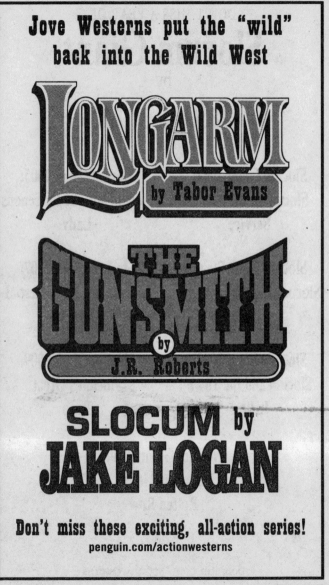

"How'd you guess?"

"Not hard."

"You don't look too good yourself, Boss," Longarm said with his typical bluntness.

Billy Vail was a good family man and he had once been a deputy marshal just like Longarm, but he had been promoted to head up their section of federal law enforcement officers. He was sober, conscientious, and smart, and best of all, Billy gave his most seasoned deputy marshals plenty of room to operate on their own as long as they produced results and their professionalism reflected well on his department.

"I had a long, sleepless night, Custis," Billy said before ducking back into his office.

Longarm poured his boss a cup of coffee and refreshed his own then strolled across the still mostly empty office feeling troubled by what Billy had just told him. Had the man experienced some deathly health issue? Or maybe his wife or one of his children had gotten sick. Was that why Billy looked so haggard and upset?

"Let's find out," Longarm said to himself as he walked into Billy's office.

"Please close the door."

"Ain't hardly anyone out there to overhear us, Boss."

"I know, but close it anyway."

Longarm closed the door and handed Billy his cup of coffee then sat down and looked his boss in the eye. "Whatever it is that has you looking so worried, it will pass and I just wanted to get that clear. So what's so wrong that you'd send a boy to wake me up at five-thirty this morning?"

"It's very personal," Billy said. "And unofficial."

Longarm blinked. "Someone from your past come to settle a deadly score?"

Chapter 1

Deputy United States Marshal Custis Long was sitting at his desk in the Federal Building waiting to be called into Billy Vail's office at the awful hour of six o'clock in the morning. Longarm wasn't an early riser and neither was Billy Vail, so he knew this meeting had to be very serious.

Longarm kicked his feet up on his old desk and sipped at a cup of coffee that he had just poured. The coffee was weak and tasted lousy, but it was either drink the stuff or dive into a stack of paperwork piled high on his desk. Doing paperwork was Longarm's least favorite pastime, so he drank the coffee and waited impatiently to find out what kind of burr was under Billy's blanket this early on a cool autumn morning.

"Custis, come on in and bring me a cup of coffee along with you."

"Will do," Longarm told his boss and best friend. "But this meeting had better be important."

"It is to me," Billy solemnly replied. "You look like something the cat dragged in. Up late with a new lady friend?"

THE BERKLEY PUBLISHING GROUP
Published by the Penguin Group
Penguin Group (USA) Inc.
375 Hudson Street, New York, New York 10014, USA

Penguin Group (Canada), 90 Eglinton Avenue East, Suite 700, Toronto, Ontario M4P 2Y3, Canada
(a division of Pearson Penguin Canada Inc.) • Penguin Books Ltd., 80 Strand, London WC2R 0RL,
England • Penguin Group Ireland, 25 St. Stephen's Green, Dublin 2, Ireland (a division of Penguin
Books Ltd.) • Penguin Group (Australia), 250 Camberwell Road, Camberwell, Victoria 3124, Australia
(a division of Pearson Australia Group Pty. Ltd.) • Penguin Books India Pvt. Ltd., 11 Community
Centre, Panchsheel Park, New Delhi—110 017, India • Penguin Group (NZ), 67 Apollo Drive,
Rosedale, Auckland 0632, New Zealand (a division of Pearson New Zealand Ltd.) • Penguin Books
(South Africa) (Pty.) Ltd., 24 Sturdee Avenue, Rosebank, Johannesburg 2196, South Africa

Penguin Books Ltd., Registered Offices: 80 Strand, London WC2R 0RL, England

This is a work of fiction. Names, characters, places, and incidents either are the product of the author's
imagination or are used fictitiously, and any resemblance to actual persons, living or dead, business
establishments, events, or locales is entirely coincidental.

LONGARM AND NAUGHTY NELLIE

A Jove Book / published by arrangement with the author

PUBLISHING HISTORY
Jove edition / July 2012

Copyright © 2012 by Penguin Group (USA) Inc.
Cover illustration by Milo Sinovcic.

ISBN: 978-0-515-15099-5

JOVE®
Jove Books are published by The Berkley Publishing Group,
a division of Penguin Group (USA) Inc.,
375 Hudson Street, New York, New York 10014.
JOVE® is a registered trademark of Penguin Group (USA) Inc.
The "J" design is a trademark of Penguin Group (USA) Inc.

PRINTED IN THE UNITED STATES OF AMERICA

10 9 8 7 6 5 4 3 2 1

ALWAYS LEARNING   **PEARSON**

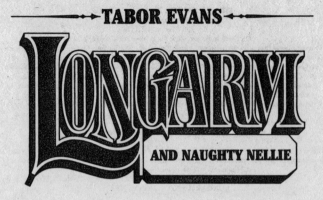

TABOR EVANS

LONGARM

AND NAUGHTY NELLIE

JOVE BOOKS, NEW YORK

Nobody Cuffs Longarm . . .

Longarm knew that if he was handcuffed, he was as good as dead. Once his hands were locked behind his back, Buck Toler was going to beat him savagely. He'd be dragged back to Carson City and then thrown in jail and abused until he was senseless and dying. Marshal Orton wouldn't stop Buck's cruelty.

Toler unlocked the cuffs with a little key and then said, "Stick your hands out here."

"Whatever you say, Buck," Longarm answered as he raised his hands wide apart.

"Put 'em together!"

"Okay," Longarm replied, suddenly making fists and then smashing them into Buck's ears.

Buck staggered and Longarm's right hand flashed across his body to his Colt, which he wore with the butt facing forward. His gun came out and the old man was already raising his shotgun and taking aim. Longarm ducked behind Buck just as the double-barreled weapon exploded . . .

THE WORLD IS BETTER WITH

Romance

Harlequin has everything from contemporary, passionate and heartwarming to suspenseful and inspirational stories.

Whatever your mood, we have a romance just for you!

Connect with us to find your next great read, special offers and more.

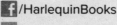